THE WILDE TRIALS

Also by Mackenzie Reed
The Rosewood Hunt

THE WILDE TRIALS

MACKENZIE REED

HARPER
An Imprint of HarperCollinsPublishers

Library of Congress Control Number: 2024942739
ISBN 978-0-06-328764-8

Typography by Catherine Lee
24 25 26 27 28 LBC 5 4 3 2 1

First Edition

To Jeff and Danny, the best big brothers a girl could ask for.
I'm forever your biggest fan and nothing makes
me happier than being your little sister.

1

This clock is trying to kill me.

Its faint *tick . . . tock* taunts me, like a literal bomb counting down to one of the most important and defining moments of the rest of my life. Maybe in a normal school, it would be the thought of summer. One last season with my friends before we all break apart for college. Melting ice cream cones and salt-textured hair; the scent of the ocean on our skin almost as strong as the sunscreen.

Despite my current rockiness in the friend department, there's still a chance for my summer to look something like that. Except hopefully with my pockets padded with cash and the title of Wilde Academy's Champion attached. But the only way to be named champion of the academy's annual seniors-only competition is to win it.

And I can't win if I'm not even chosen to compete in the first place.

"Hey," a voice to my left whispers. Emmy whacks my arm lightly. "Chill out. You're shaking the entire table."

"I can't help it," I whisper back. "I feel like I'm going to puke."

My heart thuds against my rib cage, keeping time with the

ticking of the clock. Six more minutes until I can mow down every student in the hall to get to the bulletin board in the foyer to see if my name is on it. Maybe cry in relief if it's there, and definitely cry if it's not. Either way, tears will likely be shed.

"And don't even think about skipping studying!" Professor Ruffalo reminds the class, snapping me back into the final anatomy lesson of my high school career. "Classes might be over for the year, but there are still two weeks of finals for most of you. Don't start slacking now!"

Most of you. I scrutinize her features for any kind of tell that I'm not part of that, but her poker face is strong. Professor Ruffalo is one of the main faculty who chooses the twelve students—or, Challengers, as we call them—who compete in the two-week wilderness competition that takes place deep in the forest behind campus while the rest of the school slogs through final exams.

"You have nothing to worry about," Emmy whispers. Her hand sneaks under our shared table to squeeze mine. My palms are slick with sweat from spending the entire class in fists in my lap. If she notices, she's too much of a good friend to mention it. "If anyone's going to get chosen, it's you."

Academically speaking, I *should* get chosen. In a school as elite as Wilde Academy, everyone is vying for the coveted top-of-class spot. We don't have honors like valedictorian because there are too many of us highly ranked. That's what getting named Champion is for.

"Students have been slighted before," I murmur back.

Emmy shakes her head, her ginger Dutch braids falling off her shoulders. "You're in the top one percent, you've taken every

2

extra-credit opportunity, I *know* you get 'a pleasure to have in class' on every quarterly write-up, and you've aced every single test in the two years since you've arrived. You're a shoo-in."

An uncomfortable pang spreads through me. *Almost every test.* "It's based on more than just academics," I quietly remind her. "There's also the essay."

An eight-page paper specifying why we want to be chosen to compete as a Challenger in the competition, what we'd do with the $600,000 cash prize, and what the honor of being crowned Champion means to us. Eight pages in which I stripped myself bare for judgment, admitting that had I never begged my parents to send me to Wilde the summer before junior year, maybe they'd have enough money to pay my sister's hospital bills without listing my childhood home as collateral.

Most of the students at Wilde Academy don't need the money—not like I do. But those who apply to compete desire the distinction of being a Champion and the privilege of giving the only student-led speech at graduation. And while they don't *need* the money, who'd say no to six hundred grand?

"You wrote about needing the money to help your family and your sick sister," Emmy says. "It'd be heartless *not* to choose you."

My gut twists. "I—"

"Girls, do you have something to share?" Professor Ruffalo lasers in on us. We straighten in our seats. The hall floods with noise even though one minute slowly ticks down on the clock. Some classes got let out early.

"Just happy summer!" Emmy exclaims, brighter than a ray of sunshine.

Professor Ruffalo opens her mouth but is cut off as the bell chimes, signaling the end of class. Her poker face breaks into an easy grin. "I think I've tortured you all enough for one semester. I hope you have a fantastic summer, and to my seniors, I'll see you at graduation." I fly out of my seat, slinging my backpack over my shoulder. I think it hits someone, but I can't stop to say sorry. Emmy's on my heels, her arm looping through mine so she doesn't get lost in the flood of students as we emerge into the STEM hall. Unlike Emmy, I have height on my side and can peer over most heads, but all it does is enhance my massive sense of FOMO. We have no choice but to ride the wave as everyone barrels toward the foyer.

"I don't think you're actually nervous about getting chosen," Emmy says as we enter the foyer.

A sea of students separates us from the bulletin board by the stairs, blocking it from view.

"I think you're nervous about what a certain someone will think if you do get in. *When.*"

"I don't care what he thinks." The words shoot out of me like missiles. As usual, Emmy has read me entirely too close for comfort. Her blue eyes bore into me, but I refuse to meet them. "He already hates me. It can't get any worse."

"You did throw a handful of mashed potatoes at him," she unhelpfully points out.

"And he chucked a pork tenderloin at me!" I exclaim. "Everyone forgets that part."

"I think everyone was kind of busy partaking in the most infamous food fight the school has ever seen."

A food fight that resulted in my first real relationship shattering and landed me in Principal Watershed's office. I was the only student to ever instigate such an atrocity at Wilde Academy, and I had to be reprimanded as such.

After I pulled the "my sister has cancer" card, Principal Watershed finally settled on five days of in-school suspension that wouldn't go on my permanent record. I had to spend it picking the spring harvest in the greenhouse, then catch up on the lessons and work I missed. But it could have been so much worse.

"Did you know I found a green bean in my bra that night?" Emmy continues as we push closer to the bulletin board. "A place where green beans don't belong. Ever."

"If you wanted to stuff your bra, I've heard tissues work great," I suggest.

"Shut up." She laughs, jabbing her elbow into my rib. "For what it's worth, I can't wait to see his face when your name is on that list."

I can, I think to myself. I want to hurt him as badly as he's hurt me, but not like this. Because no matter how in the right I am for wanting—no, *needing*—to apply for the competition, it doesn't change the fact that he was equally valid for not wanting me to.

"I can look first, if you want," Emmy offers as we finally cross the center of the foyer and the grand marble staircase that curves down directly across from the giant entry doors. On the floor beneath us is the Wilde Academy crest—a raven's feather crossed with a fern branch. The feather symbolizes intelligence and wisdom, and the fern symbolizes wealth and prosperity. It's the same design that's on the top left of our Oxford shirts.

"Maybe that's a good idea," I whisper, my lunch threatening to come up.

Only a few bodies stand between us and the bulletin board on the wall to the left of the staircase. Another step brings me closer, but someone knocks into me, forcing me to stumble back.

"Watch it," Dodge Chenney says, his usual sneer reserved just for me painted across his bullish features. "You're looking at a future Champion."

Of course he got chosen. Dodge, and probably all of his friends, had nothing to worry about when applying for the competition. Their politician parents are famous and wealthy and *graciously* donate large amounts of that wealth to the academy.

None of them are here on scholarship like me.

Partial scholarship, I reminded him one time after his on-and-off girlfriend Soph Gonzalez made a nasty comment about how those fronting full tuition are paying for my education. I'm one of the only students not covering my own entire enrollment, and they never let me forget it.

Unlike them, I don't spend my summers vacationing in the Hamptons or Christmas break skiing in Aspen. And honestly, I couldn't care less. Growing up in the miniscule town of Creekson in the shadow of Rosetown, a place full of some of the most ridiculously ostentatious displays of money in Massachusetts, made me realize most of the stuff rich people do is just for show. Not coming from outrageous wealth was never a sore spot for me. Until Cece's diagnosis.

The thought of my bubbly fourteen-year-old sister sitting in a hospital with a stiff gown falling off her too-thin shoulders makes my throat close. I mentally shake away the thought.

"Congratulations," I tell Dodge, not letting an ounce of emotion leak into my voice. He's already brushing past me, leaving enough room for Emmy and me to push into the front line.

"Moment of truth," Emmy says, stepping up to block it from my view.

As the milliseconds pass, hope and despair brawl inside me. My name has to be there. It just has to.

But when Emmy turns to look at me, her face is somehow paler than normal. Even the late-afternoon sun shining through the skylight overhead doesn't warm her, instead highlighting her freckles stark against her ashen face.

"I'm not on it," I assume, trying to keep my voice steady. I will not cry in front of everyone. But it must be the truth. Nothing else would warrant such a horrified look from her.

She opens her mouth, but no sound comes out. She looks more like a fish out of water than my best friend. "Um . . ."

I push her aside, needing to see for myself. My eyes skip down the list. As expected, Dodge is the first senior listed, followed by Soph, then most of his friend group. The name that follows is one I also expect, but it jumps out like a punch to the throat nonetheless. KEANA JAMES. As the other third of my roommate trio with Emmy and my former best friend, I knew she applied. But seeing she's actually been chosen leaves a tang in my mouth, our fight from last month springing to mind. We haven't had a real conversation since.

After Keana is another name that sets my teeth on edge.

CARLOS WOOLF. We spent all of junior year and the first half of senior year in our tight-knit friend group. Woolf, as he goes by, was as much my friend as anyone else. But then the Breakup happened, and his loyalty clearly didn't lie with me. He went from laughing with me to laughing at me, his teasing turned to taunting. He hates me nearly as much as Dodge does. They can bond over that while participating in the competition *I* should have been chosen for.

The next few Challengers aren't necessarily a shock, but my money wouldn't be on any of them to win. I can't believe they'd get chosen over—

My breath stops, eyes finally flicking to the second-to-last line.

CHLOE GATTI.

"That's me!" The words burst out of my mouth. I turn to Emmy, who's watching me warily. "I'm in, Em! I got chosen!" Relief floods my body as a grin splits my face. I can't wait to tell Cece that I'm now a Challenger in the annual Wilde Academy Wilderness Competition.

I don't even care that I'm up against Keana, Woolf, and the likes of Dodge and his crew. Getting chosen was half the battle. The other half, I'm prepared for. I've studied past competitions, read up on every Champion, and pored over yellowing school newspapers dating back to its inception at the turn of the twentieth century. This is just another test to ace.

But Emmy still looks at me like I'm a bomb about to detonate.

"Why aren't you happy for me?" I ask, trying not to let her kill my buzz.

She grabs my shoulders, turning me back to the list. "Look who's competing with you."

My eyes follow her finger to the paper, stomach sinking to my toes as I finally notice the name below mine.

The last Challenger is none other than my bitter, brooding ex: Hayes Stratford.

2

Hayes was the one person in the entire school I was sure would never be caught dead applying for the competition.

I've never hated being wrong as much as I do now.

Anyone else. *Anyone else.* I'd rather be locked in the kissing booth at the Fall Founding Festival with Dodge, or stuck in the broken elevator in the living hall with Keana and forced to confront weeks of passive-aggressive behavior. If I could teleport to the top of Mount Everest just to fling myself off it, I would. And I *hate* heights.

But not as much as I hate Hayes.

"He can't do that," I seethe, although of course he can.

"Chlo," Emmy warns, yanking on my arm. "Let's go."

I hear her, but the words don't click past my rage. It's like I'm ten feet underwater and can see the light of the surface but I'm unable to breach it. Her anxious eyes dart toward the stairs.

"Chlo, we really should—"

I follow her line of sight. Suddenly, it makes sense why she's trying to tug me away.

The stairs have cleared now save for the three boys walking down them. On the left is Philip James—Phlip for short. Keana's twin brother and my toughest academic competition. Like me, Phlip got accepted into a premed program. Unlike me, he's going to Harvard.

On the right is Woolf, his dark brown mocking eyes already settled on me. I set my jaw, determined not to shrink. Emmy silently tugs on my arm, but I can't leave now. That will just confirm I'm itching to run. I refuse to give them the satisfaction.

Opposed to everyone else on the list of Challengers, Woolf doesn't have the grades to warrant getting chosen. He's intelligent enough—students have to hold a 3.5 or higher to stay—but with his knack for talking back to professors and racking up detentions, not to mention his frequently skipped homework assignments, he's not the "star pupil" the school typically picks.

But like Dodge and Soph, Woolf has something I don't— powerful parents with buckets of cash. His dad joined forces with Hayes's to found the law firm Stratford & Woolf twenty years ago. Because of it, Hayes and Woolf grew up together, inseparable since birth.

Hayes.

He's in the center, one step ahead of Phlip and Woolf. Unlike Woolf's amused expression and Phlip's analytical gaze, Hayes's face is stone. His green eyes skate right over me, as if not even registering my existence. It shouldn't still sting after two months of him pretending I'm not here, but it does. I hate him all the more for it.

As usual, he's the picture-perfect boarding-academy student. While the girls need to wear plaid skirts in the signature dark blue, forest green, and black color palette, the boys get away with black slacks, their matching crisp white Oxford shirts tucked in, black suspenders optional and black ties preferred but rarely enforced. Hayes, of course, wears both the suspenders *and* the tie, his polished dress shoes gleaming almost as brightly as his perfectly styled blond hair pushed off his forehead. Paired with his pristine posture and unimpressed air, he looks like every bit the pretentious asshole he seems.

I despise knowing firsthand there's so much more to him.

He descends the last step, coming to a stop mere feet away from me in the exact spot I was in moments ago. His eyes flick over the list of Challengers. If he's shocked to see his name, he doesn't show it. But then again, he has a poker face that rivals Professor Ruffalo's.

Being this close to Hayes—closer than we've been in weeks—ignites a bright burst of anger in me. The audacity he has to spend the better half of spring semester shaming *me* for wanting to apply for the competition just for him to get in himself is so shady and manipulative that it's almost comical. What a hypocritical, self-righteous, egotistical *jerk*.

My mouth opens, whether to hurl insults or ask what the hell his game is, I don't know. But after two months of not saying a word to each other, I'm done getting frozen by his arctic shoulder. If he wants to be ice, I'll happily be fire.

I inhale, ready to scorch him with words. "What the actual fu—"

"I wasn't chosen?"

I'm interrupted by Phlip. Disappointment transforms his face, making his brows droop and eyes blink rapidly behind his glasses. "How was *Ke* chosen and not *me*?"

"Don't act so surprised." As if summoned by her brother's words, Keana weaves through the already-dispersing crowd, a satisfied smirk on her lips. Seeing her name on the list, her grin grows. She spins to face her brother. "Sorry, bro. Guess you'll have to take the L for once."

Phlip's eyes narrow, but comebacks aren't his strong suit, and he stutters over a reply. "I'm not— That's— I have better grades than you! *I'm* in the top one percent. Not you."

Keana keeps her unbothered attitude in place, but I catch the way the jab makes her fists clench.

"They clearly were selecting Challengers based on more than just grades," I say with a pointed look at Woolf.

"Right." Woolf rolls his eyes. "Or maybe they were selecting Challengers based on who has the bigger sob story. Congrats! You took the cake."

Rage boils inside me at the implication that my sister is no more than leverage. I take a step forward, but Emmy grabs my arm, nails digging into my skin to stop me.

Woolf catches the movement, a slow grin forming. He meets my eyes. "Checkmate."

Before I can channel my fury into a reply, Hayes turns his back on all of us and ascends the stairs. Woolf bounds up after him, and they both stop at the landing at the second floor where the staircase splits into two sides. Hayes looks like all of this is entirely too boring and a waste of his time. He still hasn't so much as glanced at me.

"Hell yeah! I can't wait to mess shit up in the forest. We've got this thing in the bag." Woolf whoops, slapping Hayes's back.

Hayes barely registers it.

"Not if I can help it," I mutter, but Woolf's too self-absorbed to hear it, and Hayes is already retreating up the steps that lead to the upper floors.

"It should have been me," Phlip says to Keana with an air of defeat. "Not everything is a competition, Ke."

She snorts. "Rich coming from you."

He gives her one last glare and follows Hayes up the stairs. Woolf lags on the landing, peering across the foyer.

The room isn't half as crowded as it was when we got here, and most of the excited chatter has died down. The majority of seniors aside from us have left, either ecstatic to see their names on the list or disappointed they didn't, if they applied. The remaining underclassmen milling about swap wide-eyed looks, murmuring to each other.

"Why would Hayes even want to apply for the trials?" one sophomore next to me quietly asks her friend.

"Wasn't his brother the one who—"

The friend cuts off when she notices my stare, her mouth snapping shut. I'm sure it's not lost on her the irony that after avoiding each other as much as possible, Hayes and I will be stuck together for two weeks starting tomorrow.

From the landing, Woolf howls—he doesn't have a shameful bone in his body—and spreads his arms as wide as his grin, stealing the room's attention. "Well, everybody? You're looking at this year's class of Challengers for the Wilde Trials."

The Wilde Trials. The infamous nickname students prefer for the wilderness competition due to the fact that Challengers have to compete in seven trials based off the seven traits the school values most.

It elicits the response Woolf's looking for. A wave of cheers rise from around me. He raises his arms to build the hype, and the excitement swells despite the unease coating the room mere seconds ago. *Still* coating the room for me.

I should be that excited. I should be *ecstatic*. Instead, my short-lived relief has fled and rage has won over horror. I'm mad, furious, *seething*. Was Hayes's plan all along to try to convince me not to apply for the trials so I wouldn't be competition for him? He basically tanked our relationship over it.

More likely, applying is his way of getting back at me and making me so angry it smothers my every thought in an attempt to throw me off my game.

And all the worse? It's already working. I can't believe I ever felt anything for him aside from the intense desire to shove him out of an airplane, parachute slashed.

Satisfied with the room's response, Woolf continues up the stairs. He only makes it a few more steps before he pauses. Looking over his shoulder, we lock gazes. With a condescending smirk toying at his lips, he mouths, "Good luck."

I flip my middle finger at his retreating back.

Emmy's already pulling me in the opposite direction. "He's just trying to get a reaction out of you," she tells me once we're in the hallway. When she notices Keana following us, she corrects, "*Both* of you. Don't rise to their bait. They're just boys."

Keana's cool composure slips as she stabs her finger into the elevator button. "Why can't Phlip ever be happy for me?"

Emmy sighs as we walk into the elevator. "His ego's bruised, and he feels left out because Woolf and Hayes got picked. I'm sure he is happy for you. Deep down."

Keana shakes her head so hard that her space buns bob, a few coils of black hair springing loose. "Deep down in the Mariana Trench, maybe. It's not enough that he has the best grades in the entire school and our parents' unconditional love and a full ride to Harvard. He can't let me have this one thing?"

Best grades next to me, I think to myself, but that's not something I should draw attention to. It doesn't matter. Keana and Emmy are already in their usual cadence of talking around me, not with me.

"Maybe he's slipping and hasn't admitted it to you," Emmy suggests. "Why else would Woolf get chosen over him?"

Keana huffs, blowing a loose coil out of her eye. "Slipping? Come on, Em, we're talking about Phlip, here. He has a checklist for taking a shower. He's never slipped a day in his life. Not like I have." She shifts her weight, slowly rolling her left ankle and sucking in a pained breath. It's been four years since her gymnastics injury that ended her Olympic career before it even started, but it still hurts her in more ways than one.

We stare out the glass panel of the elevator, the ground outside growing smaller as we rise four floors to get to the living hall where the dorms are. The window provides a scenic view of the miles and miles of northern New Hampshire forest that Wilde Academy butts up to. On clear days from the observation deck, we can make out the outline of the White Mountains in the distance.

Tomorrow, all the Challengers will be taken deep inside the labyrinth of spruces and maples and hemlock trees, where we'll spend the next two weeks at Wilde Estate. It was the original academy founded by Diana Wilde in the early 1900s. Diana's parents bought acres of land in northern New Hampshire toward the end of the 1800s, built their sprawling estate next to a lake in the middle of the remote forest, and then got tuberculosis before they could enjoy it, along with five out of six kids. Diana was quarantined from the rest of her family to avoid infection and lived in the library for months.

She was the only member of her family to survive. Instead of living on the big property alone, she turned it into a school for kids in need. Funny how that was the original intent behind Wilde Academy. Once she passed and the new school was built in the 1980s to expand the student population and make the campus more accessible to main roads and visitors, it had a demographic flip. By then, enough students had graduated and gone on to be successful that people were willing to pay big bucks to board their kids here. It went from being a school for children in need to hosting some of the wealthiest kids in the country.

As we exit the elevator into the living hall, I wonder what Diana would think of the school now in all its scrubbed red brick, cobblestoned path, advanced-tech glory, while her original family estate decays in the forest only to be visited for two weeks every year. Not to mention the change in economic background of most students. Me included, because while things might not be great at home, at least I have one.

For now.

"So when are we going to address the elephant in the room?" Emmy asks as we amble down the hall in silence. She brushes her braids over her shoulders so they hang down her back, all the way to her elbows. My dark brown hair used to do the same. The curls would make me shudder before realizing it was my own strands brushing my skin and not a spider crawling up my arm. Hayes used to laugh at me, asking how I could get scared by my own hair.

I wonder what he thinks of my hair now, chopped so short that the curly ends barely brush my shoulders. I like it more than I thought I would and am glad I didn't go with my plan to shave my head so I could match Cece once her hair started falling out. The day Cece heard from Mom that I was doing it to surprise her, she FaceTimed begging me not to.

"You just broke up with your boyfriend. Or, he broke up with you. I don't know, it's confusing—" It was. Still is. *"But you absolutely cannot shave your head. I don't care if you think it's solidarity or something heroic like that. You'll look like you're having a post-breakup menty b, and you can't give Hayes that satisfaction. Go get a tub of Ben and Jerry's Half Baked and cry your way through eating the entire pint in one sitting like a normal person."*

So I did, because, honestly, the decision probably was partially influenced by a post-breakup crisis. I had already cut off two ponytails, which the YouTube tutorial suggested, so the next weekend, I hopped the school shuttle to the nearby town with Keana and Emmy and let a stylist fix the rest, returning to campus with enough Ben & Jerry's to feed a small army.

"What elephant?" Keana asks Emmy.

Keana waves her hand in front of our room door. Our room keys are built into the smartwatches every student is given upon arrival, though there's still a lock for an emergency key. I follow her into our room, dropping my backpack on my bed.

Emmy stays in the doorway, arms crossed. "Really? Do I need to spell it out for you?"

She doesn't, because Keana and I are more than aware, but we're both too caught in a game of who can act more aloof. I'm not caving first.

With a huff, Emmy throws the door shut behind her and strides into the room. "Your ex-boyfriend is competing against you," she tells me, as if I'm not painfully aware. She turns to Keana, whose bed is across the room from mine. "And your ex-girlfriend is competing against you. Along with her crappy, aggressive, pompous boyfriend and equally elitist friend group."

Soph. She and Keana were together sophomore year, before I arrived at Wilde Academy. It's likely part of the reason Soph, Dodge, and the rest of their friends immediately took a dislike to me. I became fast friends with Keana and Emmy when I was added to their dorm, which made me enemies with their enemies. It didn't help that Dodge was already at odds with Hayes and Woolf because of their parents. The Stratford & Woolf firm took on a hefty allegations case against Dodge's senator father, which has been ongoing for over a year now, causing plenty of tension between the three.

"What do you want us to do about it?" Keana tosses back at Emmy. "I'm not dropping out. Besides, without a laptop and internet to hack and meddle with, Soph has no upper hand."

"I'm not dropping out, either," I state. "What's the worst that can happen? Hayes cold-shoulders me to death? Been there, done that."

"I'm not saying one of you should drop out." Emmy glances between us. From the apprehensive look on her face, I already know I'm going to hate whatever she suggests. "As two of the smartest girls in school, I don't understand how you don't see the simple solution right in front of your eyes: you should team up."

3

"Absolutely not," Keana scoffs before even a full beat passes. The sting from the rejection is immediate, something I can only salve by being equally abrasive.

"I mean, *I* was going to say absolutely not, but why did *you* say absolutely not?" I snap.

"Hey," Emmy warns. "This doesn't need to turn into a fight."

Keana ignores her. "I don't want to team up with someone who thinks I shouldn't have gotten chosen in the first place."

"I never said that," I counter. "Did you not hear me down there? I defended you."

"With the little comment about how it's not all based on grades? Yeah, thanks for that. You basically put me on the same playing field as Woolf."

"What was I supposed to say?" I ask. "Phlip's right. I'm not implying he should have been chosen over you, but it is weird he didn't get chosen."

"You didn't need to say anything!" Keana explodes. "I don't need you sticking up for me."

"We're getting off topic," Emmy snaps. It's unlike her, but it's been happening more and more lately. She's the peacekeeper of us, the gentle soul to balance out Keana's theatrics and my

heat. Now, she looks anything but gentle. "Think about it—
Challengers team up all the time. It doesn't need to be for long,
just the first few trials. Enough to get ahead."

"Then what?" Keana asks. Her brown eyes turn to me. There's
a tiredness to them I haven't noticed before. "We team up and
inevitably one of us stabs the other in the back?"

"You could stay together only through the turning point trial."

"Trial four," I say, thinking it over. There are benefits, of
course, to partnering with Keana. With no idea what the seven
trials are ahead of time, it'd be nice to have another brain to support mine. And, I suppose, to have a friend. Trial four marks the
halfway point; a chance to get over the hump with help.

"No," Keana says with an air of finality.

Emmy huffs, falling backward onto her bed. I try not to show
how hurtful it is that I'd at least contemplate teaming up but
Keana won't. She walks toward the connected bathroom. Before
going in, she looks at me.

"I can't team up with someone who won't admit the truth. I
know you're still mad at me for applying for the trials. I know
you think my reason isn't as good as yours. That no one's is. But
these aren't *your* trials, Chloe. Other people, regardless of reason,
deserve to compete. I can't team up with someone who's actively
lying to me."

The words dig deep, because of course she's not just talking
about me lying right now. The double meaning is clear in her
eyes. Our conversation from last month stretches between us.

"Are you secretly still seeing Hayes?" she asked when we were
alone after class one day.

Even his name sucked the air from my chest. The Breakup was only three weeks old, and similarly, I felt like a newborn. It was as if I had to relearn how to exist without him by my side, his presence not loud but constantly felt. People say that breakups feel like losing a limb. But *I* felt like the lost limb, discarded and useless.

I knew why she had asked. In my hand was our most recent math test bragging a 98 percent. It wouldn't have been suspicious a month prior, back when Hayes was still tutoring me. But because our breakup broke that, too, I was on my own to conquer my worst subject.

"*No. Hayes and I haven't even spoken,*" I replied to Keana truthfully.

Her next question, I didn't answer quite so honestly.

"I'm getting an early dinner so I can spend the rest of the night prepping to leave for the trials tomorrow," I say, my emotional rubber band too taut to stay in the room.

I pass Keana on my way to the door. Hand on the knob, I pause. "For what it's worth, I *am* happy for you. Because you finally got what you wanted. A leg up on your brother. I just wish *you* could be happy with that. But if we're being honest here, I don't think any win will be enough for you."

Her tone twists from tired to biting. "I guess that makes two of us."

I slam the door behind me, striding down the hall. I make it halfway when Emmy calls my name, emerging from our room.

For a fleeting moment, hope sears my chest that she's following me for once.

"Aren't you coming to the party later?" Emmy asks.

My hope plummets. Of course she's going to take Keana's side. Because no matter how close I became with them, they will always have two years of friendship without me. I'm the outsider, and the bigger the wedge between Keana and me, the more I start to lose Emmy, too.

"I need to pack," I lie. I already set aside most of the things I need for the next two weeks. All that's left to do is put them in the suitcase I keep under my bed.

"It's our last party as high schoolers," Emmy counters. "You can't miss the biggest one of the year. Especially now that you're a Challenger."

Alcohol is strictly prohibited on campus, with the severe consequence of immediate expulsion should you get caught. But despite being home to some of the country's most forward-thinking teenagers, the truth is we are still just that: teens. We have to let loose somehow, and how better than with an end-of-year blowout in the one place on campus far enough removed from the rest of the school?

And so, on the last Friday of classes, the seniors, juniors, and extra-lucky sophomores (never freshmen—they're snitches) head to the giant greenhouse tucked about a half mile into the forest. The newly declared Challengers are always treated as the guests of honor.

"Do a shot for me," I say with a tiny salute.

She deflates at my rejection. I turn my back on her, because if anyone has the puppy-dog look mastered, it's Emmy. But after what just went down with Keana, there's no way I'm about to spend the night in the same greenhouse I served five days of ISS in.

"Chlo, wait."

I sigh. Can't a girl make a dramatic exit for once? But it's Emmy, so I turn around. She glances into our suite and closes the door so it's just the two of us.

"Please promise me you'll look out for her?" she asks, big blue eyes pleading.

The sting is instantaneous, a slap I didn't expect. *Who's going to look out for me?* I want to ask. But I can't muster the courage to be so vulnerable, especially in the hallway where anyone could walk out.

"I'll try," I say.

Her shoulders sag in relief. "Thank you. You're a good friend."

I'm really not, I think. But Emmy doesn't know the specifics of my argument with Keana, though I've never understood why Keana didn't share. I'm not about to, so I smile tightly and give her the most pathetic thumbs-up ever because I don't trust my voice.

I make it safely inside the elevator when tears fall.

It'd be convenient to blame it on Keana and Emmy and how broken the three of us are, but that's not the sole cause for the uncontrollable waterworks. It's the memory of this same day a year ago that hits me like a bullet, driving deep into my splintered heart. The party.

My back collides with the glass pane, and I squeeze my eyes tight as if I can block it out. But memories are violent things, and I'm assaulted by the flashback. Meandering down the cobblestone path to the greenhouse with my fingers entwined with

25

Hayes's while Keana and Phlip bickered about something sense-less like usual. Emmy and Woolf took up the rear, placing bets on who might get the drunkest at the party. Of us, it was unani-mously Woolf. Of the entire school, Dodge had him beat.

Inside the greenhouse, a red SOLO cup pressed to my lips to hide my dopey smile as Hayes leaned down to whisper in my ear.

"Want to get out of here?"

I looped my hands behind his neck, pushing him outside and into the trees. We were nearly the same height, with him at six foot having only an inch or so on me. When my head tipped closer so our foreheads touched, I could feel his breath on my lips.

The ding of the elevator makes the memory ebb, and I make my way back to the now-empty foyer. Snapping a pic of the list, I text it to Cece. **Guess who's about to get even more insuf-ferable?** I say.

Barely twenty seconds go by before I get a response. **OMG OMG? R u serious rn?**

100000000%, I send back. **I'm in baybeeee.**

at the hospital w mom rn but call u later to screech. can i tell her?

I hesitate. I hadn't exactly kept it from Mom and Dad that I was applying for the trials, but I also hadn't been as vocal about it as I was with Cece, since we talk all the time. It's not like I don't think my parents would be proud, but there are a few . . . hesitations.

I want to tell her, I type back. **Don't spill the beans.**

She messages back with at least twenty of the zipped-lips

26

emoji, which I heart before stuffing my phone in my pocket. On my way to the dining hall, I pass through the Champions' hallway. A reverence clings to the air. The walls are lined in textured forest-green wallpaper with framed senior photos of each year's Champion and a silver plaque beneath them with their name and year. At the end of the hallway, I stare at the blank spot where mine will go if I win.

When. I need to think of this like it's already done. Winning means money. It means saving my house and my parents from even worse financial burden than they've already experienced. It means making sure my sister can continue having whatever treatments are keeping her from getting worse.

Losing is not an option.

By the time I get my food from the mostly empty dining hall and finish eating it on the patio, I feel lighter. I don't need to team up with Keana. She'd probably be a distraction, anyway.

When I get back to our room, she and Emmy are gone, which is much preferred. I shower, noticing that I can actually see our bathroom counter for once, which is usually covered in a million products.

"My twelve-step skin-care routine," Keana said when Emmy and I once called her out on the organized chaos. She gestured to her dewy brown skin. *"How else am I supposed to keep my glow?"*

By the way her suitcase bulges, I'm guessing she doesn't plan on missing a night.

I pack in peace, shoving everything I might need for the competition into the suitcase and leaving only my toiletries for the morning. Before my shower, I took off the silver chain I always wear. It's the only time it ever leaves my neck. Now, I pull it out of my underwear drawer, where I hid it in case Keana and Emmy walked in. In the dim luminescence from the fairy lights strung across the ceiling of our room, the ring looped on it gleams.

Taking it with me is a bad idea. Especially given the company I'll be keeping the next two weeks. I should leave it here. Better yet, I should throw it out.

I hold the chain with the ring dangling from it over the small trash can by my desk. All I need to do is let go. Drop it. Easy.

So why won't my fingers do it?

"I don't have a single thing to wear to the party," Keana laments, throwing the door to our suite open. She and Emmy stride in, and I curl the chain into my fist before facing them.

"Done packing?" Emmy asks brightly, ignoring the crackling tension between Keana and me.

"Yeah, but I'm waiting to talk to Cece," I say, glancing at my watch. It's after eleven. Cece should have called me back by now. "I thought you were already at the party."

"The first thirty minutes are when the sophomores and juniors show up," Keana informs me curtly.

She digs through the mountain of clothes in her closet. Emmy and I used to tease her that she was like the squirrel in *Ice Age* looking for the last acorn when trying to find a specific item in her avalanche of apparel.

"I can't find my pink tube top. Have either of you seen it?"

She says it as if we're the same size and I'd swipe it to wear. Where I'm curvy and tall, she's lithe and lean. "Can't say I have."

My phone lights up, saving me. "Cece. Gotta go."

28

Normally, I'd stay in the room, but that was before all the weirdness between the three of us, which I haven't filled Cece in on. As soon as I'm in the hallway, I answer. "Hey, everything okay? What took you so long?"

"Yeah, yeah, everything's fine," she says in her typical *Chill out* voice. She's in her favorite lemon-yellow hoodie and is curled up against her mountain of Squishmallows on her bed. Like me, she has olive-toned skin, but between her illness, the sweatshirt, and the lighting, her face has a sickly green tint. "There was a bunch of paperwork Mom had to fill out at the hospital since I got more tests done today, and then they wanted to go to dinner because I was *so brave*." She gives me her most solemn martyr look; it pulls a laugh out of me. "Obviously, I chose Cheesecake Factory."

"Obviously," I reply. "Where else could you dine with such riveting decor?"

"You get it." She smiles, but it's edged with exhaustion. "Where are you?"

"On my way outside." It wasn't my original plan, but with everyone jazzed for the party, there are too many people coming and going in the hallways.

"I thought you would have called Mom or Dad by now," she says.

"Did you tell them?"

"I'm no snitch. But Dad's already snoring on the couch, and Mom's been reading in bed for a suspiciously long time. I could wake them up—"

"No, don't do that." Relief flushes through me, doubled by the cool spring air hitting my cheeks as I step outside. "I'll text them in the morning about it. It's only two weeks, and then they'll be here for graduation anyway. Which, are you cleared to come? If it's too much, you don't have to."

"First of all, I wouldn't miss your graduation even if the sky was falling down. Second of all, don't change the subject," Cece warns, though it's hard to feel intimidated when she's frowning so adorably. "You didn't tell them on purpose, didn't you?"

"Not true," I say, though she's hit the nail on the head. "More like I omitted some facts."

"More like you didn't want them to tell you not to apply."

I hope the partial darkness hides my flinch at her bluntness. "You know how overprotective they can be."

"Oh, don't I know it. Mom doesn't even let me get out of the car on my own lately. But maybe their overprotectiveness is kind of valid for this."

"I'm not sure *overprotectiveness* is a word."

Cece ignores me. "I saw Hayes on the list."

No one's around, but I walk toward the surrounding woods that line the back of campus just in case someone overhears.

"Yeah, Hayes," I say, trying to keep my tone as casual as possible. "Surprise."

"Wasn't the competition the entire reason you guys broke up?" she puzzles.

Not even close, I think to myself. But that was the easiest explanation, especially after the food fight fiasco. It was certainly easier than explaining how my life felt perfect right up until that frigid February morning where I mentioned to Hayes that maybe, *maybe*, I wanted to apply for the wilderness competition.

The look on his face is branded on my memory, like I slapped him. *"You're joking,"* he said flatly.

I shook my head. *"They've made so many safety upgrades since—since the old trials. And they've tripled the prize money."*

"So many safety upgrades since my brother died, you mean?"

His tone was ice, so frigid it felt like the dining hall had dropped a few degrees. Even my eggs seemed colder, but I suddenly wasn't hungry anyway.

"I'd be careful," I said. It was the wrong thing to say.

"Like he wasn't careful?"

I let the conversation drop after that. But then Cece's expensive diagnosis was shared with me over a teary phone call, and suddenly the Wilde Trials went from being a nicety to the ticket to helping to pay for the hospital bills without burying my parents in debt. I had to apply. Hayes would come around. He might not ever like it, but he couldn't hate me for doing something for my family.

Apparently, he could.

Weeks of tension finally boiled over in the dining hall, where, after another attempt at getting me to back down from applying to the trials, he huffed, *"You wouldn't even be here if it weren't for your scholarship."*

The cruelty of the words still digs beneath my skin, a punch he had never thrown before because he *knew* how sensitive I was about my scholarship. He was the one who constantly stood up for me about it when Dodge and Soph took jabs.

I don't remember picking up the glob of mashed potatoes

from my plate and launching it across the table at his head. I only remember the way he slowly blinked at me while gravy dripped down his cheek.

And how the entire dining hall devolved into chaos.

"It was complicated," I answer my sister finally. "Plus, we would have never survived long distance with me going to Brown and him to Stanford."

"I thought he applied to Juilliard for their piano program?"

"Composing program," I correct. "I don't know if he got in, but it doesn't matter. He's going to go to Stanford just like his dad did, and like his brother was supposed to, and will take over his dad's half of the firm someday."

She makes a face. "Sounds boring."

"He thought so, too. I guess he changed his mind. Anyway, he really didn't want me to apply to the trials."

"Well, yeah, with good reason. His brother literally *died*, Chlo."

"You know that was an accident," I remind her, though that's part of the reason I was so surprised Hayes applied at all. I can't imagine spending two weeks in the same place where my sibling died three years prior. It just reinforces my belief that he must have applied to spite me. "Plus, the school has apparently made all these new improvements to the estate property so it's extra safe. They'd never allow us back if it wasn't."

She frowns. "I still don't get why they can't keep having them closer to the school like they did the past two years."

My nose scrunches. "Then I'd have to sleep in a tent. And last year, a snake crawled inside one. I'd much rather be in the old estate, even if it's creepy. Plus, when the trials were closer to school, it was easier for Challengers to cheat. They still had cell service."

"You won't have cell service?" She gawks. "I can't talk to you for two weeks?"

"I'm sorry it will be the most boring two weeks of your life."

"Meanwhile you'll be running around the forest like Tarzan in a trial for . . . what's one of the traits they base the trials off of again? Expert MLA formatting?"

I laugh, the kind of warm, full-belly one only my sister can draw out. "The seven traits the trials are based on each year are strength, collaboration, wit, ambition, fortitude, agility, and adaptability. You were close."

"Not all of us have textbook memories like you," she teases, but I can pick out the thread of insecurity behind it. Even before her diagnosis, Cece wasn't great at school. She spent more of class doodling in her notebooks than taking actual notes.

"Thank God for that. It'd be a pretty bland world if everyone just mouthed off facts to each other all day."

"You would love it," she counters.

"Are you calling me bland?"

She giggles. "The blandest." Her smile falls all too soon. "Just promise you'll be careful, okay? I know you're kind of doing this for me."

"Self-centered much?" Though of course she's right. "Besides, it's not dangerous. I'm pretty sure one of the trials last year was, like, doing a group project but make it woodsy."

"Sounds like your nightmare," she points out. "Or is the

nightmare part spending two weeks with Hayes?"

That part's more like my sleep paralysis demon. But I don't want her to worry. "I'll be fine. It's not like we have that much space separating us here."

"If you say so. You'll call Mom and Dad in the morning?"

"Sure thing," I promise.

A yawn escapes her. If I tell her she's tired, she'll fight me on it. I have to cut this off even though I'd talk to her all night if I could.

"I should probably head back inside," I force out. I hope Keana and Emmy are at the party by now. "But don't worry, okay? I need you to believe that I'll win, not flop."

"I always believe you'll win." She smiles sleepily. "I love you, Chlo."

My heart swells. "Love you back, Ce."

We hang up, and I realize the chain of my necklace is still in my fist. I could drop it right here in the woods among roots and dirt, kick a few fallen leaves over it, and the ring would disappear forever.

But like the numerous times I've tried to get rid of it before, I can't bring myself to do it. Slipping the chain over my head, I tuck it under my shirt so the ring rests against the bare skin of my sternum where it belongs.

As I walk back toward school, my gaze rises. I can barely make out the faint glow of the lights on the railing of the observation deck, an all-glass balcony that juts out from the roof. Even with my feet firmly planted on the ground, my stomach still swoops at the several stories between me and it. A shadow makes the light flicker, like someone might be up there. Everyone's likely at the party, so it's probably just the clouds moving across the barely-there moon.

My phone buzzes with an incoming text from Cece. A laugh escapes me at my poorly photoshopped senior picture with a crown on my head and the word *Champion* floating above it in Comic Sans.

rooting 4 u, she says with a heart.

Resolve floods me. I have to win for her.

I'll do whatever it takes.

4

SATURDAY, MAY 24, 5:50 A.M.

"I hate goodbyes." Emmy pouts, shivering against the morning chill.

We stand at the top of the stone steps leading down to the main walkway. At the end of it, a luxury bus waits.

"It's just 'see you later,'" I assure her as we hug. "We'll be back in two weeks for graduation."

I don't mention how that will be the real goodbye. Maybe not for her and Keana, but probably for me. I'll go home to Creekson, Massachusetts, for the summer before heading to Brown in the fall, and they'll go home to New York. We used to brainstorm plans to visit each other at college, but that hasn't come up in weeks.

Emmy pulls Keana into a hug next. I try not to notice how theirs is longer, but the sting is there all the same. The vibes in our suite this morning were even more bleak than usual. They got back last night when I was already asleep, and Keana barely spoke as we packed up the last of our things this morning. Though not typically a morning person, usually I can count on her to at least grumble a bit about the early hour.

When they finally part, Emmy grabs both of our hands,

tugging us together so we form a human triangle. For a disorienting moment, it feels like before our friendship splintered, when we were all three equal slices of the same pie.

"I know you don't want to team up," Emmy says.

Keana and I make eye contact and rip our gazes away just as quickly.

"But there are bigger, *meaner* fish to fry than each other, okay? Remember who you should be competing against. The Cabinet."

Emmy nods toward the bus where Dodge, Soph, Lainey, and Malcolm are boarding. We haven't used the silly nickname Woolf coined for their friend group in months, dying with everything else post-breakup. It was hilarious given the political prowess of their parents.

"Noted," Keana says dully. She glances at the double doors we emerged from, and suddenly her sullen mood makes sense. Phlip didn't come to see her off.

I want to say something to Keana about it, but after last night's argument, nothing feels right. We walk down the stone steps with our things in tow. I pause, looking back at the academy. I'll miss it, I think. Not the last two months, but when I first got admitted to the school, life was a dream. Coming to Wilde Academy was a life-changing opportunity.

But now, the true life-changing event is just a bus ride away.

At the end of the path, Professor Ruffalo and Principal Watershed stand. Beside them are the four Champions who will act as our chaperones (see also: babysitters) for the next two weeks. Carly McAster, who won last year. Jarod Lee, the year before. Trevor Kostakis, who I never went to school with but won the year Hayes's brother died. They were best friends, and he's stayed close with Hayes's family ever since. The last in the lineup is Aura Lang, the oldest.

Keana waves to Emmy and steps onto the bus. Principal Watershed wishes me luck with a tight smile. Ever since bawling my eyes out in his office, I can't look him in the eye. I'm pretty sure he regrets not expelling me after the food fight.

But when I win the trials, that'll prove to him I was worth keeping.

"Miss Gatti, fancy seeing you here." Professor Ruffalo smiles at me as I pause in front of her. "I know how hopeful you were to get chosen. Are you excited?"

"Absolutely," I say, zero hesitation. "I was so nervous I wasn't picked."

"I know," she muses. "I seem to remember you and Miss McCloud debating it in yesterday's lesson."

"Sorry about that," I say, embarrassed.

She chuckles. "Well, it's not totally up to me, but I never had a doubt." She glances around and lowers her voice. "As your teacher, I can't say I'm rooting for anyone specific. But good luck." She winks.

My mouth opens, the tiniest *thank you* escaping. She's been advocating for me since I first arrived and was behind academically, experiencing a hell of a culture shock. Back then, she told me I needed to push through. The next two weeks won't be any different. I want to give her a hug and thank her for the encouragement, but it feels inappropriate with Principal Watershed so close. We shake hands instead, and I move on to the Champions.

In Carly's hand is a clipboard. "Name?" she asks, flipping her icy-blond ponytail over her shoulder.

I have to refrain from rolling my eyes. Wilde Academy isn't big enough to pretend not to know underclassmen, plus we had an astronomy elective together last year. But for the next two weeks, she's my superior, so I have to play along.

"Chloe Gatti," I say.

Carly checks my name off as Jarod gives me an appraising look. His arms cross, muscles bulging beneath dark brown skin. Beside him, as if to counter Jarod's judgment, Trevor smiles at me. The whites of his teeth contrast with his tanned face and a spark of kindness burns in his gray eyes.

I brushed up on everything I could find on the Champions during my prep. Jarod's going into his third year of sports medicine, Carly's studying political science, and Trevor is at Brown and aiming to take over his dad's law firm someday. It's how he grew up close to Hayes's family—lawyers in SoCal travel in the same social circles. Aura was tough to find much on because she's dark on social media, but according to her senior profile, she's in veterinarian school.

She's the last Champion I pass before boarding the bus. "Find a seat," she says. Her voice is quiet and almost reluctant. Paired with her slight frame and choppy shoulder-length hair that hangs in her eyes, it's hard to believe she's the oldest.

On the bus, I shuffle down the aisle, looking for an empty spot. Keana is toward the middle. As I walk to her, I realize she stacked her bags on the free seat next to her. Message received. I hate how every slight from her is like a splinter that keeps getting wedged deeper and deeper into my skin. A nuisance and unignorable.

I could go back to the front where the Champions will probably sit once they come on, but I'm not trying to look like *that* much of a kiss-ass. Dodge and the Cabinet predictably took the back. There are several free rows in front of them, but getting to them means I'd have to pass Woolf and Hayes. Hayes already has AirPods in and is facing the window as if there's much to see when we haven't even left yet, but Woolf catches my gaze. He lifts his brow in a dare, as if he can read my internal debate on my face.

"You can sit here if you want?"

I look down at the voice. Mina Sato, a girl who was my chem partner junior year, moves her bag from the seat beside her, making room for me.

"Thanks." I drop into the seat, stuffing my suitcase below and keeping my backpack on my lap.

Three more Challengers shuffle on—Jaleigh Nelson, Charlie Giblin, and Alandra Watershed, Principal Watershed's niece, who might have exercised some light nepotism to get into the academy. I don't make that claim unfounded; she cries every time she gets under a 90 percent on a test, and her tear ducts have been putting in the work lately. I'd be shocked if she's maintaining the 3.5 GPA the rest of us need to.

The four Champions are the last to get on. Trevor stands at the front while the others sit.

"Good morning, Challengers," he greets, receiving murmured responses back. "Thanks for arriving promptly, because we weren't going to wait for you. We've got a long drive ahead of us as we head into the forest. I suggest you get some sleep. While the first trial doesn't start until tomorrow, we have a busy day planned once we arrive."

He sits down and the bus returns to low conversations and the rustling of bags as everyone gets situated. We pull out of the large looped driveway that leads to the school. It's not until we pass under the stone archway advertising "Wilde Academy" that it hits me.

I'm going to the Wilde Trials. For two weeks, it will be me, the forest, and these fifteen people. One of whom is a bully, another who used to be my best friend, a third who used to be my boyfriend, and a fourth who is annoyingly loyal to said ex-boyfriend. *Great.*

"Kind of ridiculous, isn't it?" Mina asks, gazing out the window as we turn onto a dirt road. The bus slows as it carefully weaves between large trunks and foliage. I wonder if this path used to be bigger, but each year, the trees grow and steal a little more of it.

"What part?" I ask her.

"All of it." She gestures vaguely.

In her hand is a tubed device that I recognize as an inhaler. Cece has one, too. In her other hand is an array of colored plastic strings woven together to make what's probably the beginnings of a bracelet or key chain. Boondoggle, I think it's called.

"I mean, we got chosen out of over eighty seniors to go into the forest for some weird wilderness competition."

I must make a face, glancing toward the front of the bus to

make sure the Champions didn't overhear her flippant remarks.

Her eyes widen. "Sorry. I forgot some people actually want to be here."

"If you don't want to be here, why did you apply?" I ask.

"My mom wanted me to," Mina admits. "She was a Champion her year, so she wanted me to apply to try to start a tradition. I never thought I'd get chosen, though. She was just as surprised."

"You wouldn't have been picked if you didn't deserve it."

She glances at me. "Can you keep a secret?"

I nod.

She leans in close and lowers her voice. "I don't think there were a ton of applicants this year. There hasn't been since . . . well, you know. Plus, since Challengers have to be eighteen, that narrows the pool. I went with my parents to the holiday party for the alumni society, and I overheard my mom talking to Principal Watershed about how applicant numbers have been so low, they might eventually get rid of the competition. That's why the alumni society donated more money than ever for the prize pot, but I don't know if it made a difference. I don't think I would have been chosen if it did."

Disappointment flares at her words. I wanted to think I beat out a lot of my peers. That all my relentless studying and late nights contributed. But if what she says is true, then I might have gotten picked either way based off of low applicants.

"You're really smart, though," I say, needing to cling to some piece that our academic performance was taken into consideration.

"I mean, I don't have perfect scores like you." She smiles at me teasingly. "But I'm pretty good at holding my own. I'm certainly above *him*."

She jerks her head toward the back, where Dodge is already asleep, head thrown back and snores escaping his mouth loud enough to warrant a CPAP machine.

A laugh escapes me. "I think most of us are."

That spurs a responding giggle from her. "True. But still, I was just as shocked as anyone else when I saw my name on that list. I'm not exactly cut out for forest living."

"You've got the Wi-Fi–less activities down," I say, nodding at her boondoggle.

"My therapist told me I should try tying knots to help with my anxiety, so . . ." She raises the boondoggle, shrugging. "We'll see if she's right. Camping's so not my thing."

"More of a glamper?"

"More of a 'if a bee looks at me wrong, I go into anaphylactic shock.' 'If the grass is too wet, I can't breathe out of my nose.' 'If the grass is too dry, my skin itches.' 'If I inhale too much pollen, my asthma flares up.'" She holds up her inhaler as proof.

"Dang," I say. "Your mom made you apply knowing all that?"

She shrugs. "She thinks I make up a lot of it, aside from the bee allergy. I'm the pain-in-the-ass kid compared to my siblings."

"Felt," I agree, though my parents would never purposefully make me feel that way. But between begging them to send me to the academy and the damning food fight, I can't help but feel as if I'm more of a hassle than I'm worth. "My sister has never done anything wrong a day in her life. She never asks for anything outside of what my parents can easily give her. Never gets bored or wants what she can't have. She's just . . ." I search for the right words to describe Cece. "Good. Kind. Soft."

"You don't think you're those things?" Mina asks.

"I—" I break off, unsure of my answer. With Hayes I felt soft. Like he was always a shield or shell, and I was the one taking cover behind his glares and protective energy. I didn't need it most of the time, except for when Dodge acted up. But it was still nice to know it was there. He was there.

And if I was good, or kind, or soft, wouldn't I offer to team up with Mina? It popped into my head as soon as I sat down. With all her allergies and nonexistent competitive edge, she reminds me of Cece, who I can't imagine not breaking down in a forest removed from the rest of society. If the roles were flipped, and Cece was sitting next to someone who could potentially help her, wouldn't I want them to go out of their way and do their best to make sure she did okay?

But I'm doing this *for* Cece. If I'm helping anyone but myself, that's a disservice to her and me. I have to stay focused, which means I have to be on my own.

"I don't know," I settle on. "Sometimes I feel a little too ambitious to be those things."

Mina frowns, the expression out of place on her delicate features. "I think you can be both," she says. "Or at least try. That's gotta be worth something."

"Maybe," I half-heartedly agree, no longer wanting to continue the conversation. So I do what jerks do when they don't want anyone to talk to them anymore. I stick my knockoff Air-Pods in my ears and close my eyes, pretending to fall asleep to the lull of my music as we drive deeper and deeper into the forest.

Eventually, I do fall asleep. When my eyes spring open hours later, it's to a gasp.

"Holy shit," Soph says.

The bus stops, and a hush falls. The sun is high now, streaming in through the windows and blinding me. I blink away the disorienting brightness, my mouth dropping open at the sight through the windows.

"There is no way we're about to spend two weeks here," Mina breathes as we take in a towering iron fence with ivy twisting up it, leading to barely legible words: *Wilde Estate*.

"I think . . . yes way," I say.

"We're here!" Trevor announces. The corner of his mouth lifts in a smirk as he gestures to the iron fence and the foreboding structure beyond. "Welcome to the Wilde Trials."

5

"This isn't creepy *at all*," Malcolm comments as we step off the bus, glancing around the endless trees. His red hair is mostly concealed by a dark green backward baseball cap, which he readjusts.

"Gonna piss your pants, bro?" Dodge snorts.

Soph flicks a hand toward the iron gate in front of us and, more attention-worthy, the looming estate behind it. "You don't have to be a baby to admit this place looks straight out of *The Conjuring*."

I hate to admit it, but she's right. Wilde Estate isn't just old—it's decrepit. The pictures that are hung up in the language hall and spotty views from Google Earth don't do it justice. Those have to be at least ten to twenty years old, maybe more. And that's not even a compliment. Those photos feature an estate in the woods that looks abandoned.

This is worse. Behind the iron gates is a dirt road that once was likely a manicured drive. Now, bushes climb toward the sky, creating a narrow alley leading to the porch.

With a giant ring full of keys of all styles and sizes, Trevor unlocks the massive padlock chaining the gates together. The lock and chain fall to the ground with a thud. "Well, then," he says, brushing off his hands, "time for the tour?"

Mina and I share another look, hoisting up our luggage and following the others through the gate. I glance at Keana, and she meets my eyes. My own apprehension is reflected in her expression, a mutual *What the hell is this?* passing before she looks away.

"How many spiders do we think are in this place?" Woolf asks Hayes as we walk through the alley of overgrown bushes glistening with webs.

"At least four," Hayes answers dryly.

Somehow, I think spiders will be the least of our worries.

As we emerge from the shrouded path, the estate comes in full view. It's something between a house and a castle. A plaque back at school described it as Queen Anne architecture. While originally starting as a house of decent size, Diana Wilde kept adding to it as the school expanded, room by room. Legend says there are secret passageways that serve as shortcuts from one side of the building to the other. Looking at it now, it absolutely looks like a place full of cobwebbed nooks and crannies. Probably home to a few ghosts, too.

The most concerning part of the estate isn't just the ivy swallowing it or the way moss covers more roof than not. It's the right side where the roof partially collapsed, the structure giving way to splintered wood and tangled greenery.

We stare at it as the Champions ascend the wooden porch steps. They go slowly, assessing the structural integrity before motioning the rest of us to join them on the porch beside four ancient wooden rocking chairs. They sway ominously as if someone just got up and left.

The steps creak precariously, and I am suddenly *very* aware that I am bigger than the majority of my classmates. More curvy than most of the girls, taller than most of the boys. Likely heavier, too. I quicken my pace to cut the chances of falling through.

"Over there." Trevor points to the concaved section of the house, which includes the far end of the porch. A string of caution tape blocks it off. Beyond it, wild shrubs replace what was once the end and railing. "Off-limits. Don't even think about going near it. That's the west wing."

"What's wrong with the west wing?" Charlie asks, as if it's not obvious.

"A tree fell two years ago," Mina pipes up, tucking her straight dark hair behind her ear. "That's why the trials were held in the forest closer to school the past two years. They needed to make sure the estate was totally safe before anyone came back."

"Comforting," Keana mutters.

"Professionals cordoned it off and approved the rest of the property as secure," Trevor explains, slotting a skeleton key into the lock on the front door. It's huge, more like the entrance to a church. Similar to the rest of the house, it boasts a weathered paint job, making it difficult to tell if the original color is the current homely gray or if it faded to that.

Trevor grabs the knob, giving us a conspiratorial look from over his shoulder. "Ready?"

He doesn't wait for confirmation, swinging open the giant door. As if awakening something that's been long dormant, a foreboding groan escapes from its rusted hinges, sending a shudder down my spine.

The stale air assaults me, a cloud of dust tickling my throat and making me join a chorus of coughs. Mina takes a puff from her inhaler.

"Home sweet home," Jarod declares, spreading his arms wide. We shuffle in, sunlight from a glass dome above us filtering down. Unlike the crystal clear skylights at school, the glass is covered in a film of grime, obscuring the sky. Thin snakelike shadows streak across it. Vines.

It provides enough light to see the space, which isn't quite as creepy as the outside hints. The walls are composed of wood paneling until about halfway up, and peeling floral wallpaper covers the top half. A chandelier hangs from the part of the ceiling that's not glass, covered in webs that glint in the faint light. There're bulbs in it, but when I reach for the light switch on the wall, Carly smacks my hand away.

"We have to conserve energy during the day," she scolds. "The power is generated by solar panels. Obviously, not a lot of direct sun gets through the trees. If we want light at night, don't turn it on during the day unless absolutely needed."

"Running water is a similar story," Trevor explains. "Like the new academy, the estate gets its water from Wilde Lake. Because of the minimal energy, hot water is in short supply. Keep your showers short. And don't drink the tap. We've brought bottled water. Plumbing still works, but is shitty"—he pauses, a smile toying on his lips—"pun intended."

"For best results," Jarod drawls. "Practice the courtesy flush."

"Courtesy flush?" Lainey asks, wrinkling her nose.

"When you dump," Dodge oh-so-eloquently explains. "You

flush before you wipe. It's a courtesy to the pipes."

"Thanks for that." Trevor brings us into the dining room. The table is long, like it's meant for one giant dinner party, with at least thirty seats. Hayes drags his finger across the surface, leaving a streak in the dust.

"There's a caretaker who maintains the property, but he only comes once a month." Carly frowns. From her barely concealed disgust, it's clear she had higher hopes for the estate. Since she and Jarod didn't come out here for their trials, they're exploring it in real time with us.

As I follow Aura into the kitchen, I pass a china cabinet that covers the entirety of the wall full of colorful plates. It adds some life to the lackluster space.

The kitchen is spacious, with the biggest fridge I've ever seen taking up an entire corner, though I wouldn't trust that there's not something living in it. Thanks to the surplus of windows, the space feels less creepy and just dated. Enough light streams in to highlight the cracked cream walls. There's an island in the center of the room and old Formica counters outline the perimeter. The oven in the corner opposite the fridge is an impressive retro range, the kind Dad would go nuts cooking on.

The thought of him makes guilt swarm in my gut. I broke my promise to Cece and never called my parents this morning. Partially an accident, mostly on purpose. I finally sent them a text as cell service started blinking out on the drive, and I put my phone on airplane mode. Another incentive to win has been added to the list: it's probably the only way my parents won't be too mad I came here without telling them.

"We're responsible for our own food," Trevor says. "We

brought the majority of what we need, but today will be spent prepping our meals for the next few days. I know you're probably used to Parmesan-crusted mahi and filet mignon. Here, you'll be eating even better."

"Lobster?" Alandra asks hopefully.

"Good old peanut butter and jelly," Jarod replies with matching enthusiasm.

Carly snickers as Alandra's face plummets.

"Because of the energy situation, we don't have a working fridge," Aura adds. "We have a gas stove and propane. The bus will drop off more food as we need it."

"The bus comes back before the two weeks are over?" I ask. None of the previous information I've studied said anything about that. The whole idea is for us to feel like we're literally stuck in the forest, just like the students at Wilde Estate were.

"You're not here to get spoiled," Trevor says, not hearing me.

Aura did, and her mouth parts like she wants to respond, but Trevor continues.

"The Wilde Trials are an opportunity to reflect on where you really want to be and what you're willing to do to get there. For these next two weeks, you have nothing. Just the clothes on your back, your bags, and your reputations. How you emerge will be entirely up to you. But there's only one winner. Who will it be?"

He asks the question to the room at large. When he raises a brow, I realize he's waiting for an answer.

He sighs, slowing his words down. "Who? Will? It? Be?"

"Me." It shoots out of me like a bullet. My competitors glare at me.

"There we go." Trevor looks around the room, opening his

arms wide. "Anyone else actually want this? Because here's your first hint—that's the only way you'll get anything in life. You have to want it more than anything else. You have to *take* it."

"Me," Keana follows.

"Me," Soph says, then nudges Dodge.

"Me," he says.

Malcolm and Lainey echo him, and then Mina and the other Challengers I haven't sized up much. Woolf says it, leaving Hayes as the only person who hasn't.

I only allow myself to look at him because everyone else is. Amid the dust and decay of the estate, Hayes looks out of place in his perfectly pressed shirt and slacks. I shouldn't be surprised. If he could sleep and shower in his uniform, he would.

"Me," he finally says, though the word sticks in his throat.

Trevor smiles encouragingly, an unwanted reminder that Hayes might have a leg up. Trevor likes him, knows him, and while the Champions aren't supposed to play favorites, the rules could easily get warped so far away from home.

"Glad to see some initiative," Trevor commends us. "You'll need to show a lot more if you plan to win."

We continue the tour into the living room, which has a jumbled mix of shabby furniture around a stone fireplace with a giant painting over it. The hearth is sandwiched between two floor-to-ceiling bookcases that still have a few classic titles. We loop back into the foyer and ascend the surprisingly sturdy wooden staircase. It splits down the middle of the room, with a landing for the second floor, where the Champions will stay, while Challengers occupy the third floor of the east wing. True to what Trevor said outside, the west wing is completely walled off. The scent of fresh paint battles with the stagnant air.

On the third floor, the landing is open so you can peer over the railing all the way down to the foyer. The distance to the floor makes my knees week. I turn away, following everyone down the hallway.

"You each have your own rooms but will share the two bathrooms at the end of the hall. One at a time. No funny business." Trevor gives us a stern look, eyes lingering on Soph and Dodge. "If I even hear the hinges on your doors squeak after midnight, much less catch you in each other's rooms, that's grounds for instant elimination."

"We don't need anybody getting pregnant," Carly adds, hand on her hip.

Trevor makes a face at her, as if to say *You didn't need to go that far.* She pulls out a ring of skeleton keys nearly as big as Trevor's and starts passing them out. "Your room number is engraved on the handle."

"The bow," Macolm corrects, taking his. "That's the official name of it."

"Fascinating," Carly says, not sounding the least bit interested. She jams a key into my hand. It's so old that it's difficult to see any part of the intricate design, but once I rub the dust off, I can just make out the number seven. Maybe that's a good luck sign.

When I swing the door open for room seven and am greeted by a pungent scent like something died in here, I decide seven must be an *unlucky* number. The room has a small bed with an iron frame shoved against the wall with a set of sheets sitting on it, a four-drawer dresser, a window at least 60 percent covered by ivy that blocks the only light source aside from an antiquated lamp on a rickety bedside table, and a single wooden chair in the only spare corner for peak creeptastic vibes. I'm pretty sure if I sit in it, it will disintegrate.

I try to open the window to get some fresh air in, but it's stuck. Above the door is a small horizontal glass pane that I remember my mom calling a transom window when we took a tour of a historic house for a sixth-grade field trip she chaperoned. Whatever mechanism connected to the hinge to open it is missing, and as tall as I am, I can't reach the glass itself to push. Stinky air it is.

"Off to a great start," I mumble.

"Hey, at least you have a bed," Carly says, poking her head through my open door. "Better than the tent I had to sleep in last year."

Twenty-four hours ago, I would have agreed. Now, as I sit down on the bed and the springs squeal so loudly I flinch, breaking my back on the forest ground might be preferred.

I make eye contact with Carly, who shrugs as if to say *You signed up for this.* She ducks out into the hallway.

"Meet in the foyer in ten minutes!" she announces. "Then the *real* work will begin."

6

The rest of the day flies by in a whirl of activity.

We get divided into unloading, cleaning, and cooking groups. The unloading crew spends the afternoon carrying in coolers and clear plastic totes of food, along with opaque ones that Trevor passes off to Jarod to lock away somewhere upstairs.

The cleaning group is headed by Carly and armed with dusters and brooms to freshen up the downstairs. Hayes is among them, which is the perfect fit given he hates messes and keeps his side of his room more spotless than a hospital.

It's another reason I never thought he would apply for the trials. Two weeks in the forest isn't just less than ideal for Hayes—it's anxiety-inducing. Even if he's masking it behind an impassive face.

I got put with the cooking group, which is someone's sore mistake. It takes only twenty minutes into dinner soup duty before I accidentally overboil the broth, nearly burning my fingers off in the process. Aura shifts me to join Keana at the peanut-butter-and-jelly station.

Keana shakes her head as I pick up a butter knife and start smearing. "For someone so smart," she says, a smile pulling at her lips. "You're a shit chef."

"Gordon Ramsay would be incredibly disappointed in me," I agree.

Wilde Estate might be even more decrepit than we expected, but we're still *here*. The energy in the air is infectious, despite the mundane tasks.

Keana bites back a laugh. I want to keep the conversation between us going, but we're interrupted by Malcolm complaining about his exhausted soup-stirring arm. Soph tells him he's being a little bitch, which might be the most agreeable sentiment that's ever left her lips.

For dinner, we eat around one long picnic table in the backyard, where the full extent of damage to the west side of the estate is clear. The path of destruction from the fallen tree is obvious, creating a deep V in the silhouette of the estate where one really doesn't belong. It looks as if the forest is eating the west wing, the branches and vines blending with loose shingles and splintered wood.

"When I was here for my trials, we had the run of the place," Trevor says, making me jump.

I try to cover it with the guise that my soup burned me, not wanting to appear so easy to startle.

"We could go all over. I don't suggest the basement, though. Fucking creepy." He grins at me. Between his tan skin and curling black hair, not to mention his gray eyes, which stand out starkly in contrast to the rest of him, he's what Cece would call "a hot tamale." I'd swipe right any day.

"I wouldn't say basements are typically in my top ten places to hang." I shrug, hoping I don't come off as geeked as I feel.

He laughs lightly. "Ditto. But you see those windows over there?"

He points to the far side of the west wing, past the fallen tree, where part of the building stands despite the ivy trying to swallow it. There's a giant wall of windows. Back in the day, I bet it was beautiful and let in plenty of light, easily becoming a place I could see myself spending hours in.

Most of the window is still intact, but a leaning hemlock has burst through the circular top part.

"Was it the church?" I ask.

"The library," he corrects.

"Where Diana lived while her family . . ." I trail off, not wanting to say it.

"Died? Yeah. At least she was stuck in her favorite room."

I nod. I've seen old pictures of the library, but none featuring the windows. In most, Diana sits in front of the hearth, which is framed with towering bookshelves, just like the ones in the living room.

"The library still had the majority of its books in there. No rare texts, of course. Those all got moved over to the new library. But still plenty of good options. Kind of sad they're all stuck in there forever now." He clears his throat. "Anyway, Professor Ruffalo mentioned to me you're going to Brown in the fall for premed. First year can be especially demoralizing, so if you ever need anything, I'm happy to help."

"Thank you!" I internally wince at my squeaky voice. I can't believe Professor Ruffalo brought me up to him, though since she's on the board facilitating the trials and in communication with the previous Champions, I shouldn't be surprised. I'm sure they got briefed on all of us Challengers. But still, Trevor offering to help me is another ego boost. While I'll be a freshman, he'll be a senior. And if I win, that will make two Champions at Brown at the same time. It would be nice to have a connection to somebody so I'm not totally on my own.

I think about it through the rest of dinner and cleanup, imagining life at Brown. My thoughts float to sooner—getting handed a check for $600,000 and giving a speech at graduation, one I've practiced dozens of times in front of my bathroom mirror so I'm not scrambling to come up with something on the bus ride back to school.

I'm still stuck in the fantasy when my neck prickles with the feeling of eyes on me. From across the island in the center of the kitchen, my gaze locks with Hayes's. Instead of ripping away as he usually would, he holds eye contact with me. I'll be dead before I break it first.

As if hearing my thoughts, his head tilts, eyes narrowing to see straight through me like he knows I'm daydreaming. His mouth curves upward.

The china plate I'm drying slips from my hands, shattering all over the floor in cerulean smithereens.

Lainey stares down at the shards in horror. "I just swept these floors *spotless*. Thanks a lot, butter fingers."

"Sorry!" I exclaim, looking for the broom. "I'll clean it."

"Broom's in the hall closet," Aura mentions, stooping to pick up the biggest shards.

I step out of the kitchen and into the hall. Barely any daylight is left, but I'm not about to flip on a light and get scolded for that, too. I cast my arms wide, feeling my way down the hallway.

My fingers catch on something, but it's just the edge of a gilded picture frame I looked at earlier. In it is a portrait of Diana surrounded by a small group of students, probably all somewhere between fourteen and sixteen. *The starting twelve.* They were the first students to graduate from Wilde Estate. As lore has it, they also were the first to ever engage in the wilderness competition, although back then, it was merely a game in the woods. Still, it planted the seed for decades of tradition.

It's a painting I've studied at the academy, and although I can't make out the entire thing in the dark, I know it was painted in the library. Behind Diana's wingback chair is a vine of blue flowers crawling up the wall. During literature class last year, Professor Dinero tried to convince us that Diana always kept a window in the library open for the flowers to come in through. She believed they carried the spirits of her loved ones and never wanted them to feel unwelcome. She even wrote a lullaby about it, which Professor Dinero did a very cringy ukulele cover of. I'm pretty sure the flowers were just flowers to round out a nice painting, but I needed an A, so I enthusiastically agreed.

I continue on to the hall closet the cleaning crew shoved all the supplies in. There's no light in the closet, so I fumble around until my fist closes on what I hope is a broom handle. Before I can back out, a hand wraps around my mouth.

"Don't scream," a familiar voice orders, closing the door behind us.

I don't scream—I *bite.*

"*Ow!*" Woolf yelps, releasing me to hold his freshly chomped fingers. "What's wrong with you?"

I spin to face him, fishing my phone from the pocket of my denim shorts—what I should have done as soon as I left the kitchen. I switch on the flashlight, casting his pained features in its ghoulish glow. "What's wrong with *me*? What's wrong with *you*? You can't just corner me in a closet!"

"I needed to talk to you alone," he says.

"I don't want to talk to you," I seethe, pouring on the fury so he doesn't realize how freaked out he made me.

I move to brush past him, but he grabs my arm. "Hear me out."

I raise the broom. "I have a mess to clean."

"Exactly," he hisses. "Whatever you just did, don't even think of doing it again."

My jaw drops. "What *I* did? Hayes was staring at *me*! You should go talk to him if you want to play guard dog."

He rolls his dark eyes. "As if breaking a plate isn't the oldest attention grab in the book."

"It was wet and slipped out of my hand!"

"Sure it did."

"Why are you fighting his battles for him, anyway? I know from experience he can do it himself."

Woolf shakes his head. "You have no idea what you did to him."

"What I did to him?" My cheeks are steaming. "How about what he did to me?"

"You started it."

I choke on all the words I want to say. That's how everyone views it because I'm the one who snapped first and chucked mashed potatoes at Hayes's face. It doesn't matter how he threw food back at me or that it had been an explosion building for weeks after I first told him I was thinking about applying for the wilderness competition. I was Jenga, and he was pulling me apart piece by piece with his judgmental words until I toppled right over. But I was deemed the asshole, publicly breaking up with the boy whose brother was found dead after the same competition I wouldn't back down from applying to.

I *couldn't* back down. But nobody understood what it felt like to not have enough money to solve all your problems.

"I tried to apologize," I defend. "He's the one who wouldn't take it."

Woolf scoffs. "You only apologized because you didn't want to fail math."

I've never been so grateful for shadows, hoping they conceal the truth on my face. Math wasn't the only subject I was behind in when I came to the academy, but it was easy to catch up in chemistry since Mina was my lab partner. In math, I was on my own and slipping, fast. When my math professor recommended partnering me with a tutor, I had to say yes.

I was matched with the worst possible option: the boy who walked through the halls like a cloud hung over him, a permanent bored look across his face. The boy I was warned about.

"*Hayes Stratford,*" Mina told me on my first day as my eyes tracked his movements across the chemistry lab. "*If you're into guys, I'd pick anyone to crush on but him. He hasn't been the same* since his brother died and doesn't talk to anyone aside from Phlip, who's Keana's twin, and Woolf, his childhood best friend."

"*Died?*" I asked, because surely the school would have disclosed that a student died on campus or I'd have seen it in the news.

"*Yeah, during the Wilde Trials. You've heard of those, right? It's a fun tradition for seniors to participate in if they apply and get chosen. A way to win a bunch of money and get the distinction of top of class since we don't have valedictorians here. Plus, get out of finals. Two years ago, Hayes's brother was the star—everyone thought he'd win. But he disappeared before the last trial. Everyone thought he forfeited and there was a miscommunication. They went ahead with the final trial and named the winner, but when they got back to school, he wasn't here. He missed graduation and wasn't found until a few days later. He fell through the floor of the church that was in the forest and broke his neck.*"

The memory still makes me shudder. When I had my first lesson with Hayes, I didn't know how to act. I'd never known anyone my age who lost a sibling.

Hayes sat across from me at a wooden table shoved into the corner of the library, and I was taken off guard by all the things I hadn't noticed about him from afar. The freckles that faintly dotted his nose and cheeks. That his eyes were green, a shade that reminded me of my plant-filled backyard at home Mom thoughtfully tended to. The way his fingers weren't just uselessly tapping a rhythm on the tabletop but actually moving as if pressing invisible notes.

He was even more intimidating up close. Shadows beneath

his eyes from a clear lack of sleep, though every other facet of his appearance was perfectly composed, right down to his expertly knotted tie. When he spoke, his voice was low and even. Disinterested. I was already insecure about needing a tutor. Hayes making it clear he didn't want to be there wasn't helping.

I blame that on why, when I spoke, my voice came out as faint as it did. *"Thanks for tutoring me. I'm Chloe."*

He nodded. *"Okay, Clover, let's get started."*

I was too embarrassed to correct him, so my name stayed Clover for that entire lesson, and then the next one, and then the next. It wasn't until several weeks later, when Keana, Emmy, and I got partnered with Phlip, Woolf, and Hayes for a giant group project, that Keana said my name while doling out roles.

"Chloe?" Hayes asked. *"Her name is Clover."*

Keana stared back at him. *"No, it's not. It's Chloe."*

He looked at me expectantly.

"Um, yeah. It's Chloe," I admitted, so embarrassed I wanted to shrivel up like a grape in the sun.

But he laughed, the sound so unexpected that I don't think even he saw it coming. And neither did anyone else, because they swapped perplexed looks. His laugh was nice, lighting him up and transforming his bored features.

"Okay, Chloe. You got me."

I grinned, lightly kicking his foot under the table. *"I mean, you're welcome to keep calling me Clover. I really don't mind it."*

He nudged my foot back, a smile edging his lips. *"We'll see."*

I started acing math after that, but also, falling in love. Because as soon as I heard his laugh, I knew I'd do anything to make sure I got to keep hearing it.

"I don't need Hayes anymore," I finally say back to Woolf in response to the math comment, a lie in every possible way, but especially math. Because I did need him, and it was apparent from the very first test I took post-breakup that came back riddled in red. Without Hayes helping me, my grade would drop, which would make my GPA drop, which would make my entire standing at the academy drop, which would probably mean I wouldn't get chosen for the trials, which meant I lost Hayes for absolutely nothing.

I couldn't fail math, that much I was sure of. So, when the opportunity arose, I did what I had to do.

And then I lied to my best friend about it.

"Hayes doesn't need you, either," Woolf bites back. "So that's what you need to get from this. Stay away from him. Don't mess with him, don't talk to him, don't look at him. It's going to be hard enough for him to be here without you playing your games."

I want to tell him I'm not playing games, but I'm scared that if I say a word more, my voice will crack. *Hayes doesn't need you.* I know. I've known. And it shouldn't hurt, but it does.

"And if you don't," Woolf's voice drops to a threatening tone, "you'll regret it."

"Noted," I snap, shoving him into a stack of toilet paper. Opening the closet door, I stride into the foyer.

I'm nearly to the hallway leading back to the kitchen when I pause. "Why is he here?"

Woolf knows what I'm asking—*Why would Hayes willingly spend two weeks in the same place where his big brother tragically died?*

He takes too long to answer. "He wants to finish what his brother started and win in his honor."

"Is that your lie? Or his?"

Satisfaction creeps in like shadows as I leave a speechless Woolf in the devouring dark.

When I finally retire to my room after the Champions brief us on tomorrow, I finish putting my clothes in drawers, freeing up the top of the dresser. It's full of carved initials, likely previous Champions, but some might even be old students. My eye catches on a tiny one on the corner of the dresser, fresher than the others.

HS WAS HERE ↓

HS. I'd know the initials anywhere. For a solid six months of my life, I was in a love-drunk haze penning them in the margins of my notebooks. Always *HS + CG* inside a big heart.

I'm not proud, but it was a canon event.

But it's not Hayes's carving, of course. It's his brother's— Hunter.

Three years ago, Hunter Stratford was chosen as a Challenger to compete in the Wilde Trials and stayed in this very room.

And he never came home.

7

The morning of the first trial, we meet the Champions by the iron gate where the bus dropped us off. In the muddy earth are deep treads from its tires thanks to the on-and-off rain. I'm already regretting not packing boots.

"Trial one is a test of wit," Trevor announces, voice echoing in the stillness of the morning. "Wilde Academy values clever minds."

"Being able to think on your feet is a needed skill in all manners of life," Carly adds. She cups a thermos of coffee in her hands, from which a curl of steam rises into the biting morning air. I doubt this place has a Keurig, so she must have made it the old-fashioned way by boiling water and using instant coffee. It's the stuff Dad would turn his nose up at, preferring to brew a fresh pot and pour cup after cup, which usually gets left on the counter until it's cold and he has to microwave it. Most days, he forgets it in the microwave, too.

I should have called him before I left. He would have told me to bring boots, and there's a 60 percent chance I would have listened.

"On paths to success, you'll meet all kinds of people," Jarod continues, a sinister smile on his lips. He shrugs. "If you don't learn to read between the lines, you might lose out or misplace your trust. Big-time."

"And if you can't read between the lines for this trial . . ." Trevor trails off, glancing expectantly at Aura to finish it out.

Aura swallows, looking like she'd rather be anywhere but here. I can't blame her. I'm not a morning glory, either.

"Then you lose," she says. "One of you will be going home."

My body jolts like I took a sip of Carly's coffee. "What?"

An echo rises up, all of us confused. "I thought the person who loses the trial is just at the bottom and needs to do that much better in the next ones?" Keana asks. "The winner is chosen based on who has collected the most points after trial seven, right?"

"Old rules," Carly says with a smug smile. "From now on, whoever is on the bottom is going home. We'll reveal the eliminated Challenger at the bonfire after that day's trial."

"Gives you all a little incentive to get your shit together," Jarod goads.

With this change, coming last in a trial is a green light straight to elimination.

Trevor doesn't give us any more time to lament the rule change. "For this trial, you'll have to complete a series of riddles scattered throughout the forest. Your indicators for your proximity to a riddle will be colored flags tied to trees. Orange signifies you're close and need to keep going. Red is tied to the trees where the riddles are. There are seven red flags scattered throughout the estate ground. Got that so far?"

Everyone nods.

Jarod takes over. "On each tree with a red flag, you'll find a riddle stapled to it. Solve it, and use this key"—he holds up a sheet of paper where the letters correspond with numbers—"to open the lock on the corresponding box. Inside the box, you'll find a piece of something that will help make the next two weeks easier for you. Take one piece per box. When you collect all seven pieces, make your way back. For every trial, you have from dawn to dusk to complete it and return to the gates. If you start seeing white flags, you've gone too far. Good?"

Plenty of questions brim on my lips. *How do we know where the orange flags start? How do we ensure we're not on top of each other constantly? If we can't solve a riddle, do we leave it and go to the next one? What happens if we only open some of the boxes? What if there's more than one of us with the same number of pieces but not all of them?*

But asking a mountain of questions gives the impression that I can't think critically, so I bite them back and nod with everyone else.

"Excellent." Trevor's mouth curves with a sly grin. "Let the Wilde Trials begin."

No one moves. Surely, it can't be as casual and lackluster as that, as if we're being told it's dinnertime and we should make our way to the dining hall. But when the Champions stare at us expectantly and Carly taps an invisible watch, the fire ignites under our butts. Despite having no idea where to go except away from the gates, we make a break for it.

Today's gloom makes the forest even more foreboding than

yesterday. As expected, the Cabinet moves as a unit, disappearing north down a path through the trees. Hayes and Woolf veer left, sticking to the west. Mina, Keana, and Alandra break off toward the east. Jaleigh's already vanished among the thick tree trunks.

Winning the trials isn't just about being the fastest or the smartest—it's about being cunning. Instead of following anyone else and tripping over each other, I turn on my heel, heading south. I follow the perimeter of the iron fence until the rear of the estate peeks through the thick covering. By the time most of them make their way here, I'll be circling back toward the front.

Venturing away from the fence, it only takes several paces before I stumble upon an orange plastic flag wrapped around a tree branch. Now, I just need to find the red.

I'm glad for the mission, which distracts from the supremely creepy factor that I'm literally alone in the forest. A chill walks up my arms. When briefing us last night, the Champions went over the rules. Most important—no foul play.

But as the anthem from this year's spring musical *Into the Woods* declared: "Anything can happen in the woods."

The song plays in my head on a loop as I keep walking. I pass two more orange flags before my eyes catch a flash of red in the distance.

"Yes!" I squeal, racing to the red flag tied to a low-hanging branch.

On the thick trunk a laminated sheet of paper is stapled to the bark. There's a box rigged beside it, made of heavy metal with the promised lock keeping it closed. It's attached to a chain that's looped through a branch out of reach. Clever. This way, no one can steal the entire box if they can't solve the riddle.

I crack my knuckles, analyzing the words on the page:

> What word in the English language does the following:
>
> The first two letters signify a male, the first three letters signify a female, the first four letters signify a great, while the entire word signifies a great woman. What is the word?

Hmm. One word. The lock on the box needs numbers, so I pull out the translation code from where I put it in the pocket of my jacket. If we're talking about signifying gender in the classic, dated sense, then I need to think about pronouns. *He/him.* Plenty of words start with *he*, which makes me lean toward *him*. But all I can think of is *himbo*, which I'm 99 percent sure is false. So *he*, because the next part says the third letter makes it female, which is *her*.

Four letters signifying a great, but a great what? If the entire word is a great female, then that means it's gendered language and changes subtly depending on who you're talking about.

Maybe great is meant to throw us off. I run through similes. *Excellent, amazing, super—*

Super. A superhero. A hero. No—a *heroine.*

"That's it!" I exclaim to the trees, pulling out the key code. Each letter correlates with a number up to nine, before restarting. I need seven letters in total.

It's quick work to figure out the sequence. I type it in and press the Enter button. For a drawn-out moment, nothing happens, my heart hovering in my throat as I wait.

A buzz followed by a click has the lock falling off. I catch it before it can hit the ground, stuffing it into my pocket so I can pry the heavy lid open. It's on hinges, definitely some military-grade thing. I peer inside.

The "pieces" inside are paper. I grab one, shrouding it from rain with my body since it's not laminated like the riddle, although it feels durable.

I don't know what I expected to see on the paper, but a slice of the forest wasn't it. A sketch of trees, with some fine trails woven between them. One small building is also sketched—the powerhouse, which had a fire in the late 1900s after the new academy was already finished. It was never repaired, hence the questionable power situation here at the original school.

There's a dot not too far from it, and I realize with a start that must be where I currently am. I squint into the gloom, trying to see around me. The piece has three jagged sides with one smooth edge, which is where the powerhouse is closest to. The powerhouse is south of the estate, so if this is a map, then this must be a bottom piece.

A map is clever. Giving us a way to old-school navigate the forest is another test to see how well we can use resources when supplied to us. It takes away any excuses like getting lost or turned around.

I check to make sure the remaining eleven pieces are the same, which they are. I relock the box and put my piece into my backpack. One down, six to go.

If each riddle correlates with a map piece, that means the pieces circle the estate. And since the one I found features the powerhouse, I bet the others also correlate with surrounding structures. When I was studying, I looked at maps of the grounds. The barn is also south, so that's where I head next.

I know I've gone too far when I see the powerhouse looming in the distance. It's a round building that looks more ruin than not. One entire side is scorched, with bricks toward the top crumbling inward. But what's really noteworthy is the tall, metal fence surrounding it. Unlike the ancient one bordering the estate, this one is newer, the metal still shiny with minimal ivy.

I knew the school made changes to the estate after Hunter died, but I didn't know what specifically. Now it makes sense why they would approve for us to come back out here. If these giant impenetrable fences are around everything aside from the house, it minimizes the chance of anyone wandering where they shouldn't.

I find the next riddle, which takes me longer to crack than the first, but I'm rewarded with another piece of a map, which slots perfectly to the left of the other. This one has more trees and obscure paths, but all the way toward the edge is the barn.

I'm trying to get my bearings when a branch snaps from behind me. Whipping around so quickly that my hair smacks my cheek, I relax when Jaleigh emerges from behind a hefty oak.

"Hey," she says, looking tiny next to the towering trunks. "How's it going?"

There's no rule that Challengers can't talk or team up, but I'm still wary of her. Jaleigh's one of those girls who's surface-nice but slippery, like she might compliment your outfit in the bathroom but wait till you leave to laugh about it with her friends.

"Not bad," I say. "You?"

"I've gotten three pieces so far," she proudly states. "Did you know it's a map?"

No shit. But I don't want to give away that I have fewer pieces than her, so I simply nod.

The rain has stopped, but the wind whistles through the trees. She peers around. "Is there a piece nearby? It feels like I've been walking in circles for the past hour."

The piece I just found is a few paces away, but that will award her a fourth section compared to my two.

I don't even think before the lie flies out. "Near the barn." I point in the opposite direction. Like the powerhouse, the barn is also fenced off. The only thing spared was the chicken coop, but when I poked my head in, nothing was there.

"Thanks," she says, taking off in that direction. She only gets a few paces before pausing. I brace myself, sure she'll call me out on my bullshit.

"Just so you know, Dodge and Soph and them are coming this way. They started north, moved west, and will probably be in this area soon. You might want to go east to avoid them."

She disappears into the trees just in time for guilt to hit me like a sledgehammer for messing with her. I do as she recommends and take off in the opposite direction. It's not like I screwed her up that much. She's in the right vicinity.

Besides, she could be lying about the Cabinet's whereabouts. I stay on my guard.

I find another riddle toward what I think is east of the estate, right outside an overgrown greenhouse with half the glass panels missing and only a fraction of the size of the one I spent my ISS in. Inside the lockbox are fewer pieces than the previous ones held, meaning I'm not the first to get here. I grab a map piece and slot it to the right of the powerhouse one, though the smooth edge of this one has an arrow pointing off it labeled "The Cliffs." I'll definitely be avoiding those.

My hatred of heights is the same reason I don't scale a tree for a better vantage point when an hour goes by and I have yet to find another red flag. I bet that was one of the first things Hayes did when the trial started. He loves being high up, and more days than not when the weather was decent, classes would end and I'd find him on the observation deck.

"*You're scared*," he commented the first time he took me up there. We had yet to officially label ourselves, but tutoring included a lot more yearning and footsie than normal.

"*Not scared*," I countered stubbornly, hovering near the stairs. "*Logical. Being high up is a defiance of gravity, which isn't natural. We're meant to be on the ground. Being off it is dangerous.*"

His eyes danced with mischief as he stepped farther onto the deck and away from me. The all-glass surroundings made it look like he was suspended in midair.

"*I think plenty of danger happens on the ground. Being high up gives you a vantage point. Lets you see your surroundings. This is my favorite place to come because you can see the entire forest from here, all the way to the mountains. Look.*"

He pointed far into the distance, where the snow-peaked tips were visible amid the clouds. I couldn't deny it was mesmerizing. When he held his hand out to lure me further into the sun-soaked prism, I took it.

My legs shook, the solid ground disappearing beneath me for clear glass that I was sure would shatter at any moment. People were playing soccer on the back lawn. While they weren't necessarily ants, they were still too small for comfort.

"I love coming up here." He wrapped his arms around me from behind. His warm chest against my back soothed my whirring thoughts of going splat in the middle of the soccer game.

"You're not afraid?" I asked, though the unspoken words were *"You're not afraid of dying like your brother did? By falling?"*

He always knew what I was trying to say, even if I couldn't squeak the words out. *"No, I'm not afraid of much, anymore. But especially not being high up. Hunter loved to climb. Our nanny would flip out on him because he'd go up this one giant maple tree in our backyard. Would sit all the way at the top. He taught me how to look for the best places to put your hands and feet. When I was a freshman and he was a senior, we would come up here on Thursdays and eat lunch. He was never afraid of falling, so I'm not, either."*

"I'm sorry," I said, internally wondering if Hunter had been more afraid of falling like I am, he would still be alive.

Hayes's gaze was trained on the mountains. *"Yeah,"* he said, voice detached and disbelieving. *"Me too."*

The next riddle I solve rewards me with a map piece featuring the stream, which is north, and the following piece I find includes Wilde Lake all the way to the northwest. I only have two more to go. The Champions told us last night that when the first

Challenger finishes a trial, they'll announce it with an airhorn. It's possible I'm too far away from the estate, but I haven't heard anything yet. It's nearing noon. I grab a granola bar from my backpack and keep walking, searching for an orange flag to tell me I'm close.

Or maybe I got turned around, because I hear the stream burbling again, which means I'm backtracking, since it's before the lake. Dammit. As the sun rose behind the clouds, the forest went from creepy to peaceful. It'd be a welcome change, but the shift is disorienting. The internal clock in my head urges me to figure it out, fast.

Not fast enough. Voices and footfalls float toward me, breaking up the hum of nature.

My stomach drops. Hayes and Woolf.

Before they can see me, I dive behind a fallen tree. Their footsteps grow closer. As silently as I can, I creep along the ground to put some distance between us. It feels ridiculous. I should be able to face them, just like I did Jaleigh. The estate grounds are massive, but we're still bound to run into each other. Woolf can't expect me to avoid Hayes the entire time.

But I know Woolf, and he does. I don't want to let him control me, but *"you'll regret it"* rings in my ears. It's too soon to have regrets. Whatever he means by it, I don't want to find out.

I channel Cece, pretending this is another game of spies we used to play when we were little. Being four years younger, she was small enough to move through the house soundlessly, slipping behind closed doors and locking me out while I was still scratching my head following her ghost. It worked great until

YouTube taught me how to pick the locks with a bobby pin. Ever since, I've kept one tucked into my hair to keep my curls out of my eyes.

Keeping my tread light, I walk backward, putting as much space between them and me as possible. Only when their voices fade do I turn around, releasing my held breath.

Just to suck it back in at the hulking sight before me.

8

Trapped behind the same high fence that corrals the barn and powerhouse, the church looms. Its steeple stabs the sky, the bell missing from its tower. Once the new academy was completed, the bell was taken and put outside of the chapel on campus. It's tradition to smack it at the beginning of every year. The superstition is, the louder the ding, the better the year.

Like the west wing of the estate, the forest is reclaiming its turf. Ivy clings to the eroded white paint, making the sacred place appear nightmarish. It doesn't help that some vines climb through broken panes in the stained glass windows, as if prying their way in.

The grass leading to the double wooden doors is overgrown, peppered with flowers or weeds or both. Beside the doors are smaller windows on either side. One is covered by a wooden board while the other still has a cracked glass pane in place. Threading my fingers through the fencing, I press closer to see inside. I can make out rows of pews and the altar beyond it. Above the altar is a balcony where the choir sang from.

Where Hunter *fell* from.

As if the fence burns me, I stumble back, falling onto the

ground and scooting backward. Hayes's voice rises in my head, a conversation from November 19 springing up.

"The balcony railing was broken," he told me, the darkness of his dorm cocooning us as we waited for Woolf to return from a late detention. Hayes had been off all day. Squeezed together on his small bed with my fingers raking through his hair stripped his defenses.

"They think he leaned against it and fell," he continued, voice low and choked. *"But when he hit the floor, it gave out. He went through it and landed in the basement."*

I didn't know what to say. He didn't talk about Hunter's death often and never in detail. I kept the rhythm of my fingers steady, waiting.

"Five days passed before they found him," he said. *"And sometimes all I can think about, over and over and over, is how scared Hunter must have been. If he was calling out for help and hurting. If he was cold. If he thought of me."*

Tears welled in my eyes. *"Maybe it was instant,"* I squeezed out.

"We'll never know." He got quiet for so long I thought he fell asleep. Or maybe I did, when he whispered, *"He would have been twenty-one today."*

A shudder wracks me as I push the memory away, leaving the church without looking back. I hope Hayes didn't come this way.

I need to stop getting lost in memories and focus. I find an orange flag not too far away, getting back on track when the sixth red flag pops up a few paces later. The map piece slots in between the lake and the main part of the stream, featuring more stream and, of course, the church. All the edges are filled in, and I'm missing one sole piece in the center—the estate.

I jump as a sound fills the air, echoing through the breeze. A horn signaling that the first person has returned. "Shit." Someone beat me.

I wanted to start strong and leave a good impression. Second isn't terrible, but it only gets less noticeable from there. I have to find and solve this last riddle, fast.

If the final piece is the estate, then it has to be near the gate, where we started. I make quick work of finding an orange flag, then red. Like the other red flags, a riddle is stapled to the bark.

> I have cities but no houses. I have mountains but no trees. I have water but no fish. What am I?

My brain whirrs like an old laptop after opening a chunky document in Word. "What do cities, mountains, and water have in comment?" I ask myself. But maybe I'm looking at the wrong subset. If I focus on fish, trees, and houses, the only thing that ties them together is that fish and trees are living and houses are made from wood, which is made from trees.

"That's reaching," I mutter, wishing for approximately the seventh time today that I had paper and a pencil to write this stuff down. I change course, looking for differences between all of them. Houses are part of cities, like trees are found on mountains, like water is home to fish. So whatever this "has" are the more generic things without going into detail. It *literally* has cities, mountains, and water.

Wait—it's a *map*.

"Duh." I grin, putting the corresponding code into the lock. If the Champions assumed that Challengers would start with this riddle since it's closest to the gates, then the first riddle also serves as a clue for what the pieces make.

The lock clicks open, and I dip my hand inside the box. But my hand meets the cold metal of the bottom.

It's empty.

"What the heck?" My fingers search frantically, and I tug it down to peer inside. The last piece isn't here.

Maybe it got caught with someone else's piece and fell out. Maybe I missed it somehow and it stuck to the lid. Maybe I just need to look harder.

A full lap around the tree and scan of the area proves the shattering truth that it's gone. Which means there are only two things that could have happened to it. Option A, the Champions somehow miscounted twelve pieces. Option B, someone took more pieces than they were supposed to.

A chill races down my spine. Last night, the Champions warned us that we need to play each trial exactly to their rules. Any failure to follow that would result in immediate elimination. Who would risk it all so early?

I'll just tell the Champions the truth—someone took more than one piece. Whether by accident or purpose, I don't know. They'll figure it out.

As I make my way down the treelined path leading to the iron gate, I convince myself this is good. I'll get second, which is tolerable, and whoever messed with the first trial will be the one they'll eliminate. This trial was an easy start, and if this is the only hiccup, I'll gladly take it.

"Done?" Jarod asks as I approach him and Carly. They sit on the porch in the ancient rocking chairs, a risky gamble since the wooden structures look like a strong wind could turn them to sawdust.

"Yep," I say. I take the six pieces out of my backpack, passing them to Jarod.

He fans them out, eyes flicking up. Carly's fill with glee, like she can't wait to point out my flub.

"I'm missing one." I beat her to it. "But not because I couldn't solve all the riddles."

"If you solved all the riddles, you'd have all the pieces," Carly argues. It keeps everything in me to keep my tone polite.

"I did solve all the riddles," I repeat. "But the riddle closest to the gates with the map answer didn't have any more pieces left in the box."

She raises a brow. "What are you suggesting?"

"Maybe someone else took it?" I say, because accusing them of miscounting the pieces makes it seem like I don't trust them to do their job.

They share a glance. I'm clearly telling the truth, since I knew the answer was *map*. To my annoyance, Jarod starts laughing.

"Damn," he says, pulling a twenty-dollar bill from his pocket and slapping it in Carly's hand. "You got me. I didn't think it'd start this early."

"You've gotta start listening to me more, babe." She smirks, tucking the money into the pocket of her Patagonia sweatshirt.

"You should have seen the cheating that went on last year behind the scenes."

My eyes ping-pong between them. "Excuse me?" I interrupt, trying to hold on to my temper. "You guys said last night that cheaters would immediately get eliminated."

Carly twirls one of the long strands of her white-blond ponytail, looking at Jarod to answer as if I'm boring her.

"Yeah, if we catch them," he says. "We told Trev this trial would be too easy for someone to get messy. He always has too much faith in Challengers."

"Sometimes Challengers get creative." Carly shrugs. "With no proof to tell us for certain, it's impossible to do anything about it. You'll just have to do better next time."

"If you proceed to the next trial." Jarod highlights my fear. When he smiles, it's with an edge. "Guess you'll find out later at the bonfire. In the meantime, we're supposed to urge students to eat something, shower, and rest until it's time to make dinner. But honestly, as long as you go inside so you can't disrupt anyone still in the forest, you can do whatever you want."

"Thanks," I say, swallowing past a lump as I walk inside. If I'm the only one who didn't get all the pieces, I'll get sent home. Despair courses through me. I can't get sent home this early. Not only would it be devastating to tell Cece, but it'd be downright *embarrassing*.

When I make it up all three flights of stairs to the third floor to change out of my damp clothes and shower, it's just in time for the bathroom door to open on the opposite end of the hall. Keana emerges, her shower cap still on to protect her hair and a tower wrapped around her. When she notices me, she pauses, halfway to her room.

"You finished first," I point out the obvious, envy warring with awe.

"Don't sound so impressed," she says with a guarded tone as she shuffles to her room in her fluffy pink slippers. They look incredibly out of place amid the weathered wood floors and peeling wallpaper.

The vibe between us is too strange to stomach, so I unlock my door as she swings hers open. It's like I have a mini Emmy angel sitting on my shoulder.

There are bigger, meaner *fish to fry than each other*, she told us.

Before Keana can close her door, I spin to face her. "I'm glad you won."

She blinks at me, surprise morphing into a tentative smile. "What? Like it's hard?"

"You stole that from *Legally Blonde*," I accuse, but I can't help smiling back. We watched it together for the first time on Emmy's laptop last year, the sound all the way up.

She waves, disappearing behind her door. I close mine, leaning against it.

The smile drops from my face as an unwanted thought intrudes.

What else did you steal?

"Who wants to do the honors of lighting the first fire?" Trevor asks, holding up a lighter. After showering and eating lunch, anxiety over potential elimination gnawed at me until sleep dragged me down. During dinner, I considered trying to get Trevor or Aura alone to explain what happened but decided against it in case they told Jarod and Carly. Or worse, maybe they would have turned out to be as callous about it as them.

Now, we sit on tree trunk logs around a charred pit full of wood and tinder waiting to find out which one of us is getting eliminated.

"I do!" Dodge and Woolf volunteer to take the lighter, the last two people who should ever have control of an open flame. They glare at each other from across the pit.

Woolf's closest, so Trevor passes him the lighter. In seconds, the pit exudes tendrils of warmth as the tinder burns and the wood catches. Thankfully, Trevor takes the lighter back before Woolf can set the forest ablaze.

"Before we name the eliminated Challenger," Trevor says. "I want to congratulate you all on even being here. Getting chosen for the Wilde Trials is no easy feat, and regardless of how far you make it, you should be proud. As you know, one of you won't be joining us for the rest of the competition. In fact, the bus is currently in front of the gates now ready to bring the eliminated Challenger back to school."

"And then what?" Malcolm asks. "We go back and hang out? Take finals?"

"You won't have to take your finals, but you're not allowed to mingle with anyone else," Aura says.

"It's important you stay separated until graduation," Jarod explains. "Can't have you going back to campus and spilling all the details, can we?"

"It would be bad form," Trevor smooths over. "We know not everything about the trials can stay a secret from year to year, but an unspoken eighth trait that is highly valued is discretion."

"Are you ready to see who's going home first?" Carly asks. In her hand is a silver card folded in half, as if we're at the Oscars. She clears her throat, unfolding it. Her eyebrows shoot up in surprise, as if she's not one of the people in charge of keeping track of our rankings.

Over the card, her gaze meets mine, fire glinting in it. I steel myself, waiting for the inevitable humiliation of being the first one sent home for something that wasn't even my fault.

She reads the name aloud. "Jaleigh Nelson."

My jaw snaps together so hard that an ache reverberates through my skull. I'll gladly deal with the pain. *I'm safe.* I made it to trial two.

But then the guilt hits.

I pointed Jaleigh in the wrong direction earlier. It was just to buy myself some time to get ahead, but maybe it wrecked her chances of winning. If she took too long to finish, or didn't get all the pieces, then that could partially be my fault.

No, I mentally slap myself. This is good. One Challenger down, ten to go.

I still feel terrible as tears well in her eyes, the dancing firelight making the shine more noticeable. She stands, sniffling.

"You did your best," Carly tells her, comfort overly thick in her tone. "But it wasn't good enough."

Damn, Carly. No holding back any punches, I guess.

From the glare Aura shoots at Carly, I can tell I'm not the only one thinking it. As tears spill down Jaleigh's cheeks, Aura leads her across the backyard and into the estate.

"Nice job, you little shits." Jarod breaks the silence. "You all made it past the first trial."

I glance around the fire, searching for any expression that might indicate who cheated by taking more than their map piece. Keana meets my eyes, giving me a slight nod. I don't want to entertain the thought that crossed my mind earlier. The Cabinet celebrates, existing in their own little orb. Charlie frowns at Alandra, who stares after Jaleigh. They are all friends. Woolf holds out a fist for Hayes to bump, but Hayes is too focused on the flames to notice.

The fire continues crackling into the night. Aura never returns, and Trevor, Jarod, and Carly make up the majority of the conversation reminiscing about their first trials. I finally let myself relax, mind drifting as I stare into the embers of the smoldering branches.

"I'm exhausted." Mina yawns, jarring me out of my thoughts. A quick glance around the fire shows I've blanked out for longer than I thought. At some point, a case of beer was brought out. Jarod, Carly, and Trevor crack open cans.

"You planning on sharing some of that?" Dodge calls from across the fire.

"Ask us when you're older," Jarod cackles, which is ironic given I know for a fact he and Carly aren't twenty-one yet. But I keep my mouth shut and follow Mina inside.

"This place is so creepy," she shudders as we climb the stairs. Just like Cece would, she drags out the *o*, making it sound more like "sooooooo creepy."

"We're certainly getting the full experience," I agree. What experience that is, I'm not quite sure yet. If the society wants us to feel like we're roughing it, they're doing a fantastic job.

"Good night," she says softly once we get to our floor, slipping into her room.

I unlock my own, stepping into the dark room. Immediately, I'm taken off guard by the unexpected chill. For a disorienting moment, it feels like the AC is on. But that's impossible. We're lucky to have running water, let alone the modern comforts of blissful air-conditioning.

Something crunches beneath my sneaker. I spring back, but the only light is beside my bed. I have no choice but to keep moving forward, cringing with each step. I turn on the lamp and gasp.

Across the floor of my room is glass, some pieces large and jagged, some tiny, probably thanks to me trekking across them. Where my windowpane once was, only a few sharp shards remain in the sill.

Amid the glass is a brick, just like the crumbling ones I saw at the powerhouse earlier. Carefully, I pick it up, my breath hitching at what's held to the eroding brick with a thin vine.

It's a note.

9

Heart in my throat, I break the vine. The note was folded in half, and something else slides out from inside, fluttering to the glass-strewn ground.

It's a photo. I stare down at it, trying to make out the image.

"No," I breathe. Snatching it from the ground, I stumble to the lamp, putting it right under the light. There is no way this is real.

It's a picture of me in the library. Something that wouldn't necessarily be damning. Except I'm looking over my shoulder, an expression on my face that says, *I'm doing something I shouldn't*. Because of my head tilt, the computer screen in front of me is in full view.

The only thing sparing me from a total meltdown is that it's hard to make out what is on the screen of the computer. While my expression isn't exactly innocent, it's just a picture of me in the library. Nothing to see.

Except, in black Sharpie that I can still smell the remnants of, a date is scribbled on the back—*3/13/25*. If someone really wanted to push for answers, they would know that was the night before our math midterm. The midterm I magically aced.

Still, that's a lot of hoops to jump through and would only

lead to minor suspicion. I'm unnerved that someone wasn't just watching me in the library but hiding from me. I had quadruple-checked that I was alone. If I had suspected otherwise, I would have never taken the risk.

That night rises in my memory. The panic I'd been succumbing to for days about flunking the midterm. The humiliation from the recent food fight nobody could stop talking about. The heartache from breaking up with Hayes and shattering our friend group. It all felt hopeless.

Until I saw my math professor get up from her usual spot in the library to use the bathroom.

She hadn't seen me because I was tucked away at the corner table behind the stacks that Hayes and I met at for tutoring sessions. Which, coincidentally, was also the perfect spot to make out in without getting caught. Sitting there post-breakup, alone and struggling through practice problems, left me desperate.

I was about to leave when I walked past her computer and saw what was on the screen. The master test PDF. It was wrong, but my brain wasn't listening. I plopped into the seat, still warm, and scanned the navigation pane. Every single test, with answers.

Another check ensured I was alone, just like she thought she was. She would have never left it up, otherwise. But she did, and I was here, so I made a split-second decision to do something I thought I was better than: cheat.

I sent the PDF to my email from hers, then deleted it from her sent folder. It all happened fast, thirty seconds or less. I made sure everything was how she left it, right down to the chair half pushed in.

When I got to my empty room, still reeling from my choice, I saved it to my drive and put it in a locked folder, then deleted it from my email, too. I only ever opened it in the privacy of my room when both Emmy and Keana were out.

I remember the piece of paper and unfold it, scanning the typewriter font. Hi Chloe, it starts. The damning picture and brick slamming through my window made it pretty obvious this was targeted at me, but any hope that it was bad aim flees at seeing my name. What's weird is the paper is old. Yellowed with time and rough in my hands. Dread creeping in, I keep reading.

Congrats on making it into the Wilde Trials! I know how important it was for you to get chosen. Because of your sister, right? At least, that's what you keep telling everyone.

But I know you, and I know why you're really here— you've got something to prove. Don't we all? If only everyone knew the truth. The brilliant, star-student Chloe Gatti is a CHEATER.

The picture is only a tease. I have more, and with a little zooming, it's easy to see exactly what you're doing. I bet the Champions would love to take a look. They'll naturally have to report it to Principal Watershed. Getting disqualified from the trials will be the least of your worries—you're on the road to getting expelled. And what a shame. You were so close to graduation.

Unless you keep your mouth shut. Or better yet: forfeit. If you do choose to stay, things will only get worse. That's a threat AND a promise. And don't even try to rat to the

Champions again. I'll make you regret it.

Let's have some fun, shall we?

Your Challenger

I reread the note to make sure my eyes aren't playing tricks on me. I'm being threatened. And *blackmailed*! Who does that in real life?

"What the hell?" I hiss to the brisk air. They want me to forfeit because they think I'm tough competition. My ego says that's a good thing. The rest of me knows it's not.

Then there's the fun little promise that things will get worse.

I wonder if this came from the same person who took the map pieces, though I don't see how that could have specifically been targeted at me. The only one who knew for sure that I started toward the back was Jaleigh because she did the same. But why would she target me?

Unless she knew I misled her. But even so, I don't think she had enough time between getting eliminated and being loaded onto the bus to plot a revenge scheme to scare me. Especially not if Aura was with her.

So maybe there's a cheater *and* this blackmailer. Comforting.

I reread the note for the third time, one line jumping out. *I'll make you regret it*. Hadn't Woolf said something similar when threatening me to stay away from Hayes last night? But I did. I even went out of my way to make sure we didn't run into each other in the forest during the trial today. Plus, Woolf wouldn't be caught dead in the library. I don't see how he could have gotten the picture of me.

Still, this is something he would do. Maybe a little over-the-top, even for him, but out here, without any real adults, I could see him taking extra liberties. Hayes might even be in on it.

Maybe this is why they applied for the trials. To mess with me. Well, it's not going to work.

I repeat it to myself as I use my spare towel to brush the glass into a pile, then under my bed. At some point, I'll need to really get rid of it, but with the sounds of the stairs creaking and doors closing as people trickle in from the bonfire, I don't want to risk it right now. Maybe tomorrow, I can snag a spare trash bag from the kitchen and add it to the dumpster by the door.

Wrapping my towel around my fist, I tug out the jagged shards still in the windowpane and set them on my dresser before adding them to the pile beneath my bed. The last one is nearly the length of my forearm, coming to a lethal point.

A gust of chilly night air makes goose bumps rise along my skin. Before I can think twice, I shove the shard into my bottom drawer, beneath my heaviest hoodies. "I'm not afraid," I tell myself quietly. This is just Woolf and Hayes being jerks. The ultimate get-back-at-your-ex prank.

So why does it make tears prick at my eyes?

"I'm not afraid," I repeat, still quiet but with more force, as if I can will my waterworks away. But my thoughts are already tumbling away from me. If the person who did this is serious, then I can't tell any of the Champions because I'll risk my cheating getting exposed. And if it's not Woolf and Hayes, that opens up far too many possibilities.

It's something Dodge would do, and he could have gotten

the damning evidence from Lainey or Soph, who spend more time in the library than him or Malcolm. I can't imagine Mina could even launch the brick hard enough to make it through the window, or that Alandra would risk defacing estate property given her uncle is the principal. But she is friends with Jaleigh, so if Jaleigh told her I misled her, Alandra could have done it on her behalf.

Then there's Keana. Last month, after she asked me if I was secretly still seeing Hayes, she asked if I was cheating. I was indignant and angry at the accusation, which led to me making an out-of-line comment about her inferiority complex thanks to being overshadowed by Phlip. It was cruel, and I knew it, but I had to get her attention away from the truth. The exchange started the schism in our friendship that's been yawning open ever since. But even though Keana expressed a hunch I was cheating, that was all it was. She wouldn't threaten me over it, let alone break a window.

At least, I don't think she would.

After running through potential suspects and none sticking out more, I sit on the squeaky bed. There's a 95 percent chance that this is like every other bullying attempt I've experienced since coming to the academy—cruel and meant to make me feel small but, ultimately, harmless.

Except, of course it isn't. Not if the blackmailer is serious about having more pictures to prove exactly what I did that night in the library. It could ruin everything.

Fear is simply the unknown. So, theoretically, if I want to stop being afraid, I need to find out who's actually behind this.

Maybe I can get them eliminated before they do anything else.

Eventually, someone will notice my window, and I'm not sure what to say when they do. My room faces the front of the property, overlooking the porch. The one plus is that the branches of a wily willow stretch in front of it, hopefully blocking it from view. Most of the vines that covered the glass fell away. There's still the moth-eaten velvet curtain, which might marginally keep the cold out. With the nights getting warmer, that's not what I'm worried about. Bugs and bats are an entirely different story.

Well, I did want the window open. That's one way to do it. As I stare at water droplets on the sill, it hits me that maybe I could narrow it down more. The fresh rain earlier probably left the ground muddy. Whoever stood outside to throw the brick might have left tracks.

I can't leave my bed and investigate until everyone's asleep, so I wait. Footsteps sound in the kitchen, then on the creaky stairs, then on the floor beneath me. The hum of deep voices, Jarod and Trevor, are punctuated by Carly's high-pitched giggle. Doors click shut and beds squeak. If there's one plus to being in an old-ass house, it's that every movement leaves little room for guessing.

I wait and wait, listening for any other signals that someone is still awake. But when none come and the glow-in-the-dark face of my watch shows it's well past one in the morning, I rise and slip on my sneakers. My phone might be useless as far as service, but it still has a charge thanks to me sticking it on airplane mode. Once I'm outside, I'll turn on the flashlight.

At the last second, my gaze catches on Hunter's initials carved into the dresser.

I snatch the glass shard from my bottom drawer, along with a hoodie. Shrugging the hoodie on, I carefully tuck the shard into the front pocket. It's not a weapon. I'm just taking a sharp piece of glass with me. For fun.

At the top of the stairs, I hesitate. Maybe this is exactly what my Challenger wants me to do. Run outside after curfew just to get caught by the Champions with a giant shard of glass in my pocket.

Not knowing things is my kryptonite, and the need to investigate overpowers my apprehension. Painstakingly slow, I make my way down the stairs. Each creak and groan might as well be gunshots in the stillness. I finally reach the bottom, but in the openness of the foyer, I'm certain that the front door's rusty hinges will rat me out. I shift course, making my way toward the back door in the kitchen.

The estate is almost less creepy in the dark, where I can barely make out the threadbare carpets and curling wallpaper. The back door is unlocked, which is slightly disconcerting, but I guess in the middle of the forest, there's not much to be worried about.

Except for each other, apparently.

I slip outside, stopping short at the glow from the fire in the distance. But a few steps closer proves it's just embers still burning.

Clinging to the shadows, I round the estate. The sky crackles with energy. Another rainstorm is rolling in. Only once my window comes into view do I turn my flashlight on. Thankfully, it is mostly blocked by the willow unless looking right at it.

What I didn't account for is the overgrown grass. Even with

my phone flashlight pointed directly at the ground, it's hard to make out anything telling. Hoping for muddy tracks, I'm instead granted wet weeds and wildflowers. In minutes, my sneakers are soaked.

I keep searching, careful of my own footsteps. If I can't find tracks, maybe there's something else. A memento they might have dropped, like a tube of ChapStick or—

The unmistakable snapping of a branch makes me tap my phone flashlight off, cloaking me in a darkness so black I can't even see my own hands. Pulling the sleeve of my hoodie past my fingers, I grab the shard from my pocket. Each sweep of the breeze rustles the tree branches above me, giving a new shadow to suspect. The trees are close together, providing more than enough protection for someone to hide behind. I could have been followed and not even know it. I was so worried about someone hearing me that I didn't think to listen for someone else.

Another crunch confirms my suspicions—I'm not alone. I press my back to the nearest trunk, weighing my options. If it's a Champion, they'd have no reason to be sneaky. It has to be another Challenger. Maybe even the one who threw the brick.

The sudden silence is eerie. All I can hear is the stampede of my heart, followed by a faint rustle. They're on the other side of the trunk.

Two options are clear. I can wait for them to make the first move. But didn't they already as soon as they threw that brick? Or, I can try to throw them off by springing to action first.

My brain doesn't realize that my feet choose option two until I'm swinging out from behind the trunk in a gust of movement.

But either the Challenger was closer than I thought, or they chose the exact same moment to surprise me.

We collide in a crash of darkness, a surprised yell screeching out of me until a hand slaps over my mouth to staunch it. I stumble back from the force. There is no way in hell they're getting the upper hand.

My next step back is intentional, putting me just enough out of reach that they lose their grip. I waste no time in pivoting, throwing my weight onto them so we barrel into the tree we both were just hiding behind. Their back slams against it, a whoosh of minty air fanning across my face from the breath knocking out of them. Copying moves I saw in a movie once, I place my left forearm across their collarbone to hold them still, remembering the shard in my hand. *It's not a weapon*, I repeat to myself, bringing it to their throat.

A slice of moonlight cuts through the swaying branches above us, highlighting the jagged edge of the shard pointing at a smooth Adam's apple that bobs up and down with heavy breaths.

This Adam's apple is awfully familiar. One I've kissed and cried against. One I've run my fingers over lightly, asking, *"Does it tickle?"*

Amused green eyes stared back at me, fingers coming up to tuck a rogue curl behind my ear. *"Stop trying to tickle me, Clover. It's not gonna work."*

"Sounds like a challenge."

My gaze raises, meeting those same eyes. But there's no amusement in them now. They're hard and angry and defiant, mouth twisting to match. A cold laugh breaks out of him, nothing like the sound I finally elicited that day upon winning the challenge and finding out that he was, indeed, ticklish, as any human should be.

"Tell me, Chloe," Hayes says now, head tilting toward me so the shard presses into the skin of his neck. "How long have you been dying to put a knife to my throat?"

10

"It's not a knife," I correct. "It's a glass shard."

He doesn't look surprised, as if me running around with a glass shard clenched in my fist is the norm. "And where did you get that from?"

"You should know," I seethe. "You're the one who broke my window."

"Someone broke your window?"

"*You* broke my window."

"I didn't break your window."

Right, just my heart. It hits me suddenly that this is the longest conversation we've had since the Breakup and I'm holding a sharp object to his throat. Fitting.

"Why else would you be out here in the middle of the night?" I ask.

"If I broke your window, why would I come out here? I'd be giving myself away."

"You want me to get caught and disqualified."

"Tempting," he says. "But wrong."

"Fine, then why *are* you out here?"

He glances at the shard still pressed against his throat. "I'll tell you if you let me go."

Right now, this is the only upper hand I have. "Of course that's what you want. I let you go, and you make good on your threat, right?"

If it wasn't so difficult to make out his expression thanks to the shifting shadows, I could almost fool myself that his brows pinch in concern.

"What threat? What are you talking about?"

"You and Woolf," I accuse. "The brick. The message." I leave out: *The blackmail.* "You're trying to scare me into forfeiting. You should know better than anyone that it's not going to work. I'm in this, and I'm not about to let some half-assed attempts at sabotage convince me otherwise."

"Sabotage?"

"Stop acting like you don't know what I'm talking about!" I burst out.

A bird caws from above as it soars away, spooked. I lower my voice.

"I came back from the bonfire to find glass all over my floor from my broken window and a brick with a note attached promising that things will get worse if I keep competing. Does that not sound like something you and Woolf would scheme up to scare me? Because it sure does to me."

I step back from Hayes, mostly because I can't stomach the heat rolling off his skin and seeping into mine. While the shard leaves his neck, it doesn't drop to my side, either.

"We didn't do anything," Hayes says, brushing himself off.

"Oh yeah? And you've been with Woolf all night to confirm?"

"I mean, yeah, I—" But he stops, clearly remembering a point where they must have been separated. "Fine. *I* didn't do anything. But I don't think he did, either."

"Sure." I roll my eyes. Coming out here was a bad idea. Between the failed search for tracks and literally running into Hayes, I'm more frustrated than ever. And while I don't believe Hayes is telling the truth, not even close, his insistence makes an earlier concern bloom. If it's not him and Woolf messing with me, then who is?

"Where are you going?" Hayes asks as I storm toward the back door.

"Away from you," I spit out before my face can reveal my fears.

"You don't want to know why I'm actually out here?"

I do, so badly. He knows I can't stand not knowing things. But it's for that very reason that I turn to him, hand on the doorknob, and say, "Don't care."

As I climb the stairs, a foolish piece of me expects Hayes to trail after me, if not to tell me what he was actually doing, then at least to torment me some more. By now, I should know him better than that. He didn't follow me out of the dining hall after our breakup, and he doesn't follow me now.

My room greets me with an unnatural chill even though I pulled the green velvet curtain over the window, a reminder that I better get used to it unless I want to rat to the Champions, which could lead to my Challenger ratting on *me*. It's a risk I can't take, so I carefully slide the glass shard back into its spot in the bottom drawer and climb into bed, drawing the sheets and old afghan over me.

I hate him. The poisoned thought spins in my brain over and over as tears wet my cheeks. It's the part of breakups they don't show in the movies. I've gone through the Ben & Jerry's and rom-com movie nights. I've gone through the severe haircut that—thank God—didn't end in bangs. I've gone through my healing-girl era and gotten to the point where I can pass him in the halls or accidentally look at him in class without mentally deteriorating.

But all it took was one three-minute conversation to unravel it all.

It doesn't help that my only comfort is grabbing the ring attached to the chain around my neck. If I was wise, I'd rip it off and chuck it out the window. Instead, I let the familiar shape press into my palm, soothing me the same way it does every night.

I fall into a fitful sleep, my thumb running over the ring's face: a four-leaf clover.

I'm out for an illegally short amount of time when a banging on my door wakes me up.

"Up and at 'em!" Trevor cheerily calls. "We've got a busy day ahead!"

I poke my head into the hall, several others doing the same.

"Isn't it a rest day?" Keana rubs her eyes, her hot-pink bonnet tilted on her head.

"It's a buffer day," Carly corrects, standing at the end of the hall with her hands on her hips. "Rest is for the weak."

"Everyone in the foyer in fifteen minutes! Wear your swimsuits!" Trevor orders. A chorus of groans fill the air, myself included. Going for a swim at seven in the morning isn't exactly my idea of a rest day. Downstairs, we're funneled into the kitchen, where we're given oatmeal and berries. It's as if since we're in the forest, we need to pretend we've never seen a bagel and cream cheese in our lives. I eat the oatmeal because I'm starving, but I'd prefer it if there was some maple syrup and chocolate chips thrown in.

"We're spending the day at the stream," Trevor says as we clean the dishes. Despite the storm that soaked the ground early this morning after my conversation with Hayes, the rising sun quickly burns off the lingering clouds. The trek to the stream takes longer than expected, leading me to assume that the maps we collected yesterday aren't drawn to scale. Last night after dinner, Aura passed around tape so we could connect the pieces. Mine has a hole in the center where the estate should be.

I keep to myself, sticking to the back. This morning, I tried to scrub any remnants of tears away in the bathroom, but anyone who looks too hard will be able to tell my eyes are puffy.

The stream ends up being more of a river, rushing from the recent rainfall. The Champions stop on the bank, turning to us.

"As you all know, this stream flows into Wilde Lake, which supplies the academy, estate, and surrounding areas with fresh water," Trevor explains. "Since we're on the heels of storm season, debris and branches clog up this part of the stream every year because it's the narrowest, and the school is responsible for caring for it. This year, that will be you."

"It looks like the current is moving kind of fast." Mina stares at the water uneasily.

"You can stand in it," Jarod says, which I guess is as close to reassurance as he can get. "Barely four feet deep. Maybe five."

"I'm barely five feet tall," Mina mumbles.

She takes off her T-shirt to reveal a pretty lavender two piece beneath, the same style of suit that the other girls wear. I'm hyperaware of the fact that I'm the biggest girl here. As if my curves and height don't set me apart enough, my one-piece teal-and-black bathing suit does. It's an insecurity that used to be much, much worse, but now rears its ugly head in the face of being in such little clothing.

I want to cover myself back up, but Dodge will pounce on any sign of discomfort. Strutting to the edge of the stream, I ease myself into the water.

"It's cold," I hiss. "*Really* cold." The type of cold that, were the sun not beating down, might warrant concerns of hypothermia.

"The faster you clean up the stream, the faster you get out of it." Carly shrugs. Bold of her to be so blasé about it when she didn't have to do any of this last year.

Everyone slowly enters with a huff or a hiss. There are a lot of branches, mostly broken twigs and brush caught on the embankment. I take a section on the opposite side, planting my feet in the mucky bottom to steady myself against the current and tossing sticks onto the grassy ledge. Hayes works on the opposite embankment behind me. I don't want to be so aware of him, but it's like, since last night, I have an internal compass keeping me tuned to his whereabouts. What it should be doing is pointing me toward my Challenger.

Unless, of course, they're one and the same.

The Champions watch over us on the rocks scattered around the embankment. Carly's in a black bikini sunbathing while Aura reads a book beneath a floppy hat. Jarod watches us work, yelling commands every now and then as if he's actually our boss. Trevor paces back and forth along the embankment like a lifeguard, making sure no one gets swept up in the pull of the current, which isn't as strong as it looked.

We break for lunch around midday, eating a peanut butter and jelly sandwich and a bag of chips. They're the same sandwiches we bulk-made two days ago. The bread is now soggy from the jelly.

Even after finishing the sandwich and chips, I'm still ravenous. It's the one part of the trials I didn't account for—our meals are scaled way down. I can't help the feeling that the food rations are another test I need to pass. One of the traits Wilde Academy values is adaptability, and a substantial change in diet is certainly that. It's not as if they're starving us, but it's nothing like the gourmet feasts laid out at school.

After lunch, we move down to a new section. Keana ends up beside me.

If I want to figure out who broke my window last night, I need to start collecting information. Keana and I may be on tumultuous terms, but I'm sure she didn't cheat or throw the brick. If she cheated during trial one yesterday, she's too smart to have gotten first because she knows that would make her suspicious. And last night, I can't recall a moment where she would have been gone for longer than five minutes. But that doesn't mean she didn't see anything I missed.

"Hey," I say quietly, glancing over my shoulder to confirm everyone is either sucked into their own conversations or the task at hand. Hayes is back to pretending I don't exist, which I prefer. The monotonous task of tossing branches has given me way too much time to think about our interaction last night.

"Hey," Keana says back.

"Are you okay?" I ask. She's quiet today, but so am I. Still, I can't help the distinct feeling that there's more to her silence. "Is your injury bothering you?"

The water is crystal clear, allowing full sight to the bottom. She rolls her ankle with a wince. "It's a little tender," she admits. "I ran for most of yesterday's trial. Sprinting always makes it flare up."

That explains how she finished so fast. "Being in the water has to feel good. Like a giant ice pack."

She cracks a smile. "Sort of. Although I'm a little annoyed our rest day is being spent doing manual labor."

I glance at the Champions to make sure they didn't overhear her. "It's not so bad," I counter. "Kind of like community service."

She snorts. "Yeah, is it also community service for the four most recent Champions to come back to re-create the trials every year and babysit us? Come on, Chlo, you're too smart not to realize the school dresses up the things they want done as an *honor* and *privilege*," she makes air quotations with her fingers. "When really it's just a fancy way of keeping us busy."

I don't know what to say to that. Sure, maybe the Wilde Trials haven't been as glamorous as I imagined, but I never thought of it as an opportunity for the school to use us. I figured it was all part of the game.

"Anyway"—she waves it off before I can respond—"I think maybe Em was right, you know? All those times she rolled her eyes when the Wilde Trials came up. It really is a weird tradition to keep."

"It's meant to be an honor. A distinction." I don't know why Keana is suddenly cold on the trials when I wanted her to feel this way for weeks and she was insistent on still applying.

She rolls her eyes, dropping a pile of sticks onto the embankment. "I am soooo honored right now. Truly."

We lapse into silence. This conversation got me nowhere closer to finding answers. To get her on my side without explicitly telling her about the blackmail means I need her to trust me again. So first, I have to trust her.

My eyes dart to Hayes. He's locked into a conversation with Woolf, something about brain-eating amoeba. I don't need to tell Keana *why* I was outside at two in the morning. Just who I ran into.

I take a deep breath. "So, something kind of wild happened last—"

"Chloe." She turns to me, tone sad but serious. The water rushes around us, but it doesn't chill me nearly as much as her expression does.

"What?"

"I really don't think we should talk to each other until this is over," she says, finality ringing through her words. I keep my face schooled, but an ache flares in my chest.

"Why?" I ask, though I should have been wiser than to think maybe, like me, she'd actually try to listen to Emmy.

"I can't trust you." Her words hit me like a slap. "You might pretend you care about me, asking me about my ankle and congratulating me on getting first, but I know you want me to lose just like the others. Let's just keep our distance, okay? It's easier that way."

She moves farther downstream, and I spend the rest of the day with my mind ping-ponging between her, Hayes, and the note. Maybe I was wrong about Keana being too smart to cheat and she's pushing me away so I don't find out. Maybe Hayes was honest about not throwing the brick, but his accomplice isn't Woolf. Maybe my Challenger isn't a some*one,* but a some*ones.*

Maybe I really need some sleep.

By the time I forego the nightly fire, my simmering stew of thoughts have reached a boiling point. What's spilling over is an idea I really, *really* shouldn't entertain.

Somewhere between the walk back and dinner, I realized Keana was the wrong person to want on my side. Like me, she's playing the trials as a loner. I need someone who can keep an eye on the other Challengers but also who I can keep an eye on. Someone who's close to my number one suspect, and also maybe is my number one suspect. Someone who hates me so much that it would take a miracle for them to agree to ally.

I need Hayes.

My brain hasn't fully processed the thought before I'm snatching a gel pen and notebook from my backpack. I rip out a page, laying it on top of the dresser. My pen hovers over the sheet.

Whatever I say has to be perfect because I only have one shot to convince Hayes to hear me out. I'm done running from him like I did last night. If I want to win, I need to be the one in control. The only way he'll agree is if there's something in it for him. We won't get to that point if I don't write the perfect prompt.

Not a prompt. A proposition.

The first proposition posed was late April last year. Hayes had just asked me to be his girlfriend only a few weeks prior, and we had been in the library for hours going over a particularly tough math lesson that wasn't sticking.

"I have a proposition," he said.

I was resting my head against the worn library table in full crisis mode.

"We get through two more problems and we can take a twenty-minute break to do whatever you want."

I perked up. *"Whatever I want?"*

He nudged my foot beneath the table, unable to wipe the grin off his face. *"Whatever you want, Clover."*

After that, everything became a proposition.

"Swipe me a muffin from the dining hall, and I'll let you pick our next movie to watch," I'd pitch.

"Hang out with me on the observation deck, and I'll play whatever songs you want on piano," he'd wager.

"Come spend Christmas with my family, and it will be the best Christmas ever," I swore.

He did, which led to the Christmas-night proposition, but I can't get lost in that right now.

I press my pen to the paper, scrawling a hasty note.

Before I can overthink my plan, I grab my shower things and head into the hall. I pass Hayes's room and stoop to shove the note beneath his door. When he gets back from the bonfire, he'll find it.

> H,
> Meet me by the fire at 2am. I have a proposition.
> C

11

Hayes is never late.

So when 2:10 rolls around and he has yet to show, I'm ready to leave my log by the fire's dying embers. I'm stopped by the faint sound of footsteps coming from the estate behind me.

"You're late," I say, schooling my features as my ex takes a seat on the other end of my log, as if three ghosts sit between us.

"You're lucky I'm here at all," Hayes replies, voice as neutral as mine. "What do you want?"

"I have a proposition."

"Got that." He pulls out the note I slid under his door and tosses it into the embers. It curls from the heat, immediately turning black and withering.

He's in a zip-up sweatshirt and joggers, an outfit that somehow still looks put together but I know is his definition of "dressed down." He rolls the sleeves up, and I can't help glancing at his forearms, where I used to drag my fingertips up and down the underside. Now, the minimal light highlights a cord of vein sticking out beneath his skin when he flexes his hand.

"You were right last night," I force out. I hate the admission, but this is part of the plan. He needs to think I'm giving in.

He raises a single brow, knowing all too well how unlike me the confession is. "About?"

"I do want to know why you were out," I say. "If you weren't throwing a brick through my window, that is."

"I wasn't," he says.

"Well, I didn't throw it myself."

He nods, enraptured by the embers. "So that means someone's after you. Sees you as a threat and wants you to forfeit. You won't."

"Nope," I confirm.

"That's why you went outside last night. You were trying to catch them."

I already might have. But accusing him last night got me nowhere, so I have to pretend he's off my suspect list. "Caught you instead."

"We caught each other," he parries. "What has you so curious now?"

I knew this question was coming. How I answer it will determine if my plan might actually work.

The worst part? It involves letting my guard down. Or, at least, pretending to.

I blow out a breath, a curl fluttering away from my face. "I think maybe we could help each other."

The words hang between us. If he's shocked, he'd never show it.

"What do you think you could help me with?" he finally asks.

I raise a brow in challenge. "Well, I can't know unless you tell me what you were up to, now can I?"

Instead of responding, he unzips his sweatshirt, pulling out a small leather-bound book from the inner pocket. It has a plain black front and back. He holds it out for me to take.

The leather is smooth beneath my fingers, the journal about the size of my hand. I flip open the front cover to the first page and scan the messy scrawl.

Property of Hunter Stratford.
Read at your own risk

"Your brother's journal," I realize. "Didn't he have this with him during the trials and police thought it got lost?"

Hayes nods, finally meeting my eyes. In the darkness, his pupils nearly swallow his verdant irises. "After the trials were over and they found him, my parents were given a box of everything that had been in his room at the estate. But this wasn't in it."

My room, I think. But I don't want to reveal that yet.

"So how'd you get it?" I ask.

He frowns at the book. "Someone sent it to me. I don't know who, but late March, just a few days after—" He breaks off.

"We broke up?" I supply, because I want him to know I'm not afraid to talk about it.

"Yeah," he says, voice low. "Right before the application window opened for the trials. It just showed up, no note or anything. I read it all that night. I tried not to think anything of it, but the last page stood out to me. Flip to the back."

I do carefully, as if it's a century-old artifact that might crumble to dust in my fingers. The book is full of writing, not a single page left blank. Unlike Hayes's neat script, Hunter's scrawl is rushed and borderline illegible. In the margins are doodles, reminding me that while Hayes held the talent with music, Hunter loved to draw. He must have brought his colored pencils with him to the trials. Most of the doodles are blue, winding through the words.

When I get to the last page, I glance up. "Should I read it out loud?"

"If you want."

I don't, but I clear my throat anyway, not willing to back down. I continue reading.

It's getting worse.

A comforting start.

I'm not sure what to do anymore. I don't want to forfeit, because how embarrassing is that? And not just for me. I have to think about Hayes and how all of this might affect him. I want him to be proud of me. How can you be proud of a brother who's a quitter?

Hayes shifts. It takes everything in me to keep reading and not look up.

The trials are difficult, more so than I expected. I wish I had A Good Book to read. Maybe some music to keep me company. If only my brother were here and could play me a song. I'm sure that would make me feel better.

I still plan on winning. Nothing's going to change that. Being out here in the forest makes me feel like I might never leave. Maybe I don't

want to. It is nice out here, everything aside. Peaceful and pressureless.
No Ivy Leagues or parent expectations. Just me and the trees.
And, of course, the other Challengers. I can't forget about them.
So yes, it's hard, and the mental and physical toll is getting worse.
But it will all be worth it. That's what they tell me.
I just need to stay focused, so this might be my last entry.

I lower the journal, a sour taste in my mouth.

"I don't think I ever told you this, because I never believed it myself," Hayes breaks my stunned silence. "When the police gave my parents Hunter's things, they told my parents the Champions said Hunter had been acting weird before he disappeared. Reckless. And that's what everyone thinks, don't they?" There's venom in Hayes's voice and an underlying hiss that says, *That's what* you *think.* "He went into the off-limits church, a dangerous thing to do. The Champions said he was losing, and that he was getting careless."

I don't realize we've both been leaning closer across the log until I look up and his face is inches from mine. The shadows sharpen his features. "Do you think that's true?"

"Hunter never lost. Kind of like someone else I know."

I lost you, I bite back. I don't want him to think his words mean anything to me. "He said his trials were getting harder, though, so someone else might have been outdoing him."

"Maybe there's a world where I could have believed that, too. If for nothing else than to get the closure everybody keeps telling me I need. But I can't. Not after getting sent this. Because there's more."

I frown, letting him take the book. "What do you mean?"

He folds the spine, making me cringe. But then I see why—it looks like there are pages missing.

"Whoever sent it to you could have ripped them out," I suggest.

He shakes his head, climbing onto the ground to get closer to the ember's dying glow. It's so unlike him to willingly sit in the dirt that I immediately follow.

He points to the last page. "Do you see how some letters are in cursive instead of print?"

I nod, though I originally thought that was just Hunter's messy writing.

"That used to be a thing we did," Hayes continues. "Hunter was trying to teach me how to read cursive because I had a teacher in elementary school who only wrote in it, so he'd randomly mix cursive letters in with the regular ones. Look at what the cursive ones spell."

I follow the movement of his finger, highlighting a cursive *I*, followed by an *L*, and another *I*. All almost imperceptible unless you know what to look for.

I suck in a breath as Hayes points at the final letter, realizing what it spells. *ILIED.*

"'I lied'? What does he mean?"

"Could be anything," Hayes says. "But I think he's telling me not to believe that it's his last entry. That there's more."

"You're not here to win, are you?"

He pauses, eyes crashing with mine. "No. I'm here to find out what actually happened to my brother because I know in my gut his death wasn't an accident. He was so many things, but reckless wasn't one of them." He drags in a breath, raising the journal. "These pages prove something was up. Whoever sent this to me must agree because the timing of getting it right before the application opened can't be a coincidence. And the only reason I can think of that they'd push me to apply for the trials is because they know I need to be here. Which leads me to believe that Hunter hid the ripped out pages somewhere on the estate grounds." He sets his jaw with determination. "So I'm going to find the missing pages and discover the truth."

My brain can hardly process his words, especially when he's so close I can smell the minty scent of his toothpaste. "You need to find out the truth about your brother," I say. "I need to win for Cece."

He eyes me warily. I continue.

"I need extra eyes, because right now my biggest roadblock to winning might be whoever threw that brick. If you help me figure out who it is so I can win, I'll help you search for the pages."

"The proposition."

I nod. "The proposition."

He shifts, as if literally weighing the pros and cons. "We meet at night and don't talk during the day," he says, which sounds a lot like an agreement.

"I wouldn't have it any other way," I say, though my chest twinges.

"There's just one problem," he says. "You hate me."

"True." *Lie.*

"And I hate you." *Ouch.*

"True."

"So how are we supposed to work together if we can't stand each other?"

I hadn't thought of that.

We look for answers in the embers.

After a few long moments, his eyes meet mine. "We need a truce."

"A truce?" I ponder it. "To put aside our differences. Just until the trials are over."

He holds out his hand. Before I can betray how shocked I am that he's actually agreeing, I slot my palm against his, giving him a firm shake. It's weird.

"Truce," I say.

"Truce."

"It's too fucking early for this."

Hayes and I freeze, hands still clasped together as Jarod stumbles out of the back door with a yawn. I thought he was speaking to us, but Carly follows him out.

"Tell me about it," she groans. "But we've gotta get everything ready for trial two before the campers wake up."

"The trials starting at dawn is a dumb tradition," Jarod whines. "Why can't they start at, like, noon?"

"All of this is a dumb tradition," Aura corrects, one of the opaque plastic totes in her arms.

"The trees," I whisper to Hayes, nudging him toward the thick foliage. As soon as they look our way, we're toast. We sneak behind an oak, barely breathing.

A twig snaps in the distance, stealing the Champions' attention.

"What was that?" Carly asks.

"Probably just a bear with a late night craving for blonds," Jarod snickers. A whack sounds, followed by a groan. "Owww."

"There aren't bears out here," Trevor says, the back door clicking shut. He doles out orders, though I can't gather what the trial might be from the broken sentences I catch. Their voices lower, then fade as they walk around to the front of the property. The unmistakable scream of the gate's hinges is a cue that they're far enough away from the estate and it should be safe for us to return.

Hayes and I stick to the tree line before sprinting across the dew-soaked grass, slipping through the back door, and hurrying up the stairs. We don't say a word the entire time, as if our daytime truce to keep ignoring each other is already activated.

When we get back to our rooms, we both pause.

"Same time tomorrow?" I whisper.

He nods, stepping halfway into his room before poking his head back out. "As long as you don't get eliminated in trial two."

I roll my eyes as he slips into his room. My door clicks shut behind me. I drop my head back against it, still shocked that Hayes actually agreed to my scheme.

I can't help thinking of all the ways that this could go south. He could use this as an opportunity just to mess with me. He could set me up to get caught.

Or, a secret third thing, the worst option of all: I could fall back in love with him.

12

"Is this not just a giant game of Mad Libs?" Keana asks, staring at the stack of papers in her hand.

"It's a test of knowledge," Trevor reminds us, having just given the spiel that knowledge is the trait that trial two aligns with. There's respect in history, and we need to prove we're willing to remember. "Not a children's game."

"But if it was," Soph goads, a grin curving on her lips. "It'd be Mad Libs."

"Call it whatever you want." Carly shrugs. "Point is, same rules as last time. You have until dusk to fill in the blanks. You can go pretty much anywhere. Use your maps to find the landmarks throughout the forest where you might find clues. Go in the estate and roam the main and east wing. We'll grade your answers like a test. You're all good at that, aren't you?"

"This is dumb," Woolf mutters. He's never been a good test taker. It wouldn't surprise me if he applied for the competition just to get out of finals.

If I'm lucky, this is the trial that sends him home. I don't plan on a soul discovering the deal Hayes and I made, much less seeing us together.

As with trial one, I expect some sort of dramatic start, but the

Champions tell us we're free to go and to return to the gates when we're finished. Using my map, I follow a path into the woods toward the lake as other Challengers branch off around me. It's a few miles away, and I don't plan on walking all the way there, but I want peace and quiet while I read through what's essentially a mega-test booklet.

And a test booklet it is. Twenty pages, single spaced. Paragraphs and paragraphs of information, all about Wilde Estate and Wilde Academy. Everything from founding dates to the names of random professors and previous Champions to questions about specific architectural decisions. Gaps in the sentences around dates and names are most common, as well as specific trials from past years or awards and accolades students have received through the past century.

As I flip through it, I'm relieved to see ones I'm 100 percent sure of, which is a good chunk since I read all the books on Wilde history in the library and made color-coded flash cards. If only I had them now. I expected the Champions to be more strict when it came to backpacks and checking what we're carrying during the actual trials, but they don't bother. Cheating would have been easy.

Then again, I thought cheating was easy the first time I did it. Apparently not, if my secret Challenger and their blackmail is any indication.

I find a secluded nook between two trees to sit. Taking out my pencil, I spend the next hour scribbling in the answers I'm sure of, feeling like I'm taking the world's weirdest SAT. Keana was right—it's basically Mad Libs.

I stay vigilant of the sounds around me, never letting too much time go by without lifting my head, though all I hear are occasional footsteps in the distance.

As soon as I finish the ones I'm sure of, I start making a game plan on how to tackle the rest. There are three that all mention the church, so I should go there despite how badly I want to steer clear. There's also a question about Diana Wilde's suite, along with one regarding the artist who painted the portrait of her with the inaugural twelve students. I think I know the answer to the latter, but if I need to go back to the estate anyway, I might as well check for a clue.

The sun rises higher as I trek toward the church. Today is humid, the sky cloudless though the trees provide decent coverage. I thought I would run into someone by now, but with only eleven Challengers left and miles of forest to explore, it's easy for us to spread out. And anytime I do hear someone, I veer off the path into the trees. I don't know what else my Challenger has up their sleeve, but it's probably best not to go out of my way to get noticed given I don't know who it is.

When I get to the church, the clues are easy to find and written on whiteboard plaques staked into the ground behind the fence.

Booklet in hand, I flip to the section that asks what's the largest number of students the choir has ever had. The whiteboard closest to me reads:

Dulcet tones for every key, a voice to match do-re-mi.

123

"More riddles," I huff, running the nub of my eraser across my bottom lip. "Key must be the piano," I brainstorm out loud, checking my six to make sure I'm truly alone. "So that could mean either there was one student for literally every key, or just for one octave. Do sharps and flats count?"

No one replies, of course. Hayes taught me that every piano has eight notes in an octave. Or was it a scale? Are they the same? I can't remember. But how am I supposed to know how many octaves are in a piano? And doesn't it vary depending on the piano's size?

Hayes would know thanks to his years of classical piano lessons. I wonder if Trevor remembered that and purposefully chose a question Hayes would ace.

I might need to do my least favorite thing: guess. My pencil presses to the paper, but I pause, looking through the fence's posts to the freaky church. The sun's rays hit a broken portion of window and highlight the room within. It's off the side of the church, an alcove that doubled as the music room. In it is a piano.

"Yes!" I celebrate, trying to get closer to count the keys. But with the fence in the way, it's impossible.

Unless I get higher up. That could give me the perfect vantage point to see through the window while still staying on the right side of the fence. There's a tree right next to the fence with a branch fairly low to the ground. I really, *really* don't want to climb. But the need for a correct answer wins out. All I have to do is get five or so feet off the ground. I can manage that.

My limbs say differently. They shake as I pull myself higher, my stomach twisting into knots. There's a natural knob above my nose. I reach for it—

And my feet slip. I fall, landing roughly on my side. The breath shoots out of me and spurs on a coughing fit. I lay on the ground for an embarrassing amount of time, making sure nothing's broken and that I'll live to see another day. Realistically, I only fell a handful of feet. Unrelated: I *hate* climbing.

Guessing it is. I'm gearing to sit up when a shadow hovers over me, an upside-down face peering down.

"Did you fall out of the tree?"

Mina cocks her head to the side, offering me a hand.

"It's not a habit, trust me," I say, taking her hand. "Was it loud?"

"You did scream," she says. "And swear."

"Oops. What are you doing all the way out here?" She flips the pages of her own booklet, which, to my surprise, is mostly filled out in *ink*. That's a level of confidence I haven't yet mastered.

"I'm looking for how many piano keys there are," she says.

"Me too," I admit. "That's why I was in the tree."

"In the tree?"

I almost don't expand, but maybe she could help. It can't hurt to ally for this one thing.

I explain how the higher branches of the tree should give a good vantage point to see the piano, but I can't reach them because I hate heights. Mina cracks her knuckles, scaling the tree like a spider monkey while I watch in awe. "Are we counting the black keys?"

"Yes." I make an executive decision. "The riddle says every key."

I uselessly stand by the trunk as she counts, ready to at least try to catch her if she falls. But she shimmies down in no time.

"Eighty-eight keys," she announces.

While I have no reason to assume Mina might lie to me, I purposefully take a long time to pull out my mechanical pencil, adjusting the graphite so I can watch her write *88* down in pen. Once she does, I do, too.

"That was the only one I had for here," she says. "You?"

"I have two more." I'm not as careless as her to show my entire sheet, which makes me feel like a jerk, since she just showed me hers. She trusts me, but she shouldn't. "The year the church was built and what was used to build it."

"Oh, I got those. Oak was used to build it, and it was finished in 1893."

I blink at her, unable to believe she just gave me the answers. At least with the piano keys, it was a mutual need. "Oh. Thanks."

"No problem. I've gotta get going. Have to go all the way to the lake in hopes that there's an answer about what year the flood happened."

I shouldn't help her. She's my competition, and she's clearly more prepared than I gave her credit for. But she did just help me, and I don't want any debts. Maybe this can be my repentance for misleading Jaleigh.

"The flood happened in 1928," I say. "April, to be exact."

She scribbles that down, flashing me a smile. "Thanks. I'll see you on the other side."

"See ya," I echo, going the opposite direction.

I pull a twig from my hair, a pep in my step because I only have two questions left. I don't want to get cocky, but this trial feels made for me.

Some of my arrogance withers during the thirty-minute jog back to the estate, which leaves me with a stitch in my side despite my numerous walking breaks. Unlike Keana, I'm not a runner. My lack of speed might be my downfall.

I'm a sweaty mess when I finally pass Carly sunbathing on a towel by the gates. She lowers her sunglasses as I walk by.

"Done?" she drawls.

"Almost," I say. "Has anyone else finished yet?"

"Have you heard the horn?"

I smile. "I have not. Thank you."

She raises her sunglasses, lying back down. If someone told me that Carly won her trials by being the bitchiest Challenger, I'd believe it.

When I enter the estate, it's much less quiet than I hoped. Woolf and Hayes confer in the common room. They must not know what country the rug was made in. Iran, duh.

To stay out of their way, I start upstairs. I'll have to circle back to the painting, but that can be last. Right now, my biggest prerogative is getting the answer to the question about Diana's suite. When I get to the Champions' hall on the second floor, I hurry all the way to the end where the suite is, something I only know because I found scans of the estate's blueprints in the library at school. This area is deserted, making me wonder if the other Challengers automatically know the answer (unlikely), came here first while I was in the forest (more likely), or are choosing to guess because they don't know where Diana's suite is since it's tucked away (most likely). The question asks, "In honor of her parents, Diana kept things in the room mostly the same.

Including the blueprints for the library expansion, which were finished in _____."

When I try the door, it's locked, of course. But there is a small whiteboard stuck to it that reads:

I'm the year the Second World War ended. What am I?

That's easy. 1945. I'd never forget it after countless history lessons where Professor Asad drilled it into our brains.

I go to write it down, but my pencil hesitates. There's something not right about it. It's too late, I think. Diana would have been older than she was in the portrait downstairs, and that portrait was painted right after the expansion. It had to have been earlier.

An internal clock ticks as I debate the answer. I'm almost positive it was after the First World War, actually. And that would have been 1918.

In a snap decision, I trust my gut, going with 1918. I fly down the stairs, sprinting to the hallway with the painting. As I remembered, it shows a younger Diana surrounded by the first class of students in the new library. There's a whiteboard beside it that correlates with the question on the sheet:

In a portrait painted by _____ that Diana cherished deeply featuring the first class, one can find her favorite spot to be the _____.

I got the second part, which is the library. I think I know the first part, but I want the clue to confirm.

This Spanish artist is best known for his paintings during the early twentieth century.

"Spanish artist?" I ask. I was so sure it was a woman, and French. And what Spanish artist could it be? The only one who comes to mind for this time period is Picasso, and it's certainly not his style.

The artist doesn't have their signature on the painting, but more of an indiscernible scribble in the corner. No matter how hard I try to read it, I can't even figure out the letters.

But it is familiar. I close my eyes, trying to picture it. I can see the painting on the wall, a black-and-white grave with flowers and vines wrapped around it. Morbid, for sure. But from where? I try to picture the flowers, and—

"Rosetown." My eyes spring open, my seventh-grade field trip to the Rosetown Museum of Fine Art snapping into focus. The most famous painting there was by Amelie LaFramboise. I remember learning about that in art history my junior year and thinking it was funny that a little piece of home followed me all the way over here.

So why does the clue say Spanish? I don't know, but I know it's wrong, just like the one upstairs. Maybe this is another part of the trial. To test how sure we are of ourselves.

I write what my gut tells me. Usually I double-check answers, but I can't waste the time. I sprint outside to where Carly still lounges, though now she's joined by Aura and Jarod.

"I'm done," I pant, holding the packet out. "Everything is filled in."

Carly takes it with a catlike smile. "But is it filled in correctly?"

"You can finish first, but the person who gets first has to also have everything correct," Aura states, as if she's reading from the Wilde Academy Wilderness Competition rule book.

"Check my answers, then," I say, stomach flipping as I overthink the last two questions.

As I watch Carly compare my sheets with the answer packet she pulls out from under her towel, Mina emerges from the trees.

"Congrats on finishing first," she tells me, handing her own packet to Aura. Jarod has his sunglasses on and hasn't moved an inch since I showed up. I'm pretty sure he's asleep.

"Thanks," I say. I'm not sure I would have finished first if she didn't give me the answers at the church. "Congrats on finishing second."

She beams, the face so similar to how Cece looked at me after I commended her on getting a B on a science test—her toughest subject—that I have to look away. There's been plenty to distract me from missing out on my daily chats with my sister, but now the reminder hits like a fist. If there's an emergency, I won't even know until the two weeks are up.

"Okay," Carly says, tucking my packet under her towel and taking Mina's. She starts scanning hers.

"Did I win?" I ask. "Were the answers correct?"

"Oh, yeah," Carly says, not bothering to look up. "Congrats."

Aura blows the horn. A smile breaks out on my face. *Finally.*

I turn to Mina. "See ya."

I strut inside, pleased that all my hours of studying random Wilde lore to prep for the competition—even the kooky bit about how Diana would leave a window open in the library so the spirits of her family could come in and out, which was a question on page nine—paid off.

On the way into the estate I pass Hayes and Woolf, now debating the whereabouts of Diana's suite and if they should bullshit an answer or keep looking.

"No way." Woolf scowls. "*You* finished first?"

"Yep. And Mina already got second. But maybe you both can secure third and fourth. You know, as long as all your answers are right."

Stopping at the top of the steps, I look back just in time to watch them share an apprehensive look. They definitely aren't confident they nailed everything.

"Good luck!" I call.

Inside, Lainey and Soph stand by the painting, scribbling down an answer. They give me scathing looks as they pass, hurrying outside.

On the way to the kitchen to get a snack, I walk by the painting and glance at the whiteboard. I stop short.

This French artist is best known for her paintings during the early twentieth century.

French artist. Someone changed the clue.

I skip the snack, running upstairs to check the clue by Diana's suite.

I'm the year the First World War ended. What am I?

Somehow, somebody changed those two clues. It would have been easy enough as long as they had a dry-erase marker. But was this done to trick me, specifically? If so, that means they were watching me so they could change things before I went to it, then back to the right answer after I was gone. And did they try to change others but I didn't notice because I didn't need the clues? Whether my Challenger or just a cheater out to cut the competition, this was an attempt at sabotage.

If I hadn't trusted my gut, it would have worked.

13

Lainey gets eliminated.

I'm happy to see her go, but it doesn't make sense. There were only four Challengers in the estate between the time when I was looking at the clues and when I came back: Hayes, Woolf, Soph, and Lainey.

Soph has a track record of tearing people down, something I experienced firsthand junior year when she hacked into my classroom profile and fudged a bunch of my grades, sending me into a spiral when my email lit up with zero after zero. The only reason she got caught was because Keana recognized her handiwork since Soph had cooked up a similar scheme while they were dating. After we reported it, Soph got a week of detentions, but her senator mom got her out of anything too harsh.

So while trying to sabotage another Challenger is something Soph would do, I can't imagine she'd do it at the expense of Lainey, her best friend. Assuming they were together for the whole trial, if Lainey came in last, Soph should have, too, since they were working together. Their answers couldn't have varied that much.

I studied Soph's face for any hint of remorse as Lainey cried, getting led away. Soph looked as shocked as Dodge and Malcolm.

Which brings me back to suspecting Hayes and Woolf.

After waiting for the sounds of the Champions settling in their rooms later that night, I sneak out of mine.

"I know," I say to Hayes, throwing my hands up as I approach the fading fire. "I'm late. But Carly took forever to stop flirting with Jarod in the hall and go into her room."

"I came out here early and had to sneak around them," Hayes says, voice emotionless as ever. "Figured you'd want to sleep more."

If he hadn't just admitted to hating me last night, he could have almost fooled me into thinking he still cares about my well-being. I take a seat on the log. "I slept after the trial for a bit. I've been thinking over the last page of the journal and have some ideas on where to start."

"Yeah?" He quirks a brow, passing the journal into my waiting hands.

I reread the last page. "Hunter said, 'I wish I had A Good Book to read.' Why would he capitalize *A Good Book* if he wasn't talking about a literal book? The other night, Trevor told me that during his trials they used to have access to the library before the tree fell and the west wing was blocked off. So what if Hunter hid the pages somewhere in the library?"

It's not like I expected Hayes to call me a genius, but his slow nod makes frustration bloom.

"You don't think it's a good place to look?"

"I think it's the best place to look," he replies. "If it wasn't walled off."

"That's why you were outside the other night," I realize. "You were looking for a way into the library from outside."

"There isn't one," he confirms. "It's so overgrown around the west wing that it's impossible to get closer. I was on my way back in when we"—he trails off, looking to the stars for the right word—"rendezvoused."

"So what were you planning to do tonight?"

He gives me a dry look. "I was hoping my new associate might have a trick up her sleeve."

"Maybe I do, but remember the rules of the proposition. You're supposed to help me, too."

"I did," he says. "You really think I didn't know the rug in the living room was made in Iran? Of course I did. I distracted Woolf long enough so you could get upstairs and do whatever you had to do. I figured you were nearly done."

"That didn't help that much," I say. "Especially because someone gave me false clues."

I catch him up on my assumptions, because in a truce, I guess laying all the cards on the table might be helpful. But it's more so I can carefully watch his features for any tells *he* changed the clues and tried to trick me.

"It couldn't have been Woolf. He was with me the whole time," Hayes says.

"The only other two people in the estate were Soph and Lainey," I push.

"And Keana. She was coming from the kitchen when Woolf and I got downstairs."

"I didn't see her."

A huff escapes him. "Take my word for it or don't. I don't care. But if you haven't noticed, your saboteur sucks. You got first place today."

"It's almost like I don't need your help."

He gestures lazily back toward the estate. "By all means, call it quits. The truce lasted a whole twenty-four hours. A good run."

I'm tempted, but breaking the truce feels like letting him win. "Actually, this associate does have a trick up her sleeve."

His stone expression fractures, interest piqued. "Do tell."

"It will involve some minor breaking and entering," I warn.

"I seem to remember you're good at that," he says.

I flush, recalling the time I picked the lock on his dorm while he and Woolf were in a night class to decorate it for his birthday.

"If we get caught, we're toast."

His mouth curves in a smirk that makes my stomach flip. "So we don't get caught."

"And also—"

"Chloe, *spit it out*."

My heart leaps at my name pouring from his mouth. He rarely called me it, always preferring my four-leafed nickname. I wonder if it's as strange to say as it is to hear.

I take a deep breath. "If we want to get into the library, we have to find the tunnels."

His face falls. "Aren't those made up just to buy into the creepy-house vibe?"

I shake my head. "They exist. I'm sure of it. While prepping for the trials, I studied everything I could find about the estate, and one source mentioned that Diana had a set of blueprints that show the hidden entrances to get into the tunnels. And as we know from today's trial, Diana kept blueprints in her room."

He nods, meeting my eyes. "You can get past the locked door?"

I pull a bobby pin from my hair. "This should do the trick. I looked at the lock earlier. It's the same kind on my attic door that I used to break into when Cece and I played our spy game."

His gaze softens at my sister's name. A blink later, he's back to normal. "We'll have to sneak past the Champions' rooms."

"Good thing we're well-versed in sneaking around authority."

I start toward the estate, not wanting to give him the satisfaction of waiting for a reaction. I hope the statement floods his thoughts with all the memories that haunt me—slipping into each other's rooms past curfew and stealing kisses in storage closets.

After a split-second hesitation, he follows me inside.

We sneak up the stairs, collectively wincing at the creaks and groans. Pausing at the second-floor landing, I stare down the dark corridor where the Champions are staying.

"Come on," I whisper, taking the lead. We creep down, passing door after door. This hallway is almost the exact same as ours on the floor above, but there're fewer doors, leading me to believe the rooms are bigger. That checks out, given it's where the faculty stayed.

I stop short, causing Hayes to bump into me. He hisses out a swear, the breath of it breezing across the back of my neck.

"Why'd you st—"

My elbow connects with his stomach, more breath shooting out of him. I emphasize the motion of keeping my lips zipped, then gesture to the two doors we have yet to pass.

The one to my right is ajar, moonlight spilling through the gap. The door on the left is closed, but the unmistakable sound of kissing comes from within. Followed by a *groan*.

Hayes and I hit the same conclusion simultaneously, mouths falling open. I'm pushed forward by his hand, propelling me down the rest of the hallway. It's not until we get all the way down the twists and turns and find Diana's locked door that we stop.

I spin to face Hayes, eyes wide. "Do you think they were—"

"Shhh!" Hayes orders, pressing a finger to my lips. "Let's hope that keeps them busy and they didn't hear you."

"You talked, too," I whisper against his finger.

He grimaces as if my lips burned him and he's not the one who put the digit there, removing his hand to gesture to the door. "Do your worst."

Feeling the pressure of his expectant gaze burning into my back, I drop to my knees, bend the bobby pin into shape, and thread it through the hole fit for a skeleton key. While I didn't exactly lie about the spy game, I might have stretched the truth. Cece always wanted me to be the bad spy because I was worse at picking the lock and usually had to give up. She likes an easy win, and she's the only person I'd ever give it to.

Now, I wish she were here to effortlessly pick the lock for me. Even the lock on Hayes's dorm didn't take this long. Seconds tick by, quickly morphing to minutes. Hayes huffs behind me, a cross between impatience and nerves. In the stillness of the hallway, the scraping of the bobby pin inside the lock sounds like fireworks.

And then, the most miraculous sound—a click. The bobby pin catches just right, freeing the lock. I turn the crystal knob and the door swings open.

"Gotcha," I whisper, bouncing to my feet and pushing into the room.

Hayes closes the door behind us.

"Creepy," I breathe.

Enough moonlight streams through the windows that I don't need to use my phone flashlight, which is the only reason I'm keeping my phone charged since it's useless otherwise.

The room is more of a suite with multiple sections. The first part is a sitting room with a velvet couch riddled with moth holes and two wingback chairs across from a hearth framed by bookshelves, though they're bare. Whatever texts were once in here probably got moved into the academy's archives. On top of the mantel sits a crooked candelabra with wax dripping down the sticks, as if Diana lit it just the other night.

"It feels like the pictures are watching us," Hayes mutters.

He's not wrong. The walls are lined with eerie portraits. Some are recognizable as Diana and her family, but others obscure and older. Probably relatives. The Wilde family came from old wealth, the kind of money that sticks for generations. At least Diana used that money to help others.

"It makes me sad," I comment, running my finger along the dusty shelves as I follow Hayes deeper into the suite.

"What? That she's dead?" he asks.

"No," I ponder it. "So much of her is still in this room and no one bothered to put this stuff in a museum or the academy, or even give it away. It's decaying with the estate."

"Feels like a grave," he agrees.

The next room is a hallway with a bathroom off the side of it. I peek inside, confirming there's nothing but cobwebs and a claw-foot bathtub that Mom would die for. She's always on Pinterest dreaming of fancy, luxury bathrooms where she can relax after submitting a new article.

"Diana's bedroom," Hayes states as the hallway opens into a space that rivals the size of the kitchen. A giant four-poster bed sits in the middle draped with faded pink—or maybe red, once upon a time—velvet. The same fabric hangs in thick curtains around the windows, all of which boast enviable window seats. On one side of the room is a giant wardrobe with a closet door beside it. The quilts on the bed are mismatched, showing a hint that a real person lived and slept in this room and it's not an elaborately staged haunted house.

"There's what we're looking for." Hayes points to the walls. On every available stretch of space are giant framed sketches. Blueprints.

"Eight in total," I count. "You take four and I take four?"

"Deal."

He takes the ones on the right side of the room, and I tackle the ones on the left. To view the one hanging over Diana's dramatic bed, I have to climb on top of it. The springs squeal in protest like the entire thing might collapse beneath me.

Hayes shoots me a stern look at the noise.

"Sorry," I mouth.

A few more squeaks and I'm tapping on my flashlight to

illuminate the huge drawings. In the bottom left corner in faded pencil markings are the words *Wilde Estate, floor 2, east wing.*

The sketches don't show me much aside from what I already knew. This is the largest suite by far, but the other rooms on this floor are decently sized with their own bathrooms. One even has a sitting room like Diana's. I hoped it might show secret doors or hidden hallways, but nothing stands out. Regardless, I snap a picture so I can study the layout later.

I move off the bed and to the next blueprint: first floor, west side. It shows the path to the library, game room, and gymnasium, which doubled as a ballroom. If it wasn't now walled off, it'd be helpful.

The third blueprint highlights the basement, east wing. I didn't expect the basement to be divided into wings like the rest of the estate, but it seems to be. Even more strange is that it doesn't split right down the foyer like the other blueprints. Instead, the side closest to the center ends in a half moon, as if carved around the foyer.

My last blueprint is the third floor on the west side, which used to be more student housing as the school grew.

"Anything?" Hayes asks.

"No," I sigh, meeting him in the middle of the room. "You?"

"No." Even the dark can't hide the disappointment in his eyes. "A bust."

"We got the layout of the estate," I say, holding my phone up. "I took pictures."

"That will give the Champions evidence we were sneaking around if we get caught."

"We're not going to get caught," I argue. "Maybe we should start looking in—"

I break off, my gaze catching on the desk shoved into the corner of the room by the wardrobe. And, more important, the thing on the desk.

Hayes waves a hand in front of my face. "What? You think the entrance to the tunnels is in Diana's wardrobe? This isn't Narnia."

I swat his hand away, rushing to it. The desk was on Hayes's side, in the shadows.

"What are you doing?" Hayes asks, exasperated. "Can you stop being so freaky—"

"This is a typewriter," I say, pointing to the old-school writing device on the desk.

"I know what a typewriter looks like."

I shake myself out of my stupor. "No—I know—I mean"—a frustrated breath escapes me—"whoever threw the brick through my window attached a note with it that looks like it was written on a typewriter. They signed it *Your Challenger.*"

Hayes frowns, taking out a flashlight—a real flashlight, not his phone—and capturing the old system in its cone of light. "That's weird."

"It's not just weird, it's suspicious."

"That's not what I meant. Look at the keys."

They're worn, which is unsurprising given Diana probably wrote everything on here. She was always drawing up papers and plans, most of which are preserved in the archives. Some keys don't even have legible letters on them.

"They're well-used," I observe.

"Not just that. Every single thing in this entire suite is disgusting. Full of dust and dirt and grime." He shudders. "But there's no dust on the keys."

I take his flashlight, confirming it for myself. "Not on the lever for the paper, either."

He nods. "Someone's been here."

"My Challenger?" I guess.

"Maybe. But how'd they get in?"

"The bobby pin trick isn't exactly a science," I admit.

"How would they relock the door?"

"They wouldn't. We can't. They must have a key."

"Or *found* a key," he corrects. "But what were they doing in here?"

Writing a blackmail letter to me, I want to say, but he still doesn't know about that.

"Maybe they'll come back," I choose instead.

He checks his watch. "We can't wait until they do. Trevor's an early riser, and I don't want to sneak past his room once he's up. We'll have to circle back tomorrow."

We creep back to the sitting room, but as we pass the hearth, something catches my eye.

"Do you see that?" I point to the fireplace. "That brick is darker, isn't it?"

He scans his flashlight over the facade. "I guess?"

I press on it, then pull, waiting for something to happen. Nothing does.

"Anticlimactic," I huff.

"If Diana's ghost is around, I wonder if this crooked-candle thing bothers her as much as it does me," Hayes says, grabbing the tarnished candelabra on the mantel and straightening it.

A series of clicks ricochet through the air, making us jump. Hayes stumbles back into me as the bookcase on the right yawns open with a groan of rusted hinges.

It's a *door*. We share a glance before staring into the dark depths beyond.

14

"We obviously have to see where it goes," I say, stepping through the secret door. I make it a few paces before realizing Hayes isn't following me. Turning to him, I flash my phone light in his eyes. "You coming? Someone might have heard that, so we better hurry."

"Yeah," he says, unable to mask the unease in his tone. I glance around me, taking note of the cobwebs and general grime, all things high on Hayes's *no thanks* list.

"If it helps to close your eyes, I can lead the way," I offer.

He scoffs, breaking out of his apprehension and pushing past me. "And lead me right into a snake pit? I don't think so."

"Probably more like a spider pit," I reason, using a lever on the other side of the sneaky bookcase to swing it closed behind me. It latches with a foreboding clank.

"Not helping," he huffs. I hurry to catch up to him, flashing my light around the decrepit space.

"I think we're between the walls," I comment. The ceiling hangs low, only a foot or so above our heads, and there isn't enough room to walk side by side.

"You think this leads to the library?" Hayes asks. For once, the disinterest has slipped from his tone, replaced with disgust at every new web our light shines upon.

"According to what I read, there are multiple entrances," I say. "I'm sure one goes to the library, but figuring out which it is might be tricky. In one article—"

"Stop!" He grabs my arm, his whisper-yell caught in an echo.

"What?" I ask.

He nods at the floor before us. Or, more important, the lack of. I shine my light directly underfoot, highlighting a narrow stairwell going down.

"You could have fallen down the stairs," he says, taking a careful step down.

I follow him, though now I'm the apprehensive one. There must be a bottom, but since I can't see it, this feels a lot like being on a roller coaster plunging down the biggest dip. "You probably would have gotten a good laugh if I had."

"It would have been hilarious," he mutters, shoulders tensing.

Too late, I realize the insensitivity of my words. Hayes is certainly not the audience for falling jokes.

"Concrete," I comment when my feet finally touch solid ground.

"Must be the basement," Hayes points out, flashing his light around. "Or . . . some of it?"

Whatever space we're in is strange. The area is too small to be the full basement, and in every direction are slim stairways like the one we just descended. I count six in total.

"It's the center point," I realize. "We must be right beneath the foyer. Look at this."

Hayes comes close enough to peer over my shoulder, and I find the photo of the basement blueprint I snapped. I point to the east section that makes a C, then scroll to the matching blueprint, which makes a backward C on the west section. "If you were to nudge these blueprints together, there would be a circular gap," I point out.

"But not a circle," Hayes corrects, glancing around us. "A hexagon."

I nod. "These staircases must lead up to different floors and the tunnels within the walls for that wing. There're six, which matches up with the six blueprints for east and west wings, floors one through three. We just need to figure out where each staircase goes."

"Can I see the other blueprint pictures?" Hayes asks. I pass him my phone.

"They don't show the tunnels," I sigh. "That would have made it too easy, I suppose."

"We don't need it," he says, a hint of excitement in his tone as he holds my phone out so we can both see. The blueprint is east wing, floor two. Where we just came from.

"Notice anything odd about these blueprints?"

I take the phone back but shake my head. He points at the fireplace in Diana's room. "No furniture is on them except for where there's a fireplace. For every fireplace, two bookcases frame it. But there are other bookcases around the estate that aren't on the blueprints."

"Which could mean only the ones by fireplaces are secret doors," I realize, smiling up at him. He cracks one back, but it falls too fast. He steps away, putting distance between us.

"I don't know if every fireplace means there's a corresponding tunnel and secret door, because this place has tons of fireplaces," he says, voice serious again. "But if that's true, then another secret entrance to the tunnels is in Trevor's room." He points to the other room in the blueprint with a fireplace framed by bookcases.

I scroll through the blueprint pictures, stopping at west wing, floor one. I point at the fireplace in the faded drawings of the library. "I'd bet everything this is another door. We just need to figure out which stairway takes us to that wing."

Hayes looks around at the stairways. "Process of elimination? We could go up each one to see what floor it takes us to."

"Maybe we should split up to save time?" I suggest.

"I know for a fact you've seen horror movies," he states dryly.

It's too casual a comment for the memory it unveils. A chilly October night snuggled in his bed in the nook between his left arm and side with my laptop propped on our stomachs streaming a recent low-budget horror flick. The lights off and covers pulled to our chins. Me nearly peeing the bed when Woolf burst into the room, moaning like a zombie before dissolving into cackles.

The memory makes me want to split up even more. As it is, we've spent entirely too much time together tonight and I've dropped my guard. He's so much better at playing the angry ex than I am.

I fold my arms, wanting to fight him just to gain some ground back. "I think splitting up is a good idea. And since *I'm* the one who found the tunnels, what I say goes."

His eyes narrow. "*I* was the one who moved the candlestick to reveal the hidden door."

"Which you would have never done if I hadn't pointed out the discolored brick. And it's not a candlestick—it's a *candelabra*."

"Is there even a difference?"

"Of course there's a difference!" I hiss. I'm not sure why I'm willing to die on the candelabra hill, but when it comes to Hayes, all hills seem worth perishing on. "A candelabra—"

I break off as a low murmur of voices floats toward us from the staircase we came from. From the panic in Hayes's eyes, I can tell he hears it, too.

"I think that's Trevor," he whispers, our candelabra quarrel falling to the wayside. He climbs up a few steps to get closer to listen.

"Do you think he heard us?" I creep up behind him.

He glares down at me. "If we get foiled because you were yelling about candelabras or whatever they're called, I'll never forgive you."

"Add it to the list."

Something between a huff and a laugh escapes him, but he clears his throat and ascends a few more steps before I can overanalyze. We stop halfway up once the voices get clearer.

"I'm fucking exhausted, man. Can't we chill out for one day?"

The voice is distinctly Jarod's, an edge of a whine to it.

"You know we have a list of things that the school is expecting to be complete by the end of these two weeks," Trevor says. "We need to stay on track."

"We are kind of doing free labor on the off days," I whisper to Hayes.

"Fucked up," he agrees.

I don't know if it's the rare swear word leaving his lips or the fact that he's actually agreeing with me for once, but a warmth spreads, tingling to my fingertips. I shake them at my sides, as if I can dispel whatever weirdness hit me.

"Also," Jarod sounds cautious, which seems so unlike him. "Aura's pissed that we changed the rest of the trials to be harder than the original seven we pitched the school. Carly's worried she's going to rat."

"I wonder what that means," I murmur. "Why would they make them harder?"

"Don't know, but can't be anything good for us," Hayes forebodes.

"She's not going to rat." Weariness seeps from Trevor's tone. "This is just her last year as Champion, so she doesn't want to put any real effort into it."

Jarod huffs. "Kinda can't blame her, man. This is way more work than last year. And for my trials, the Champions made it look like a vacation."

"Your year was light," Trevor says.

"What's that supposed to mean? It still took a lot to win," Jarod argues, ego bruised.

Trevor sighs. "I'm not saying it didn't. I just mean that being a Champion overseeing the trials isn't meant to be a vacation. It's an honor and expectation. Besides, even the changed trials aren't as difficult as the ones I went through during my year. I would never let it get to that point. Nobody is going to get hurt."

Hayes flinches. My fingers itch to reach out, to brush his arm in some sort of acknowledgment of his flash of grief, but I think better of it. It's not my job to comfort him anymore.

"And we are loosening the reins," Trevor adds. "Why do you think we're sending the losing Challenger home? I don't want anyone competing if they don't have an honest shot."

Jarod sucks air between his teeth. "I don't know if anyone has an honest shot with some of the later trials."

Even in the dark, my eyes find Hayes's, alarm thrumming through me.

"They'll rise to the challenge," Trevor says confidently. "It's what they do. Now please go wake them up and do a room check while you're at it. Bring Carly with you, since it seems like you two enjoy spending time together."

Hayes and I jerk to attention. I glance at my glow-in-the-dark watch, flashing it in Hayes's face. It's nearly five.

"We aren't, uh—nothing is happening between us," Jarod stammers.

"It better not be," Trevor says. "It's bad enough we have to babysit the Challengers and make sure they all stick to their own beds. Don't make me need to babysit you two, too."

"Oh, don't worry about me, man; I'm not into blonds," Jarod lies through his teeth.

"We need to go!" I whisper, dragging Hayes down the stairs.

"We can't go back out through Diana's room without crossing the Champions' hallway again," Hayes frets.

"Then we need to find a different door," I say. "There are two other staircases on the east side. One of these should lead to the first or third floor."

"We can't chance the third floor," Hayes counters. "The only fireplace on the map is in Dodge's room."

"First floor it is," I say, choosing the staircase closest to me. When we reach the top we sprint down another narrow corridor as quietly as possible, coming to a door with a lever. It's rusty from disuse, and I have to shove my shoulder into the door to get it to nudge open. We spill into the living room.

"I told you," I brag as we sneak through the downstairs. At the base of the stairs, Hayes pauses. Footsteps sound overhead.

"We have to risk it," I whisper, nodding at the stairs. "If Carly and Jarod wake everyone up and our doors are still closed, they'll get suspicious."

"I hate this," Hayes huffs, creeping up the stairs. If we go fast, we're loud. If we go slow, we're sure to get caught. Hanging out in the openness of the grand staircase is a dead giveaway.

"I could say I got thirsty." I start mustering excuses as to why I was out of my room.

"And me?"

"More than one person can get thirsty."

"Impossible."

I can feel Hayes's eye roll through his back.

Holding my breath as we pass the landing for the second floor, I risk a peek down the hallway. And seriously shouldn't have.

"Jarod and Carly are coming," I whisper to Hayes. He picks up the pace. "We'll never make it to our rooms in time."

The whine of Carly's voice mixes with Jarod's as they exit the hallway. If my heart wasn't pounding in my ears, maybe I could make out their conversation.

We reach the top of the stairs as they step onto the second-floor landing and start ascending. All they'd have to do is look up to see us.

Hayes tugs me to the mouth of our hallway, but my room is halfway down, and his two doors farther. Plus, my door is locked. To make it to my room, fish my skeleton key from my pocket, and slip inside before Carly and Jarod see? That's a problem.

We're still two doors away from mine and out of time. I yank on Hayes's arm so he stumbles back into me.

"You need to kiss me," I hiss.

His eyes blow wide. *"What?"*

"We need to redirect them so they don't suspect what we're *actually* doing."

I don't have time to point out that we're coated in cobwebs and dust. If they look too closely, we'll have a lot of questions to answer.

Hayes follows my frame of thought, reluctant understanding filling his gaze. I don't need to turn my head to know Carly and Jarod are about to turn the corner. We're in full view.

"It's your idea." He is not seriously still arguing right now when we're heartbeats away from getting caught. But he's Hayes, so of course he is. "You should be the one initiating—"

"Fine," I snarl against his mouth and crash our lips together. My fingers come up to thread in his hair, purely for the purpose of making this look as real as possible. It's not like I've missed the softness of the strands gliding past my fingers, and I definitely haven't missed the way his lips warm mine. I haven't missed kissing Hayes Stratford one bit. I'd rather gouge my eyes out. And I would, if so much wasn't riding on the line that I need my eyesight for.

I expected to do the legwork, but to my surprise, Hayes kisses me just as hard. The force makes me stumble back until my spine hits the wall, probably waking up whoever's room it is. His hand presses into my waist, pulling me closer, while his other hand cups my jaw, thumb on my cheek and fingers reaching past my ear to tangle in my short curls. When his head tilts to deepen the kiss, my brain short-circuits, the familiarity of him dangerous.

This was a bad idea. This was a very, *very* bad idea.

"Hey! What are you two doing?"

When we break apart at Carly's voice, there's a split second where all I see is Hayes. His green eyes hook on mine, lids half lowered, like he's drunk. Lips red, a sheen of saliva—probably mine—still on them. Hair tousled, cheeks pink.

I don't even want to know how I look, but if my burning mouth is any indication, I'm sure my appearance is a hot mess.

"Sorry," Hayes apologizes, not sounding very sorry at all. I'm not sure where my voice went. Maybe he sucked it down his throat. Probably a little bit of my soul, too.

"You guys are out of your rooms breaking curfew *and* hooking up," Carly accuses. "That's two strikes in one."

"We aim for efficiency," Hayes says, calm and collected.

How? *How?* If I opened my mouth, I'm pretty sure nothing but nonsense would tumble out.

"Way to go, dude," Jarod commends, holding his fist out for Hayes to bump. Hayes hesitates but obliges.

"Seriously?" Carly turns on Jarod. "We're supposed to be reprimanding them. This is grounds for elimination. No hook-ups allowed."

"Does that also hold true for Champions?" I ask innocently,

finally digging my voice out of whatever grave Hayes's tongue buried it in.

Carly blanks, sharing a startled glance with Jarod. "How would you—"

"Sound travels easily through the vents," I say, sweet as pie.

Hayes meets my eyes for the briefest moment, looking mildly impressed before his face flashes to an expression I've never seen on him before. He smiles coyly at Jarod.

"I'm really sorry, dude," he drawls to Jarod, his expression only clicking once his tone hits me. It's a classic *boys will be boys*. Like they're two bros having a chat and Carly and I might as well be invisible. "You know how it is."

Jarod chuckles, going for another fist bump. "Don't I know it."

Carly's jaw drops. She smacks Jarod's arm. "What's that supposed to mean?"

Jarod flinches. "Uh, nothing, just—"

"Asshole," Carly bites, turning on her heel and continuing down the hall. She starts banging on doors, screaming for everyone to get up.

"So . . . we good?" Hayes asks, going for another fist bump.

Yeesh, three is laying it on way too thick.

But Jarod's unable to resist. "We won't snitch on you if you don't on us," he says, casting me an uneasy glance. I mime zipping my lips.

"Deal," Hayes half-heartedly salutes him.

Jarod catches up to Carly, who is clearly cold-shouldering him. She's still yelling.

"That was close," I blow out a tense breath.

"That was the worst decoy plan ever." Hayes storms off to his room.

He can say whatever he wants, but that doesn't negate the truth:

It worked. And tonight, we can pick up right where we left off.

15

For the rest of the day, we become a landscaping crew.

We're split into groups and doled out rakes, hedge trimmers, and other maintenance equipment. My group is taken to the church, where Trevor unlocks the gate with a silver key on the big ring he keeps hooked on his belt loop. With strict orders not to venture inside the church and that we're meant to clean up the lawn and cut down on some of the overgrowth, we get to work under his supervision while the other groups tend to the estate grounds. Whispers float around me about Hunter's place of death, and Trevor shuts them up every time.

At this point, I'm really starting to doubt the competence of the estate's caretaker, but at least the activity keeps my mind from thinking too hard about the kiss between Hayes and me.

I'm scared of what will happen if I do.

When I get out of bed hours later to meet Hayes in the living room, my bones are heavy with exhaustion. We moved our meeting time up to one, the earliest we dared since the Champions don't come inside until after midnight. Hayes went down first so we would avoid getting caught in the hall together again. I don't have another decoy kiss in me.

As I pad into the living room, he turns to me. "Hey, you're—"

"I'm not late," I cut him off, flashing my watch.

"I know," he says, showing me his own watch strapped to his wrist. "I was going to say you're not going to want to hear this, but the door doesn't open the same way."

He points to the perfectly straight candelabra in the middle of the mantel. I tug on the bookcase we bolted out of this morning, but the door doesn't swing open.

"It has to be another trick," I reason, looking for a sign that anything looks amiss. But when dealing with a decaying estate that's over a century old, everything looks amiss.

"The bookcases in Diana's suite didn't still have books on the shelves," Hayes points out, starting to tug out the dusty tomes. As he makes his way down the shelves, I turn my flashlight on to analyze the giant painting hanging above. It's in greens and blues of a forest of trees with a single path slicing through the center. Super boring, as if we don't see enough of the same view outside.

In the bottom right corner, the canvas is peeling away from the frame. I pick at it. "That's weird, isn't it?"

"I guess. Nothing here," he replies, sitting back on his haunches as he puts the last book on the shelf. I pinch the peeling corner of the painting and pull.

He slaps my hand lightly. "You're going to ruin it."

"Maybe," I agree.

Instead, the canvas peels out of the frame, revealing a recessed area with a hidden lever.

"Or maybe I'll find exactly what we're looking for."

Hayes rolls his eyes, but from the corner of my eye, I catch the hint of a smile.

I pull down on the lever, and the mechanism clicks, the bookcase to our right popping out. Hayes enters the tunnel while I smooth the painting back into the frame to conceal the lever again. On the back of the canvas is a sticky substance, like double-sided tape. If it wasn't for the corner unsticking, I would have never suspected what it was hiding.

We sneak through the narrow path, descending the staircase into the hexagon basement. Only once my feet touch the concrete do I let the tension slip from my shoulders, the pressure to be quiet easing.

In its place, an awkward silence mixes with the musty air as we stop in the center, unsure where to go next. From the way neither of us can make eye contact or find something to say, I'm starting to wonder if getting caught sneaking around last night would have been the preferable choice.

Finally, Hayes clears his throat. "The staircase we need should only go up one flight, right?"

"Right," I say, internally shrugging off all thoughts of his warm lips against mine or fingers threading into my hair in favor of inspecting the west-side staircases. I shine my light up the one closest to me, its path going up, up, up and disappearing from view. "Not this one. Too steep. Must go to the third floor."

"Same with this one," Hayes says. His flashlight points upward, highlighting an identical staircase to the one we came down yesterday after finding the entrance in Diana's suite.

"So that just leaves—"

We both step toward the middle one, coming face-to-face. In the shadows cast by our lights, his fair eyelashes look longer than ever, spiderwebbing past his brow bone.

"This one," I say, ripping my gaze away to flash my light up the staircase. It's less steep than the other two, more like the one that leads to the living room entrance.

"Then let's go," he says, though his voice betrays a hint of hesitancy. I take the initiative, testing the old steps before continuing up. It's not that far before we reach the top, entering the same dusty in-between wall space as the other tunnels.

"I was looking at the blueprints last night," I say to fill the silence. "On the first-floor west side, the only fireplace is in the library. This should lead us right to it."

As if to emphasize my point, a chill sweeps through me. Like I passed through a ghost.

"The broken windows," Hayes says, shivering. We have to stand way too close in the narrow space, making it impossible to miss any of his movements. "When I looked at the forecast for this week, it predicted a cold front moving in toward the weekend. The next few days are going to be chilly."

"You looked at the forecast?"

"As if you didn't," he throws back. He has me there, because of course I did. And I packed appropriately. I just didn't realize I'd be missing a window.

The tunnel comes to an abrupt end with another levered door. I move aside to let Hayes do the honors of opening it since it feels momentous. He could be on the precipice of getting the closure he's craved for three years.

He pushes on the lever, using his entire body to force the door open. While the others were sealed shut from the passage of time, this one is worse off, with something blocking it even after Hayes manages to inch it open. I throw my body against the door in sync with Hayes, and between the two of us, we finally break through. I turn to see what was halting us.

Vines. The secret door was covered in *vines*.

Not just the secret door. As I take in the rest of the library, my jaw drops. The floor-to-ceiling wall of windows let in ample moonlight, enough to cast the space in an eerie blue glow. The library is three stories tall, rows and rows of bookshelves crammed in. Some are empty or sparse, but many are full. Vines climb through broken wooden spokes of the railing on the upper floor mezzanines, tangling with each other and spreading over the walls. Green grows all the way up to the ceiling, where a chandelier that rivals the one in the foyer hangs. The vines have claimed that, too, hanging off its tarnished arms in twisting tendrils.

A shudder races through me, partly from the obscure beauty of it, and partly from the cold. The vines pour in through several broken windows, a tree branch bursting through the top one. The ground sparkles with the broken glass, like snow.

"So," I say to break the silence. It feels as if I'm disrupting a graveyard, but replacing tombs for tomes. "Where should we start?"

It's a loaded question. There's a reason this was Diana's favorite room in the house. It's bursting with knowledge, the kind of place that can never warrant boredom. I imagine her wandering through the stacks, running her finger against the spines. I used to wonder how she wasn't sick of the place after being quarantined here while her family died in the rest of the estate. Now, it makes sense. The library is so big, it could be its own house.

"Let's work our way up," Hayes says, nodding at the iron spiral staircase in the corner. The vines winding through the staircase have splotches of white flowers. I move closer, cupping one in my hand.

"I think this is moonflower," I say, running my thumb over the white petals. "My mom liked to keep them in the garden."

The bud is hungry to drink in the moonlight, head tilted toward the windows. The cloying scent fills my nose. There's also the faintest tinge of old books, like a library should smell, but it's overpowered by the musk of the outdoors. Of air that bites and rain-soaked earth and a wildflower sweetness.

"This too?" Hayes asks, pointing to another stretch of vine that scales the staircase, climbing all the way to the third floor and disappearing into the shelves. Unlike the other vines that are strictly shades of green or spotted with white moonflowers, this one is riddled with bright, brilliant bursts of blue. It's a shade so pigmented it looks fake, as if a kid pulled the cornflower crayon from a box of Crayola and colored in the petals.

"I think so." I glance back at the white ones, comparing the two. They appear mostly the same save for their color. "I've never seen blue ones before."

"Must be rare," he murmurs. "That vine's the only one."

"Let's start scanning books and see what we find. You take this end, I take the other?" I gesture to the bookshelves nestled between where we stand near the windows and the opposite side of the room where the closed double doors lead to the rest of the west side. To our right is a collection of tables with chairs pushed out, as if students left for class and never came back.

"Meet in the middle." He nods.

"We know we're looking for missing pages, and that they're hopefully tucked inside 'a good book.' But a good book is subjective. What did Hunter like to read?"

Hayes is already dissecting the first shelf. A book opens, pages flip, and then thunks with a close. He moves onto the next.

"Hello?" I call out, confident we're out of earshot from the east side. I'm pretty sure if the tree leaning through the window fell to the ground, no one but us would even hear it. Or our screams if it crushed us. "What are we—"

"I don't know," Hayes snaps. "Hunter was always drawing. I don't know what he liked to read. I didn't even know he *liked* to read."

There's despair buried in his voice, as if he also can't believe that he doesn't know the answer to such a simple question.

"I don't know what Cece likes to read, either," I admit, a feeble attempt to ease his guilt.

"Well at least you can still ask her," he mutters, snapping the book in his hands shut with an air of finality.

"Maybe not for much longer," I whisper, too quiet for him to hear. I've been so busy since the start of the trials that I haven't had time to truly miss my sister's nightly video calls or texts. Now, the absence of her from my daily life slams into me, an unwanted reminder that if all the treatments keeping her alive should stop working, this could be my new forever. Silence.

I can't lose sight that she's the reason I'm here.

Like him, I start at the top of a shelf, working my way left to right, then down, before doing the whole thing again on the next one. I open books, flip through them, close them. Rinse and repeat. Most reek of dampness and decay; must and mold. Some I recognize, like Fitzgerald and Homer and Brontë, and others are names and titles that turn into one gigantic blur. Many I almost skip, sure that Hunter wouldn't possibly have picked the tome on the bottom shelf detailing eight hundred pages of Mayan history, but it could be *the* book. The one hopefully holding Hunter's missing journal pages.

It's not. None are.

As shadows shift across the room, Hayes and I meet in the middle. Wordlessly, he climbs the spiral staircase. I take it much slower, uneasy at the way the floor beneath us gets smaller. Even up on the mezzanine, I can't relax. My fear of heights rears its head, pressing on my chest as I stare over the edge.

"Let's switch sides," Hayes suggests, nudging me toward the deeper section of the stacks while he stays closer to the railing. Whether he does it because he notices my agitation or because he prefers the moonlight, I don't know, but I'm grateful nonetheless.

My angst subsides as I get lost in the rhythm of checking books, but his grows. When we meet in the middle of the second floor an hour later, arms sore and fingers peppered with paper cuts, he groans in frustration.

"It has to be here," he says, more to himself than me. "Hunter wouldn't have worded the last page of his journal like that if it wasn't. We're not looking hard enough. We need to find it."

"We still have another floor to look through." I tread lightly, sensing the fragility of his mood. This isn't just about Hayes finding the pages; it's about Hayes knowing his brother well enough to be right about Hunter's hints. "Let's come back tomorrow."

Hayes's eyes flash with anger. "We can't. One of us could get eliminated in the trial. We need to keep searching."

"We've been here for hours, and the Champions are getting unpredictable with their wake-up times. We shouldn't push our luck."

His gaze trails to the final floor of books to flip through. I need to get him out of here so I can get out of here. Maybe I can even squeeze in an hour of sleep.

"We can cut it close like last night and almost get caught," I suggest, the edge of a taunt in my voice. "But if you're that desperate to kiss me again, you should just say so."

His jaw drops open. "I'm not—I don't want to—" He stammers, the denials tripping over each other on their way out of his mouth. "That's the *last* thing I want to happen again."

"Suuuure," I say, making my way down the spiral staircase and white-knuckling the railing. "Whatever you say."

"I mean it," he growls, following me all the way to the fireplace. We didn't close it all the way, so it's easy to tug open. "I'd rather get caught."

"Then you really wouldn't get to look on the third floor tomorrow night," I wager. "According to Carly, we got two strikes last night. Strike three means we're out."

He follows me all the way into the tunnel and down the stairs into the basement, debating with me the whole time. I humor him, enjoying it entirely too much, grinning ear to ear in the darkness as we bicker.

As we get to the secret door to the living room, the smile slides off my face. I'm not supposed to enjoy it. I'm not supposed to like anything when it comes to Hayes. I'm supposed to vehemently hate him as much as he hates me.

But last night's kiss—

"What do you think the third trial will be?" he asks, interrupting a self-destructive thought.

"No idea. There are five values left—adaptability, agility, ambition, collaboration, and fortitude. It could be any of them."

Sneaking around every night has its advantages. I'm figuring out where to step to make the least amount of noise and what floorboards feel more dependable than others. When Hayes and I get to our rooms, it feels too easy.

"See you tomorrow," I say, even though tomorrow is today.

"Whatever happens today, you can't get eliminated."

The way his eyes cut through the dark makes my heart rate pick up. Of course he only means it because he needs my help. After we find the pages, he won't care what happens to me. And there's still the potential that *he's* my Challenger. Maybe that's why things have been quiet. He doesn't want to scare me out of the competition until he gets what he wants.

Exhaustion is my friend, leaving no room for spare thoughts of Hayes as I collapse in my bed, the chilly air wrapping around me. I dream of flowers, of white and blue petals and moonlight. It's all in flashes, a kaleidoscope of soft edges and colors. I'm wandering through the forest, but it's something else. In the same way that the woods took over the library in real life, in my dreams, the library grows in the woods. Books sprout from the ground like mushrooms, split down the spine so their pages are the underside and their leather covers face the sky. I want to stoop down to pluck one up, but I'm too busy following a trail of blue flowers.

Too soon, I'm woken by yelling and knocking, jerking out of the dream. Everything is sore, but especially my arms. The motion of sliding books on and off shelves for hours last night has taken an unexpected toll. Librarians seriously don't get enough credit.

I'm the last person to drag myself into the foyer. Hayes doesn't have a hair out of place, as if he got a full eight hours of REM. Beside him, Woolf's tired brown eyes narrow at me.

"Good morning," Trevor says, too loud given the sun isn't even up yet. Dawn sneaks through the skylight, extra faded thanks to the film of grime. When he's not satisfied with our grumbled response, he repeats it louder.

"Good morning," we echo a few decibels above the previous greeting.

"Today is trial three, and we're focusing on collaboration. It's a trait often overlooked, as many assume the way to the top is paved on your own. But we can attest that's not true. Being able to work together is a skill that will serve you well throughout all of life. It's not just about being friendly, it's about politics. Navigating situations with ease and a smile goes a long way."

"For this next challenge, we'll be going to the stream," Carly takes over. "Which you all so helpfully cleaned up the other day."

"An honorable sport where collaboration is a must is rowing."

I don't like where they're going with this. Suddenly, I am very awake.

"Today, you'll be put into predetermined pairs," Aura takes over, voice soft. "You need to row downriver. At certain points, you and your partner will stop to collect assets. These assets will be useful to you in your next trial."

"Since you're working in teams," Jarod says, "it's only fair that you're punished in teams, too. At the end of the day, two people will get eliminated instead of one."

Gasps resound, mine included. The chances of getting sent home just rose exponentially.

"The stream lets out into the lake, where one of us will be stationed until the last pair returns." Trevor holds a hand out, and Aura passes him a sheet. "Now for your teams."

I wait anxiously, not sure which match would be my best-case scenario. Keana, maybe. Or Mina. But Mina gets matched with Hayes. Keana gets paired with Malcolm. Not ideal for her, but it could have been worse. Soph is still an option, as is Dodge.

"Chloe Gatti and Carlos Woolf," Trevor reads.

My gaze snaps to Woolf across the room to see he's already looking at me. A slow grin spreads over his face.

From over Woolf's shoulder, Hayes flashes me a worried look. It's all the confirmation I need to know that my rough day is just getting started.

The malicious glint in Woolf's eyes promises it's about to get a whole lot worse.

16

Of all the things I studied, how to expertly row a canoe wasn't one of them.

But clearly it should have been, because when we arrive at the stream, we're greeted by five canoes. Or, as Jarod corrects, *shells*. That's what they call it in rich-boy-crew world.

"Each team will get one of these," Trevor says, holding up a translucent page. "It's a map for your map. Lay it on top and it shows the stops for your team's specific assets. Everyone has different stops in an attempt to make sure you all stay out of each other's way as much as possible. While you start together, you should end up pretty staggered depending on how long it takes you to find and make your stops."

"Are all routes equally timed?" Keana asks, arms folded across her chest.

"As close as possible," Carly confirms. "And everyone has the same number of stops."

Trevor passes out the sheets, but before I can grab ours, Woolf reaches over me to snatch it. "I'll keep this," he says, loading himself into the canoe and nearly tipping it over. He laughs, like this is all one big game.

"We'll both need to consult it," I reason, plopping into the canoe in the least graceful way possible. True to Hayes's weather forecast, today is cooler than the other day when we were at the stream. The sun hides behind the clouds and the chilly water nips my fingertips. I suppress a shiver, not wanting to give Woolf any more incentive to throw me in than he already has.

"Don't forget your life vests," Aura reminds us, standing on the bank. Her mouth is set in a grim line. The concerned look seems to be as permanent on her face as Carly's RBF. "And downstream, when you near the fork, stay left."

We shrug on the orange devices, although I'm one of the few who actually buckles mine. The water might be shallow here, but there's no telling what it will be like closer to the lake.

"Remember, you're a team," Trevor says. "Act like it."

Jarod sends us off with a fling of his arm. I use the oars to push against the embankment until we're fully floating. Our canoe—shell, whatever—bumps into Charlie and Alandra's. They throw dirty looks our way, rowing ahead of us.

"You suck at this," Woolf comments as I try to find a rhythm. Other teams are pulling ahead, forcing us to take up the rear. The waterway is so narrow that the rush of movement makes it wavy, rocking the boat. It's a good thing that all we ate on the way were granola bars. If it's possible to get seasick before seven in the morning, I'm there.

"We need to sync up to glide," I say, glancing at him from over my shoulder. I'm seated in front facing forward, but I wish we were facing each other. I feel too vulnerable with my back to him. "Follow Soph and Dodge's movements."

"Seems like a waste of time to me," Woolf says, continuing his sporadic, lazy rowing. It does nothing but splash me with icy spurts, soaking my sneakers in seconds.

"Soph's mom was a national regatta champion," I counter, remembering the accolade from Senator Gonzalez's campaign. "I think she knows what she's doing."

He snorts. "Yes, and my dad plays golf with PGA champs. But you don't see me hitting hole-in-ones on the daily. Being like our parents means nothing."

Bringing up parents was a bad move in front of Woolf. While Hayes succumbed to the pressure of following his dad's footsteps all the way to Stanford, Woolf would never give his father the satisfaction of walking in his shoes. His disdain for his parents runs deep, a well I could never find the bottom of even when we were friends. He does everything in his power to be a headache for them.

But right now, he's a headache for me. I need to twist his anger into something that can help me win. Help *us* win.

"Are your parents letting you take flying seriously yet?" I ask him.

"Why do you care?"

I shrug. "Last I heard you were having a tough time convincing them to let you go to aviation college."

"They should be lucky I want to go to *any* college," he spits out, picking up the pace so our strokes finally match. "I'm taking a semester off."

"Really? You're going to go live at home with them?"

Hayes once told me that Woolf practically lived at the

Stratford house when they were growing up. As kids, Woolf's parents were always taking trips without him, leaving him with a nanny. An only child, he had no one to play with, so he would spend his days with Hayes. Last summer, during the week when Hayes came to visit me in Creekson, Woolf blew up our group chat with how bored he was at home. While Woolf didn't particularly care for the actual school part of living at the academy, he loved being away.

"Fuck no," he says. We're making strides toward catching up to the others. I wish he'd actually take out the map. If I bring it up, he'll probably toss it overboard just to spite me. "There's no way in hell I'm moving home."

"Not even for the summer?" *Take out the freaking map.*

"No, for the summer I'm . . ." He trails off. "Stop trying to weasel information out of me."

"I don't know what you're talking about."

I can hear the eye roll in his voice. "You're trying to get me to let my guard down. Too bad. My lips are sealed."

"Fine," I huff. "Let's spend the entire day in silence if you prefer that."

"Absolutely," he says. Finally, he tugs out the map, but when I turn around to get a peek, he holds it at such an angle that I can't see. I can't grab it from him without releasing the oars and losing precious rowing time. "Our first stop is up ahead."

I don't trust him one bit, but there's not much I can do about it. When he orders us to stop ten minutes later, we leave our canoe to wander through the trees. I'm starting to doubt his map-reading skills as we work our way farther from the bank, fanning out to cover more ground, though I never let him leave my sight. Minutes tick by. With each lost, it grows harder not to vent my frustrations on him. I need to keep whatever fragile peace we have.

"There," he says, pointing to a dying maple. It's split down the middle, as if maybe it was struck by lightning. Tucked between the severed trunk are two bright orange bags.

"They're sleeping bags," I realize, passing him one.

He frowns. "Why? It's hot in the rooms."

Speak for yourself. He's not the one dealing with a broken window.

But since the tree outside my room has concealed it enough that no one but Hayes and I seem to know, I keep my mouth shut.

Slowly, we gain on the others. First, we pass Charlie and Alandra, who stand on the bank arguing over their map. Then, Dodge and Soph, whose canoe is pulled onto the grass, though they're nowhere to be seen. I wouldn't be surprised if they got distracted in the woods hooking up. Woolf and I make five more successful stops, the supplies we collect taking theme. Fire starter at one, a flashlight at the next. Some type of reflective tarp thing at the fourth. Stop five is a reusable metal water bottle with water purifying tablets. Stop six grants a bag of nonperishables, like ramen in a cup, granola bars, and cans of beans.

"I think we might be going camping for the next trial," I say as we slide back into our canoe, staring at the contents strewn over the bottom of it.

"I prefer glamping," Woolf replies. He's not as good at giving me the cold shoulder as Hayes is. Woolf can't resist cracking a quip, or pointing out a moment where I mess up, like at stop four where I slipped in a mud patch. (*"Walk much?"* he snorted.) It's things that used to wear me down after the breakup, but here, it's oddly comforting.

A strange sadness spreads through me. This is the most time we've spent together one-on-one since March. A piece of me misses his ever-ready stream of remarks and ability to turn even the worst situations humorous.

But then I remember he might have thrown a brick through my window, and I get angry with him all over again.

When we get to a marshy part of the stream, the sun pokes out from behind the clouds right above us. "It's noon," I say, glancing at my watch. "We must be getting close to the lake."

I don't know what aches more—my arms, legs, back, or butt. We've taken breaks, and each time we make a stop, it usually turns into at least thirty minutes of wandering before we find what we need. Stop five was nearly an hour itself. Even so, sitting in the canoe for long stretches is killer.

"It goes way deeper into the forest before coming back to empty into the lake." Woolf points at the map. I twist around to look. "See how the mouth is cut off? We'll just have to follow the stream at that point. It's taking so long because the stream isn't a straight shot. We entered it at one of the farthest points. That hour we walked to it this morning was putting us farther away from the lake."

"Because the Champions can't make anything easy." I sigh, recalling what Hayes and I overheard the other night when they talked about making the trials harder. "I think my arms are going to fall off if we have to do this much longer."

He snorts, but quickly covers it with a cough. We pass Keana and Malcolm, who are stuck in the marsh.

"Move your damn oar!" Keana yells at him.

"I'm trying! It's suctioned in the muck!" Malcolm cries. For a second, I think he's literally crying. But no, his face is just so red because it's burned. Badly. Even with the sun spending the majority of the day behind the clouds, his fair skin is no match.

"Then get out and pull it free," Keana grinds out.

"I can't swim!" Malcolm shoots back.

"You can literally *stand*!"

"Good luck with that!" Woolf taunts as we glide past.

Keana throws us a glare.

We pass another empty canoe, which must belong to Hayes and Mina, since they're the only pair we haven't seen. They've held on to first, but I'm ready to keep my streak going.

At the last stop, I pick up our pace, and Woolf and I literally run through the woods. We find two whistles dangling from a branch, black cord attached to silver metal. I hang mine around my neck.

"We're going to get first," I tell Woolf, unable to keep the excitement from my tone as we hurry back to the embankment and hop into our shell.

When we round the bend, we're greeted with the fork Aura warned us about. "Stay left," I remind Woolf, shifting my technique to maneuver us that way. The current's faster here, a sure sign we're close to the lake.

"No, thanks," Woolf says from behind me. Before I can react, he smacks my left hand with his oar so hard I drop mine. It sinks, disappearing into the deeper water.

"What the hell?" I shriek, pulling my stinging hand close to my chest. "You could have broken my fingers!"

"Looks fine to me," he cackles. I want to turn around, but I still have my right oar to man. Without my left one, though, we're immediately shifting course, aiming down the wrong path.

"We need to stay left," I say, furious that my voice wavers. This morning, he warned me about making him let his guard down. I didn't realize he was doing the same to me.

"Too late!" he exclaims. I watch helplessly as we soar past the fork, entering the shaded way of the right path. It's significantly more narrow, to the point where if I stretch my arms out on either side, my fingertips brush the low branches off the embankment.

I scramble around in the canoe to face Woolf, nearly capsizing it in the process. "We were winning," I snarl, the diplomatic mask sliding off. "What the fuck is your problem?"

"There she is!" he laughs, mirth in his eyes. "You know, I've been watching you and all the acts you pull. Concerned Chloe on the bus, talking to poor, weeny little Mina. Loner Chloe at meal times and fires, barely talking to anyone at all. Competitive Chloe during the trials, where your sole focus is to win. But I've been waiting for Vicious Chloe to make an appearance. I knew I could knock her loose."

"What do you want?" I ask, fear pressing on my chest. Today went smoothly—too smoothly. And here I thought, so close to being done, that we could win together.

"I told you what I wanted," he says. "It's on you for not listening."

Hayes. This is always going to be about Hayes.

"I don't know what you're talking about," I say, not wanting to admit to more than I need to.

He scoffs. "Hayes has been sneaking out at night, and so have you. One night, I saw you both by the fire. Then the last two, I've waited. First his footsteps, then yours. But where have you gone? It's like you've disappeared."

"If Hayes wanted you to know, he'd tell you," I say, keeping a tight grip on my lone oar in case I need to use it against him. The night Hayes showed me Hunter's journal, I heard something in the trees. Jarod joked it was a hungry animal, and he was partially right. Woolf was ravenous to catch me disregarding his conditions so he could act on his threat.

"Actually, you're going to tell me," Woolf states surely. I start to protest but am struck by a swell of water courtesy of him whipping his oars out. He stabs them into the muddy embankment on either side of us, bringing the shell to a jerking halt. "Because if you don't, I'm going to make you lose."

17

"If I lose, you lose," I remind Woolf, trying to find ground to stand on. In fact, this would be a whole lot easier if I actually did have ground to stand on. Canoes or shells or whatever are the least ideal place to be when faced with a threat.

"I'm happy to get eliminated if it means taking you down with me. I consider it my civic duty."

"Why are you here?" I snap. "If you don't even care to win, what are you playing for?"

"Must everyone have a heroic reason?" He raises a thick dark brow. "Fuck finals."

"There's no way the school chose you based on you wanting to skip out on finals," I scoff. "What did you write about in your application essay?"

His smile slips off. "I wrote about something you would never understand. About being willing to do anything to protect someone who's been there for you since day one, even if they're not your blood. If it wasn't for Hayes, I would have grown up with nobody, and honestly? I'd probably be in juvie by now. And Hunter was like my own big brother. After he died, I made a promise to myself to always stick by Hayes's side. In my essay, I straight up said I don't care about winning. But I do care about Hayes."

"Hayes can take care of himself. He doesn't need a babysitter."

"Most of the time, I'd agree. But when it comes to you, all bets are off. Once he decided he was applying for the trials, I couldn't change his mind for shit. I knew you'd get chosen, and I couldn't risk him being alone with you. So I convinced Phlip to apply with me, figuring he'd have a better shot than I would. But somehow, I got chosen. Good thing because Phlip is way too oblivious and would have never picked up on you and Hayes sneaking around."

I don't bother denying it at this point. "What are you so afraid will happen? If you haven't noticed, Hayes doesn't care!"

Care escapes like a strangled scream. I don't like that I'm losing control. That I'm revealing that *I* care.

Woolf stares at me. "You really think so?"

"I know so!" I burst, horrified at the press of tears behind my eyes. "We had that fight in the dining hall and broke up, and he didn't care. He didn't want to talk after, or even look at me. He made you and Phlip ice me out. He cut me out of his life like I was never there at all." I suck in a ragged breath. "You both used to stand up for me against Dodge, and now you treat me even worse."

"I'm not like Dodge," Woolf growls, bristling at the mention of his nemesis.

"Then stop acting like him."

"How about you?" he asks. "You remained perfect, polished Chloe. Not even your grades dipped."

It takes everything in me not to react to that, because of course they did. But it's an odd thing for the person I suspect as my blackmailer to point out.

"Then I guess we both came out of it fine," I lie. "So why do you have to keep torturing me over it?"

"Because Hayes isn't fine!" Woolf explodes. A raven screeches from the branch above, taking off at the loudness.

"What do you mean?"

I watch the debate happen on Woolf's face. Another difference between him and Hayes—Woolf can't play poker. Hayes could rob his opponents clean.

"He isn't fine," Woolf repeats, quieter. He won't look at me now, instead focusing on the burbling water. "When Hunter died, Hayes changed. He was always chill and quiet, while Hunter was the loud one who challenged their parents. But he was always *Hayes*. And then Hunter died, and he wasn't. He didn't laugh anymore, or smile. He didn't care about anything. He did his work, but only because his parents kept threatening to bring him home if he fell too much behind. And he hated being home with Hunter not there. He still does."

Hayes told me as much. Our video chats last summer made my heart bleed. "*I miss you*," he'd say. "*When can I visit? I hate it here. The house is so empty with just me.*"

"He was like that for all of sophomore year," Woolf says. "Just . . . blank. Doing the things he needed to do to get by without anyone getting too suspicious that he wasn't okay. But I could tell. When you know someone since before you can even walk, you know who they really are."

"I know," I say quietly, thinking of my sister. Since getting sick, some days she's herself, but most days she's not. I can see through the cracks.

"And then junior year starts, and you're there," he continues as if I hadn't spoken. "At first, you're just the girl he has to tutor. Then the girl we have to do a group project with. But suddenly, he starts becoming Hayes again. Laughing, joking, being sarcastic. Playing piano. Things I thought were dead and buried with Hunter. You brought them back. You brought *him* back."

"I . . ." I don't know what to say. In the whispered moments of the dark, Hayes had hinted that same truth to me. *"I finally feel like myself again."* When he slid my clover ring on my finger on Christmas Eve, he said, *"You make me feel lucky, Clover. I haven't felt this way in a long time."* I felt too small and insignificant at the time to believe him, but I should have.

"And then you snuffed him back out," Woolf says, disgust morphing his face. "He wasn't fucking *fine.* He stopped caring about everything. He was barely eating, he skipped class, he tried to bribe a sophomore to buy him alcohol from the store in town. I even had to do his homework for him for a week. I don't even do my own homework!"

He breathes heavily, knuckles white around the oars. "You wrecked him, Chloe. And *I* had to pick up the pieces. But even worse than the breakup was the fact that you didn't listen to him. You knew applying for the trials would hurt him, and you did it anyway. And now, for some reason I can't figure out for the life of me, he's gotten dragged into it, too. So whatever you're playing at here—"

"I was wrong," I say. It's the only three words in the world that could get Woolf to shut up, and it works. "I shouldn't have snapped at Hayes in the dining hall that day." *And you shouldn't have supplied him with a pork tenderloin to lob at me.* I leave that part out.

I could sit here and argue with Woolf until we're both blue in the face. We both lose, we both get eliminated. Hayes is here alone. Maybe he finds what he's looking for, maybe he wins.

Or, maybe, if I'm out of the way, my Challenger will choose a new target. If Woolf truly isn't behind the blackmail, then eliminating him does no favors. Not to me, and certainly not to Hayes, who could get targeted next.

I'm not supposed to care what happens to Hayes. But I do. And right now, I'm facing the only other person who cares about him just as much, if not more. He also happens to be the same person standing between me and winning.

I meet Woolf's dark eyes with my own, praying there's a scrap of my old friend somewhere in there. "Here's the truth."

I tell him everything. Well, almost everything. I leave out my blackmail note, and the kiss. Because it's not like the kiss was real, anyway. Even if every time I think of Hayes's lips on mine, a flush falls over me like a fever.

"Let me get this straight," Woolf says as I finish spilling to him what Hayes and I have been up to the past few nights. "There's a secret tunnel system and I have yet to see it?"

I fold my arms across my chest. "Out of everything I just told you, *that's* what you picked up?"

"It's fucking awesome!"

"It's actually pretty gross, so don't get your hopes up."

"Still, I—"

A horn blows. The first pair of Challengers made it to the end. Woolf's eyes widen at my murderous face.

"Are you kidding me?" I snap. "You just made us lose. Our deal was I would tell you and you wouldn't sabotage us. I held up my half."

He rips his oars free from where they were lodged into the embankment. "That's just one team," he reasons. "We could get second. We found all the things on the map. Second is safe."

We're gliding at a good clip now, but it still doesn't feel fast enough. "Second sucks," I counter. "We don't even know where this path leads. It could take us longer."

"It won't," Woolf says. "I studied maps back at school that show the entire forest. More than just the Wilde land that this shows. This way is actually a shortcut."

"Why would Aura warn us from taking a shortcut?"

His reckless grin doesn't put me at ease one bit. Paired with the sudden sound of rushing water, I know it's not going to be good.

"Probably because of that." He points behind me.

I turn around and feel the exact moment my soul leaves my body.

The stream *falls*. Not like a waterfall, but something worse. Rocky and frothing with foam. Like the mouth of a hungry beast and we're a juicy steak heading inside.

"Those are—"

"Rapids," he announces. "Hold on!"

"There's nothing to hold on to!" I yell. But it's too late. We're catapulted over the first swell, our tiny shell fragile as an egg. When it hits back down, it's with a worrisome *crack* that I feel in my bones.

I don't know what's worse: my current position with my back to the rapids where I can only see Woolf's gleeful face as he tries to maneuver us with his oars, or if I were to turn around for full view.

I'm soaked in seconds, and the bottom of the shell is filling with water. My stomach somersaults, my grip so tight on the sides that my hands cramp. While not the same as my fear of heights, it's certainly triggering it. The same weightless feeling, the possibility of getting tossed out, of shattering my body on the rocks—

I squeeze my eyes shut. Partly to keep out the spray of water, but mostly because the tilting of the shell is more than enough to feel without seeing the dips and turns. Woolf's laugh rings out, like he's having the time of his life. I'm pretty sure I'm about to die.

One final plunge has water pouring in on all sides, the iciness of it making my eyes spring open. "Having fun?" Woolf howls.

"I hate you," I rasp, voice gone from screaming.

It takes several moments to realize we're past the rapids, gliding into the middle of the lake. The sun blazes across our wet skin as the roar of the rapids fades the further we get from the outlet.

"That wasn't so bad," Woolf says, rowing a steady rhythm. I smack his arm, realizing my single remaining oar fell out during our adventure.

"That sucked." My stomach rocks dangerously. I sort through the soaked belongings in the bottom of the boat, making sure we didn't lose anything. We didn't, but there's a bigger problem. "We're taking on water."

"How much?"

"It's already up to our ankles!" I exclaim. "We're *sinking*."

"Guess I better row faster."

"Hurry!"

I turn around, finding Aura and Jarod on the beach and waving frantically at them. "We're sinking!" I yell.

"Good job!" Jarod waves back, clearly not hearing me. Or maybe he did, and this is my payback for blackmailing him the other night.

"At least we're getting back before them."

I follow Woolf's nod to where the other, correct outlet is. Dodge and Soph flow out of it. When they see us, their faces transform from triumph to fury. I smile back, waving cheerily despite the dire state of our boat.

"Are they pissed?" Woolf asks, rowing steadily.

"Steaming," I confirm.

"Excellent."

Before we sink, we nudge onto the shore. Aura and Jarod scratch their heads at our banged-up boat but don't say much else. We gather our supplies in our arms and begin the long trek back to the estate just as Soph and Dodge beach their own shell.

I'm still mad at Woolf for the rapids stunt so I walk ahead of him in silence. Given the fact that each step is accompanied by a squelching sound as water squishes out of my sneakers, I don't have much dignity going for me.

"Wait," Woolf says when we reach the estate.

I stride through the gates, pausing to glance back at him lingering at the entrance. "What?"

"You know that truce you told me you and Hayes agreed on? The one that lasts only through the end of the trials?" Woolf meets my gaze with daring eyes. "I want in."

18

Hours later, I drag myself up to my room after the bonfire. Alandra and Charlie got eliminated. While I wasn't worried in the least about Charlie and kind of forgot he was here, Alandra was on the suspect list. I didn't get sabotaged today, which could mean three things:

1. The antagonist is Woolf, and he couldn't act without giving himself away.

2. The antagonist couldn't act because of the nature of the challenge. Either they were paired with someone who might have told me the truth, or they couldn't figure out a way to sabotage me without bringing Woolf down with me. And the only person who cares if Woolf stays is Hayes, so that would mean Hayes is my Challenger.

3. The antagonist was Lainey or Alandra and is no longer my problem.

I want option three to be right, but I'm doubtful. When Hayes and I meet tonight, maybe he'll say something that will reveal himself if it is him. Right now, wading through my tired brain feels like walking through Jell-O.

Without turning on the light, I strip off my clothes, the cool air from my window ghosting across my skin as I tug on shorts and a T-shirt. I slide under the covers, settling in.

I'm nearly asleep when I feel it. The worst possible sensation when lying in the dark: Something crawling on my leg.

There's a point of being tired where you don't care, and I'm nearly to that point. Nearly.

And then it bites me.

"Ouch!" I yelp. I kick and detangle myself from the sheets, crashing to the floor. Fumbling for the lamp switch, I finally flick it on. My bleary eyes dissect my rumpled sheets, but nothing is there. The growing red welt on my calf proves otherwise.

"Shit." Panic grips me as I analyze the wound in the dim light. There are *bite marks*. Two tiny punctures in the center of the bump, which stings when I touch it. My breaths turn shallow as I glance at my open window. Anything could have crawled in. If whatever bit me is poisonous—

A knock against my door makes me jump. With my light on, it's useless pretending I'm asleep. But my broken window is on full display, and I have yet to dispose of the glass under the bed. If it's a Champion and they start asking questions—

The knock comes again. "Hey, it's . . . me."

Hayes. He says it as if he can't believe himself that he's on the other side. Life is so weird. Once, we used to walk into each other's rooms with barely a hello like it was our own dorm. Now, we knock stiffly and announce ourselves.

I open the door, but only a crack. "Hi."

He tries to see over my head into my room, but I stand my full height so he can't. "Did you scream?"

"No," I say quickly. "Must have been someone else."

"Everyone else is still at the fire," Hayes points out.

"Why aren't you?"

"I guess I'm a little sleepy." His tone is dry as bones.

"You should get some rest, then." I start closing the door, but his hand shoots through the crack, stopping me. "I'm not afraid to crush your precious piano fingers, you know."

"I don't doubt it," he says, nudging his way in. I finally relent, tugging my shorts down from where they rode up and closing the door behind him. "Why did you—"

He stops, taking in the scene. My afghan and sheets in a tangle, half on my bed, half on the floor. His eyes pass over me in a quick assessment and hone in on my swelling left leg. "What happened?"

"I don't . . ." I trail off, zeroing in on something past him. It crawls out from beneath my twisted bedding and starts scaling the wall. All the saliva in my mouth turns to dust as I point at it. *"That."*

He follows my gaze and startles at the sight of the spider. "That was in your *bed*?"

"Yep," I realize quietly. My brain sifts through everything I know about spider bites. The two most deadly kinds are black widows and brown recluses.

This spider looks a hell of a lot like the latter.

"Okay," Hayes says, an air of forced calm overtaking him. "This is fine."

"It's not fine," I counter. Hysteria bubbles up my throat. "It *bit me*. I think it's a brown recluse."

His eyes widen imperceptibly. "In New Hampshire? Don't they prefer warmer climates?"

"I don't know!" I begin to hyperventilate. "But if it is, I need to go to a hospital. Their bites become ulcers, which lead to necrosis, which means my skin will literally start *decaying*—" I gag.

Hayes warily inches closer to the spider to inspect it, and it scoots farther up on the wall, away from him. "I saw a brown recluse when my family vacationed in South America. This isn't it."

"Since when did you become a spider expert? You hate bugs. And why did you follow me up here, anyway?"

He bites his lip, still staring at the spider. "I wanted to know how things went with you and Woolf today."

"He didn't tell you?"

Hayes shakes his head. "We both slept most of the afternoon after showering. Then there was dinner and the fire. No time to debrief."

I fold my arms across my chest, just realizing now how half-dressed I am. "I told him."

"Told him what?"

"Everything," I say. Then I think about how, like with Hayes, I left out the specifics of my blackmail. And also the kiss. "Almost everything."

"Why would you do that?" he asks between clenched teeth, poker face slipping.

"He was going to make us both get eliminated." I still feel like it's a mistake, but there's no going back now. "I had no choice."

Hayes blows out a frustrated breath. "I was worried you two

were going to kill each other. Not—this!"

I throw my hands into the air. "Well, lucky for you it might not matter now if I'm about to die from a poisonous spider bite."

He rolls his eyes. "It's not a poisonous spider. I'm pretty sure it's a—"

A knock comes from the other side of the door, stealing our attention.

"Answer it," Hayes hisses, nodding to the door.

"If you're found in my room, that's strike three," I counter.

"Where am I supposed to go? I'm not hiding under your bed," he states firmly.

"There's a pile of glass there anyway."

His brows raise. "Seriously?"

Another knock sounds.

"*Hide*," I command, striding toward the door. Before I open it, I glance over my shoulder, blinking at the sudden emptiness of the room. He disappeared.

I swing my door open to reveal the conversation culprit. Woolf leans against the doorway, the amused smirk on his mouth a sure sign he's been eavesdropping. "Hey, Nancy Drews," he says, grossly optimistic. "Are we solving a mystery tonight?"

Hayes's head pokes through the window. "Will you shut up before someone hears you?"

I tug Woolf into the room and lock the door behind him before turning to Hayes. "Get back in here before you fall off the roof," I scold.

"The porch roof is a story below. I'm on a ledge," Hayes corrects.

"That's not better."

He swings a leg through the window, stepping back in and coming face-to-face with Woolf since three's a crowd in the tiny room. Woolf glares at him.

"Hey," Hayes greets casually.

"Hey?" Woolf echoes back. "Is that all you have to say to me? You've been sneaking around with your ex-girlfriend—worst idea ever, by the way—trying to find some missing message from your brother, and you couldn't tell me? Your best friend?"

Hayes lets out a breath. "I'm sorry, okay? I can explain."

Woolf stabs a finger into Hayes's chest. "Explaining would have maybe—*maybe*—covered speaking to her again."

"I have a name, you know," I state indignantly.

Woolf ignores me. "But, dude, to find a secret tunnel system and not tell me? That's too fucking far, bro."

Hayes throws his head back with a groan. "I know I should have said something. But in my defense, she wasn't supposed to get involved, either."

"My name is Chloe," I interject. It's useless. I might as well not even be here.

Woolf shakes his head. "You find a whole-ass secret tunnel system *and* fraternize with the enemy without saying a word. I don't even know you anymore."

Hayes rolls his eyes. "It was one kiss."

Woolf's jaw drops. He looks from Hayes, to me, back to Hayes. "You *kissed her*?"

Hayes spins on me. "You said you told him everything!"

"I said *almost* everything!"

"You should have been more specific!"

"This is so bad," Woolf groans. "She's playing you, man. She just wants to win!"

"Hey!" I stomp my foot. "I'm not playing anybody. What happened to the truce?"

Hayes looks like he might toss me out the window. "You told him about the truce?"

"She didn't just tell me," Woolf brags. "I'm part of it now. Whatever you guys are up to, so am I."

"No," Hayes says sharply. "That's not . . ." He trails off, gaze zeroing in on my dresser behind Woolf.

"That's not what?" Woolf asks. "Because whatever you were going to say, I don't care. I'm in this."

Hayes pushes us aside to inspect the top of the dresser.

"This was Hunter's room," I say. Suddenly, our argument feels years away, a stillness settling as Hayes traces his brother's carved initials.

"Was there anything in the drawers?" Hayes asks.

I shake my head. "Nothing."

He nods, only ripping his eyes away from the letters when Woolf plops down on my bed, springs squealing in protest. "Gatti says you went to the library last night."

"We did," Hayes confirms. "And don't sit there unless you want that spider to come bite you, too."

"Spider?" Woolf asks, gaze trailing to where the questionable creature sits high on the wall. He hops up, but instead of keeping a wide berth like Hayes and I did, he pinches it between two fingers and gently places it in his cupped hand, stepping off the bed and bringing it closer to us. "This little guy?"

"That *little guy* bit me," I defend, stepping back so my spine presses into the dresser.

He strokes a finger down the arachnid's back. "It's just a wolf spider. They're harmless."

"Wolf spiders aren't poisonous," I state, more as a reassurance to myself than anyone else. Woolf takes it to the window and releases it outside.

"Told you you're not about to lose a leg," Hayes says. "The bite will probably just itch. When you got back from the bonfire, was your door locked?"

I frown, trying to remember. "Yes."

"So they came in through the window, then."

"Who?" I ask.

Hayes raises a brow. "You really think that spider crawled under your covers on its own? Someone obviously put it there. The bigger question is if *they* knew it wasn't poisonous."

I hadn't thought of that, but I should have. "Great," I say. "If that's the case, they can get to me whenever they want. I'm never safe."

"Whoever's messing with you is getting desperate."

"Wow, that really sucks for them. It must be so hard when the person you're trying to ruin is making it difficult. How rude of me."

"Why would they wait until after the trial?" Woolf asks. "It's riskier for them. They could have taken us both out today."

"Unless it's you," I accuse, pieces sliding together as I glare at him. "Because who else would put a *wolf* spider in my bed?

You probably saw it the first day when you mentioned something about spiders. The same day you threatened me to stay away from Hayes."

Hayes glares at Woolf. "You *what*?"

Woolf raises his hands in defense. "I might have done some light intimidation. But only with your best interests in mind!"

Hayes pinches the bridge of his nose. "We've talked about this."

"Have you?" I fume. "Is this a usual conversation between you two? *Woolf, you can torment Chloe, but not too much.*"

"Look, I didn't put the spider in your bed," Woolf defends. "It would have had to happen between dinner and the bonfire, and I was downstairs the entire time."

He's right. I showered when we returned from the lake and slept until dinner. If the spider had been in my bed before, it probably would have bit me then.

"Soph wasn't," Hayes points out. "I saw her come back upstairs."

"So did Keana," I admit.

"Charlie and Alandra came up to get their things after getting eliminated," Woolf adds.

"Fine, it could be anyone," I snap. "We're no closer to revealing the identity of my Challenger today than we were yesterday."

"But with each trial, the pool of suspects gets smaller," Hayes says. "And our time to find whatever Hunter left gets shorter."

"Gatti said that Hunter ripped out the pages and hid them because something was off. But if that was true, wouldn't he have told someone?" Woolf asks. He turns to me. "Why won't you tell the Champions you're being messed with?"

Hayes looks at me sharply. It's a question he hasn't asked yet, but he should have. "Why haven't you?"

"I'm not a snitch," I lie.

Woolf guffaws. We scold him to be quiet.

"Sorry," Woolf whispers. "It's just, if anyone here would take any chance to rat someone out, it'd be you. In fact, if this was happening to anyone else, I'd assume *you* were behind it."

"Hey," I whine. "I don't need to sabotage anyone to win."

He snorts, eyes flicking to Hayes. "Jury's still out on that one."

Hayes gives him a very mean, middle-finger gesture and turns to me. "Why haven't you told Trevor?"

I can't tell them about the blackmail when I still can't fully trust either of them. "My Challenger said it would only get worse if I did," I partially tell the truth. "I don't want to risk it until I know who it is."

They both nod, buying it.

"As the pool of Challengers gets smaller, it will be harder for them to keep messing with you without it becoming obvious. For now, we need to go back to the library." Hayes turns to Woolf. "We've been meeting after everyone comes in from the fire, usually around one or two."

"Probably two. Tomorrow's a rest day, so the Champions will likely hang out later," I say, mentioning the pattern I've noticed.

"Why wait?" Woolf asks. "Let's go now."

"We can't go now," I say. "It's too early. What if the Champions do a room check?"

"They're getting plastered out there," Woolf says. "Let's take advantage of it."

Hayes and I share a look, then promptly rip our gazes away when we realize it. "More time could be useful," is all he says, leaving it up to me. Woolf raises a brow in challenge.

I glance at my mangled bed, the pain in my leg subsiding to an annoying itch. Sleep is off the table anyway. "Fine," I relent. "Let's go break some rules."

19

"This place is awesome," Woolf says, awe dripping from his tone as he takes in the library. We came through Diana's suite, since the Champions are still by the fire. The door was still unlocked, making it difficult to tell if anyone else had been there since we last were.

"It's . . . something," Hayes comments, nose scrunched in distaste. "Don't be too loud. The fire is far, but most of the windows are broken, so let's not risk it."

"I can't believe Diana was locked in here for months," Woolf gawks. "Where did she even sleep?"

"Maybe they brought a bed in," I suggest. I glance at my watch. "Let's get going."

"You already checked the first two floors?" Woolf asks.

"Just floor three is left," I confirm.

Woolf takes the spiral staircase two steps at a time, and Hayes follows. I make the same treacherous climb that I did last night, clinging to the railing. The blue moonflowers are just starting to open up. Counting their vibrant blooms as I ascend is a good distraction.

"Hunter said he wished he had A Good Book," Hayes tells

Woolf. "So that's what we're looking for."

Woolf waltzes past the row of shelves. "Literally or figuratively?"

"Both," Hayes and I reply at the same time. I say, "I'll take the four shelves closest to the back, Hayes will do the middle four, and you'll do the ends. Good?"

They nod, splitting off down their respective aisles. I repeat the same actions I did last night, except now, it's ten times more painful. My arms scream after spending the day rowing. By the time I finish one aisle, I need to take a break.

"Anything?" Hayes calls quietly after fifteen minutes.

"No," Woolf and I both reply.

It only takes an hour for us to finish. We rub our sore shoulders, meeting in the center.

"What's plan B?" Woolf asks.

"That was plan B." Hayes paces away from us before spinning back around. "It should have been here. *Something* should have been here."

"Maybe you both missed something on the shelves below," Woolf suggests. "Probably Gatti's fault. Want me to look?"

"I didn't miss anything," I grouch, but it's half-hearted. Hayes doesn't look at either of us, frustration steaming off him. He takes his brother's journal out from where he tucked it in his pocket, rereading the last page.

"There's nothing else," he says, defeated. "He didn't write any other hints."

"Can I see?"

He passes the journal to me, stalking away and running his

fingers through his already-messy strands. It's so un-Hayes it might as well be a crisis smoke signal.

"What if we need to read more into the music part?" I ask, flipping backward through the pages. "There had to be a music room somewhere."

"There was a music room," Hayes says flatly. "At the church."

I deflate, continuing to scan Hunter's pages. It's mostly the musings of a teenage boy. Him being hungry, him being clever, him hinting he had feelings for a girl that was in the trials with him. *We have to sneak around because we'll get in trouble if we're caught together*, he said. How star-crossed-lovers of them.

"What's that?" Woolf asks, reading over my shoulder. He points at a random doodle in the margins.

"The journal is full of them," I say, flipping through the pages to show him.

"Yeah, but that one is the same on every page," he mentions, circling a blue dot with his finger.

I bring the journal closer to the window so the moonlight can better illuminate the page. It's not just blue dots. It's flowers.

"Moonflowers," I realize, flipping through to watch the vine weave through the entire journal. Hayes and Woolf crowd around me to see. "Sometimes at the bottom, sometimes at the top, and sometimes right through the middle. But always there. Right up until the last page, although it looks like maybe it would have kept going onto more."

"And always blue," Hayes says.

"Why does the color matter?" Woolf asks.

"Because it's a hint." I hurry to the railing. My vision swims as I peer down, but I force myself to focus. "There's only one vine of blue moonflowers among all these white ones. Look!" I point to where it sneaks in from outside. It doesn't come from one of the broken windows but instead from an open one. "Don't you see? This vine has always been here. It's the blue moon that Diana talked about looking at when she would miss her family. Remember? There's a rhyme."

"It's a lullaby," Hayes corrects, looking at the ceiling as if it has the notes painted on it. "It goes, 'When I miss them, I stare at winter's blue moon, and remember those who leave us, come back with spring bloom.'"

Woolf raises his brows. "Bloom as in flowers?"

"*Moon* as in flowers." I follow the path of the blue moonflower vine with my finger. Through the open window, across a bookshelf, up all three floors of the spiral staircase, and onto the cracked ceiling over us. "Everyone thought Diana kept the window open as a way to let the spirits of her family come and go as they pleased. But really, it was to let the flower in. Because she thought they lived in the blue flowers."

Woolf makes a face. "We're getting kind of out there, don't you think?"

"Diana was kind of out there," Hayes reminds him. "Hunter knew the song. When I applied for the academy, he told me to learn it to impress Principal Watershed."

"And did it?"

Hayes shakes his head with a half-laugh. "Of course not. He was messing with me."

"If Hunter remembered you knew the legend about the blue

moon, then it's not that wild he would have left a clue on it . . ." I flip through the journal. "On every page."

"We need to follow the vines," Hayes says. The blue vine splits off in three different directions, scattering across the ceiling and down the walls. I follow one vine, and Hayes and Woolf split off to trace the meandering paths of the other two.

"I don't get it," Woolf says from a few shelves over. "How could Hunter have known that the vine would still be here? It's been years."

I pause at my vine. It goes all the way to the end of the wall, but in the middle is a portrait. It's huge, stretching from the ceiling to the floor. It's an acrylic painting of a bookshelf.

And on the shelf is a blue book with the spine reading, *A Good Book.*

"I found it!" I call, forgetting to keep my voice quiet. They rush over, eyes widening at the book in the painting. I point to the vine, which goes beyond it. "Look at where the vine is now. I don't know how fast they grow, but three years ago, it probably ended here. I bet it led right to this painting. And Hunter would have had no reason to think it would have taken Hayes three years to come searching, because he probably thought the journal would get to him immediately. But it didn't because . . ."

I trail off, not sure of the answer.

"Because someone else had it," Hayes says. "And only just sent it to me right before the application period opened for the trials."

"Whoever it was must have been here with Hunter," I reason. "Maybe they even know something happened to him but need *you* to discover it."

"Who would keep the journal for years and only just send it to you now?" Woolf asks.

Hayes and I lock eyes, jumping to the same conclusion. "Trevor."

"It makes sense," I follow up. "He was in the trials Hunter's year. He's stayed close with you ever since, and Hunter was his best friend. If he knew something happened to Hunter that could look bad on the trials and the school, he wouldn't be able to outright say it without jeopardizing the school's reputation, and maybe his own."

Hayes nods. "Trevor sent this to me trusting that I would come here and finish what he couldn't. And I think . . . I think he's been looking out for me to make sure I wouldn't get eliminated. I was paired with Mina today, and she was amazing at finding all the map stops. And for trial two, I felt like there were some questions specifically meant for me, like the ones about the piano and music. Stuff that anyone who knew my brother would have known about me."

"In the beginning, I was afraid Trevor would favor you," I admit.

Hayes meets my eyes. "If he helps me stay in, then that gives me more time to help you win."

I nod. "Then I guess I have a truce to uphold."

A smile flickers across Hayes's face; there and gone. Woolf scratches his stubble. "So we found 'A Good Book,' but what does it mean?"

Hayes pushes on the book, but all it does is indent the canvas. "It has to be hiding something."

I inspect the frame, which is oddly close to the wall. So close that there isn't a centimeter of space between the back and the plaster, both blending into one. When I pull on it, it doesn't move.

But when I push, despite the resistance, I feel it budge. "Help me," I say, pushing harder. Slowly, with their help, it folds inward.

Another trick door. But this one doesn't lead to a tunnel.

It reveals a hidden room.

"I guess this answers your question about where Diana slept," I say to Woolf, taking in the single bed shoved into the corner of the room. The space is tiny, with just a rickety dresser, an easel, and a small desk in addition to the bed. It looks suspended in time. Unlike the library, it hasn't been touched by the elements, the only window a grime-covered rectangle out of reach. The room itself is a small square, each wall displaying a selection of pictures, some painted, but most black and white photographs.

"Do you think students knew about this?" Woolf asks. "Because imagine the hookup potential. If only our library at school had a good secret spot."

Hayes and I lock eyes, because, of course, we have firsthand knowledge that there is a good secret spot.

He rips his gaze away first but not before his flashlight reveals a hint of pink across his cheeks.

"This was her family, huh?" Woolf continues, peering at a picture on the wall with Diana and her siblings. "They all died, and that led to the tradition of the Wilde Trials because . . . ?"

"Diana wanted students to remember to always be grateful. That the school and estate and knowledge were gifts that could be taken away. Things that not everyone got to live long enough to experience. It is, admittedly, a little messed up."

"I think being locked in a library might make you a little messed up," Hayes points out. He crosses the room quickly. "Hey, look at this."

Clipped on the easel are a bunch of sketches. The paper is yellowed and curling at the edges. Hayes unclips the top one carefully. "Hunter did this."

"He did?" I ask.

Hayes nods, breezing through the others to see for himself.

"The style is different," Hayes points out. "The others look older, all depicting similar nature settings with trees and streams and lakes. The one Hunter did is the only one centered around birds."

"I don't get it," Woolf says. "Why birds?"

"And why are they on wires?" I ask. It's a mix of ravens and doves spanning five evenly spaced wires. It's pretty in a simple way, similar to the drawings of Hunter's that I've seen in Hayes's room. Where Diana's portraits lean toward realism, Hunter's has an animated quality.

"No clue," Hayes says. He flips the painting over to reveal writing, sucking in a shocked breath. "Another message."

"What's it say?" Woolf and I ask.

Birds have the most beautiful tunes. It's the only thing that makes being here somewhat bearable. I could listen to them sing all day. There's only one person I know with better songs. I hope I live to hear another.

And, by the way, if you've found this, you're nearly there. What you're missing is where I was.

HS

"Another clue." I meet Hayes's eyes. "You must be the person with better songs."

He shrugs. "Could have been whatever artist he was into at the time."

"Doubt it," I say. "What about the last part? What's that mean?"

"Where I was? Like, in this room?" Woolf suggests.

We search the rest of it. It's full of things: old paints, brushes, a fountain pen, even a couple ancient cameras. After a while of quiet shuffling, we determine everything else belonged to Diana.

As we close the hidden door behind us, an ache shoots through me. All those paintings and pictures should be preserved. Everything in this entire library should be. Instead, it's going to rot here.

"Trevor is putting out the fire," Woolf says, peering through the windows. "What should we do?"

"I don't think anything else is here," I say. "Maybe we go back to our rooms and think through the new clue? Reconvene tomorrow?"

Hayes nods, glancing down. "How's your leg?"

Tonight has been so long, I already forgot about the spider fiasco. "I'll live."

We sneak through the tunnels, going back to the entrance in Diana's suite. It's a risky move, but the Champions are still meandering downstairs, giving us enough time to sneak down their hall and up to ours.

"Do you hear that?" Hayes asks, perking to attention. We pause, listening.

"They're going up to our floor," I realize when the footsteps continue up the stairs past floor two.

We dash to our rooms, and I turn off my light just in time for footsteps to sound right outside my door. Sitting on my bed at this point would be too loud thanks to the springs, so instead I sit on my floor beside my backpack stuffed with my newly acquired sleeping bag rolled up with everything I got from today's trial. Leaning against it, I listen to two pairs of feet pacing our hallway. Not a room check, exactly, but still a check to make sure all our doors are closed and the lights are out. If we hadn't come back, mine would have surely caught their attention.

"Everyone's asleep," Carly says, stopping right outside my door. "Whatever you saw through the window was probably just the light flickering."

"Probably," Aura echoes. We tried to sneak past windows as best we could, but if she was looking, she might have caught a glimpse.

"Are you okay?" Carly asks, sounding more caring than I thought was possible. "You seem stressed. Do you want to do Pilates with me on the grass in the morning?"

"I'm nervous for the next trials," Aura says, ignoring the Pilates offer. "I'm so afraid of something bad happening."

She was a new Champion when Hunter was in the trials, and I'm sure that ordeal was nothing short of traumatic. The

Champions all got questioned by police and the school, and her ex-boyfriend Ravi was also in the trials as a Challenger. I heard she had broken up with him right before they started, likely because Champions and Challengers can't date, for obvious reasons.

"It won't," Carly assures. "That was an accident that will never happen again. Anyway, Jarod's pretty drunk, so I better go make sure he makes it to his room."

Carly's steps retreat until they fade down the stairs, but Aura doesn't follow. Long seconds pass, as if she's waiting for Carly to be truly gone. I start to drift off.

Until Aura's cryptic whisper hits my ears like a warning bell, jolting me awake.

"It was no accident."

20

I'm rooted to the floor.

Aura's footsteps finally disappear down the hall, but that doesn't stop my swirling thoughts. Hayes is right that Hunter's death wasn't an accident. But if Aura knows, that begs the questions: Why would she stay quiet about it? And, most important, if it wasn't an accident, does that mean he was murdered?

A sound outside my window makes me scramble to my feet. I brace myself, wondering if I have time to dig the glass shard from my bottom drawer.

I'm about to try when a blond head pops in, face shrouded in shadows but silhouette unmistakable.

"Hey," Hayes whispers, holding out a hand in a way that makes him look like Peter Pan. "Come with me."

I stare at the hand. "Where?"

"The ledge."

I take a step back. "I don't do ledges."

He raises a brow. "You do when you have no other options. You can't sleep here tonight. It's way too cold and unsafe with your window. Your Challenger can get you too easily."

"You'd like that," I whisper back, more for his reaction than anything else.

Even in the dark, I can feel his glare. "I'm not going to beg."

"It's a *ledge*. You shouldn't be out there, either."

"There's plenty of space," Hayes assures. "You can't walk in the hall. The floors are too creaky, and the Champions are still awake."

Don't I know.

"Where am I walking to?" I ask, but I'm smart enough to connect the dots. I just can't quite believe it.

"Let's go before we get caught."

I grab his hand, trying to ignore the shock of touching him. He tugs me through the window, helping me step over the sill and onto the ledge.

"It's slanted," I whisper, unable to hide the panic in my voice. My legs shake, breath coming in short spurts. The reaction is instantaneous. I can't catch up with my brain, can't stop the intrusive thoughts of slipping off and falling to my death. A brutal vision crosses my mind of Hayes laughing in my face and shoving me off. I turn back to my window.

"Just walk," he orders, turning me around so he's behind me and his breath heats my ear. I take a step, then another, letting him guide me. His hands are on my shoulders, warm and reassuring. "My window's the next one."

We're one room away from each other, so the window we pass belongs to Soph. I crouch as low as I dare, moving at a glacial pace. Hayes tenses behind me but doesn't urge me faster.

The good thing about having small rooms is that the windows are close together. Only a few more steps, and we're at Hayes's. I crawl in as quietly as possible. He locks it behind us.

Since he doesn't have the big tree covering most of his window, he gets a lot more moonlight. As expected, the space is pristine. His shoes are neatly arranged by the door, his suitcase closed and tucked into the corner. The top of his dresser is bare and dust-free. When I turn to the bed, my jaw drops at the bleached white sheets.

"You brought your own sheets?" I ask, realizing he brought his own pillow, too.

"Didn't you?" He looks genuinely perplexed that anyone would go anywhere without doing such a thing. The expression is so Hayes-from-before, the type of face I thought I'd never see again post-breakup. For a moment, my breath is short for an entirely different reason than the risky walk.

"No," I say. "But I don't want to take back spider eggs in my sheets, so maybe it's a good thing."

His face darkens. "If they snuck into your room from the window, they probably didn't come from far."

We both look at the wall, where Soph's room is on the other side. "It'd be like her to try to break me down."

"Is it working?" Hayes asks.

I grin at him. "She'll have to try a lot harder."

He starts to smile back, then clears this throat. "So, anyway, I didn't think too much further ahead aside from that you should maybe sleep here. For protection."

"You're going to protect me?"

I wish there was enough light so I could see if his cheeks turn red. It used to be my favorite thing. Nobody could ever make Hayes blush like me.

"The locked window will," he points out.

"Right." I look around the cramped room. "Thanks. I can take the floor."

It's warmer here, but I still wish I brought my sleeping bag. Hayes must have gotten one today, along with the rest of the trial assets. Knowing him, they're probably alphabetically organized inside the drawers of his dresser.

He sits on the bed. "Do you want to sleep on the floor?"

"When faced with a choice of a floor beneath a broken breezy window and a floor that's not, I'd much rather take the second option. I can use the sheets and pillow we were given the first day, wherever you put them."

I sit down, careful not to make the boards creak.

"Chloe," Hayes's voice is low, his use of my name disarming. With my back to the window, hopefully he can't see. "You can sleep in the bed."

"And you sleep on the floor? I'm not going to make you do that."

Nobody likes sleeping on floors, but at least I'd probably sleep. Hayes's mind would run ragged thinking about the dirt.

He swallows. "I mean . . . we could both sleep in the bed."

Our eyes meet in the dark. I hope he can't hear my heart racing. "It's a small bed."

"It's the same size as our beds at school," he says. "And we've slept in those before."

He's right, but admitting it out loud feels like unlocking a Pandora's box of memories I've kept tucked away. Like opening them might literally destroy me, and maybe the world, too. "This one looks smaller" is all I say.

He pats the spot beside him, a daring tilt to his head. "Why don't you get up here and see for yourself?"

He knows me so disgustingly well. I'm not going to turn that down. I unfold myself from the ground, climbing onto the bed with him. The sheets are already folded back, so I go all the way to the wall, which was always my spot when we shared beds back at school. Hayes didn't like feeling closed in, and I didn't like the potential of falling off during the night.

I lie down stiffly on my back, and so does he, his entire left side pressed against my right. Heat radiates from his body, warming my chilled bones that haven't totally defrosted since being doused in stream water earlier today. Or yesterday. I'm not sure what time it is, and I don't want to move my arm to check and end up even closer to Hayes.

He pulls the covers over us, his sheets carrying his scent straight to my nose. Laundry detergent, like fresh linens, and pine from his cologne.

"It's definitely smaller," I say to break the awkward silence. I wiggle around, trying to get comfortable. But every time I move, his left arm is *right there*. It feels bigger than I remember. "Have you been working out?"

"Uh, maybe a little?"

I huff. "Yeah, I can tell. Your arm is like, all over the place."

"I haven't moved an inch since lying down."

"I don't remember it being there."

"I've actually always had this arm." His voice is full of amusement. "Grew it myself."

A laugh escapes, but I quickly cover it with a cough, which he immediately hushes me for. "I *mean* your arm feels bigger. Like it's taking up more space than it used to. It's annoying."

"You're annoyed that I work out now?"

"Very," I say, turning onto my side so my back—and, unfortunately, my butt—is pressed to his side. "We used to fit fine."

"We used to lie differently," he says quietly. As if I didn't spend weeks missing the feeling of our legs tangled together and his shoulder beneath my cheek, even though he'd always whine about his arm falling asleep. As if I still don't miss it every night and fall asleep clutching my clover ring for that exact reason.

My fist closes around the ring beneath my shirt, hoping it doesn't fall out during the night. He can't see that I still wear it.

"Maybe this bed is smaller," he agrees when I don't respond. "Probably the smallest space we've had to share."

"Probably," I lie. Pandora's box is open, so the memory comes easy to me. Winter break, when Hayes came home with me for Christmas with way too many presents for Cece and a gift basket for my parents. When he gave me the ring.

It's after that burns brightest in my memory. When we left my house to go for a drive. I drove us all the way to the boardwalk in Rosetown, where the waves reach out for miles. There was a party happening at the fancy venue nearby, and faint music surrounded us. It was snowing, so no one else was outside. It felt like we were in a snow globe.

We didn't dance, 'cause we aren't dancers, but we chatted and dreamed out loud for so long our fingers went numb. When we dashed into the car, we blasted the heat and threw ourselves in the small back seat so we could get closer. For warmth, obviously.

Your dad scares me. Hayes laughed against my neck, pressing a kiss into my skin. *"We should probably get back before they won-der where we are."*

"He's a softy," I countered, trying to breathe normally despite all the very not-normal feelings thrumming through me. *"And did you see how much eggnog and brandy my parents were slurping down? They're definitely out for the night. Dad's probably been snor-ing on the couch for at least an hour."*

"What about Cece?"

"Cece is going to be very preoccupied for a long time with all the gifts you got her." I pulled back to meet his eyes. *"That was really sweet of you. You didn't need to do all that."*

He shrugged, pink blooming on his cheeks. *"Figured she could use some pick-me-ups since she's been getting sick so much lately. Besides, I need her to like me. I kind of plan on sticking around."*

"You're the big brother she never had. She loves you."

He smiled. *"And does her sister?"*

I pretended to think about it. *"Jury's still out."*

He laughed, and I pulled him in for a kiss. Lately, our kisses were different. We'd been dating for nearly a year, and in the weeks leading up to the holidays, we were sneaking off more than ever to make out. In broom closets, under the bleachers. On the observation deck, in the greenhouse. I couldn't get enough of Hayes, and he couldn't get enough of me. But we never had enough time to take it further. I was always too anxious we'd get caught, and maybe a little scared myself. Feeling confident in my body was an uphill battle some days, and despite plenty of research, there was so much I felt like I didn't know. Like with everything, I wanted to get an A+ in sex. But I'd never done it before, or even wanted to before Hayes. And though it came up a few times, he never pressured me.

But that night, with the stars and the snow and the music, his ring sitting on my finger like a promise, I felt different. I wanted Hayes, and I wanted to be with him forever. So I kissed him harder, my fingers dipping lower toward his belt until he caught them in his hand that wasn't being used to prop him over me.

"Clover." His voice was teasing, raspy and rough with a hint of warning underneath. *"What are you doing?"*

He knew what I was doing. The real question was, *What do you want to do?*

I leaned up, my lips brushing his ear as I whispered, *"I have a proposition."*

"Oh?" His breaths came short and quick as I told him my thoughts. His Adam's apple bobbed, green eyes meeting mine. *"You're sure?"*

I pulled him in for a kiss. *"Only if you are."*

He kissed me back, his answer soft and sweet. *"I'm always sure when it comes to you."*

My heart fluttered. *"I love you."*

"I love you," he said, then laughed against my mouth, glancing around the back seat of my mom's SUV. *"It's a little cramped."*

I dragged him back to my lips. *"I think it's perfect."*

It was, and we were, too. Perfect and whole. And now, as I lay in the dark pretending to be asleep while he pretends to be asleep next to me, nearly as cramped in his bed as we were in that back seat, all I can think of is how imperfect and broken we are now.

21

"You have to wake up." Someone shakes me roughly, but I'm too tired to open my eyes.

"Snooze," I mumble, patting the hand shaking me like it's an alarm clock. "Snoooooze."

"Chloe, wake up." The voice is quiet, but urgent. "It's dinnertime."

"What?" I shoot straight up, smacking foreheads with Hayes. "Ow!"

"Shh!" he scolds, glancing pointedly at the door and rubbing his own forehead. "We slept really late."

"How?" Panic grips me as last night rushes back. I'm not even in my own *room*. I slept for over twelve hours. "What have we missed? Has anyone noticed?"

He shushes me again. "I don't know. I just woke up from all the noise."

He nods at the door, where the sounds of other Challengers scurrying back and forth from their rooms to the bathrooms and downstairs is easy to hear thanks to the old floorboards. There's chatter below, likely the group congregating in the kitchen.

"Should we wait until everyone's gone?" I whisper.

His mouth opens, but he's cut off by Carly outside. "Come on, campers! I'm not leaving until you're all downstairs. You won't want to miss this meal we've got prepped. Trust me."

"The window," Hayes urges, opening it as quietly as possible.

I shake my head, but he gestures through it. We soundlessly argue, with me waving frantically at the ground outside, which looks even more far away in the daylight, and him blowing out a frustrated breath.

Carly knocks on Hayes's door. "You alive in there?"

Hayes and I share a wide-eyed glance. I gesture for him to reply. "Uh, yeah," he calls, voice scratchy with sleep. He clears his throat. "Just changing. Out in a sec."

"Dinner's in five!"

"Got it." He grabs my arm, tugging me toward the window. With no other choice, I step through, clinging to the frame for dear life.

I expect him to close his window and leave me to fall off, but he follows me out. His hands guide me by my upper arms, urging me back toward my room.

"What about Soph?" I whisper, the sound strangled in my throat. I don't know what I'm more afraid of—getting caught or falling to my death.

"We have to risk it. She might already be downstairs." His fingers press into my skin. "Stop shaking. You're going to throw us both off."

"Well, sorry," I sass. "All I can think about is falling to my death."

He tenses behind me. I immediately regret my word choice. "Distract yourself with thoughts of something else."

We inch down the ledge, slowly passing Soph's window. I mentally claw for something to distract me from my physical impending doom, landing on the realization that Hayes and I just slept in a bed together for over half a day, and it was the best sleep I've gotten since being here. Actually, in months.

My mind wanders to if we shifted positions at all during the night. I remember being warm, and I can't tell if it's my imagination or not, but I could have sworn I felt a weight over my waist at one point, like his arm was thrown over me. But I'm sure that's not right. He obviously woke up first. I hope I wasn't drooling.

Or worse—I hope he didn't see my ring.

I glance down to make sure it's still tucked inside my shirt. It is, but the action is a mistake. The ground swims below me.

But not enough that I don't notice someone walking along the path toward us.

Hayes feels my gasp, eyes following mine. It's Keana coming in from the woods, though I don't know what she'd be doing out there by herself. All she'd have to do is look up and she'd see us.

Our only saving grace is the big tree, which might provide enough coverage to not make us immediately apparent, but not enough to conceal us entirely. The Keana who was my friend would never rat us out. This newer Keana, I'm not so sure about. Especially since what she said to me about keeping our distance.

"Go!" Hayes urges, pushing me faster. My fingers scramble for my windowsill and I don't waste a second hauling myself through.

Hayes tumbles in after me, the force making me collide with my dresser. It bangs against the wall, way too loud in the small room.

"Hey!" Carly bangs on my door. "What's going on in there?"

"Sorry!" I yell back. "Tripped while putting my shoes on!"

"Let's go!" she says, an eye roll evident in her tone. Her steps retreat toward the other end of the hall.

I watch as Keana disappears onto the porch and out of sight. A sigh of relief escapes. "That was way too close. You better go back while the coast is clear."

When Hayes doesn't respond, I glance over my shoulder. He's staring at my dresser.

"Hayes," I say as loud as I dare. "Hello?"

"The top moved." His finger pushes the corner of the carved wooden surface.

"I must have knocked it loose when I ran into it."

He shakes his head, pointing at Hunter's initials. "What if you didn't? What if it was already loose? What if this is what Hunter meant in the message on the back of the drawing we found last night? He said, 'What you're missing is where I was.' And this says he was *here*."

I push at the top of the dresser. There's a shallow space beneath.

And a key.

"Oh my God," I breathe as Hayes grabs it.

He holds it up so it glints in the late-afternoon light streaming in. It's an old barrel key, its brassy finish darkened with age. Through the key's hole in the bow, Hayes and I lock eyes.

"Where do you think it leads to?" I ask, but a piece of me knows his answer before he even says it.

"The church." He looks back at Hunter's carving on the wood.

"After they found Hunter, the biggest question was how he got in because they never found a key, but the door was unlocked and there was no evidence of him breaking in. Police searched everywhere and everyone. The key never showed up."

"Until now," I say. "Something tells me if we can get into the church, the drawing we found last night might make sense."

Hayes's shoulders slump. "But Hunter hid this three years ago before the huge fence around the church was added."

"Another lock to get past," I murmur.

"Can you pick it?"

"Unlikely. Those locks are a whole lot sturdier than a doorknob lock. Harder to crack."

"Hey!" Carly's voice resumes on the other side of my door. "Let's get going!"

"Coming!" I yell back.

"We'll have to find another way into the church," Hayes whispers, pocketing the key on his way to the window. With one foot out, he turns back to me. "By the way, you snore now."

Blood rushes to my face. *"Go!"*

He ducks out, and I don't see him again until we're congregating in the kitchen filling our plates. I pile mine with mashed potatoes, gravy, green beans, and plenty of bread. There's also pork tenderloin, which must have been dropped off yesterday when Alandra and Charlie were taken away. I barely even taste it as I scarf it down. A forkful of mashed potatoes is halfway to my lips when I catch Hayes's eye from across the picnic table. He fake flinches, throwing his hands up and concealing the motion by taking a bite of bread. I blink at him, confused—

Oh. Mashed potatoes. Pork tenderloin. Last time we ate this meal across from each other, it didn't end well.

His tease shouldn't make me smile, but it does. I pick up my last hunk of pork with my fingers, baring my teeth. His eyes widen, his amusement switching to *Don't you dare.*

I plop the piece of pork into my mouth. His shoulders slump in relief.

But as I take a sip of my water, I feel another gaze on me. My eyes meet Keana's, her brows tugged into a confused V. She shakes her head, turning back to her food.

"Everyone good out here?" Trevor asks, always the last to get a plate. He rounds my side of the table to sit in his usual spot beside Hayes. As he does, something at his side flashes in the setting sun.

His key ring.

The same one he used to open the fence around the church the other day. Our way in.

I try to emphasize the discovery with my eyes to Hayes, but he's wrapped up in a conversation with Woolf. All he'd need to do is unclip it from Trevor's belt and we'd be golden. We could sneak into the church tonight and have the key back by morning. Trevor would never know it left him.

But I need Hayes's attention first.

Scooting to the edge of the bench, I stretch my leg out in Hayes's direction, mindful not to hit Trevor. I kick out lightly, the toe of my sneaker connecting with a foot.

Hayes doesn't even wince.

Trying to seem inconspicuous, I stuff my last forkful of

mashed potatoes in my mouth and deliver a real kick, not holding back.

"Fucking hell!" Dodge yells, leaping to his feet and holding
his shin. The motion shakes the table. Soph gasps, her full glass
of water tipping over and spilling into Trevor's food.

"Shit," Trevor swears, water dripping into his lap. "What happened?"

"Somebody kicked my fucking shin," Dodge whines. I
couldn't have kicked him *that* hard. But it doesn't matter, because
the perfect moment to snag Trevor's keys is ruined. Trevor goes
inside, Dodge limps off toward the fire as if his leg is broken, and
Aura and Carly start sopping up the water.

"Can you help?" Carly snaps at Jarod.

Jarod places both hands on the end of the table, looking at all
of us. "Most of you are done with dinner anyway," he says. "Start
cleaning up."

Carly and Aura glare at him, clearly looking for more assis-
tance. I sidle up behind Hayes as we bring our plates to the sink.

"Trevor has the key to the church's fence on him," I whisper.
"I was trying to kick you to get your attention so you would steal
the key ring."

"Terrible aim," he critiques.

"I couldn't see!"

I shut my mouth as Trevor enters the kitchen, freshly changed.
Hayes zeroes in on the key ring. Trevor gets more food and nods
at us before going back outside.

"We need that key ring," I emphasize.

"Leave it to me," Hayes says.

We clean up and have our nightly bonfire. A few times I catch Hayes eyeing the keys, but there's never a good opportunity. I stay at the fire later than usual until it's just Soph, Dodge, Malcolm, Woolf, Hayes, and me with the Champions, sans Aura.

"You're going to want to get your beauty sleep," Carly says. "Tomorrow's trial is no joke."

Trial four, a.k.a., the infamous turning-point trial, when things get harder.

"Don't scare them," Trevor chides. "They'll be fine."

"I'm not scared." Dodge puffs out his chest. "Bring it on."

Jarod smirks. "Gladly."

"Guess I should go to bed, then." I'm not actually tired, but I say good night, disappointed that we'll have to wait until after the trial tomorrow to get the key. All my sleep from last night has left me fully energized with nowhere to go. For once, a rest day was actually a rest day. I'm ascending the stairs when Dodge, Soph, and Malcolm come in.

Suddenly, footsteps pound up behind me. I pick up my pace, but it's too late. As I reach the third floor and cross the landing to enter our hallway, Dodge grabs my arm. He tugs me back, the force throwing me into the railing that protects me from a three-story drop. It groans beneath my weight.

"Running from me, Gatti?" Dodge asks with a sneer, blocking me against it before I can move away.

"Just tired," I lie, hoping he can't hear the tremor in my voice. The last thing I need is Dodge picking up on my fear of heights. Though if he's my blackmailer and he already knows one secret, maybe he knows them all.

"You've been doing well in the trials," he says. A compliment, but coming from him, it isn't. "I hope you don't actually expect to win."

"I am here, aren't I?"

He leans over me so I have no choice but to bend backward against the wooden railing. It creaks dangerously behind my back.

"I know it was you who kicked me at dinner," he growls, so close to my face I can feel the heat of his breath. And smell it. "What are you trying to do, huh? Cut down the competition? You starting to sweat? Realizing you don't even deserve to win because you shouldn't have gotten into the academy in the first place? That you'll never be good enough because you don't have what it takes? You don't *come from* what it takes."

Anger rises quicker than a flash flood. His words are knives meant to hit arteries. "I don't want to come from whatever made you."

"Because what made you is so much better, huh? Aren't your parents, like, snitches?"

He says it with a disgusted curl of his lip. I don't need to answer him, and I shouldn't, but bringing my family into this makes it impossible to back down.

"Journalists," I snarl right back. "And they *love* discovering the truth."

He reads between my lines, laughing in my face. "You're going to take it there, huh? Unlike you, I don't need to hurt my competition to win. But if I did"—a sickening grin crosses his face—"just remember that one's an accident, two's a coincidence, and it's not until three that people start paying attention."

Fear snatches my voice, the implication a slap. His expression

225

turns smug. "Suddenly that smart mouth has nothing to say? That's what I fucking thought—"

The words break off as his weight leaves me, cool air filling the space he was in. I stumble away from the railing, disoriented and gasping.

"Tell me exactly what you fucking thought. I'm dying to know."

My head snaps up at Hayes's voice, dangerously low and deadly calm. He shoves Dodge into the adjacent wall, keeping Dodge's shirt in his fist.

"Get the fuck off of me," Dodge raises his voice. "Let go!"

"There will be no accidents," Hayes continues, slamming Dodge into the wall again. Dodge is bigger than him in every way, but right now, Hayes is terrifying. There's a darkness over him. "Got it?"

"You wanna go?" Dodge asks, but his voice shakes. He doesn't recognize this Hayes, either. At the academy, Hayes verbally stood up for me, but never like this.

Knuckles crack from behind me. "Hell yeah, I do," Woolf says.

Soph steps forward, reminding me she and Malcolm are here. "Maybe we should—"

"What's going on?" Aura pushes them aside to take in the current scene of Hayes with a fistful of Dodge's shirt. She pries them apart. For a moment, Hayes doesn't release Dodge and the two hold eye contact. But Aura digs her nails into Hayes's bicep and he finally lets go.

"Is anyone going to tell me what the problem is?" she demands, glancing between the three of us. Her short hair is mussed, and her face is shiny with the remnants of a skin routine.

"Nothing," Dodge says, smoothing his shirt from where Hayes grasped it. "All good."

Aura looks at Hayes. He releases a long breath, taking another step back. "All good."

She looks at me. "Chloe?"

I swallow, my insides in shambles. But saying so could get my cheating exposed if Dodge is my blackmailer. "All good," I force out.

Aura clearly doesn't believe it. "Everyone go to bed. I don't want to hear a thing from any of you until morning."

We mumble affirmatives, and she waits at the end of the hall until we're in our respective rooms. I lock my door behind me, as if it will do anything when my broken window blowing cold air is an ever-present reminder that anyone can get to me.

In the sudden silence, the ordeal catches up to me. Dodge's words burrow under my skin, the cruelty in his threat enough to make me quake. My arms wrap around me as if to hold my fracturing emotions in. Like the rapids, they bubble and froth, dangerously close to spilling over.

"Hey."

I spin, sucking my tears back in as Hayes leans through my window.

"What are you doing?" I grit out.

He frowns. "You can't sleep in here after *that*. I think Dodge is your Challenger."

"I'm not sleeping with you again," I snap.

"I'll sleep on the floor if last night was too . . . weird," he says.

That's the whole problem. It wasn't too weird. Maybe at first, but then it was blissful.

I can't get used to it.

"I'm sleeping in my bed," I state firmly. "In my room. Alone."

His eyes narrow. "Are you mad at me?"

"We never stopped being mad at each other," I remind him, though suddenly, I can't remember the last hateful thought I had about him. "You're not my boyfriend anymore. I don't need you fighting my battles for me. I was handling it fine."

He rolls his eyes. "Yeah, sure looked like it. When Woolf and I came inside, Dodge had you pushed up against the railing."

The railing. The same thing that broke under Hunter. Of course the sight pushed Hayes over the edge. It had nothing to do with me.

"I don't need you" is all I say. The lie is bitter in my mouth. The truth is I will always need Hayes more than he ever needs me.

Something flashes in his eyes, but it can't be hurt. Hayes doesn't hurt; he shuts down. The poker face pulls up. "Fine. Stay here. Don't get any sleep because I know you won't. Be tired for tomorrow's challenge."

"Fine." I shrug.

"Fine," he repeats.

I take my pajamas from my dresser. When I look back up, he's gone.

Which is good, because the tears come. And this time, I can't stop them.

22

Thunder rumbles overhead as we congregate outside the gates the next morning.

Dragging myself out of bed was an Olympic feat. As Hayes foreshadowed, I didn't sleep last night. I cried out every ounce of water in me and scrolled through my thousands of photos, the only thing I can access without Wi-Fi. Every one I came across with Cece, I saved to an album for her. Then I scrolled through that album over and over again until my phone finally died.

The past few days, I've let myself get distracted by Hayes and the missing pages and the truce. But no more. Unlike Hayes, I don't need answers. I need money.

"Welcome to trial four," Trevor announces, having to raise his voice to be heard over the wind. "A test of fortitude."

"Fortitude is about strength and perseverance," Jarod takes over. "It's about pushing through despite the pain, despite the heartbreak." Thunder rumbles again, perfectly timed. He grins. "Despite the elements."

"Your sole mission for this next trial is just to exist in the forest," Carly says. "Everything from the main gates inward is off-limits. If you cross the gates before the end of the trial, you're eliminated."

"Wait." I raise my hand. "So if someone is eliminated, is the trial over?"

Jarod shakes his head. "That's one of the catches. Multiple people can get eliminated. If you cross the gates early, you're forfeiting, so you're going home."

"What if it's an emergency? Keana asks.

"We encourage you to definitely come in if you feel unsafe or injured," Trevor says. "We don't want anyone getting hurt."

"But"—Jarod drags the word out—"you're still going home. Survival of the fittest, baby."

"What's the other catch?" I ask. "You said this was only one of them."

Trevor nods. "The other catch is that this trial doesn't end at dusk tonight like the others. You need to survive the night in the forest and through the day tomorrow. We'll blow the horn at dusk tomorrow, and that'll be your cue to return."

"So how do we win?" Woolf asks.

"You don't come back to the estate until it's over," Trevor says. "If no one does before the end of the trial, then no one gets eliminated. Your future is entirely in your hands."

"And there're no tricks?" Malcolm asks. "Nothing in the forest that could trip us up? No chupacabras?"

"Um, no," Trevor says. "We asked Big Foot to sit this one out."

"What about food?" Dodge asks.

Carly nods at the backpack in his hands. "As long as you didn't skip any stops in trial three, you should have enough to last thirty-six hours."

Dodge shares a panicked look with Soph. They either skipped

a stop along the stream or he ate his portions already. Good. I'll take any legs up I can get.

"And you're welcome to hunt," Jarod says. "Set traps or whatever."

"For animals," Aura clarifies, which I didn't think needed clarification, but now I'm not so sure.

"We'll have someone stationed by the gates at all times," Trevor says. "And if there's an emergency and you can't make it back on foot, blow the whistle. Keep blowing till we come. We'll find you."

"And if you pass the white flags, you're too deep," Aura says. "Don't cross the stream."

"Understand?" Carly asks.

We all nod.

"All right, Challengers. Good luck out there."

First thing's first: I need shelter. I have the tarp from yesterday rolled up in my sleeping bag with everything else we got. I'll need water eventually, because my full bottle won't last me through tomorrow. If I can find a good spot by the stream to set up camp, maybe I can sit there until this is over.

Using my map, I make my way there. I'm glad for the silence around me. The others might stick close to the gates or go toward the lake, where there's plenty of water and clearings. The land by the stream is rocky and rooty and not what I'd call great for sleeping. But it covers the necessities, and that's all that matters. I want nothing more than to be on my own today.

Despite the fact that it's still morning, the sky gets darker. I pick up my pace, hoping to beat the rain. During the night, a chill settled over my bones. With the wind ghosting through the trees, I doubt I'll warm up anytime soon.

I walk along the edge of the stream until I find a place that might work. It's mossy and reasonably dry, with two big trees blocking it in. If I nestle myself between them, I should be able to throw the tarp over their low hanging branches in a makeshift tent. From my backpack, I take the sleeping bag out. I carefully unroll it so nothing spills out.

But it's empty.

I remember tucking the food, flashlight, tarp, purifying tablets, and fire starter within. The only things I left out were the water bottle and the whistle, which hangs off my neck. Everything else is gone.

Not just gone—taken.

"The spider," I gasp. It wasn't just a weird form of torment; it was a distraction. I haven't touched the sleeping bag since folding everything in it after trial three. When my Challenger snuck into my room to plant the spider, they must have unrolled the sleeping bag to take my supplies but not the bag itself because I would have noticed that. I should have realized it was lighter, but after barely sleeping, it didn't register.

"Fuck you," I seethe out loud as if my Challenger might be listening. For all I know, they really could be. Taking away my supplies might be their most clever act yet. Theoretically, I should be able to survive with no food until tomorrow night, though it will leave me weak. But dehydration is a different story. I'm saved by it not being a scorcher, but one bottle of water for thirty-six hours is pushing it.

Dodge's words come back to me. *"One's an accident, two's a coincidence . . ."* If he tried anything, by tomorrow afternoon, I might not have the energy to deal with him.

I have to do my least favorite thing: ask for help.

Per the truce, Hayes needs to help me win, and keeping me fed and watered is a start. But given how we ended things last night, I'll have to do some heavy groveling and bury my dignity to get his help.

Under any other circumstances, I'd never do it. But this is for Cece, not me.

I grit my teeth, shoving my sleeping bag into my backpack and starting toward the church. I'm 99 percent sure Hayes and Woolf went there to scope out other ways to get past the fence. If they find one, I don't want them to go in without me.

The rain miraculously holds off and the thunder rolls away, though the clouds stay. When I get to the church, I walk the perimeter of the fence, but it's empty. The lock is as I thought— difficult. I tug a bobby pin free to try it anyway, but after a few minutes of poking, I give up and tuck it back among my strands.

I consider calling out for Hayes and Woolf, but I'm not trying to draw the attention of the Cabinet. Instead, I find a tree a bit closer to the estate and sit against the trunk. If they're coming, they'll hopefully pass this way.

It only takes thirty minutes before I hear them.

But they're not alone.

"If I bribe you with a granola bar, will you leave me alone?"

Keana. I bristle, trying to gauge where they're coming from

and if they'll see me. Quietly, I get to my feet, shifting so the tree stays between us.

"How many granola bars are we talking about?" Woolf inquires.

"No," Hayes says at the same time. "You're limping."

"So observant," Keana mocks.

"Your ankle?" Hayes asks.

"Obviously," she says, voice softer. "It's fine. Just a flare-up from all the running."

"We should team up for this trial," Woolf suggests.

Why suddenly drag Keana into this?

"Funny," Keana says. "Kind of thought you were secretly teaming up with Chloe."

I slap my hand over my mouth to cover my surprise. Woolf laughs too loudly, but Hayes rebounds.

"I haven't talked to her in weeks," Hayes says. "Why would I start now when I'm so close to being free of her?"

An ache ricochets through my chest. *Free of her.* As if I'm clinging to him, holding him back and stamping him down. *Needy.*

"Kind of thought *you* were going to team up with her," Woolf adds.

Keana's quiet for a long moment. They're stopped on the other side of the tree. I wish I could risk a peek to see her face.

"Yeah," she finally says. "I did, too. But you know how Chloe is. She wanted to be on her own."

They start walking again, but I drop to my knees, pressing my forehead to the rough bark. That's not what happened at *all*.

She's the one who didn't want to team up with *me*.

I want to tell them so, but it's too late to reveal myself. And whatever Hayes and Woolf are playing, I want no part of it. Dodge and Soph have been highest on my antagonist list, but Keana just skyrocketed to the top. Why lie about me wanting to team up unless it's to throw suspicion off herself? She wouldn't be able to anonymously sabotage me if we were allies.

I squeeze my eyes shut against the tears. I know I haven't been the most supportive friend lately, but I didn't think we were this broken. That she would go as far as to blackmail me with the worst thing I've ever done.

But now that I'm sure it's her, I'm missing one thing—proof.

"Are you okay?"

I spring to my feet, but it's just Mina. Quickly, I swipe at my eyes. "Yeah. What are you doing here?"

Her map is in her hand. "I'm out of water so trying to get to the stream. I went to the lake first, but Dodge, Soph, and Malcolm are there. Didn't really want to mess with them."

I nod. "Wise."

Her top teeth sink into her bottom lip. "I heard what happened last night. I'm really sorry. I should have come out of my room to stick up for you, but I . . ."

She trails off, but I get it. "You didn't want to be his next target," I say.

Pink spreads across her cheeks, but she nods. "Sorry. I'm not great at being brave."

"Spending the night in a forest you're mostly allergic to is pretty brave."

She laughs, jiggling her backpack. "Well, I do have my EpiPen. Hopefully I'll have time to stab myself with it before it's too late."

I swallow, trying not to think of all the times I've carried Cece's EpiPen around because she never remembered it. "My sister has a bee allergy. I'm happy to stab you if you need it."

"Almost sounds like you're suggesting to ally," she teases.

I realize suddenly it wouldn't be the worst thing. Plus, it would prove to Hayes that I don't need him. If everyone else is allying, why shouldn't I? "Almost sounds like you might say yes," I wager. "I should probably tell you I have no food or water, though."

She blinks. "Really? Didn't you finish second in trial three?"

I don't want to give too much away, so I shrug. "Yeah. Kind of went MIA."

"Well, I have more than enough. What I can't do is make a fire. I know there's fire starter but I'm pretty sure I'll light the entire forest ablaze if I use it."

I've never lit a fire in my life, but if Jarod and Carly can do it every night, it can't be that hard. "I can help with that."

She sticks her hand out. "It's going to be cold tonight, so that's enough for me. Just for this trial, right?"

I fit my hand to hers, shaking it. If Hayes and Woolf want to replace me with Keana, I'll replace them right back. "Just for this trial."

23

Teaming up with Mina was the best decision I've ever made.

We made a game plan and stuck to it, prioritizing finding dry wood, a good place for a fire, purifying more water, and planning our next meals. She doesn't eat beans, so those get passed off to me. Not my favorite, but it's surprising what tastes good when there's no other option.

Now she rests, cocooned in her sleeping bag while I take first watch. She's convinced we don't need watches, but I'm not taking any chances. Teaming up with her may have worked out for the better on my end, but she's also a liability. I don't want her getting tied up in anything my saboteur pulls.

A rustle of leaves steals my attention from the embers of the fire I made. I wiggle out of my sleeping bag, and the cold air wraps around me as I stand. I grab Mina's flashlight, since mine was taken, clicking it on to shine through the trees.

In the distance, an owl hoots, adding to the chorus of chirping crickets and the nearby burble of the stream. Another rustle makes me spin, sweeping the beam of the flashlight at the endless trees. My free hand closes around the whistle. I don't want to use it, but maybe it would scare whatever's out here. Or whoever.

Because I'm definitely not alone. The hair on the back of my neck stands at attention, my light arcing across—

"Ah!" I gasp as the beam hits a face.

From behind a split trunk, Woolf stands, mouth gaping and eyes wide. At my shock, his terrifying expression cracks. Silent laughter wracks his body.

"Holy shit," he cries, wiping literal tears from his eyes. "You look like you peed a little. You were so scared!"

"You," I'm still catching my breath. "*Jerk.*"

"Dude, tell me you saw that," Woolf asks, gripping his stomach as if all the laughing is giving him abs. He wishes.

Hayes steps out from behind the trunk. "Hilarious." To me, he says, "We've been looking everywhere for you."

"I bet," I shoot back, thinking about them wandering the woods with Keana. "It's a big forest. What do you want?"

"We thought you'd want to come to the church."

"Yeah, but we need the key to the gate first," I remind him. "It's too high to climb."

"We don't need to climb," Hayes says.

Woolf, who's finally pulled himself together, grins. Hayes holds out his hand.

Hanging off his finger is Trevor's key ring.

"How'd you get that?" I ask, swiping it to inspect myself. There're only six silver keys, narrowing our options down since the others are barrel-style.

"Are you coming or not?" Hayes asks. "I'll tell you on the way."

I glance back toward Mina and the fire. Leaving her alone feels like a shitty thing to do when we agreed to be allies. But I'll probably be back before she even wakes up.

I have to risk it.

"Let's hurry," I say, striding past them.

Woolf clears his throat, holding up the map. "You're going the wrong way. We need to keep the stream to our right."

With a groan, I follow him. His flashlight leads us while Hayes falls into step beside me.

"What do you keep looking back for?" Hayes asks.

"I feel bad for leaving Mina. We allied."

Woolf snorts. "Well, we're sure as hell not taking her."

"I didn't suggest that," I say.

"She can hold her own," Hayes assures. "I was actually pretty impressed by how well she did during trial three. She's good with a map."

"Not as good as me." Woolf puffs up his chest.

"Probably better," I say just to get under his skin. I'm still confused where Keana falls in all this and why she's not with them now. "How'd you get the key?"

"We borrowed it," Hayes says simply, keeping his voice low.

"What's that mean?"

"Stole it right from under Trevor's nose." Woolf laughs.

"When did you do that?"

"An hour ago?" Hayes guesses.

I stop. "How'd you get back into the estate?"

"Walked in," Woolf grins.

They don't stop, so I have no choice but to keep going.

"How?"

"Jarod's shift at the gates is from midnight to six," Hayes says.

"And he's pretty much been drinking and sleeping the whole time."

"That doesn't explain how you got the keys."

"Sure it does," Woolf says easily. "We snuck into the estate. The light in Trevor's room was off, and he was snoring, so we knew he was asleep. We went into the tunnels to find the right passage to get to his room and swiped the key ring from his nightstand. He slept like a baby the whole time."

"You could have gotten caught!"

"Tonight's the perfect opportunity to go into the church," Hayes says. "We can't waste another night."

"Besides, being out here is boring," Woolf says. "What else are we supposed to do?"

"Do you have the drawing?" I ask Hayes.

He nods.

"And the journal?"

Another nod.

"We have to return the key ring by five before Jarod's shift ends, maybe sooner," Hayes says. He glances up at the moon as if to gauge the time. The storm rolled away by dinnertime and left a cloudless sky, giving us plenty of natural light to navigate by.

"I can't believe you allied with *Mina*," Woolf chortles. "She's a nerd."

"I can't believe you allied with Keana," I spit back. I wasn't going to say anything, but there goes that plan.

"We didn't ally with Keana," Hayes says, but there's a hint of defensiveness in his tone.

"Whatever," I huff, quickening my pace. It's immature, but

the sting of knowing they chose her over me earlier is too strong. Plus, now they're lying about it. Why would they lie if they had nothing to hide?

As we slip through the dark forest, the air around us shifts. Hayes grows on edge, and for once, Woolf seems serious. When we break into the clearing that leads to the fenced-in church, a shudder ripples over me.

The church gives off a ghastly glow in the beam of the moon, its peeling white paint casting speckled shadows down its facade. The broken edges of the stained glass windows catch the flashlight's beam, sharp as knives. The red ones look dipped in blood, still shiny and wet, though it must just be the light playing tricks on the glass.

"Here goes nothing." Woolf takes the key ring from Hayes and sticks one of the modern silver ones into the lock. It takes three different keys before we find the right one. The gate opens surprisingly quietly, and we walk inside, nudging it closed behind us.

Hayes strides ahead, quickly closing the distance between the gate and the five crumbling stone steps leading to the wooden doors of the church. He jogs up them, as if any lull will give him time to rethink everything and turn around.

His hand shakes as he tugs from his pocket the church key Hunter hid in my dresser. It takes a few tries before he fits it in the lock. He has to jiggle it, but it finally turns. It takes all three of us pushing on the splintered wood to get the door's rusted hinges to creak open.

We hesitate, no one wanting to be the first to step in. Hayes stares at his feet, as if willing them to move. I want to tell him we can turn around, either come back another time or leave this all behind. But we've discovered too much to stop here. Instead, all I can do is take the first step.

The air inside is stale and musty, but a reverence still clings. Entering from the back, we can see the entire church spread before us. Rows of pews lead up to a raised altar. Two sets of staircases frame it to form a balcony. On all sides of us are stained glass windows depicting the stations of the cross. The largest window over the balcony is broken in too many spots, making it impossible to decipher what biblical scene it originally depicted.

The altar is bare, all religious paraphernalia gone. The only thing remaining is a stone slab. Hayes leads the way to it down the center aisle. Beneath our feet, the planks are surprisingly sturdy. I expected each step to feel like the ground might cave under me, but these floorboards protest less than the ones in the estate.

"That's it," Hayes says quietly, stopping halfway down the aisle. In the center of the altar behind the stone slab is an unmistakably person-size hole in the floor framed by broken and jagged boards.

Hayes's eyes are glued to it. I itch to take his hand and thread my fingers through his own. My gaze rises up the two staircases to the balcony where the choir sang. A wooden railing frames it, but a chunk is missing right above the hole in the floor.

"Hunter fell from there?" I ask Hayes, nodding at the balcony. Goose bumps prickle my skin, as if mentioning Hunter might call forth his ghost.

"Yeah," Hayes says, voice rough. "They think he was leaning on it and it gave out."

A flashback of Friday night hits, when Dodge pressed into

me, bending my back over the railing. If he had pushed just a little harder, or that wood was a little weaker, would I even be here right now?

"Shit, man," Woolf sighs, placing an awkward hand on Hayes's shoulder, which in boy world I guess equates to a sympathy hug. "That's rough."

Hayes nods, tearing his eyes away. "Let's not waste time."

Woolf and I follow him up the balcony steps. There isn't much up here aside from some old music stands shoved against the window. But it does give us a full view of the church. Enough moonlight filters in that it might as well be day. Dust motes dance in the air, drifting around us in a slow waltz.

"What are we looking for again?" Woolf asks. We're all pointedly avoiding peering down into the hole.

"A piano, I think." Hayes gestures to the stands. "In Hunter's journal, he said, 'If only my brother were here and could play me a song.' I thought it'd be up here."

I perk up. "There is a piano. I saw it in the second trial."

I get as close to the edge of the balcony as I dare, peering over the railing. When I spot the side room, I point at it. "I think it's in there. I'm pretty sure that used to be the music room, and then for services, they would roll the piano out."

We hurry down the other staircase and into the room. On the walls are curling posters, yellow with age and water damage. Some show simple song sequences and notes on a staff, and others are so worn away they're illegible. One entire wall is a blackboard, mussed chalk scribbles still visible on it. Some of the ivy that crawled through the busted windows of the church sneaks through the doorway, spreading out across the ceiling.

In the center of the room is a grand piano, its dark wooden top covered in moss and warped from water. A glance up makes my stomach queasy. Beyond the devouring vines, the ceiling is crumbling, some chunks suspended thanks to the greenery.

"This looks like birds, doesn't it?" Woolf asks, peering at scribbles on the blackboard. "Maybe Hunter drew them to match the drawing."

Hayes pulls out the drawing and the journal, laying them on top of the portion of the piano not yet eaten by moss and mold. We look down and up, comparing the drawing with the chalkboard.

"I don't see it," I finally say.

Hayes agrees, shoulders slumping.

"Did he have a favorite song that he always asked you to play? Maybe the right tune will unlock something."

"Would it even still work after all these years?" Hayes counters.

"We have to try something." Using my foot to nudge out the bench, I push him onto it. He wobbles, throwing me a glare.

Once he finds his balance, he places his hands on the keys. His left thumb presses down. A sour note rings out, making us flinch.

"Maybe not that one?" Woolf suggests.

"They're all bad," Hayes comments, playing a quick scale. Each sounds worse than the last. "It hasn't been tuned in years. Maybe he meant an organ?"

"But you can't play the organ," I say. "Can you?"

He shakes his head.

"Then Hunter wouldn't have done that. It must be this piano," I say, sure of it. I just wish I knew what exactly "it" was.

Hayes sighs, glancing at his watch. "We're running out of time."

"Maybe there are more secret rooms," Woolf suggests. "I bet these posters are hiding something."

He gets to work on peeling them off, and Hayes directs him around the room, pointing to different potential hiding spots. I pick up Hunter's drawing, as if looking at it hard enough might make something pop out that I didn't see before. There's really not that much to it. It's simple, something that probably only took him five minutes and a pen to sketch. From the black ink-blots on the paper, he might have even used the fountain pen we found in the secret library room. Spanning across the five tele-phone wires are twelve birds. Some are ravens, some are doves. There doesn't seem to be a rhyme or reason to their positioning.

"Damn," Woolf says from the other side of the room. He holds up the last poster he just stripped from the wall of a music staff. "Nothing was behind this one, either."

He crumples it up. "Wait!" I shout, the sound way too loud for such a sacred, dormant place. They both tell me to shush, but I barely hear past the blood pounding in my ears. I hold the draw-ing up so I can see it better in the moonlight, glancing between it and the wrinkled poster in Woolf's hands.

"It's a staff," I realize. I flip it so Hayes can see, excitement coating my words. "Look, the wires make up the five lines, and the ravens are sharp notes, and the doves are . . . non-sharp notes?"

"Naturals," Hayes breathes, taking the drawing from my hands. "Holy shit, you're right. Hunter drew sheet music."

"Could he have maybe made it a little more obvious?" Woolf scratches his head.

Hayes plops on the unsteady bench, nearly falling backward in his haste. He rights himself, shoving the drawing onto the music holder. Fingers perfectly placed, he plays the notes in accordance with what's written. It sounds vaguely familiar, but I'd need more to pin it. When he gets to the end, he laughs.

"What?" Woolf and I ask.

Hayes shakes his head, eyes fluttering closed. "It's Diana's song. The one about blue moonflowers that Hunter tricked me into learning to impress Principal Watershed."

Woolf chuckles. "He always did like to mess with you."

"Never let anything go, either," Hayes says. He plays the string of notes again, frowning.

"What is it?" I ask.

"The last note. It's a D sharp. But listen." He presses it, but nothing happens. "It's stuck."

We come to the same conclusion at the same time. Hayes scrambles off the bench as Woolf and I wipe debris from the piano top. We pry it open, staring inside at the rusted strings.

"This is D sharp," Hayes says, pointing to the corresponding string. We follow it down toward the back of the piano. Wedged between two of the strings is what looks like a small plastic baggie.

Hayes tugs it free and pulls out the contents. I shine the flashlight down, illuminating what he holds:

A small stack of papers the size of Hunter's journal tied together with a dirty shoelace.

The missing pages.

24

"We did it!" I cheer, bouncing on the balls of my feet. "We found the pages! You were right!"

A brilliant grin breaks out across Hayes's face. "I was right. They exist! I was *right*!"

"Fuck yeah!" Woolf exclaims, fist pumping the air. "Take that, Nancy Drew."

Before I can think twice, I throw my arms around Hayes. To my surprise, his wind around me, and he bends back so my feet lift from the ground, twisting me in a spin. I laugh, clinging to his neck until he sets me down.

"You did it," I grin, squeezing his hands. "You knew."

"But you solved his final puzzle," he says, eyes full of awe. "In your genius hours."

I flip my short hair over my shoulder. "Aren't I always?"

Woolf aggressively clears his throat. The flirtatious spell breaks, and we release each other, jumping back like we're both matches in the presence of a spark. Hayes coughs, and I can't help noticing how very concerning the state of the ceiling is.

"So," Woolf says, dragging the word out. "We gonna read them?"

"Only if you want to," I tell Hayes. "I get it if you want to read them on your own or in private first."

Woolf casts me a judgy look. "Speak for yourself. I wanna know what they say."

"I want to do it together," Hayes says.

I'm glad, because I may not lack as much tact as Woolf, but I also really want to know what they say. We close the piano top, spreading the pages out. There's only four, but they're covered in writing.

"I can read them."

Woolf and I nod. Hunter's scrawl is so messy, I'm not sure I could decipher it. Hayes takes a deep breath and begins.

I never know how to start these things, because it's not like I'm going to ~~Dear Diary~~ this shit and spill my feelings. I don't even know why I'm keeping this journal, anyway. In the beginning, I thought it'd be a cool thing to look back on. Like someday, I could pull it out at a dinner party and be like, "Wow, remember the Wilde Trials? What a time!" It'd be a good conversation starter.

Now, I'm not sure I'll even survive the Wilde Trials, let alone win.

Hayes pauses, his breath shuddering out before continuing.

Okay, that's dramatic. But something is seriously wrong. I should be winning. I was. But every time I win, bad things happen. First, it was the dead rabbit. Weird, but whatever, basically prep for hazing next year. But then there was the giant spider. How did someone get a key to

248

my room and know to put my worst fear under the blankets with me? Barely anyone even knows I'm afraid of them.

We all meet eyes. "That sounds familiar," Woolf says. "But it's been three years. How could it be connected with your spider surprise?"

"Keep reading," I urge Hayes, hoping the other pages bring answers.

But the rocks were the first time things got dangerous. I mean, the challenge was senseless, sure. Who needs to prove their fortitude by rolling rocks up a hill like Sisyphus? But then for someone to be hiding at the top rolling them down at me? What the hell was up with that?

They want me to forfeit. That much is clear. Well, too damn bad. They'll have to try a whole lot harder.

"That's the first one," Hayes says, putting the page down. He picks up the next, glancing up to meet my eyes.

I nod at him to continue.

I jinxed it.

The champions told us trial four was a turning-point trial, and they weren't kidding. On top of needing to do a high-ropes course in the trees for agility, my stalker got crafty. They must have been just ahead of me and dropped a beehive right beneath the path. I didn't realize until it was too late.

I'm not allergic to bees, but I wonder if they knew that. The stings hurt like a bitch. I got at least ten. I managed to not place last, but I'm seriously lagging.

It might not have sent me into anaphylactic shock, but the outcome is nearly just as bad: Aura knows something's up. She's worried about

"Woah, wait," Woolf says. "When did Aura enter the chat?"

"Maybe we'd find out if you didn't just interrupt," I huff.

Woolf raises his hands in an innocent gesture. "Sorry, sorry. Keep going."

Hayes nods, returning to the sheet.

She's worried about me. I told her I accidentally ran into the hive while on the ropes course, but she didn't buy it. I guess it's a compliment. She said I'm way too smart to have done something so clumsy.

We only had a few minutes together in the secret library room, and I didn't want to spend it with her being upset. She's already stressed enough having Ravi here. I know I should be glad that him being chosen as a Challenger finally gave her a legit reason to cut things off with him so we can finally be together, but now we have to be even more careful. Aura keeps denying it, but I'm pretty sure Ravi is following her. Every time I try to get her alone, he's conveniently there with his staple glare.

If he found out about us, he'd be furious given the entire reason Aura told him they needed to break up is because he's a Challenger. He'd realize she lied and was willing to risk it for me but not him. And when I win, it will look even worse, as if she helped me. I hate it, but Aura's right that we have to keep our relationship secret a while longer and at least get past graduation so no one gets suspicious.

That's what keeps me going. Before, I wanted to win the trials like I wanted everything else—to prove I could. But now, I want to win to be a Champion with her. And for Hayes. Because how embarrassing of a big brother would I be if I backed out now? I can't bring that shame on him. And Mom and Dad wouldn't take it well, either.

But if something really bad happens to me, that's not going to help Hayes, either. Dad will expect him to take over the firm in my place. It's not like I want to do it and spend the rest of my life in a suit and tie making people sweat on the witness stand, but art school was never in the cards for me. Hayes could be different. He's so good at piano. I bet if he applied to some fancy school like Juilliard, he'd get in. Mom and Dad wouldn't say no to that as long as I'm taking over the firm.

It's depressing to think about my future and how it's been decided for me since before I was even born. Maybe that's another reason I want to win. With the money, I could run off with Aura. Elope. Become travel social media influencers or run foodie blogs or whatever the hell people do to get rich on the run these days. We could give our parents and Ravi a big middle finger and be happy.

But that would mean leaving Hayes. And I'd never do that.

Hayes drops the page to the piano, a sheen over his eyes.

I bump my shoulder to his. "I can read the next one, if you want?"

He swallows, handing it to me. I clear my throat.

I might have just made a huge mistake, but I had to do it.
I told other Challengers about what's been happening to me.
And I'm shook off my ass to find out—it's not just me getting targeted.
It's not everyone, but the few people I've asked have consistently been in the top five and been dealing with extra shit behind the scenes.

251

Tricks, sabotage, attacks. Jackson forfeited two days ago. I can't stop thinking about why.

But Aura never mentioned anything strange happening during last year's trials, so I don't know what to think.

Me and some of the other Challengers have been meeting up in the church to talk through our experiences and next steps. I swiped the key even though it's off-limits. It's the only place we can meet without the risk of the Champions overhearing. I don't trust them, except for Aura. But she can't know things are this bad. She already wants me to throw it all away. I won't.

I've been keeping a closer eye on Ravi. Aura and I are so careful, but the way he's always hovering makes me feel like he knows about us. Maybe even figured it out before the trials. But if he does know, that doesn't explain why he would target any of the others. At least with me, he has a solid incentive to give me shit.

I caught Trev up on what's going on. He's pissed and wants to confront Ravi outright, but leading with a hot head will get us nowhere. I still have a few other suspects I'm considering.

I replace the third page with the fourth. "Let's see if his final entry tells us."

Everything hurts.

We all flinch at the dismal opening. I push on.

Only one trial left. I can make it. I have to. But at what cost? Aura's begging me to forfeit. We got in a fight tonight because of it.

252

She's scared. Said she tried to tell the other Champions that something dangerous is going on, but because she's the youngest, they don't believe her. Or maybe they do, but they don't care. Maybe the glory and fun of the trials have always been a lie. A glittering skin to hide a rotten core.

Even as I write this, my ribs ache. Trial six took place in the dark. I thought I was keeping tabs on everywhere around me. Until I got jumped.

Whoever got me, got me good. My ribs are bruised, if not broken. They stayed away from my face, but my torso is a purpling mess. I think something major tore in my shoulder.

"He had all those injuries when he was found," Hayes says, voice numb. "The police said it was from the two-story fall."

"Maybe they didn't know better," I try to reason.

Woolf scoffs. "Or maybe they were paid off."

I keep reading.

Aura doesn't get it. She doesn't understand the need to prove herself To be the older sibling and have the pressure of the world sitting on your shoulders. I have to win. Because I'm sure as hell not about to keep my mouth shut about this for the rest of my life. But if I walk out of this anything but a Champion and try to explain what happened, I'll sound like a sore loser.

Winning gives me leverage. It gives me respect. Winning is the key. I thought I was winning for Aura, or for Hayes. Now, I'm winning to blow this messed-up thing wide open.

Fuck the Wilde Trials. It's time for this tradition to crumble.

I'm close to the truth. Tonight, before the seventh trial begins, I'll know if my assumptions are correct.

I squint at the page. "I thought that was the last entry, but there's another at the bottom of the page. Probably the same night."

"Read it," Hayes urges.

I've always loved being right. But not now.
I know who my attacker is. I guess it should have been obvious it's been him all along. I'm going to confront him at the church and force him to admit to everything.

Everything is underlined four times for emphasis. I lower the sheet. "Do we think he meant Ravi?"

Hayes is already pacing. "He must have, right?"

"So Ravi finds out that his girl lied and was sneaking around with Hunter and goes nuclear?" Woolf asks. "He pushes Hunter off the balcony so it looks like an accident and leaves him here. But if Aura knew something was going on and then Hunter went missing, wouldn't she immediately suspect Ravi was behind it? Why not ship his ass off to jail?"

"Because she's scared," I realize. Suddenly, Aura's timidness makes sense, along with her words the other night. "And she's traumatized. She knows the truth of what happened to Hunter and that it was no accident because it partially revolved around her."

"Do you think Trevor knows the truth?" Woolf asks Hayes.

Hayes nods. "I think he knows something happened. Maybe

he's been trying to figure it out ever since but couldn't, so he sent the journal to me."

"You mentioned he might be looking out for you," I remind him. "It could also be him feeling guilty that he couldn't help Hunter, so he wants to make sure the same thing doesn't happen to you."

"Speaking of Trev, we need to get these keys back." Hayes glances at his watch, eyes growing wide. "Like, now."

He gathers the pages and the drawing, fleeing the room without waiting for Woolf and me. We share a look of concern but follow him.

When Woolf and I finally make it out of the church, Hayes is already by the fence. I don't mention the glimmer of a tear track down his cheek, or that his inhales are accompanied by a faint sniffle.

The strangest thing happens on the walk back. While Hayes silently grieves a few steps in front of us, Woolf talks to me as if we're still friends, sometimes even looping Hayes into the conversation. By the time we reach the gates to the estate, the air has shifted from grim and wretched to cautiously cloudy.

Hayes stops before we can get close enough to be heard by Jarod. "I'll take it from here."

"Alone?" I ask.

"We're late. If Trevor's already up, it'll be a lot harder for three of us to sneak around him than one. I got the answers I wanted. If I'm caught and eliminated, it is what it is."

"I'll come with you," Woolf offers. "I don't care if I get eliminated."

Hayes's eyes flicker to me before locking on Woolf. "I'm going by myself."

"But—"

Words die on my tongue as Hayes walks away, leaving no room for arguing.

"Do you think he's okay?" Woolf asks me, staying by my side. "This was . . . a lot."

"I don't think so," I say quietly, worry worming inside me as Hayes disappears past the gates. "But hopefully it gives him the closure he needs and he *will* be okay."

25

"What's taking him so long?" I fret to Woolf, pacing in the same spot Hayes left us. That was at least twenty minutes ago. My heart races, wondering if Hayes got caught. Him getting eliminated theoretically is something I should want, but I don't.

"I should have gone with him," Woolf says.

"Yeah, you should have," I agree. "Why did you back down so easily?"

Woolf's eyes flash. "Because of you."

"Me?"

Woolf groans. "You are so smart and somehow so dumb at the same time. If Hayes and I both went and we both got caught, that would leave you to finish the trials by yourself. When is it going to click that he's trying to protect you?"

I blink at him, sure he can't be serious. Yes, we have a truce, but protection doesn't fall under it. "No, he's not."

"Of course he is. It's the same reason he didn't sleep the night before this trial started. He was up all night making sure whatever shithead is messing with you didn't come back through your window during the night."

My mouth drops open. "He told you that?"

"We swore no more secrets."

I have so many more questions to ask, but suddenly Hayes emerges from the line of trees separating us from the gates.

"You took forever," I accuse, an edge of anger in my voice to disguise the tidal wave of relief I feel. "What happened?"

"I got caught," Hayes says.

I suck in a breath. "By Trevor?"

"What'd you say?" Woolf asks.

"I told him—"

A horn blows through the air, the signal to mark the end of the trial. Except, that can't be right. It hasn't even been a full twenty-four hours yet.

"Return to the estate," Trevor's voice carries through the trees. He must be using a megaphone; I didn't even know he *had* a megaphone. "Trial four is over. This is not a test. Return to the estate *now*."

"Come on." Hayes turns back the way he just came. "You'll find out soon enough."

All the Champions are gathered on the porch. Jarod blinks sleepily, and Carly rubs her eyes, but Trevor's gaze is alight with fury. Aura's arms wrap around herself. She looks like she's going to be sick.

I stare at Hayes, trying to decipher what he could have said to warrant a reaction like this. The rising sun brightens the sky, illuminating the grounds just enough to reveal Soph, Dodge, and Malcolm striding down the path looking as confused as Woolf and me. I'm surprised they even heard the megaphone all the way near the lake.

Keana arrives next, frowning as she takes us all in. "Why did the trial end early?"

Jarod ignores her, turning to Trevor. "Is that everyone?"

"We're missing Mina," I say, a knot forming in my stomach.

Moments stretch out as angst swirls inside me. Despite leaving Mina safe and asleep a few hours ago, anything could have happened between now and then. I didn't even leave her with her own flashlight. She could be *dead* for all I know. If a bee stung her—

"Is it over?" Mina breaks through the trees with a twig in her hair and an air of confusion. A breath shoots out of me.

"Congratulations, you all won trial four and will be going on to trial five," Trevor announces, but nothing about his cool tone feels celebratory. "But because we can't trust you to behave on your own like adults, you'll spend the rest of the day cleaning the estate."

"We already cleaned the estate," Malcolm counters.

Trevor stares so hard at him that Malcolm visibly shrinks. "Clean it again." He steps back, looking at each and every one of us. "If you want to act like animals in the woods and hurt each other, then you don't deserve the honor of seeing a trial through to the end. Don't ever attempt to mar the reputation of the trials again. There will be no sabotaging each other, or fighting, or whatever the fuck else happened. Understood?"

Everyone quickly nods in agreement, but mine feels mechanical. The only reason Trevor would end the trial early is if Hayes told him I'm getting sabotaged. But telling Trevor goes against the terms of my Challenger's blackmail, where they threatened to

259

rat about my cheating to the Champions. They'll think I caved and snitched about their antagonizing.

Fury storms through me, but it has nowhere to go. Hayes doesn't know about the blackmail, so he couldn't have known that telling Trevor could get me disqualified. Hell, if it makes it back to Principal Watershed, I might not be allowed to graduate.

I glance at Keana. If she really is my Challenger, maybe I can talk to her. Beg her not to tell the Champions my secret. We could reach a compromise. I'll swear not to tell the Champions it was her specifically sabotaging me as long as she deletes all evidence I cheated.

But she doesn't even look my way as we walk inside. Carly assigns us our cleaning duties, and I get the third-floor bathrooms while Keana gets the kitchen. I'll have to wait until later to confront her.

"I'd rather spend the day in the woods," Dodge mutters, hefting up his rake to tend to the backyard.

Hayes tries to meet my eyes, but I avoid him, taking my cleaning equipment from the hall closet and escaping upstairs. I'm halfway to the bathrooms when Mina's voice stops me.

"You weren't there when I woke up this morning," she accuses.

"I'm really sorry," I reply, wishing I could say more because she doesn't deserve my ambiguity after the kindness she showed me yesterday as my ally.

Conflict crosses her face, as if she wants to hold out and cold-shoulder me, but it's not her nature. In her hands is a broom and Clorox wipes, since she's tasked with cleaning the empty Challenger rooms. She blows out a big breath. "I was worried. I thought something happened."

Plenty happened, I think, picturing my eventful night in the church with Hayes and Woolf. I shake my head. "I'm okay."

She nods, gaze flickering back toward the stairs. "Did it have to do with whatever Trevor was talking about?"

"No," I lie. "I don't know what that was about."

Her frown deepens. "Maybe Aura told him about Dodge cornering you."

"Maybe." I wish it were as simple as that.

"Chloe?"

Trevor's voice comes from the end of the hall as he crests the top of the stairs. Mina slips into Lainey's empty room to clean.

I swallow past a growing lump, turning to him. Maybe this is it and my Challenger has already told him that I'm a cheater. Maybe I'm going home.

With just the two of us in the small hallway, it's more apparent than ever how tall he is. It's as if the hallway is folding in around us, the peeling wallpaper like fingers reaching out.

"Let's go in your room," he says, nodding at my door.

My broken window. "Um, actually, I'm supposed to clean the bathroom. Whoever did it last time did a pretty subpar job, so—"

Trevor sidesteps me, opening my door. I know I locked it, so that means he's already been in here. A blast of cold air hits me, sneaking right through my jacket.

He points at the glassless window. "Got an explanation for that?"

"I didn't do it," I say carefully, still not sure how much Hayes told him.

"Who did?"

"I don't know." That's true, at least.

"Chloe, I really need you to be honest with me. Is something happening?"

"Like?"

He looks around the room. "Like . . . have the other Challengers been treating you poorly?"

"No." I don't deny it quickly enough. "Why would you ask that?"

He sighs, scrubbing a hand down his face. Stubble lines his jaw. "One of the other Challengers said they're being messed with. I want to make sure it isn't a widespread issue."

I try to hide my surprise. Hayes didn't say *I* was being sabotaged. He told Trevor he was.

"No, not for me," I say. "I think the window shattered because of the tree. Do you see how close it is? I think a branch smacked the glass during a storm."

Trevor nods, not pushing it. "Well, either way, you can't sleep in here. We're going to board it up. You can move your things into Lainey's old room when Mina's done cleaning it."

"Got it." Lainey's room. Across the hall. No more window visits from Hayes.

Maybe that's good. Now that he got answers about Hunter, we can cut our truce short.

By the time I slide into Lainey's bed hours later after dinner and a shower, sleep takes me immediately. I dream of Keana and her hot-pink scrunchies, of Hayes and his verdant eyes, of Woolf and his namesake grin. But mostly, I dream of wandering through the forest, both chasing someone and being chased. Every time I grab them to finally see their face, they explode into spiders, or ravens' feathers, or dust.

I grab them again, sure that this is the time I will see their face and know for certain who knows my worst secret. I spin them around and—

Wake up.

"Come on!" Jarod calls, banging on our doors as he paces the hall. I'm more disoriented than usual, feeling as if I only closed my eyes minutes ago. I squint at the time on my watch. It's two in the morning.

"What's going on?" Keana asks as we open our doors.

"Trial five, that's what," Jarod says, stopping at the end of the hall where Carly and Aura wait by the top of the stairs. "You have ten minutes to be downstairs. Swimsuits encouraged."

"It's the middle of the night," Soph states the obvious.

"Welcome to the adaptability trial," Carly says, raising a brow in challenge. "Care for a night swim?"

An hour later, we stand on the shore of the lake. The water is still, the ripples from the two mouths of the stream smoothing out by the time it reaches the point we're at. While there's a decent amount of light from the half-moon, all it does is reflect off the surface, making the inky darkness even more prominent. I wish I had thought to do more research on what exactly is in the lake. I'm not trying to get my leg bit off by a beaver.

"On the other side of the lake, you'll find two types of shells— eight golden seashells and the five shells you used to get down the river in trial three. To win this trial, don't be the last one to deliver a golden seashell to us," Trevor says. "To get back, you can use the canoes, but since there are eight of you, three will either have to share with someone else or swim back."

"We're supposed to swim to the other side of the lake?" Malcolm squeaks.

"Or, get crafty," Carly suggests. "Anything's game. This trial is all about adapting to the circumstances. All that matters is that we get a seashell from you."

"Can we use that rowboat?" Woolf nods at a small metal boat between two trees.

"That's for us," Aura says.

"In case we need to fish anyone out," Jarod adds.

"The last person to get back on this shore or return without a seashell loses." Trevor says. "If you need us to come get you, yell."

"Ready to go?" Jarod asks. We all give varying levels of agreement. "Swim fast."

I kick my shoes and socks off, nudging my toes into the water. Without the warmth of the sun, it might as well be an ice bath.

Dodge wades out, unfazed. "Come on!" he calls to Soph. "Let's just swim it."

Soph cringes at the cold. "Maybe there's a faster way?"

"Doubt it." Dodge dives, resurfacing several feet away. "You get used to it!"

"You get used to it," Hayes echoes next to me, taking his shirt off. We haven't had a chance to talk since coming in from trial four. Depending on how this trial goes, this could be my only opportunity.

"You shouldn't have said anything to Trevor about the sabotage," I tell him quietly, walking until the water is up to my waist. I should remove my shirt, but I can't without risking my ring out in the open. Woolf takes off, splashing us as he passes. Keeping my upper half dry is useless, so I submerge myself up to my neck. The mushy ground disappears beneath my feet as the bottom drops off quickly.

"I had to tell him something worthy of breaking the rules to sneak back into the estate during the trial," Hayes defends. "Otherwise, he would have had no choice but to eliminate me."

"I thought you were fine with getting eliminated?" I challenge what he told Woolf and me. "You got what you came here for. The sooner you get out of the forest, the sooner you can share the truth about Hunter's death."

He's still stuck in the muck, glancing down into the water like he might be able to see what's beneath us. "You held up your end of the truce. I plan to hold up mine."

"No need. I'm pretty sure I know," I say. My gaze sweeps the lake, trying to pinpoint Keana. But even with the moonlight, everyone is still inky blobs. The only two I can tell are Dodge and Woolf shredding through the water. I'm a strong swimmer, but I need to shut this conversation down so I still have hopes of catching up.

I do a slow backstroke so I still face Hayes. He's fully illuminated thanks to the moon, brows tugged in a V and his torso exposed. I force my eyes not to dip below his face.

"I didn't mention your name to Trevor because I know there's something else you're keeping from me," Hayes says, glossing over my Challenger's identity.

I wish I could blame the icy water for the way my breath freezes in my chest. It's not like Hayes not to push if he thinks there's something he doesn't know. The only reason he would leave it be for this long is if there's something *he's* not telling *me*.

Keana comes to mind, romping through the woods with him and Woolf yesterday afternoon. How he denied it. Why would he lie about that?

Sickness rolls in my stomach. If I can't trust her, then maybe I can't trust him, either.

And with six hundred grand on the line, I can't risk a loose end.

My gaze levels with his as I force the chill in my veins into my tone. "The truce is over."

26

I don't look back, kicking as hard as I can and cycling between freestyle and breaststroke. By the time I reach the midpoint, a stitch attacks my side.

I try to scout the competition again with minimal luck. In front of me, Woolf and Dodge are still trapped in some weird competition between the two of them. A head bobs several yards away from me, though I can't tell if it's Soph or Mina from the silhouette of a high ponytail. Who I think is Keana is even further away, clinging to the outskirts of the lake. It's fine by me. I want as much distance between us as possible.

Pushing on, I cross the lake as quickly as the throb in my side allows. It's not that large of a body of water, but the cold paired with the lack of sleep and darkness make it feel bigger. By the time I'm finally dragging myself onto the opposite shore, I'm gasping for breath, my fingers digging into the smooth pebbles that compose it.

The only ones to beat me are Woolf and Dodge. I cling close to the trees to avoid their attention. Grabbing a gold seashell and tucking it into the top of my bathing suit, I push out the nearest canoe. I'm halfway into the water when the moonlight reveals the roughed-up bottom. This is the one Woolf and I beat up that started sinking.

I leave it to ruin someone else's success, moving to the next one. By the time Dodge and Woolf notice me, I'm already several strokes from shore.

This is so much easier by myself, although my arms still haven't recovered from the other day. I push through the pain, gunning for first. If I can keep proving myself, maybe it won't matter what my Challenger spills to the Champions about me. Being first has to count for something.

In minutes, I'm halfway across the lake. I keep my eyes trained on the shore, where the lanterns the Champions were carrying glow. This trial is short. Maybe it's intentional. I have a feeling they want this whole thing over just as much as we do.

I'm not aware of anything aside from my own strokes, the smack of the paddles entering the water nearly as loud as the chirp of the crickets echoing in the still night. The glow of the lanterns shifts from pinpricks to golf balls, growing bigger by the minute. I'm going to win this.

A scream breaks through my heaving breaths and splashing water. I slow my oars, trying to locate the source. Everything is so dark suddenly. I've been so focused on the lanterns that I've missed the clouds rolling over the moon, blocking what little light we had.

"Help!" someone screams, voice frail and coughing. Mina. I try to find her behind me, but all I can see are shadows. We're all spread out across the lake.

"Help!" she calls again. "I'm sinking!"

"Shit," I breathe. She must have taken the wrecked canoe and not realized she was taking on water until she got too far from the shore.

"Please!" she yells.

There's movement by the shore. One of the lanterns is floating into the lake. I squint, trying to see through the darkness. They should be coming my way. But the lantern moves farther away, carried by the rowboat. Malcolm's voice breaks through the night.

"I'm drowning!" he sputters. "Help! I'm drowning!"

Whoever is in the boat is going to him. Of course they are— they likely can't even hear Mina. Meanwhile, Malcolm's barely offshore. He could probably still touch the bottom if he would just stand up.

I start rowing again. It's not like Mina's going to die. She can clearly swim since she made it to the other side of the lake. Besides, this is why I left the broken canoe. I want it to mess someone up.

But I was hoping for anyone but Mina.

"Help!" she screams, coughing harder. "Please!"

Her voice grows faint as I get farther away. But that last call didn't sound right. It wasn't just a cry for help. She was *begging*.

And the coughing is strange. Even if she took in a mouthful of water, she shouldn't be that bad off. It's strangely familiar, something caught between a gasp and a wheeze.

I ditched Mina last night. Something bad could have happened to her, and I was lucky it didn't. Would I really get that lucky again?

With a frustrated breath, I turn my canoe. I can catch only glimpses of her position, like the shift in water but paired with the coughing, it's enough. I row to her, trying not to think about what a massive mistake I'm making.

When I get close, my bleeding heart emphasizes that this was the right thing to do. Her breaths are ragged, wheezing gasps, punctuated by a harsh cough every other second. Its familiarity hits me in a horrible way that has Cece's face springing to mind.

Mina's having an asthma attack.

"Mina!" I call, finally able to make her out in the dark. Her canoe is gone, swallowed by the lake. She treads water, but her head barely bobs above the surface. I stick out my oar for her to grab. "Can you get in?"

She clutches the oar for dear life. "Can't breathe," she chokes out. "Asthma."

"Where's your inhaler?" I ask.

"With Aura," she coughs. "On shore. Can't get wet."

"If you can kick, I might be able to pull you up."

I give her my hand and tug, lifting her small frame out of the water. "Almost there," I reassure her through gritted teeth, trying to balance the canoe. We get halfway, enough so that she can let go of my hand and pull herself in. She tumbles to the floor, shivering and wheezing.

"I'm gonna get us back," I tell her, reaching for my oars. "You're going to be—"

I don't have time to scream. One second, I'm above water, and the next I'm not.

The canoe capsizes, dumping us into the lake. I was out

long enough to mostly dry off and the cold goes straight to my bones. It makes me forget how to work my limbs, numbing me. I only realize I'm sinking when my bare feet brush the weeds beneath me.

I kick up hard, a mouthful of water spilling from my lips as I break the surface. "Mina?!" I sputter. "Where are—"

Hands fist my hair, shoving me under. I lash out and feel the unmistakable slide of wet flesh as my elbow hits something. When my hand closes around what might be an arm, instead of pushing it away, I tug it closer. I can't hear anything except my pounding blood, can't see past the dark murkiness that burns my open eyes. The fingers knotted in my wet curls push me deeper, but I'm still holding on to them. I rake my nails along whatever skin I can reach.

They let go of me with one last shove, kicking out of my hold. A scream of bubbles escapes my lips as a foot hits me square in the stomach. Water slides down my throat in an arctic waterfall, short-circuiting my brain. Only one thought prevails:

This is my Challenger.

And they just tried to drown me.

The clarity propels me up, and I break the surface, coughing up so much water that bile joins it. It takes everything in me to stay afloat as I get a hold of myself. I whip from side to side, trying to see through the darkness. A head bobs several feet away from me before diving back under.

"Chloe?!" Mina's voice is frantic. My head jerks away from the bobbing head to face her. "What's going on? Are you okay?"

"I'm here!" I sputter. Confusion rocks me. Could Mina have

tipped us and held me under? Was the asthma attack an elaborate plan to get me alone?

But she still wheezes and coughs, clinging to the now-righted boat several yards away from me. Someone else was definitely here. Whoever held me under was bigger than Mina.

"The boat." She pushes it toward me, struggling to stay afloat. "Can you get in?"

It takes a lot of shimmying, but I finally pull myself up. I turn to Mina and do the same, careful to make sure no one is around to capsize us again. Her breathing is even worse and her body quivers with every gasp.

When we get within hearing distance, I start screaming for help. Jarod and Trevor splash into the water to pull us the rest of the way.

"She needs her inhaler," I gasp, sweat coating my skin from the exertion.

"I have it!" Aura says. They pick up Mina, sitting her on the ground. I climb out, but my legs buckle beneath me. Pebbles dig into my hands and knees as I vomit onto the shore.

A warm palm rubs my back. "Easy there," Trevor says gently. "What happened to you?"

Tears spring to my eyes. I wipe my mouth and raise my head, the lanterns providing enough light for me to make out that every other Challenger stares at Mina in varying levels of horror as she puffs on her inhaler.

The only one who's looking at me is Hayes.

"I'm fine," I force out, unable to meet Trevor's concerned gaze.

"I told you this trial was a bad idea," Aura bites out at Trevor.

She helps Mina stand and wraps a towel around her, leading her back to the estate. Over her shoulder, she yells, "I hope you're fucking happy!"

Trevor rakes a hand through his hair, gesturing us to go before him. The entire walk back is dead silent.

By the time we're passing the gates, the sky glows with dawn. As we walk up the porch steps, Soph's long black hair shifts, falling off her shoulder and down her back. She took it out of her ponytail. She never takes it out of her ponytail.

She hurries to fix it, but not before I see the four weeping red scratches running the side of her throat.

27

I wait more patiently than I ever have in my life.

Through the rest of the day, through dinner, through the bonfire and Malcolm's elimination. A somberness clings to the air, subduing even Woolf and Dodge. Gone are the mocking conversations and jabs. It's easy to crawl into myself and be left alone. Everyone's doing the same thing.

Mina's been resting since we got back. She refused Aura's concerned suggestion that she go home, insisting she'll be fine by the next trial. The inhaler did its job, but I can't help but think maybe she wouldn't have needed it at all if I had turned back when I first heard her yell for help. I'm starting to realize the price of winning might be more than I bargained for.

And then there's the drowning, which could have killed me *and* her. I glance at Soph throughout the night when she's not looking. There's no remorse, no guilt. Even if she didn't know Mina was having an asthma attack, she had to have realized Mina was in the canoe. If her absurd hatred for me knows no bounds, there's no telling who she might wrap up next in her sabotage attempts.

I have to stop her.

I leave the bonfire first, then sneak into her room. She should lock her door, but she doesn't. Up until now, she's been on the offense. Not anymore.

So, I wait. In my right hand is the glass shard I saved from my broken window. I almost left it, but then I coughed. Despite the hours that have passed since morning, it still feels like water clogs my lungs, all because of her. I took the shard.

Her door opens, and I press myself against the wall. I have no idea what I'm about to do, only that I can't come back from it.

I slam into her back, pressing my hand to her mouth and making sure to cover her nose. It muffles her scream and gives me enough time to wrap my other arm around her front, bringing the glass shard to her throat.

"I know it's you," I whisper. "But I have the upper hand now. So you're going to do exactly as I say. Got it?"

I feel her fear through the quiver of her body against mine as she nods.

It feels good.

Maybe that's why she's been tormenting me the past week. When you're something to fear, you hold power. It's not quite serotonin, but more sinister. More addicting, too.

I could get used to this.

"You tried to drown me in the water earlier. Yes or no?" I ask her.

She tries to jerk out of my hold, but I'm bigger than her and keep the glass against her throat.

When she doesn't reply, I press the edge into her skin. "Lying isn't going to save you. I see my nail marks on your neck. I just want you to admit it. Yes or no?" I repeat.

She nods, trying to speak against my hand, but I'm not finished yet.

"And you put the spider in my bed and stole my supplies?"

She hesitates, then nods.

"What about messing with clues for trial two?"

Another nod.

"And stealing the map piece for trial one?"

A shake this time. Three yeses, one no.

Pain radiates through my hand. She *bit* me. I release her mouth but keep the shard to her throat.

"You can't kill me," she rasps, wise enough to keep her voice low. I don't think killing her is part of my plan, because that wouldn't really solve anything. Not to mention it would definitely ruin my future forever. But if that's what she thinks, I'm not going to be the one to correct her. "I know something you don't about Hayes."

"Like what?" I ask. I knew he was keeping something from me. This could be it.

"Why don't you remove whatever's on my throat and I'll tell you."

"And risk you screaming for help? I don't think so."

"And risk *you* stabbing that thing into my stomach? Yeah, I'll keep my mouth shut, thanks."

Even scared, she's a sassy brat. I loosen my hold on her but keep the shard held high, as a threat. She glances at it as she faces me.

"Looks familiar, right?" I ask. "As the person who broke my window with a brick, you should have known I would use it to my advantage."

Her dark eyes betray bewilderment. "I didn't break your window."

"Right." I don't believe her one bit. "Just like you didn't shove my head underwater in the lake."

"I had no choice, okay?" she snaps. "What do you want me to say? Sorry? Besides, you got me back. It's going to take so much makeup to cover these. I bet they'll scar." She brushes her glossy hair over her shoulder to reveal the red scratches.

"Oh, I'm so sorry that when I was terrified I was going to end up at the bottom of the lake *forever*, I didn't think about how my last-ditch effort to save my life might mess up your perfect skin," I snark. "You could have killed me. And Mina."

"Don't be so dramatic. I was just trying to scare you. I had no choice."

I can't help it; I laugh. "No choice? You really expect me to believe someone's been putting you up to all this?"

"Someone has." She warily glances at the shard. Seeming to decide I'm not going to use it right at this second, she goes to her backpack, digging around. From the very bottom, she pulls a folded-up piece of paper. When she holds it up for me to see, the unmistakable typewriter font reads:

I have another task for you to protect your secret since
you failed the last time. Don't fail again. Make Chloe terrified.

"Who gave you this?" I ask, scanning it for anything that might tell, but the paper is blank aside from the words, and looks like the same parchment from the typewriter in Diana's room.

"I don't know," she admits. "It was slid under my door at some point between going to bed and waking up for the trial."

"And what about trial two? That's what they're talking about, right? I outsmarted you."

Her face sours. "Yeah. That one wasn't as harsh. They told me to trick you."

I don't know if I should believe her or not. Soph likes messing with people, and I've never been an exception. But I can't imagine she'd go through the trouble of planting a fake note to herself on the off chance I'd catch her. Although, if she really knew who she was messing with, she should have known I would.

"What's your secret?" I ask.

She chews on the inside of her cheek, glancing out the window. Since I block the door, maybe she's gauging if she'd be able to open it and slip onto the ledge before I get her. She doesn't know I'm afraid of heights and wouldn't follow her out anyway.

"My mom," she finally says, taking me off guard; I didn't think she'd tell me. "I did something I shouldn't have to boost her campaign. Hacked a confidential system. It would come back bad on me but worse on her."

"So you hurt me to try to protect your mom?"

Soph meets my eyes with a ferocity that makes me step back. "And I'd do it again, and again, and again. I'd do anything for my mom. I know you think I'm just like Dodge and Lainey and Malcolm, but I'm not. My abuela came to the States as a teenager with nothing. She had to build her own way, and so did my mom. I'm not going to let some faceless bitch take away every-thing we've worked for because I made a mistake."

"What about Dodge?" I ask. "If you're not the only one work-ing for this person, is he, too?"

"I don't know," Soph says, but something's off about her tone. "I haven't told him about it, and he hasn't told me. We kind of . . . broke up before the trials. For good."

For good is debatable with the two of them, but it's news to me nonetheless. "Does he know your mom's secret?"

She swallows, then nods.

"Would he ever use that against you?"

She meets my gaze with bitterness. "Don't ask stupid questions."

"Who else knows?"

Her eyelids flutter shut. "Keana."

I blink, not expecting that. Keana was already topping my list. Now, she's highlighted.

"Anyone else?"

Soph groans. "I don't know, okay? If I did, we wouldn't be here right now."

"I'm just trying to figure out who might know your secret and mine."

My mistake is immediate in the way Soph's face lights up. "You have a secret, too? I knew it made no sense why you hadn't told anyone yet about what's happening to you. What's yours?"

"Like I'm going to tell you," I snap.

She opens her mouth to protest, but I raise the shard and talk over her. "You said you knew something I don't about Hayes. What is it?"

She smirks. "I'll tell you if you tell me your secret. I told you mine."

"You probably shouldn't have," I say even though I'm not going to do anything with it. I just want to keep her afraid. "I'll find out Hayes's secret myself."

"Good luck with that."

I finally lower the shard, walking to the door. I got as much as I'm going to get tonight. Peering into the hall to make sure it's empty, I'm one step out when I turn back to face her.

"By the way," I say. "If you do anything else to me, or Mina, or anyone around me during the rest of the time we're in the forest, those scars won't be the only ones from me."

Soph's sharp intake of breath echoes in my ear as I close her door behind me. I should go back to my room, but I don't. Instead, I pass Hayes's door and stop at Keana's.

There's no answer when I knock, but the door is locked. Glancing at the empty hallway, I pull my bobby pin from my hair and make quick work of it, letting myself in and using my phone flashlight. The empty room greets me, the space so Keana-fied that my chest squeezes. Her various skin-care bottles are strewn across the dresser along with spare hot-pink scrunchies. The bed is unmade—Keana would rather die than make a bed every morning—but tucked into the corner is her ratty baby blanket that she sleeps with every night.

On the nightstand is a Polaroid that makes my throat close. It's of her and Emmy, and must be recent because Emmy has bangs, which she got only a few months ago. They're in our room, but it's just of the two of them cheesing. They took it without me.

I still have the shard of glass, but carefully tuck it into my hoodie pouch. All I want is a conversation. If Keana is behind anything that's happened to me, maybe like Soph, she's being put up to it.

I cling to that hope as minutes tick by, turning into hours. Sitting on her bed with my back against the wall, I listen as people come in. First Challengers, then Champions. At one point, I hear the door to Hayes's room open, then close. He paces on the other side of the wall. His door opens again, and moments drag out before his footsteps reenter his room and the door closes for a final time.

I'm drifting off when I jerk awake, the glow of my watch proving it's after one. Keana should have come in by now. Another hour passes before I finally go back to my room, unable to keep my eyes open and not wanting her to catch me with my guard down. I have no way to lock her door again, so she'll know someone was there.

My eyelids are heavy and sleep tugs me under, but still I listen for her footsteps to creak down the hall.

She never comes.

28

"Eat some breakfast." Aura passes us granola bars as we shuffle downstairs the next morning. "You've got a long walk ahead of you."

Jarod woke us up for trial six even though it should be a rest day. I'm not sure if it's on purpose to throw us all off or because the Champions are trying to get us home sooner.

"Where are we going?" I ask, taking one.

She's back to her quiet, reluctant self. "East."

I unwrap my bar, taking a bite. East is the greenhouse, more forest, then a part of the stream we haven't visited yet on the outskirts of the grounds. Maybe after trial five's fiasco, they're keeping today easy for us.

I'm so, *so* wrong.

After hours of walking, to the point where the map is useless because we're off it, we come to a stop at a clearing. The hike became noticeably downhill once we crossed the stream on a wooden footbridge a few miles back. A plus for my hammies in the moment, but I'm already dreading the elevated walk back.

Mina white-knuckles her inhaler, deep-purple eye bags marring her features. I wanted to check on her last night, but she holed herself up in her room. And I guess I was a little busy threatening Soph and waiting out Keana, who emerged from her room this morning as if she'd been there the entire night when I know she wasn't.

Soph hasn't so much as glanced at me today, always keeping a few bodies between us. But she doesn't stay close to Dodge, either. Just like I'm trying to stay outside of speaking distance to Hayes.

Soph's words about him rang through my muddled dreams. *"I know something you don't about Hayes."* I'm itching to find out what, but I can't give her the satisfaction of asking.

"Welcome to trial six," Jarod announces. "A test of agility."

"As you've probably guessed, we're miles from the estate," Trevor explains. "Your sole mission is to get back. The last one who passes through the gates gets eliminated. You could return the way we just came. That's how we'll be getting back. But that will take hours of walking. In a race against each other, time is of the essence."

"So you might want to put your agility to the test." Jarod rubs his hands together, a mischievous spark in his eyes. "It's time to climb."

There's no way I heard him right. *"Climb?"*

"The shortcut back is climbing the cliffs. Follow the path we've been on and you'll reach the bottom of them. Some of my pro climbing buddies rigged up seven secure ropes. Here are your harnesses." Jarod unzips his backpack, pulling out multicolored harnesses and passing them out. He hands me the blue one, my favorite color; it's a small comfort as I take it numbly. "I'll show you how to put these on, and then all you'll have to do is clip into the rope with the same color. If you lose your grip on the cliffs, stay calm. Swing a bit and then get your holding again. It's an easy climb that isn't as steep as it looks. I could do it in my sleep."

If that's meant to reassure me, it doesn't. The harness feels flimsy, like it could never support my body. What's the weight max on these things? I'm probably heavier than I look.

"Sick," Dodge says. "That's all we have to do?"

Trevor nods. "Once you crest the top of the cliffs, stay on the path. You'll eventually hear the stream again. Cross it and keep it to your right. It will lead you all the way to the lake, so pay attention to your maps to make sure you don't overshoot the path that will take you back to the estate. Carly and Aura will be waiting there for you if we're not back yet."

Jarod does a too-quick tutorial of how to wear the harness and clip it into the rope, but I feel like I'm at the back of an airplane watching the flight attendant run through the safety measures should the engines fail. I'm watching, I'm trying to remember every little detail, but I know as soon as catastrophe strikes, I'm doomed.

I don't realize we're told to start until everyone's running. My legs move, but I'm already taking up the rear. As I jog down the path, lungs burning, I try to think of what Cece would tell me. If I focus on her, maybe I can do this. I *have* to do this.

She'd tell me I should avoid all thoughts of plummeting to my death. That's what she told me at her thirteenth birthday party at a rock-climbing gym, right before the diagnosis hit and everything went to shit. "*If you think too hard about failing, then you probably will*," she said, putting her waist-length brown hair into a braid. It's lighter in color than mine and less curly. Consequently, less frizzy, which I was always jealous of. Since she shaved it, it's been growing back in spirally tufts. *"And we both know you're not the failing type."*

"No, I'm not," I huff to myself. Of all I've been through, I can't let this be the thing that stands between me and winning.

Today is warmer than any other so far. It's like now that it's June, Mother Nature cranked the defrosters to max. By the time I see the cliffs poking through the trees, I'm drenched in sweat and the ground turns from dirt to rock.

I gawk at the cliffs. Everyone is already hooked in and at least halfway up. Woolf and Dodge are still in their own race from last night. They scramble at the top, pulling themselves over the ledge and racing to unclip. Keana's in third, Soph and Hayes are even for fourth, and Mina is exactly halfway.

Mina clings to the rockface, resting her forehead against it to take a breather. While she's not making the horrible wheezing sounds from the lake, she still doesn't look good. But no more looking out for her today. At this rate, she's the only one I can beat. I just need to catch up.

I stuff my terror down as deep as it goes and grab on to my rope, tightening my harness until it cuts into me. I hook the rope onto the loop in the front like Jarod showed us, tugging on it to confirm it's secure. Wiping my sweaty hands on my shorts, I find my first handholds and pull myself up.

My progress is painstaking. Finding handholds is a chore, and getting the right divots for my feet is even worse. I'm barely ten feet off the ground, but even falling from this height would surely bruise, if not break something.

"You have a rope," I remind myself when a bout of anxious nausea hits so hard that black dots dance across my vision. "And soon, you're going to have a lot of money."

Soph snorts from above me. "I wouldn't be so cocky," she says. "You're still in last."

"Not for long," I grit out, climbing higher. The need to show her up—show them *all* up—soars through me. Sweat drips down my forehead and into my eyes, my palms slick with it. It makes holding on even more precarious. Now I get why rock climbers are always carrying around chalk. I never expected rough rock to get so slippery.

The easiest way for me to keep moving quickly is to lift my leg as high as I can, find a good placement for my foot, and push up. It raises me at least a couple of feet every time, and as long as I don't look down, I can keep a steady rhythm. But my arms ache, especially after all the rowing. Letting go for a second to let them rest while I hang is tempting, but I have to push through.

Keana and Mina are already gone, making my hopes of at least beating Mina plummet. Only Soph and Hayes remain, but both are nearly to the top while I'm just passing halfway.

I'm going to lose, and there's nothing I can do about it.

"Hey, Gatti! Look who has the upper hand now!" Soph brags, hauling herself over the ledge.

"Congrats," I yell back. "Your mom would be so proud!"

I hoped bringing her mom up would deflate her, but it just goads her on.

"You can't do anything to me now. You're going to lose this trial, and go home, and . . ."

Her voice dips off. I pull myself a little higher. "You can't leave me on a cliffhanger."

She makes a choked sound. Jeez, the joke was bad, but I'm the one about to lose. I squint past the sun's glare to see her staring somewhere between me and the top, which is still another ten feet away. The only one between us is Hayes.

"Don't" is all he says to Soph. He's a fast climber and should have finished by now.

"What's happening?" I ask, suddenly remembering where I am, the burn of my muscles, the daunting expanse between the ground and me.

Soph's mouth is open in a small *o*, eyes wide in shock. "Your rope," is all she says.

"Don't," Hayes repeats, more forceful this time.

"What about my rope?" I ask, trying to maneuver away from the sun to get a good look. And then I see it.

It's frayed. Badly. Right where it's pulled taut against the sharp edge of the cliff.

My breath comes quick, harsh, shallow, *desperate*. "Wait," I plead as she backs up.

I don't know what I expect her to do.

"I didn't do this." She shakes her head. "I swear I didn't do this. I didn't cut your rope. I promise."

And then she runs. Leaving Hayes and me, and a rope about to snap.

29

"You have to stay calm."

I can barely hear Hayes over the roar of blood in my ears. My head swims, my hands cramp, my legs quiver. The several feet separating me from safety might as well be a mountain. I'm never going to make it.

"Chloe, you have to keep climbing. You were doing fine."

"I'm going to die."

The words burst out of me with an avalanche of intrusive visions of my body splattering on the ground. "I'm going to fall and get really hurt. I'm going to break something. My neck, my spine, my legs. I'm going to *die*."

He flinches, and there's a buried piece of me that knows how triggering my words are. But I can't stop them. The thoughts hit me, fear wrapping around my throat until I can't breathe. "I'm losing my grip. I can't do it."

I squeeze my eyes closed, trying to take a deep breath, trying to hold on. Wishing for anger to come, anything that could ignite some sense into me. But nothing is there aside from the panic. I've had panic attacks before. Over grades, and Cece being sick, and wondering if anything I do will ever be good enough to make me matter. But I can't sort through my jumbled brain to remember how to get through them. I'm frozen.

"You're going to listen to everything I'm about to say, okay?" Hayes asks. His voice is closer now, low and even and *Hayes*. He climbed down to me.

"It's hard to breathe," I cry, my breath trapped inside my chest.

"You can do it," Hayes reassures me. "You're not going to fall. I won't let you. But you need to do exactly as I say. Got it, Clover?"

My eyes snap open, hooking on his green irises. He called me Clover. He hasn't called me that in months. I never thought I'd hear the nickname from his mouth again.

From the conflicted expression on his face, he knows. "You with me?" he asks.

I force a shaky nod, clinging to the rock.

"First, you need to get your mind away. Remember where we went after you found out Cece was sick? Where did we go?"

He's testing me. Tests, I can do. "The auditorium."

"And what did we do?"

I force the blackness edging my mind back to the corners. "We sat on the piano bench in the band pit, and you played for me. For hours."

"And what did I play?"

"Taylor Swift." Something between a laugh and a sob escapes. "I begged you to play me her songs for months, but that day you finally caved."

"What albums?"

I got the news from Mom after breakfast, and we skipped all

our classes that day. "*Evermore. Red. Midnights.*"

In my ear, the songs still play. All instrumentals, just his fingers on the keys. His hands must have ached by the end of the day, but he didn't complain. He looked up the music on his phone, or played some by ear since he was good at that. Then, he made me guess the songs just based on chords and melody. It was a game. A test. Just like this one.

"Right," he says. "Hold on to that. Now lift your hand and grab here."

I raise my head to see where he points, a little over my right shoulder where the rock juts out. I try to keep the phantom music in one ear, his steady instructions in the other. When I have a firm grip, he nods.

"Good. Now with your left, reach up to that outcropping on your other side."

I grab it, pulling myself up.

"You're doing great. See that indent above your nose? Hold on there and push yourself up."

I do, and I keep following his instructions little by little until the only place left to go is over the ledge. Up close, I can see the frayed threads of the rope sticking out like the frizz of my hair. I shut my eyes, not wanting to plummet into panic again.

"Hold on," Hayes says, climbing over the top. He reaches a hand down for me to grab.

"What if I pull you over the edge?" I ask.

"Is that a threat or a concern?" he teases, smiling down at me. A real Hayes smile, with one dimple popping. His blond head of unusually mussed hair is highlighted by the sun behind him, creating a halo effect. When he leans lower so his hand is within reach, I grab it.

"More concern, with room for threat," I tell him. He pulls me up, and the force of our conjoined efforts has me tumbling into him, knocking him over. We both go down, rolling over each other on the ground until we come to a stop several yards from the edge, limbs tangled and me on top.

I know I should get off him, but for this moment, with his heartbeat beneath my ear and my own still thrumming inside my chest, I finally feel safe. The realization cracks me open with relief. Tears spring to my eyes.

"You're okay," Hayes murmurs, running his hand over my back while I shake against his chest. "You're okay. I knew you could do it."

I lift my head to meet his reassuring gaze. The majority of my short hair fell out of my stubby ponytail and hangs in my eyes.

"Thanks to you," I whisper. With my head raised, our lips are close. If I leaned forward a little bit, they might brush. Even though we're sweaty and gross and I shake from adrenaline, I want them to. I could have just died without ever kissing Hayes again. That feels illegal.

"I like your hair." He says it like a secret, twirling a stray piece around his finger before tucking it behind my ear.

"Really? I thought you'd prefer it long."

"I liked it long, too," he agrees. "But this is so . . . you."

Me. "It is." I try to pull away, but his hand on my back keeps me close.

"I'm sorry I wasn't there," he chokes out.

I frown. "You were. You saved—"

"Not now," he interrupts. "Trial five. Whatever happened that made you sick on the shore. I'm sorry I didn't stay by your side for that trial. I should have."

"I ended the truce," I remind him.

"I don't care," he counters. His knuckles brush my cheek, and I lean into his touch. "And you can't just end a truce cold turkey. I get a say, too."

"I don't remember that in the truce rule book," I deny him, but our lips are too close to be denying him anything. Paired with the fact I'm lying on top of him, it's a dangerous position to be in. The way he's looking at me has my breath sticking in my lungs. His lips are *right there.*

"Maybe we should stop playing by the rules," he suggests.

People like us don't ever stop playing by the rules. But maybe we aren't the same people we once were. Maybe our time in the forest has stripped us down to our wildest selves. Maybe nothing matters, because at the end of the day, one of us will be going home. And deep down, I know it should be me.

Maybe one kiss can't hurt. As a goodbye.

I lean down to press our lips together, but a patch of red catches my eye. Jerking back, I take in the stain blooming across his white shirt. "You're bleeding!"

"I am?"

I scurry off him as he sits up. Tilting his body so he faces the sun, I inspect the tear in his shirt on his right shoulder and the blood soaking through.

"I don't know what happened," he says, wincing as he moves his arm to look.

"The branch got you," I assume, picking up a broken branch lying on the ground. The end of the wooden stick is jagged and sharp, stained red.

"Must have while we were rolling."

Whatever moment we had fizzles. He blinks as if waking up from a dream. I stand, and now it's my turn to pull him up. "We should clean it."

"We can when we get back."

"You saw the frayed rope," I realize as we unclip ourselves, leaving our harnesses with the ropes. "You waited for me."

"I didn't see it until you were already halfway up. But I thought if I didn't say anything, you'd make it all the way without knowing. Soph ruined that."

We start walking down the path. "I'm sure she wishes it took me out since her attempt at drowning me didn't do much."

"Her attempt at *what*?"

As we walk back to the estate, I tell him everything about the lake trial and last night when I threatened Soph. It's a good distraction to get the last of my panic out, along with whatever weirdness had me almost kissing him. Hayes agrees that Keana and Dodge are my biggest suspects, although he's more doubtful of Keana than I am.

"She doesn't have a real motive to hurt you, does she?" he asks.

Of course she does. I lied about cheating, which impacted her, too.

Hayes picks up on my silence. "What haven't you told me?"

"What haven't you told me?" I fire back, thinking of what Soph said last night. *I know something you don't about Hayes.*

He sighs. "It's not important."

I want to push him on it, but then he'd push me back, and I can't admit the truth. It's not even because I don't want him to know I cheated. I'm so past caring about that at this point.

What I don't want him to know is how badly I needed him. That I could keep up pretenses only by doing something awful that's currently haunting me.

We make it to the stream. The chilly, hip-high water actually feels good as we wade through it to cross to the other side. But as soon as we're out, an unbearable sadness strikes.

I'll see Hayes at graduation, but by then, the truce will be over for real. I have no idea where we'll stand with each other, or what will happen in the aftermath of everything we've discovered about Hunter's death and my antagonist.

"We should really take care of your injury," I decide. I don't wait for him to agree with me, just hope he follows as I meander back to the stream and find a good spot with plenty of sunlight.

"It's really okay," he assures me. "I'm not bleeding out or anything."

Regardless, he lets me plop him onto a stump by the embankment. "What's the rush?" I ask. "We're the last two. No difference between us finishing now or an hour from now."

If he can read between the lines that I'm trying to stretch our time together, he doesn't say so. He lets me inspect his shoulder and winces as I peel the torn edges of his shirt away from the wound. "This is really dirty," I comment. "You should probably take it off."

He gives me a wry look.

"For medical purposes only, of course," I defend. "Don't

worry, I'm not that desperate to take your shirt off."

"I mean, I can't blame you. I have been working out."

I can't help but smile, helping him peel off the sweat-soaked cotton. The smile slips as I try not to look anywhere but the gash on his shoulder. I crouch to get a better view.

"How's it look, Doc?" he asks.

"Kind of terrible."

He flinches as I pluck out a splinter.

"How's it feel?"

"Kind of terrible," he grumbles.

"I'm going to clean it."

His shirt is so dirty that using it would be a moot point, so I discard it on the grass beside us. Before I can think too hard, I pull mine off, leaving me in my sports bra. It's full coverage and longline, but I can't help but feel like I'm undressing for him.

I wet it in the stream, then carefully dab it around the gash, wiping as much of the blood away as I can. "It's already stopped bleeding," I tell him. "So you probably won't die from blood loss."

"I was really worried for a second there," he says, sarcastic as ever. He sucks air between his teeth as I get close to the actual wound.

"Sorry," I say. "I think that's as clean as I can get it. Maybe I should wrap it?"

"Whatever you think is best." His voice sounds weird and pinched suddenly. I glance up at him, but he's already looking at me. Lower than my eyes. My chest.

I look down to see my chain with the ring he gave me in full view. With all the climbing and tumbling, it must have fallen out of where I tucked it inside my sports bra.

He reaches for it, running his thumb over the silver clover on the face of the ring. "You still wear it."

"I do." I pull back so it falls out of his hands, but there's no use tucking it back in.

He stares at his hand like it's still there. "Why?"

Because it makes me feel safe. Because I don't want to forget. Because I miss you.

I clear my throat. "It's a nice ring."

He nods, leaning back so we aren't as close. I wring my shirt out again in the water until the blood is gone, then carefully wrap it around his shoulder. His eyes flutter shut, blond lashes resting on the tops of his cheeks. This close to him, I can make out the faint dusting of freckles across his nose. He hates them, but I don't.

"It's just . . ." His eyes are still closed, but he makes a pained expression when I tighten the makeshift bandage. "I didn't expect you to still wear it. I thought you threw it out."

"Never," I say, although I realize never is like forever—infinite. But it's time I admit it to myself. If I couldn't throw it out the first thirty times I've tried, I don't think I ever will.

I finish tying the bandage and go to stand, but he stops me. His palms are warm on my arms, but not nearly as hot as the intensity of his gaze. "I have a proposition."

My breath catches. "You know I can't say no to that."

He almost smiles. "I'm going to ask you a question, and you're going to tell me the truth."

"What's in it for me?"

"I'm going to tell you the truth back."

This is a dangerous game to play. I nod at him. "Go."

"Did we only break up because of the Wilde Trials?"

It's not the question I expect, though I don't know what is. "No."

"No," he agrees. "Why else?"

I can't crouch any longer, so I move next to him on the stump. This way, at least I don't need to look at him. "School. I got accepted to Brown, and I thought"—I feel so ridiculous saying it out loud—"I thought you were going to go to Juilliard so we could stay on the same coast. And then all of a sudden, you said you applied to Stanford, and then you got in, and then apparently wanted to go, and I just felt like it'd be too hard being that far away from each other."

He frowns. "You didn't get my letter, then?"

"What letter?"

He shakes his head. "It doesn't matter now. Is that all?"

He owes me an answer, but the rest spills out. "I felt like I was losing you."

It's a whisper caught in the breeze, but he hears it, bristling. "How so?"

"All of it," I tell him. The climbing incident has left me raw, my walls cracked and crumbling. "Getting into Stanford was only the start. Suddenly, it seemed like all you cared about was law school and doing what your parents wanted you to. That day in the auditorium when you played piano for me was one of the last times I heard you play. You stopped. And you stopped talking to me, too. I mean, sure, we talked, but it wasn't like before. I was watching from the sidelines while you pulled away from me, losing more of yourself to fill the gap Hunter left to make your parents happy. Toward the end, it felt like I was in love with a ghost. Like the real you wasn't even there anymore."

I suck in a breath, and so does he. "And then what you said in the dining hall about my scholarship." My throat tightens. "You would have never said that to me a year ago. And that's when I knew I really lost you. So it made *me* lose it. And then everyone thought I was a crazy bitch for it, and the unfairness of it all made me hate you. Plus, you wouldn't even talk to me after. I felt like I meant nothing to you."

"That's not true," he says fiercely. "You meant *everything* to me. You—"

He cuts himself off.

"I what?" I ask, searching his face for answers.

"You insisting on applying for the Wilde Trials made me feel like *I* was nothing to you. I was so scared you'd end up like Hunter. And I couldn't lose another person I loved, and it didn't feel fair that you didn't see how terrifying that was for me."

"Yeah, well, I see it now. And you were right." My voice quiets as the severity of today hits me. "If you weren't there, I don't know what would have happened. I would have died."

"They'll have to try harder next time."

A laugh escapes, but it bleeds dry. "I think this is it for me. I'm going to get eliminated."

"Maybe I will," he says. "I got what I came here for. I know what happened to Hunter, and I can figure out a way to make sure the truth gets into the hands of the people who can spread it. You could still win."

"After today, I'm not sure I want to anymore," I admit. "I want to win for Cece, but more than anything, I want to go *home* to Cece. I didn't think the two were mutually exclusive, but now I'm not so sure."

Even as I say it, I know that's not the whole truth. He peers at me, knowing me well enough to make the rest dump out.

"I wanted to prove I could do it," I add quietly. "Win the Wilde Trials and be a Champion. I wanted to show my parents sending me to the academy was worth it and be remembered."

Hayes stands, grabbing his shirt from the ground and holding his hand out to help me up. When I rise, we're face-to-face, our mouths dangerously close again.

"For the record, Clover, I think you're impossible to forget. Champion or not."

"Maybe you're biased," I say to cover the way my cheeks heat.

"Maybe I am," he agrees.

We walk back to the estate together, conversation flowing as easily as it used to. When we get to the gates, he turns to me. "You go first. You can still win."

My heart aches at the offer. A week ago, I would have taken him up on it. Now, I can't bring my legs to push me forward without him.

"We should walk through at the same time," I say. "Maybe it will force them to let us both stay. Or at the very least, leave it up to them to choose."

He raises a brow. "Like a proposition?"

I nod. "Like a proposition."

We take a deep breath and, together, enter the estate.

30

Trevor rises from his log, mouth set in a grim line that the flickering flames from the bonfire accentuates. When Hayes and I strode through the gates together, it did throw the Champions. But not enough to let us both stay.

"*We can't have ties*," Carly said, sounding apologetic for once.

"*Then choose*," I bit back, tired of playing nice.

"*We'll discuss it*," Aura intervened. She gave Hayes and I a once-over, taking in our filthy, sweat-soaked clothes. "*Why don't you guys get cleaned up before dinner.*"

So we did, breaking apart in the hall to shower and change. A numbness has fallen over me since. Like my brain already knows the outcome and is protecting my heart from the truth.

"Before announcing the final Challenger to leave us, I want you to know that you've all done amazing," Trevor commends, meeting our eyes. "The academy is proud of you. *We're* proud of you."

I brace myself, forcing my breaths to stay even. I can cry on the ride out of the forest. Think about how close I got and how I'll break the news to Cece. I'll never tell her what I went through, but I won't need to. She'd never be mad at me for losing. I can only expect that anger from myself.

"I'm sorry to say," Trevor somberly starts. "The person going home is—"

"I forfeit."

Everyone's eyes snap to Soph. She stands, expression sure.

"I'm sorry." Trevor blinks. "What?"

"I forfeit," Soph repeats.

Dodge's mouth is wide open in shock. He tries to say something, but she talks over him. "I don't want to continue competing. You'll still have your six Challengers to finish out the final trial. You don't need me."

She's not asking for permission. If I had to admire anything about Soph, it's her resolve.

"You can forfeit." Aura stands.

Carly and Jarod swap surprised looks. "Let's get your things."

The two of them leave. Trevor looks up from the fire, clearing his throat. He glances at me, and it's all the confirmation I need that Soph just saved me from getting eliminated.

But *why*?

My eyes slide away from Trevor and land on Keana. The look on her face is full of anger and spite, eyes like fire. It's the most emotive she's been since we got here.

It's the face of somebody who was sure they were rid of me.

"I'm going to bed," I announce, jumping to my feet. Hayes's eyes follow me. Relief radiates from him that we both are still in it. But suddenly, I'm not very relieved at all.

I need to talk to Soph.

Thunder rumbles as I hurry inside, a storm brewing. I pass

Aura in the foyer and take the old stairs two at a time before she can say anything to me. When I get to the third floor, Soph's already walking out of her room, things in hand. She planned this and packed before the bonfire. Upon seeing me, she stops.

"Why?" is all I say, breathing hard.

"Not for you," she replies, meeting me in the middle of the hallway. "For my mom. Because sometimes doing the best thing is doing nothing at all."

"Thank you," I whisper. She swallows, pushing past me. When she gets to the top of the stairs, she looks back.

"After I saw your frayed rope, I realized how psycho this mystery person is," she says. "I don't want any part of it anymore. The only thing worse than my mom's secrets getting out is if her daughter is roped into a murder investigation."

I huff out a laugh. "It'd be quite the PR scandal."

"Tell me about it."

I expect her to leave, but she's rooted to the step, her features twisting with an internal debate. Finally, her eyes meet mine. "There's one more thing."

"What?" I ask, placing my palms on the railing and looking down at her.

"You want to know Hayes's secret?"

I blink but nod. Between that and the mysterious letter he mentioned earlier, I can't help wondering if they're the same or connected somehow. "Yes."

She grins. "He cheated. And I helped him."

"How? When?"

"Think about it," she says. "If you were a school that was

finally salvaging your reputation after a student died in the forest in a legendary competition, would you really want that student's younger brother participating in the same thing that killed him?"

"No," I say, realization dawning. "Hayes wasn't actually chosen to compete."

"Oh, he was," Soph says. "Because he chose himself. I hacked into the submission system for him, and he handpicked everyone here and discarded all the other applicants. Puppeteered the whole thing. The academy needed twelve students. Tradition, and all that. So he made sure to give them exactly that. And because applicant numbers have been low since Hunter's death, nobody questioned it. They were probably grateful they even had twelve."

"I don't believe you," I say. "If Hayes chose the Challengers, I wouldn't be here."

She tilts her head. "Funny. You were the first one he picked."

I don't know what to say. Did he want me because he planned to make my life horrible? Is he my Challenger? Is this some elaborate plan to get back at me? But after everything we've been through today—everything we've been through in general—I know in my heart it's not him.

"Why tell me this now?" I ask.

She bites her lip, dark eyes reflecting remorse. "Because I'm sorry."

Before I can reply, she rushes down the stairs. The front door opens and closes seconds later, then the hum of the bus waiting by the gates fades. I'm frozen, a million thoughts running through my head. Outshining all of them is:

I made it to the last trial. I can win.

The truth both thrills me and makes my pit of anxiety crack open within. My fingers reach for my ring beneath my shirt, needing the comfort of the clover.

But nothing's there.

I tug my top away from my body, looking down to confirm the chain and ring are gone. But I was wearing the chain all day. Hayes even saw it. I never took it off—

Except to shower.

I rush into my new room. The corner of my dresser where I placed it is empty. I'm sure I left it there, meaning to put it back on before dinner, but I was rushing so I forgot. I never forget. If it was here after my shower, I would have seen it and put it on.

Panic claws up my throat. Of all the times I've tried to throw it away, I can't lose it now. I open drawers and shake out my backpack on the off chance I tucked it away. I get on my hands and knees, searching under the bed or dresser in case somehow it fell.

Despite my frantic hunt, I know none of those things happened. Someone snuck in and stole it. And I know who.

There is no ring under my bed, but there is a pink scrunchie.

A scrunchie I've seen in my room at the academy every day for the past two years. A scrunchie I've wound around hair before, laughing while watching rom-coms. A scrunchie I used to put my elbow-length curls into pigtails before chopping them off.

My brain can't catch up with my feet as I storm out of my room and throw open the door to Keana's room. It's not locked, but it is empty. I want to trash it, to rip it apart in search of my ring and make her feel as violated as she's made me. Because no matter how much I've tried to deny it, the glaring truth is she's the only one who knows Soph's secret and somehow mine, along with my crippling fear of heights. And she's the only one with a vendetta against us both.

Movement outside her window catches my eye. Someone runs toward the gates. A flash of pink stands out in the darkness. A scrunchie. The same one I hold in my hand.

I sprint down the stairs and out the front door. For once in my life, I don't have a plan. All I know is it's time to finish this.

31

In the forest, I search the shadows in the trees. I'm far enough away that anyone at the fire won't hear us. I don't know if that's a good or bad thing.

Sick of playing defense, I take the offensive position.

"I know you're out here!" I yell. "Why don't you face me for once?!"

Nothing. Just me and the wind and a perfectly timed crack of thunder that makes me jump out of my skin. I hope she didn't see it.

"I just want to talk," I say. "Come *on*, Keana! Stop running from me!"

Not even a rustle. If I want to lure her out, I need to hit her where it hurts. "For the record? Phlip was right. It should have been him here."

With the wind swaying the branches, the shadows shift and shiver, looking as human as me. It's the perfect camouflage. She could be anywhere.

Fear creeps in with a bout of clarity. Maybe coming out here alone was a bad idea. She did try to kill me today with the frayed-rope stunt. I should at least tell Hayes and Woolf so someone knows where I am.

I turn back toward the estate and *duck*. A branch whips my way, entirely too fast to be propelled by the breeze. I narrowly avoid it, stumbling back before finding my footing.

"Stay away," Keana threatens. She brandishes the branch like a sword, swinging it in an arc that forces me backward until my spine hits a trunk.

"Wait," I say, throwing my hands up. "I just want to talk."

"The time for talking is over," she snarls, but tears fill her eyes. "How could you?"

She swings again, and with the trunk behind me, I have nowhere to go. I sidestep, but the branch collides with my ribs. My breath shoots out at the burst of pain and I fall to my knees.

"I'm sorry," I gasp, searching the ground for an adequate opposing branch. All I grasp are sticks and leaves. I shouldn't have lied to her about cheating, but I never thought it'd warrant a reaction like this. Between her brother pushing her to the edge and me, she finally snapped.

"I know I shouldn't have done it," I cry, holding my side. "I've regretted it ever since, but you don't understand—"

"Bullshit." She swings again, but I roll out of the way, scrambling to my feet. "You're a fucking liar. You're manipulative, and selfish, and a *cheater*. But I'm not letting you get away with it anymore."

Her words are like left hooks beating me down, but I need to avoid the thing that will *actually* beat me down. Another swing, another dodge. We're parrying around the trees, only bits of moonlight breaking through the clouds highlighting her furious features.

"I might be a cheater," I admit, the words freeing when finally spoken aloud as I evade another swing, "but you don't consider this cheating? Trying to take me out with a tree?"

"As if you haven't been doing worse!" A clap of thunder reverberates. "The changed clues? The threatening messages? The *snakes*? I didn't want to think it was you at first, but you're the only one here who knows I'm terrified of them!"

I blink at her. "What?"

"And then—" She ignores me and swings again.

The edge catches my arm, my confusion delaying my evasion. I yelp at the pain, glancing down to see a scratch well with blood. "As if all that isn't terrible enough, you have to drag Emmy into it? Ever since I caught you cheating, I knew you'd go to any lengths to be on top. But blackmailing me by threatening to out my relationship with Emmy to her strict parents is fucking foul."

"What?"

When she swings this time, I expect it and grab the end of the branch. Her eyes fill with fear as I tug it toward me, ripping it from her hands. I step toward her, and she trips over a root as she stumbles back, falling to the ground.

She stares up at me in terror. Tears drip down her cheeks, streams of silver in the moonlight. I raise the branch higher, and she flinches.

I throw it to the side. Her eyes follow it in confusion before flicking back to me.

"Enough with trying to kill me," I pant. *"What are you talking about?"*

"You know," she fires back.

"I thought I did," I agree. "I came out here because I was sick of *you* messing with *me*. Changing *my* clues and stealing *my* map piece. Throwing a fucking brick through my window threatening to tell everyone I cheated and get me expelled before graduation. Or how about the spider in my bed? Stealing my trial supplies from my room? Siccing Soph on my ass to drown me?" My voice shakes with unmoored emotion. "What about earlier today when you frayed my rope? If Hayes didn't help me get to the top of those cliffs, I could have fallen and *died*."

Her mouth drops open. "I . . . didn't do any of that."

"Liar," I seethe. "You said it yourself. You saw me cheating in the library and you're the only one who knew. You've been blackmailing me with it. And then I come out here to confront you on it and you attack me with a *branch*? I'm pretty sure you broke my rib!"

Her brows knit in confusion. "I knew you cheated because I saw the answer key on your laptop in our room one night when you fell asleep studying it. I asked you about it that day in the dining hall because I was worried. You'd been so off since everything went down with Hayes and cheating wasn't like you. But then you flipped your shit on me and everything just got weirder from there."

Suddenly, standing feels like too much. I plop down onto the ground, keeping a healthy distance between us.

"I'm sorry I lied," I confess. "I was embarrassed and I've never been very good at asking for help. After Hayes and I broke up, staying on top felt like all I had."

"You had *us*. Emmy and me. We wanted to be there for you, but you acted fine."

"I wasn't fine," my voice cracks. "I felt like a third wheel. Like suddenly all you cared about was each other and I was just there."

Keana's eyes soften. "I'm sorry. I promise it's not you, though. I mean, with the cheating and stuff, I guess it kind of was. But before that, it wasn't." She takes a deep breath. "When you were dating Hayes, it left me and Emmy hanging out in our room alone a lot. And, I guess somewhere along the way, around Christmastime, we realized we had feelings for each other. Like, more than friends."

"Oh." Suddenly, certain things click into place. Emmy giving Keana longer hugs. Me walking into the room feeling like I interrupted something. Maybe I was, but not them talking shit about me like I always assumed. The Polaroid on Keana's nightstand flashes in my mind.

"Why didn't—I mean, it's not like you were obligated to tell me. But you could have."

"Emmy wanted to. With her not being out, we've had to keep it on the down-low. But she really wanted to. I was the one who held her back."

"You didn't trust me."

"When you didn't admit to cheating, it felt like you didn't trust *me*. So I didn't want to trust you. Before we left school, I did feel guilty competing against you when I know you're trying to win for Cece. But when I got here"—she gestures around—"and someone started blackmailing me with my secret relationship, I figured it had to be you."

"I would have never done that," I swear, meaning it.

"Deep down, I didn't think you would. But I've been trying to figure out who else might, and you were the only one who I knew was clever enough to get away with it."

I manage a grin. "Sounds like a compliment."

She laughs, wiping the tears from her cheeks. "Don't let it go to your head."

"Is that why you really applied for the trials?" I ask, slotting together the puzzle pieces I could never find. "For Emmy?"

Keana hesitates. "Originally, yes. Emmy doesn't want to date in secret anymore, but she's scared of how her parents will react. Her mom is a Champion, so I figured if I became one, maybe her parents would be more accepting of our relationship. But . . ." She sighs. "The night of the party before we left school, Emmy figured out the truth. She asked me not to come. But when I saw my name on the list of Challengers and not Phlip's, it felt so good. I texted my parents, and they were so happy, they even called me. I guess that's when I realized you were right. This was just another competition between my brother and me. A chance to prove myself so I could finally do something that would make my parents proud again."

"I wanted to prove myself, too," I admit. "I think I was giving you so much shit for it because deep down, even though I am here for Cece, I'm here for me, too."

"I know." Keana gives me a small smile. "And for the record, I never planned to keep all the money if I won. I wanted to give some to you. Until I came to the assumption you were blackmailing me, that is."

My vision blurs with tears. "Really? You would have done that?"

"I still will, if I win. But honestly? I don't even care about winning anymore. I just want to get home to Emmy."

Another rumble of thunder rolls, accompanied by a flash of lightning. I crawl across the ground to sit beside her, wincing at the movement.

"Did I really break your ribs?" she asks, guilt dripping from her voice.

"They're probably just bruised," I say, my side aching as I take a deep breath. "Don't feel too bad. I might have done the same. I was convinced it was you."

"We should go tell someone." She starts to get up but pauses when a branch snaps nearby. We jump to our feet, backs pressed against each other as a truth hits us at the same time. If I'm not her antagonist, and she's not mine, then they're still out there.

The glare of a flashlight forces us to shield our eyes.

"Found her!" Woolf announces. "And Keana?"

"There you are," Hayes says, relief clear in his voice as he emerges from the trees. He frowns, giving us a once over. "What happened?"

Keana and I look at each other, taking in the twigs in her hair and blood dripping from the scratch on my arm.

"We had a misunderstanding," I say. "Good now, though. Right?"

"Right." She huffs out a laugh, and so do I. Hayes and Woolf swap confused looks.

"Girls are so weird," Woolf mutters.

"Keana's not my Challenger," I say. "And I'm not hers. We need to figure out who it is."

"Not here." Hayes glances up as a raindrop plops down, followed by a second and third.

"I know a place," Keana says. She starts walking deeper into the forest. "Follow me."

32

"I've been coming here since the first time someone snuck into my room last week," Keana says as we step into the overgrown greenhouse. Rain still trickles in thanks to the broken and missing glass panels, but it provides enough protection for us to stay mostly dry. Keana lights a few candles, casting the space in a dim glow.

"This is where you slept last night?" I ask.

She nods. "I sneak out here after the fire, then go back inside before the Champions wake up. I thought it was *you* sneaking into my room to plant things."

"Why'd you think that?" Hayes asks before I can admit that last night, it was me. At least the sneaking part.

Keana casts him a wary glance, pulling something out of her pocket. "I found this on the floor of my room."

"My ring!" I gasp at the glint of silver, taking the chain and putting it back around my neck. "It disappeared after my shower today."

She gawks at Hayes and me. "Are you guys back together?"

"No!" we say too quickly.

Hayes aggressively clears his throat.

"We made a truce," I explain, though that doesn't even begin to cover why I still wear the ring. In an attempt to salvage some scrap of dignity, I gesture to Woolf. "He's in on it, too."

Woolf gives me a look as if to say, *Don't drag me into this.*

"Uh-huh," Keana says, completely unconvinced. She looks at Hayes and me. "I knew something weird was up when I saw you two outside one night. I figured the only way you would talk to each other again was if there was something of equal benefit to go after."

"There was." Hayes pulls out his brother's journal, passing it to Keana. "This."

He recounts everything we've discovered since teaming up, and Keana fills in with her side of things. "What I don't get is why you guys were suddenly all over me during trial four?" she asks Hayes and Woolf.

I turn to them. "Yeah, why were you so shady about that? It made me suspect her more."

"I didn't want to tell you the truth because I know you two have been on the outs and didn't want to risk you backing out of the truce," Hayes says to me.

"And the truth is?" Keana prods.

Woolf shrugs. "Making good on our promise to Phlip to look after you."

Her eyes soften in surprise. "He asked that of you?"

Hayes nods. "We swore we would. But we obviously didn't do a very good job."

"Horrible job," she agrees, but she looks away, a film of tears shining in her eyes.

I redirect the conversation. "So, if it's not us who are doing these attacks, that only leaves two people. Mina and Dodge."

Woolf snorts. "Is that even a question? It's obviously Dodge. He's an asshole."

"So are you," Keana, Hayes, and I point out simultaneously.

"Yeah, but I'm like a mid-tier asshole," Woolf defends. He raises a hand higher. "Dodge is up here. Platinum status."

"It has to be Dodge," I agree. "Mina was attacked with me in trial five. And she has no motive. She's been nice to me, and I've been nice to her."

"I also say Dodge," Keana votes.

"So what do we do from here?" Woolf asks. "Just, like, storm his room or something?"

"What do you think?" I ask Hayes—he's been too quiet.

"I think . . . there's something I need to tell you." He rubs his jaw, meeting my eyes. "I rigged the trials."

"You *what?*"

I try to act as shocked as Woolf and Keana, but he's carefully watching my reaction. "You knew."

"Soph told me," I admit.

"Well, good, I'm glad someone was in the loop." Keana rolls her eyes.

"Do you tell me anything anymore?" Woolf complains.

"I didn't want you involved if I got caught. Applying was a last-minute decision because of the journal showing up, and I knew I wouldn't get picked unless they had exactly twelve applicants," Hayes explains. "I bribed Soph to hack into the system, and I picked all of you."

But me first. I want to say it, to find out—

"Why didn't you leave Chloe out?" Keana asks, beating me to it.

"It would have been too obvious," Hayes says smoothly. "Everyone knew she wanted to apply. If she didn't get in, she'd make too much of a scene."

He's right. But still, I wish there was more to it.

"I had to choose the Cabinet. With their parents and the money they put into the school, leaving them out would have been suspicious. And then I tried to pick people unlikely to win."

"That's where Mina comes in?" Woolf assumes.

Hayes shakes his head. "That's the thing. I didn't pick Mina at all. I picked Phlip. So when the Challengers were announced and he was the only one who didn't get included, I didn't know what happened. Just that she was there in his place. I didn't think much of it at first. But now . . . I don't know."

"How would Mina have known I'm afraid of snakes?" Keana asks. "And that Chloe's afraid of heights?"

"She did know about me," I realize suddenly. "Trial two. I tried to climb a tree and epically failed. She helped me get the right answers anyway. I think I said something then about hating heights. But . . ." I can't picture Mina, who reminds me so much of Cece, being behind all this. "Why? And how? I don't think she could have pulled this off by herself."

"She didn't, right?" Woolf asks. "She was using Soph. Maybe Dodge, too."

"And you told me earlier that Soph didn't know who was blackmailing her," Hayes reminds me. "So when Soph tipped your canoe during trial five, she wouldn't have known she was also sabotaging her own blackmailer."

"We're still missing a motive," I say, trying to find some hole to prove it's not Mina.

"There's something else," Keana says. "Aside from last night, all the times my room was broken into, I came back to the door still locked. That means she had a key."

"Which means she had help from a Champion." I deflate. It's bad enough to think Mina could actually be the mastermind behind our blackmail, but to not be able to trust the Champions, the only adults we have, is a jab I didn't expect.

"My bets are on Carly," Woolf says.

Keana shakes her head. "I think it's Jarod. Think about it. A Champion had to have been the one to fray Chloe's rope today since the trial was so far away. Jarod said his friends set it up. If he helped them, he could have frayed it."

"But why?" I ask. "What's in it for him?"

"Maybe Mina promised him something if she wins?" Keana guesses. "At this rate, she's going to win. And then it will be obvious it was her behind everything, but we won't be able to say shit without looking like sore losers."

"Hunter thought the same," I murmur. This feels almost like a multiple-choice test when none of the bubbles seem like the right answer. But maybe I'm the one reading the question wrong.

"Red string and Post-its would be so clutch right now," Woolf says.

"Wait . . . ," I say. Keana's words tug at me. "Mina wants to win. If she's really my Challenger, she did all of this *to* win." I bring a candle closer to Hunter's missing pages that we set on a table with his journal to scan his final entry.

I've always loved being right. But not now.

I know who my attacker is. I guess it should have been obvious it's been him all along. I'm going to confront him at the church and force him to admit to everything.

A chill races down my spine. "What if we were wrong?"

"About what?" Woolf asks.

"All of it," I whisper, horror stealing my voice. Because the more I think about it, the more I'm sure I'm right. "I don't think Ravi killed Hunter. Trevor did."

33

"No way." Woolf points to the journal pages. "Trevor would have never hurt Hunter. Reread the pages. Trev was the one who wanted to go after Ravi."

"Because Ravi was the perfect suspect," I counter. "Trevor wanted Hunter to think it was Ravi messing with him. Maybe Trevor even *told* Ravi about Hunter and Aura. But we missed the biggest red flag. Ravi didn't win the trials. Trevor did. That's who Hunter was going to confront the night he died. It was never Ravi. It was Trevor."

"He's also the key keeper," Keana adds. "He could have given Mina keys to unlock my room to sneak in."

"And to Diana's suite if Mina was writing our blackmail notes on the typewriter so we wouldn't recognize her handwriting." I remember another thing. "When Hayes and I found the tunnels, we overheard Jarod telling Trevor that Aura was mad they changed the rest of the trials from the ones they originally pitched the school. I didn't get why they would change them, but now I do. Trevor needed to make them harder so he could help Mina win. And that was after trial two, which was when I told Mina I hated heights. I bet that led to them adding the cliff trial."

"Why would Trevor help Mina cheat?" Woolf asks.

"I don't know," I admit. "Hayes, do you— Hayes?"

I jerk upright from where we're huddled over the journal pages. Hayes is gone.

"Where the fuck did he go?" Woolf asks, voice laced with rare panic.

"I didn't even know he left," Keana says. "The rain is so loud—"

I sprint into the downpour. Keana and Woolf match me step for step. "Hayes figured it out," I realize too late. "He must have gone after Trevor!"

"We have to stop him!" Woolf's voice is barely audible over the rain.

"Spread out!" I order, peeling off to put distance between myself and Keana and Woolf. Hayes could have taken the path back, but if he didn't tell us he was going to go after Trevor, he's not going to want us to follow him easily.

Woolf veers right so I stay left while Keana takes the path. With the rain and rolling thunder, I can't see them at all. I'm alone, the darkness all-consuming thanks to the clouds.

"Hayes!" I scream, my voice stolen by the wind. "Hayes!"

I flip my wet hair out of my eyes and squint into the darkness, catching the movement of a shadow far in front of me.

"Hayes!" I yell, pushing myself faster. "Stop!"

My feet slip and slide, catching on roots and uneven ground. Ahead of me, he stumbles over a fallen branch. By the time he regains his speed, I've caught up.

It's too late to slow down, so I slam into him, my speed propelling us forward. We roll, just like we did earlier, and I end up on top again. I scramble to straddle his waist as he writhes beneath me to throw me off.

"Stop!" I shout above the wind. "You can't go after Trevor. Not tonight."

"He killed Hunter," Hayes bites. "He was my brother's best friend. But he was the one who killed him and then pretended to grieve and mourn and look out for me ever since. He's a liar, and he needs to pay."

"He will," I swear, pinning his wrists down so he stops trying to push me off. "But not like this. When we get home, we can tell people. You can show the journal pages to the police. We can try to get the other Challengers from Hunter's year to speak up. But if you confront Trevor when we still have a trial left before going home, you might not even make it home. If he killed his best friend, what do you think he'd do to you?"

Hayes rips his wrists free, covering his eyes with his hands. "I don't care anymore."

My heart aches at the hopelessness in his voice.

"I just want him to know his time is up. I'm willing to suffer the consequences."

"I'm not," I say, standing up and taking him with me. "We've gotten too close for you to throw it all away now."

He wrenches out of my hold, pacing a few steps away before facing me again. "You don't get it, Chloe. I don't fucking care about anything anymore. Hunter never should have died. *He* was the perfect student, *he* was the perfect son. My parents want *him*, not me. The least I can do is make sure the person who killed him knows what it's like to be afraid."

He starts toward the estate again, but I storm after him. "And what about you? You think Hunter would want you to sacrifice yourself to get revenge? You think that will solve anything?"

"It doesn't matter! Nothing matters! I have nothing left to lose!" He spins to face me, a flash of lightning fully illuminating him. This isn't a Hayes I've ever seen. His hair is flattened and dark with rain; his eyes feral and features contorted with anger and betrayal. Gone is the poker face and the perfectly put together, impassive air. This Hayes is raw and wild and hurting.

"Everyone loved him. Everyone needed him. *I* needed him." His words break on a sob. "Nobody needs me."

"That's not true," I burst out. Before I can fully think, I've closed the gap between us. I cup his cheeks in my palms, thumbs catching tears or raindrops or maybe both. "I need you. And I—" My voice catches. "I love you."

I press my lips to his, waiting for him to pull away. Maybe it's wrong of me to kiss him when he's like this, but I don't know how else to convince him that I've never stopped loving him even for a second, never stopped needing him. This is the only way I can try.

There's a brief hesitation, but when I try to pull away, he tugs me closer, finally kissing me back. Something snaps between us. Maybe the truce, maybe the weeks of tension. My spine hits the rough bark of the tree behind me as he pushes me backward, deepening the rain-soaked kiss. My fingers find his hair, knotting in his dripping strands. Through our drenched clothes, I feel the rush of his heart pressed to mine, like our blood is beating to the same song.

I want to kiss him until all his hurt washes away with the rain; until we're home and safe and everything's okay. I want to kiss him until we're back to what we used to be.

I try to convey all of it, pulling him closer and closer until the familiar planes of his body mold to mine. When our mouths finally break apart, I cling to his shoulders, my gasps sending throbs of pain through my bruised side.

"I need you," I repeat, pressing my forehead to his. Each breath brings our lips close enough to touch, then apart again. "I need you so badly it's the whole reason this is happening."

His brows furrow. "What do you mean?"

My last secret spills out. "The entire reason I couldn't tell the Champions what was happening to me is because I'm being blackmailed. After we broke up, I was going to fail math without your help. I only passed because I emailed the answer key for the tests to myself one night in the library. But someone saw—" I break off, forcing myself to come to terms with the face behind my blackmail. I'm still rocked by disbelief, but it's another piece I hadn't considered—Mina's always in the library. It's much more likely that she saw me the night I sent myself the answer key than Dodge.

"Mina saw and she threatened to show evidence of my cheating to the Champions if I told anyone about the sabotage so I'd get disqualified from the trials, or maybe even expelled." I squeeze my eyes shut, shaking my head. "I never suspected her because she's been helping with the trials and making me trust her. Hell, I wanted to protect her because she reminded me so much of Cece. But she's been playing me the whole time."

"She's been manipulating you." Hayes pulls me close again so my face presses into his neck. "I'm sorry you felt you had to cheat."

"I need you for other reasons, too," I cry. "You make me feel like I'm someone deserving of being protected and defended. I've never felt that before because—" Tears clog my throat, but I force myself to get the words out. "I've never felt like I'm enough. Like I have to keep proving myself and being perfect and getting amazing grades. But with you, I never felt that pressure. I'm sorry I applied for the trials, because you were right that it wasn't just for Cece. It was for me. Another chance to prove myself. I shouldn't have needed it, and I wish I had seen that I don't need to be enough for everybody, just for those who don't care if I am or not."

"You're always enough for me." He kisses me again. This one's softer, sweeter. Lighter, and so is the rain.

"I never stopped loving you," I admit against his mouth. "And I'm sorry I threw mashed potatoes at you."

"I'm sorry I threw pork tenderloin at you." A shaky laugh escapes him. "I never stopped loving you, either, Clover. I think that's why I've been awful to you since the breakup. I had no choice but to be angry and hate you, otherwise I might have admitted to myself I still love you. And that felt dangerous. But I'm sorry. That wasn't fair."

"I forgive you," I breathe against his mouth, a wave of relief surging through me. "But promise me—"

"Hayes?!"

Woolf sprints into the clearing, skidding to a stop as he takes in how Hayes and I cling to each other. I expect Hayes to pull away, but he doesn't.

"I'm okay," Hayes says. It's meant for Woolf but directed at me.

"Oh, thank goodness," Keana pants, only a few paces behind Woolf. "I thought we were too late."

Hayes finally backs away so I can unglue my spine from where it's pressed against the tree. But his hand finds mine, our fingers intertwining.

"You still at vigilante risk?" Woolf warily asks.

Hayes shakes his head, glancing at me. "Not at the moment."

"Wait," I realize. "Did anyone grab the journal?"

We trade panicked looks and take off running. When we get back to the greenhouse, we suck in a collective gasp at the person standing inside.

Aura looks up from the journal in her hand, her eyes shining and short dark strands plastered to her cheeks. "Hi, Hayes," she says. "I see you got what I sent you."

34

"You sent Hunter's journal to me?" Hayes asks. "I thought—"

"It was Trevor?" Aura interjects.

He nods.

"I was worried about that. Thought you might ask him about it and raise suspicion. But it was a risk I had to take. Your brother would have wanted you to have it."

"So you know that Trevor killed Hunter?" I assume.

Aura swallows, tracing the side of the journal page in her hand. One of Hunter's moonflower doodles, no doubt. "I saw it happen," she chokes out.

"I want to know everything," Hayes pleads. "Please tell me the truth."

"I will," Aura promises. "But we need to get inside before Trevor starts setting up for the final trial. I know you figured out a way into the west wing. Take me to the library."

We jog the path back to the estate, the rain more of a mist now. Inside, the house is dead silent. It's hard enough to sneak around as two people, let alone five. When we finally emerge from the library's hidden bookcase door, relief floods me.

Heartbreak and longing mar Aura's pretty features as she

takes in the space. She squeezes her eyes shut as if she can block out whatever memories cling to the air.

"How did you know where we were?" Hayes asks.

She opens her eyes. "I haven't slept much since being here. I've heard you leave your room. Sometimes even heard you in the walls. But when Soph forfeited, I knew something was going down. I heard yelling in the forest and followed it, but by the time I got to greenhouse, it was empty. Then I saw the pages."

"Did you know Hunter left a mystery?" Woolf asks.

"Only because I knew Hunter." She takes a seat on the musty couch, and we gather around her. "The night he . . . died, I tore his room apart looking for his journal. I found it, but the last handful of pages were ripped out. I took the journal and hid it.

"But I couldn't figure out what Hunter did with the rest of the pages. I thought about sending it to you right away," she tells Hayes. "But when the police deemed his death an accident, I got scared. I wasn't sure if pulling you into it could put you in harm's way. You weren't even sixteen. Maybe thinking it was a tragic accident was better than the truth."

"I knew deep down it wasn't an accident," Hayes confesses.

A humorless smile flits across Aura's face. "Hunter always said you were too smart for your own good. The next two years, when the trials took place close to the school, I thought that was it. We'd never be able to get back to the forest to look for the missing pages. But when we were told this year that we'd be going back to the estate, I saw an opportunity since it was your senior year. Maybe it was selfish, but I sent the journal in hopes you would apply."

"And I did," Hayes says. "As soon as I read the last page, I knew there was more."

"I wasn't sure the pages would still be here," Aura admits. "Three years had passed, after all. I could have been luring you out for nothing."

"But they were here," I say. "And we found them."

"We're going to ruin Trevor," Woolf adds, slamming his fist into his hand.

"No disrespect," Keana says to Aura. "But why didn't you say something?"

Sadness fills Aura's gaze. "I was a coward. And at the time, confused. Hunter had only told me bits and pieces about what was happening to him. I didn't even know he was confronting Trevor until I went to find him that night and realized they were both missing. I knew they must have gone to the church, so I ran all the way there, but when I walked in . . ."

She trails off, tears brimming.

Beside me, Hayes stiffens. "They were already fighting?"

Aura nods. "They were on the balcony yelling and hitting each other. Hunter had confided everything in Trevor the whole time and was betrayed. But Trevor was mad, too. They were best friends, but Hunter was always one-upping him. Hunter was never supposed to apply for the trials—that was going to be Trevor's thing. His dad was a Champion and put a lot of pressure on Trevor to continue the legacy. But Hunter wouldn't back down. The way he saw it, the best person would win fairly."

"He was always the best at everything," Hayes murmurs.

Aura nods. "Trevor knew that better than anyone. When I

finally connected the dots, it was too late. I saw them fighting and called for them to stop. It distracted Hunter, giving Trevor enough time to get the upper hand. He shoved Hunter into the railing."

Hayes's breath hitches. I reach for his hand, squeezing.

"The thing is . . ." Aura's voice gets so soft we have to lean in. "It *was* partly an accident. The railing wasn't supposed to break. But it did. Hunter fell, and Trevor tried to reach out for him. I was too far away. Neither of us could stop him, but I thought the floor would. And then he went through it."

We flinch.

"And then what happened?" Hayes urges her on.

"For a second, nothing. I'll never forget the silence, how it felt like the entire world turned off. But then Trevor was swearing, running to the edge of the balcony and looking down into the hole Hunter fell through to the basement. And then he was crying. I raced up the stairs to look down beside him and—" She covers her mouth with her hand, tears leaking out of the corners of her eye. "Hunter was gone. Just like that. It all happened so fast."

"He was dead?" Hayes asks, the word making me jolt. "You were sure?"

Aura closes her eyes like she's seeing it all again. "I would have never left him there if there was even a sliver of a chance he could be saved."

A breath shudders out of Hayes. "All this time I've wondered how long he was awake down there. If he was hurting or cold. If he was crying out for help and nobody heard him."

Aura sniffles, shaking her head. "It was instant."

I'm glad Hayes gets peace on what's tormented him most—Hunter didn't suffer.

"Even so, we should have told someone that night," Aura continues. "But Trevor freaked out, going off about how our lives would be ruined. He said if I came forward with the truth, he'd make sure nobody would believe me. We couldn't tell a soul. And foolishly, I agreed. I was terrified. If I tried to tell the truth, it would be Trevor's word against mine. Without proof, I didn't know if I had any ground to stand on. I needed the right evidence."

"You needed the missing pages," I realize.

She nods. "The pages are a firsthand account that someone was out to get Hunter. I think paired with me as a witness, it could be enough."

Hayes tucks the missing pages into the journal and hands it to Aura. "Keep it safe until we get back," he tells her.

She takes it from him. Before his hands retreat, she grabs them.

Fresh tears sparkle in her eyes. "I just want you to know Hunter loved you so much. More than anyone else, even me. He's forever your biggest fan and nothing made him happier than being your big brother."

"I miss him so much," Hayes whispers, tears dripping down his cheeks. In another world, Aura might have become his sister-in-law one day. I'm sure she's thought of the same thing. She squeezes his hands before releasing them.

Hayes walks a few paces toward the window so his back's to us.

Aura wipes her eyes. "I'm sorry," she tells us. "I swore that nothing like that would ever happen again. But I was wrong, wasn't I?"

"A bit," Woolf admits.

"We figured it out this time," I say. "We think Mina has been sabotaging us. And that Trevor might be helping her behind-the-scenes. We just don't know why. It seems like a risky thing to get involved with, especially now that we know what he did to Hunter. Unless . . ."

Hayes comes back over to us as a realization slams into me. I turn to Keana. "If Mina's been blackmailing us, what's to say she's not blackmailing Trevor? She must know what he did to Hunter."

"How could she know if we didn't even know?" Keana asks.

"She does know," Aura sucks in a breath, eyes wide. "During the alumni holiday party, it was announced that the trials would take place at the estate again. I freaked out thinking about coming back here, and Trevor took me outside and told me I had to get a grip. It was the first time we had talked about Hunter's death since the night it happened. I accused him of killing Hunter, and he agreed he did but that the whole thing was dead and buried, just like Hunter. I thought we were alone, but Mina was at that party, too, since her mom's a Champion. Maybe she was lurking and overheard?"

"That's on brand for her," I confirm.

Keana nods, no stranger to being a victim of Mina's spying. "If she got proof, she's holding it over Trevor. And, Hayes, when Soph hacked the applicants and you left Mina out, she probably made Trevor add her back in."

"That makes sense," Hayes realizes. "The most recent Champions help pick the students, right?"

"Not usually. It's up to teachers, but this year, Trevor did want to help. Now I know why." Aura's teeth dig into her bottom lip. "If that's all true, then Trevor's going to give Mina the best chance he can at winning the last trial."

We reluctantly nod.

"It's not looking good," I admit.

Resolve fills Aura's gaze, and she strides toward the fireplace before turning to face us, arms crossed in front of her chest. For the first time, I see the fierce, savvy Champion Hunter must have fallen in love with.

"If Trevor's going to help Mina cheat, then I'm going to help you," she tells us. "Here's everything you need to know about the final trial."

35

"Congratulations on making it to the final trial. Welcome to a test of ambition."

Trevor's voice echoes in the morning stillness of the forest. We're outside the gates, the sun brightening the sky. It looks like a watercolor painting, something Diana herself might have made. In the wake of the rain, everything smells fresh and deceivingly hopeful. Like maybe we can win.

If all goes to plan, we will.

After Aura ran through everything she knew about trial seven and we debated different scenarios, we slunk back to our rooms. Hayes slipped into mine, but even snuggled against his side with our arms around each other, I couldn't sleep. He faded in and out, the emotions of the day taking their toll. I raked my fingers through his hair and wondered if it'd be the last time I'd ever get to be that close to him. After today, we'll return to the academy and the truce will be over. I don't know what we are outside of the forest.

Now, Hayes stares at Trevor, his poker face pulled up as Trevor drones on. Trevor commends us on our perseverance and progress, reassuring us we are all Champions in their eyes. It all sounds like bullshit now that we know the truth. He's a liar, and he's good at it.

Speaking of good liars, Mina glances at me with a small smile. I smile back. With teeth.

I rip my gaze away, glancing from Hayes to Woolf to Keana. I have a lot more to lose now than I did when I started the trials.

"Since the final trial is ambition," Trevor continues. "We thought the perfect test was answering a simple question: How much do you want it? Bad enough to get it yourself?"

"That's exactly what you'll do if you want to win," Carly says. There's less sass in her tone than usual. Deep half-moons rest beneath her eyes, and whatever tan she came in here with seems to have faded. "You need to find the prize money."

I try to look surprised, as if Aura hadn't told us last night.

"Spread across the forest is six hundred thousand dollars," Trevor explains. "It's divided into six one-hundred-K chunks in bags. Whoever finds the largest sum gets it all."

"What if we all find a bag?" Keana asks. "There are six of us."

Jarod nods. "Which is why there's a seventh, tiebreaker bag inside the gates. The winner will get an extra reward, as the last bag will include an additional fifty thousand dollars. But you can only get it at the end of the trial. Once you go past the gates, there's no going back, so make sure you have enough. You could have one bag plus the seventh, but if someone else collected two or three bags, they'll still win."

This trial is my worst nightmare: math.

Trevor looks at Aura, clearly expecting her to add something else. She stares ahead, her mouth set. Annoyance flickers across his face, but he turns to us with a smile. "The way you'll find the money bags is simple. They're all in places you've been before that are on your maps."

"We don't get clues?" I ask.

This was the one part Aura couldn't help us with. She knew the money would be spread out across the forest, but Trevor was secretive about its exact whereabouts and wanted to set up the trial himself.

Dodge casts me a withering glance. "Not all of us need clues to win."

I narrow my eyes, wondering if he knows where everything's hidden. If Mina does, and he's helping her, then he might. It's ironic to stand here and act like we have no idea what's ahead of us when we all have varying degrees of information.

But he and Mina don't know that, and per the plan, we need to keep it that way.

"If you want it badly enough, you'll figure out the right places to look," Trevor says. "Like all the other trials, you have until dusk."

"How do we know when all the bags are collected?" Hayes asks.

Trevor looks at him. I wait for Hayes to crack and all his anger and betrayal to pour out of him like lava erupting. If it was me, it would. But he holds eye contact, not revealing a thing.

"We'll blow the horn when the first person finishes like with the other trials, then again once the majority of the money has been returned. Unless, of course, the first person wins by having the greater sum." Trevor's gaze sweeps across us. "Ready to begin your last trial?"

We nod, sizing each other up. Keana narrows her eyes at me. I narrow mine back. Step one of the plan: make Mina think her attempts at framing us were successful.

I can feel her eyes boring into me, and maybe it's my imagination, but there's an air of self-satisfaction there. I can't wait to prove her wrong.

"Challengers," Trevor says. "Go forth and good luck."

Dodge, Mina, and Woolf immediately take off in a sprint. I'm slower, sharing a glance with Hayes before turning off the path. Now for step two of the plan: start out alone.

Aura knew the money would be spread out between the four cardinal directions, and since there are four of us, we each took a point so we don't double up on efforts. Hayes took north, Keana east, Woolf the lake and west, and I volunteered for south—the barn and powerhouse.

"What if one of us gets in trouble or hurt?" Hayes asked last night.

"Use your whistle," I said. *"Three consecutive long blows means something's wrong and we need to find each other."*

The barn is closer than the powerhouse, so I head there first. I try to move at a good pace, but every bone in my body aches from yesterday's climb and the pain in my ribs flares with each gasp for breath. I don't think any are broken, but when I lifted my shirt this morning, the area Keana whacked was purple and red.

When I finally get to the barn, I walk the perimeter. Since it's surrounded by a fence like the other crumbling structures, I can't get inside. No bags of money are hanging from the trees nearby.

Aura hoped Trevor would give clues, but of course he didn't.

Except, maybe we did have clues. Thinking back to trial two, the Mad Libs challenge, I mentally sift through the questions regarding the barn.

"Think," I scold myself, pacing in front of the locked fence. "One question was about the animals kept, and the answer was cows, pigs, horses, and—" I stop. "Chickens."

The coop. That's not within the fenced area but behind. I saw it in my perimeter search but didn't check it since like everything else, it's falling apart.

I sprint to it, slowing as I approach the small graying structure. The metal wiring on the coop is riddled with holes and peeling away, leaving jagged pointy barbs. I carefully pull a corner back, stepping inside.

"Ah!" I yelp, attacked by a flapping creature. Only once it soars past me and through the opening do I realize it was a trapped raven. I stare after it, its caw grating on my ears as it settles on a nearby branch.

"Get out of here," I tell it, suddenly jealous of the fact that it can go anywhere, yet it chooses to stay close to the exact place it just escaped from, as if it doesn't know it could have died in the coop had I not come along.

But maybe I'm just like it. I could have forfeited at any point in the past week and a half, but I didn't. I stayed in the trials for this exact moment. Maybe there's a reason it's staying, too.

I don't know its reason, but I know mine. And it hangs from a rope in the center of the coop.

Significantly lighter than I expected, the sack swings thanks to the raven's disruption. I grab it, peering at the beam across the ceiling that it's tied to.

Tugging lightly makes the entire coop creak. With zero interest in pulling the weak structure down on top of me, I let go of the bag to reach into my backpack for the thing I debated on bringing all morning.

I know I should have thrown the glass shard out, but after everything we discovered, I couldn't enter the final trial without something to defend myself with.

It comes in handy for cutting the rope, which would have taken time I don't want to waste working through the knot to untie. I open the bag to peek inside.

Holy crap, they actually put money in here. I expected it to be a decoy. But when I pull out a $100 bill, the blue stripe on it is all the confirmation I need. This is real.

I'm tempted to pocket a few of them on the off chance I don't win, but I'm sure the Champions would know. Instead, I stuff the small bag into my backpack with the shard. One bag down, five to go.

I wiggle through the wiring out of the coop, the change in light from the dimness inside disorienting. Blinking to adjust my sight, I pull my map from where I tucked it into my pocket—

And gasp as something swings toward me, blocking the sun. I twist away, but it still clips me, a razor-sharp sting near my hairline. My fingers prod the spot, coming away wet with blood. Zipping the shard in my backpack was a rookie mistake, so I whip the bag off my shoulder and smash it into my attacker's stomach. They let out an oof, doubling over. Thanks to my full water bottle, it's packing extra weight.

I put more space between us, wiping the trickling blood from my forehead before it drips into my eyes. The cut isn't deep, but if I hadn't reacted so quickly, it might have been worse. As my attacker straightens, I take in the sneer reserved just for me.

"What happened to not needing to hurt your competition to win?" I throw Dodge's words back at him.

"If you knew your fucking place, I wouldn't have to," he snarls. Clenched in his hands is a rake, the metal prongs raised like the tip of a sword. The red sheen on the ends makes my stomach curl.

"Really?" I ask, backing up to put more space between us. "You're resorting to using yard equipment as a weapon? You must be really scared of losing to me now."

"Shut up," he barks. "Give me the money. You're not going to win. Trust me."

"Why? Because the trials are rigged and Mina's supposed to?"

It wasn't part of the plan to reveal my hand so early, but the shocked expression on his face is so worth it. "How did you—"

"Assume I know everything," I brag, continuing to back up. He stalks forward, following me step for step. "But maybe elaborate on what role you're playing in this."

He takes another swing at me. I avoid it, but the reach is much longer than Keana's branch last night. I'll need to figure out a way to get away, and fast.

"I'm not some pawn," he seethes. Another missed swing. His anger makes him sloppy. "Just received a more interesting offer to focus my efforts elsewhere."

"On going after me instead of the money?"

"I don't need money like you," he jabs, both verbally and physically. I dodge both, no longer letting his belittling remarks get to me.

Knowing his words are powerless makes him even madder and he swings again. I leap back to avoid it, but I don't realize where we are until it's too late. He's backed me up against the fence.

"What are you going to do?" I ask. "Kill me?"

"I was supposed to hold you off. Scare you. But now you know everything." He swallows, the ferocity in his eyes dimming. I realize my mistake too late. I revealed just how much I know, and it makes me a threat.

"I won't tell anyone," I lie.

"Of course you will," he spits out, as if trying to keep his rage even though I can see something like fear flickering behind it. "You're going to go back and tell everyone. And I can't have that happen."

Despite his hatred of me, he doesn't want to be a killer. No one does.

But that didn't stop Trevor from killing Hunter, accident or not. And it doesn't stop Dodge from raising the rake as his fury and fear win out.

"Two's a coincidence," he repeats his threat from the other night, as if trying to convince himself it's true. "Besides, anything can happen in the forest."

Something over his shoulder in the distance makes me pause. "Wrong line," I say.

His brow furrows and the rake pauses above our heads. "What?"

"Wrong line," I repeat, heart hammering. Almost there. "The right line is 'anything can happen in the woods.' You would have known that had you gone to the spring musical. You should try and be more supportive of your peers instead of tearing people down."

He stares at me like I just suggested we eat lead. "Why the fuck would I—"

Woolf tackles Dodge, the two of them flying to the ground. I duck to avoid the falling rake, throwing my arms over my head as it thunks down beside me.

"Get off me!" Dodge roars, wrestling Woolf.

"Knew there was a reason you ditched Mina at the lake after she got the bag just now," Woolf says, managing to pin Dodge down. He glances over at me, eyes widening at the cut on my head. "Sorry I was late."

"You weren't," I say. "I got one bag of money but still need to check the powerhouse."

"I bet Mina got it already!" Dodge spits, confirming my suspicion that another bag is there. "You're never going to beat her. She knows everything."

"That makes two of us," I lie.

To Woolf, I say, "Are you coming with me?"

Woolf looks down at Dodge, who writhes beneath him. He grins, as wolfish as ever. "And miss finally beating the shit out of this asswipe? Hard pass."

Dodge bares his teeth. "Let's fucking go."

"Let's." Woolf gives me a smile—a real one, like the kind he gave me when we were friends. It falls as Dodge wiggles out of his hold, scrambling to stand.

"Go," Woolf orders before throwing himself back at Dodge.

They collide in a whirl of limbs, scrambling for the upper hand. If anyone can hold their own against Dodge in a fight that's been brewing for months, it's Woolf.

As I pass the chicken coop and enter the forest again, I spot the raven. Poking out of its beak is the tail of an unlucky field mouse.

It got its reward. Now, I'm going to get mine.

36

By the powerhouse, I find the next bag of money hanging from a tree. It's an easy grab, filling me with delusion that I might really win. Or maybe my head wound is worse than I thought and I'm starting to hallucinate.

I'm tempted to gamble my chances with the pot I currently have, plus the additional fifty thousand I'd get for passing the gates first. But if Mina got three of the other bags, it won't be enough. I need to find Keana and Hayes to see what they collected or find more money.

A shrill sound hits my ears. In the distance, a whistle blows three times, all long. Our SOS signal.

I sprint toward the sound, panic bubbling as it repeats. It's in the opposite direction than Woolf, meaning it must be Hayes or Keana.

My heart screams in my chest, side burning to the point where the pain is nearly unbearable. Sweat makes the cut on my forehead sting worse than it already does. But I can't let any of it stop me, especially when the SOS signal repeats for a third time, much closer now. I push myself faster, bursting through the trees—

And collide with someone. Instead of tumbling to the ground, they absorb the force of my pace and stumble back.

"You're okay," Hayes exclaims, gripping my arms both to steady me and reassure himself, giving me a once-over. His eyes widen when they land on my cut. "You're not okay."

"That wasn't me," I rush out, stepping back to scan him for injuries.

"It wasn't me," he denies.

"It was me!" Keana cries from *above.*

We look up, jaws dropping. She dangles upside down, swinging several feet off the ground. Her foot is caught in a rope tied to a branch.

"What happened?" Hayes asks, reaching up to brush fingertips with hers.

"My ankle," she whimpers. "It's my bad one from my gymnastics injury. I stepped on something to trigger the trap, and there was this awful snapping sound when I flipped."

It doesn't look good, that's for sure. It's already swelling.

"I can get her down," I say, swinging my backpack off my shoulder and pulling out the shard.

I wince as Hayes's fingertips ghost over my cut. "Who did this?"

"Thank Dodge," I say.

He stiffens.

"Woolf's currently giving him a taste of his own medicine."

"He's probably the only one who can," Hayes says.

I pass the shard to Keana. "Can you cut yourself free?"

She sniffles. "Yeah, but I'll fall."

"We'll catch you."

We arrange ourselves beneath her as she saws at the rope. "Do you think Mina set this trap?" Hayes asks me.

I think about her on the bus with her boondoggle. *"My therapist told me I should try tying knots to help with my anxiety,"* she said.

"She pretty much told me as much," I say.

"It's just about— Ah!"

Keana yelps as the rope snaps. While the shard falls to my left, she falls into Hayes's arms. Mine are beneath his, but more for moral support.

"Good thing you've been working out," I commend as he gently lowers her to the ground. I pick up the shard and return it to my backpack.

Something between a huff and a laugh escapes him. "Good thing."

"Ow." Keana unwraps the rope from her ankle. "I don't think I can walk on it."

Hayes and I crouch on either side of her, sharing a concerned look over her head. I'm not a doctor yet, but it's definitely broken.

"I can carry you," Hayes offers. "We're only a mile or two away from the gates. If you get on my back, we can make it."

"I'd slow you down," Keana says.

"I could run to get Aura," I say. As the words leave my lips, I know it would mean losing. Still, I'd do it for her. "She could get real help."

"And let that sneaky cheater win? No way." Keana sniffles, composing herself. "You need to leave me here. If Woolf is with Dodge, I'll be okay. You take on Mina together and get me after. I don't care about winning anymore. I just want this to be over."

I chew on the inside of my cheek. "We swore we wouldn't leave each other behind."

"That was before the girl who has made our life suck the past week and a half rigged the forest with booby traps. We can't let her win."

"I only got two money bags," I admit.

"I got one by the church," Hayes adds.

"Mina already got the one in the greenhouse," Keana says. "I was too late. But the horn hasn't blown yet, meaning there's still time to get the seventh tiebreaker bag. If we have three and she has three, it'll come down to that. You have to hurry!"

"She's right. We have to go," Hayes tells me.

"If anything happens, you whistle," I order Keana. "Got it?"

"Got it," she promises. "Make her pay."

We leave her, but I glance back before she's out of sight. She grimaces, tears sliding down her cheeks as she props herself up against a tree trunk.

Emmy's words ring in my ear. *"Please promise me you'll look out for her."*

We're barely half a mile away when I stop. Hayes jogs a few paces ahead before realizing, turning back to face me. "What is it?"

"I can't ditch her," I say, motioning in the direction we left Keana. From my backpack, I pull out the two bags of money, stuffing them into his hands. "I made a promise to Emmy to look out for her. You're faster than me. If you take these, you can win."

He stares at them, then shakes his head and drops them back into my hands. Pulling out the one he found, he adds it to the bunch. "I made a promise, too. Let me go back. You deserve to win. It was always meant to be you."

Tears well in my eyes. "What's that mean?"

He takes my face between his hands. "The real reason I chose you first when Soph hacked the system is because I knew you could win. That you *would* win. And a piece of me hoped maybe if we were in this together, we'd find our way back to each other. So I got more than I came here for. But you haven't."

"I have," I say, tears spilling over. "I got you back, and fixed things with Keana, and Woolf is Woolf."

We both laugh, but mine dies in my throat as I remember Cece and the money.

He presses a kiss to my lips, there and gone. "Go do what Clover Gatti does best: win."

I run and don't look back.

By the time I get close enough to see the estate, I'm on edge and exhausted. I'm working on borrowed time.

I turn down the last bend in the path, and the gate looms in the distance. From the iron arch in the center hangs the final bag. It sways in the breeze, a tantalizing prize. All that separates me from it is one last stretch.

I'm halfway down the path when I stop suddenly. Beneath my feet are leaves. It's the forest, so there's always leaves, but some of these ones don't even match up with the surrounding trees. I don't remember this many.

Using the toe of my sneaker, I nudge some aside. Beneath is exactly as I feared. A rope.

I carefully step around it, walking a few more feet before finding another one. The path is riddled in traps, just like the one Keana got caught in. Maybe Mina wasn't lying when she said tying knots helps her anxiety. She certainly tied enough of them.

And if I was laying traps, wouldn't I want to see them work?

I duck off the path, pressing myself behind the trunk of an exceptionally large oak tree. The space between the trees lining the path is minimal, their branches intertwining and overlapping. It's the perfect place to hide.

I could go around the path. Cut through the forest and hope that I don't get caught in any other booby traps Mina set.

Or I could beat her at her own game.

I find a fallen tree and step onto its trunk so I can grab a low-hanging branch and haul myself up. My hands sweat and the nausea returns, but I shove my fear down and climb higher. I imagine Hayes's voice in my ear directing me. *Grab this branch, pull. Put your foot here, step up.* My limbs shake, but I repeat the same rhythm over and over. By the time I look down, I'm at least twenty feet off the ground.

From up here, I can see all the traps Mina laid. They're made of sticks and rope and something translucent, like fishing line. No—boondoggle string. There's one every several feet right up until the last trees before the gate. That's the trip wire.

"Where are you?" I murmur, peering through the leaves.

In the corner of my eye, I catch movement. Mina crouches on a branch two trees away from me, closer to the gate. Her head slowly moves from side to side as she scans the length of the path. I got off it just in time.

Now for the hard part. A neighboring branch from the tree between us crosses under my current one. I step onto it carefully, feeling it bend beneath my weight.

I hate everything about this.

But Mina clearly wants to see me get close enough to think I have winning in the bag, just to get it literally pulled from my hands.

It takes me forever to reach the trunk and transfer to another branch. I'm lucky that the breeze creates a constant rustling sound to disguise my own. The branches creak without my help, so she has no reason to suspect me.

I make it to her tree and spot where she sits near the end of the branch. She's farther to the edge than I would ever go, her legs dangling on either side of the branch. Even if I wanted to, I couldn't go after her.

So I do something I would never do otherwise: I climb higher.

It's the worst, but I know it's the right move when I nudge onto a branch just a little above her and to the left. All she'd have to do is look up and she'd see me. But she's spent the entire trials being the predator. Predators have no reason to watch their backs.

"Looking for someone?"

Mina startles at my voice, nearly losing her balance. She catches herself at the last second, scrambling to remain upright.

"Chloe!" she exclaims, spotting me and putting on her wide-eyed innocent act. "I thought you don't like climbing?"

"Hate it," I state simply. "But after somebody forced me to climb a cliff essentially ropeless, I guess some of the terror ebbed.

You wouldn't happen to know who, would you?"

Her lips part.

"It might be the same person who blackmailed Soph to drown me," I continue before she can deny it. "Or the person who blackmailed Keana, threatening to out her secret relationship. Could be the same person who blackmailed me with my worst secret that I cheated at math." I smile at her. "But that would never be you, right?"

Her face transforms. Sweet, innocent, asthmatic Mina falls away to reveal my scheming Challenger. Well, I guess she's still asthmatic, but she clenches her jaw and narrows her eyes. Her shoulders push back, and her chin raises, posture straightening. She's every bit the entitled tormentor who's been messing with me.

"Took you long enough to figure it out," she snarks. "I thought you'd be smarter. But you and Keana fell right into the trap of assuming each other. It was perfect."

"Until we realized exactly what it was: a trap."

"One of many." She grows serious. "But for the record, I never thought you'd actually climb using a busted rope. I wasn't trying to kill you. I needed you to give up. But you and Keana kept pushing me to get worse and worse. I was running out of ideas."

"I couldn't even *see* the rope until it was too late. Your ideas sucked."

"They seemed to have done the job."

"And yet here I am, still about to win."

"Bullshit." She laughs, but the sound dies instantly. The look she trains on me is full of so much vehement hatred, it could have Dodge taking notes. "That's all you ever care about, isn't it? Being the best. Acing every test. *Winning.*"

"It's something I should probably unpack eventually," I admit. "But you're one to talk. You did all of this just so *you* could win."

"Not at first. In the beginning, I just wanted to prove to my mom I could get in."

"And you couldn't even do that on your own," I say, because she doesn't know Hayes rigged the applicants. "You needed to blackmail Trevor into making you a Challenger and helping you."

I expect her to be surprised I know, but instead, her eyes light up. "When I overheard Trevor and Aura arguing at the holiday party and followed them outside, I never expected that bomb to drop. I got Trevor's entire admission of guilt on video. Once he saw that, he was pretty willing to work together. Though the cliff trial did take some heavy convincing."

"Why me?" I snap, my patience waning. "I thought we were friends."

Her eyes flash, and she stands suddenly. The branch sways beneath her, but she pays it no mind. "So did I. *I* was the one who was nice to you when you first arrived at the academy. *I* helped you catch up in chem. Scratch that—I'm the reason you *aced* chem. But then as soon as a better, bigger friend group came along, you ditched me."

She starts climbing higher, putting several branches between us in minutes. I follow her, but not nearly as quickly.

"Emmy and Keana were my roommates," I remind her, pulling myself up another branch. "We naturally became close."

"Emmy and Keana gave you a status I couldn't," she spits back, looking down at me. "They didn't spend hours alone in the library like me. They had friends, which means you had friends. But most important, they had a connection to Hayes."

His name takes me off guard. I crouch, gripping the branch beneath my feet. "What does he have to do with this?"

She scoffs. "You can't play dumb half as well as me. I used to watch you in chem looking at him. You had barely been at the academy two weeks and were already obsessed with him. I warned you not to go after him."

"Please do not tell me this entire thing is over a *boy*."

She scrunches her nose. "Of course not. It's over you being a shitty, self-serving person. You wanted Hayes, so you ditched me for Keana and Emmy so you'd have an in. You wanted to apply for the trials, so you disregarded Hayes's feelings about it because you can never be wrong. You couldn't admit to not being smart enough in math without him, so you cheated to keep your perfect grades. It doesn't matter who you step on or throw to the side in the process. You will always do whatever it takes to get exactly what you want. You're ambitious to a fault. I wanted to give you a taste of what it's like to fail and let down the people who matter most."

"Because that's how you feel, isn't it?" I ask. "Like no matter what you do, it will never be enough for your parents. So when you were nice to me and helped me with chemistry but I still didn't become your best friend, you saw it as me reinforcing how they make you feel: like you will never be enough."

"You have no idea how I feel," she snaps, but her voice sounds choked. "You might be a know-it-all, but you don't know shit about me."

"You're right," I agree. "I'm sorry about that. And for the record, I feel like that, too. We're alike. But I know now that perfect grades and winning and a fancy title isn't going to change that. I'm not trying to win to fix the piece of me that always has something to prove. I need to win for the money. Please, Mina."

I crack myself open, doing the thing I hate maybe even more than math: asking for help.

We lock eyes, mine pleading and hers conflicted. I almost have her.

"We are alike," she agrees quietly. "But with one big difference."

I'm desperate to hang onto the hope that I can turn this around. "What?"

She smiles sweetly. "I'm not afraid of heights."

The truth is a swift kick to my aching ribs, knocking the breath from my lungs.

"Wait!" I yell after her, but it's too late.

Dashing toward the trunk, she quickly drops down to the branch below. By the time I scramble down one, she's down five.

"Mina!"

Her laugh rings out, carried on the breeze and circling me. Panic squeezes my chest as I look down, the ground so very far away. I'm only halfway when she's already dropping onto the dirt in a low crouch.

She takes off toward the gate, carefully dancing around the trip wires. I'm still too high. I'll never outrun her.

But maybe I don't have to.

Instead of continuing my descent, I step onto a branch belonging to the next tree on the path. As quickly as I dare, I make it to the trunk, then onto the branch that overlaps with the tree beside it, the last one before the gate. I start climbing down again, stopping on a thick lower branch just as Mina rushes past on the path below.

I unzip my backpack to pull out the glass shard. In my rush, the jagged edge slices my palm. I wince, wiping the welling blood on my bare thigh.

I only have one shot, and if my aim is off, this could end very badly. I have to be careful, but quick. Zeroing in on my target, I wind back.

There's only a small stretch of path between Mina and the seventh money bag when I launch the shard. The sunlight glints off it as it soars in the air. It passes Mina, its sharp edge wedging into the ground. She looks at it and laughs.

"You missed!" she calls.

I tilt my head. "Did I?"

She doesn't see the movement of leaves until it's too late. The glass shard cut one of the trip wires, just like I hoped. Her own trap wraps around her foot, jerking her upside down. She screams, swinging from the rope.

I shimmy down the rest of the tree, leaving bloody handprints as I go, more thankful than ever when my feet touch the forest floor. Carefully avoiding the rest of her traps, I make my way down the remainder of the path.

"Cut me down," she demands, voice wavering. "Cut me down right now."

"I'm sorry I wasn't a truer friend to you," I tell her, because maybe there's some truth in what she said about me casting her aside for more. "But not sorry enough to cut you down."

She screams after me as I untie the final bag of money hanging from the arch. Turning to her, I raise my left middle finger. "This is for Woolf and Hayes." And then I raise my right. "This is for Keana and me." Lastly, I raise the final bag. "And this is for my sister." Her shouts fade behind me as I strut along the path back to the estate. I can still hear her faintly when I reach the steps of the porch.

The four Champions sit in the ancient rockers. They gawk at me covered in blood. Jarod starts a slow clap. Carly and Aura join. Trevor looks like he's seen a ghost.

In front of them, I drop the four bags of money. "I'm not great at math," I say, something I should have admitted a long time ago. "But I believe that's three hundred fifty thousand dollars."

37

The thin red line across my palm stares back at me from where my hands rest in my lap against the fabric of my green-and-silver graduation dress.

"I am so proud to present to you this year's graduating class of Wilde Academy, our dear seniors."

The crowd explodes in applause at Principal Watershed's announcement. From where I sit on the stage of the auditorium with the rest of the seniors, I find my parents and Cece seated in the middle. She waves excitedly at me, her spiral tufts bouncing.

I give a teeny wave back, but nerves swarm my gut like wasps. I wonder if Principal Watershed noticed how sweaty my hand was when he shook it before handing me my diploma.

"And now I'm going to invite prior Champion Aura Lang onto the stage for the annual Wilde Champion Crowning Ceremony."

Everyone claps as Aura leaves her front-row seat with the other Champions to take the stage. It's customary for the oldest of the most recent four Champions to introduce the newest one, kind of like they're passing the baton down.

She's in a stylish, loose-fitting red dress that stops just before her knees and has pockets, which one hand is in. Right before she turns to face the audience, we meet eyes.

After returning to the academy and sleeping through most of yesterday, Hayes met up with Aura, since the Champions have to stay until graduation. She said immediately after, she's going to bring the journal to the police and tell them everything.

"She thinks it will be enough evidence," Hayes relayed last night.

While Hayes was with Aura, Woolf, Keana, and I convened in my room with Phlip and Emmy to catch them up on everything. Woolf had just finished a very in-depth and dramatized reenactment of his brawl with Dodge—which resulted in both sporting black eyes—when Hayes walked in.

"She thinks it will be enough? That's not super reassuring," Phlip commented, his concerned gaze locked on Keana and her swollen, propped-up ankle.

She visited the hospital on her way back from the trials and found out it was fractured. They wrapped it, but she'll need to go again after graduation for a cast.

Hayes's shoulders slumped in disappointment. "Aura said the police will have to investigate further before things go to trial. They'll likely reach out to other Challengers from Hunter's year, and probably us, too. If they do, that could take months, and the trial might take even longer."

"So we just . . . wait?" Woolf asked in disbelief. "Graduate tomorrow and pretend everything's normal?"

"I don't know what else we can do."

"What if we had a confession?"

Silence met my question. Finally, Emmy, who had cried all night after hearing everything we went through and wouldn't leave Keana's side, said, *"But you don't. Do you?"*

"No. But we know who does."

Realization dawned in Hayes's eyes. *"Mina."*

I nodded. *"She told me she has it. It's either on her phone or laptop. If we could get them, we could get the video, and that would be the final damning piece of evidence."*

"She's been holed up in her room ever since we got back," Keana pointed out. *"We'd have to lure her out somehow."*

Woolf's eyes lit up. *"I could start a fire—"*

"No!" The rest of us unanimously shut him down.

"Nobody ever lets me do anything fun," he whined, flopping back onto Emmy's bed.

"Mina can't know we stole it," Hayes said. *"At least, not until it's too late."*

I met his gaze, a very precarious plan taking shape. *"Sounds like we need a hacker."*

My mind spins over the rest of last night as Aura explains to the audience why the Wilde Academy Wilderness Competition is an honored tradition. She speaks clearly and kindly, though I know she doesn't agree with any of it. If it were up to her, the Wilde Trials would have ended after Hunter's death. If all goes to plan, they'll end today.

"And now it's time for me to crown our newest Champion," Aura says. She turns to me, waving me forward. "Congratulations, Chloe Gatti!"

My parents and Cece stand and holler amid the sea of polite clapping, which would have embarrassed me two weeks ago, but now, my heart swells with love for them. It takes everything in me to keep the tears inside my ducts as I amble down the stage to the podium.

I feel a gaze burning into me and glance back to see Mina's scorching glare. She managed to get herself out of her trap, but I had already been deemed winner by the Champions. Telling on me meant telling on herself, since she was the one who set them. We were at a draw.

Music from the band pit plays as a crown is placed on my head. I watched this same thing take place at last year's graduation for Carly and couldn't wait for it to be me. Now that it is, I can't help feeling ridiculous. The crown is made of metal with emeralds and diamonds studded throughout. It's the same crown that's been placed on every Champion's head since the new school was built. It's as heavy as it looks.

People clap as I step up to the mic for my speech. I grip the side of the wooden podium because if I don't, I might pass out. To center myself, my thumb runs over my clover ring. It sits on my finger again, where it belongs.

"Hi, everyone," I start, hoping my words aren't as breathy as they sound to my ears. "I'm so honored to be standing here right now. You have no idea. I applied to the Wilde Tr—Wilderness Competition in the hopes of winning for my sister. But I felt like it was a long shot since I was up against such talented competition."

People aww and ooh, and my parents smile proudly. Cece gives me a thumbs-up.

"I think I was a different person two weeks ago. A little selfish, a lot arrogant." That scores some laughs. I loosen up. "I felt like I had something to prove. I always do. So I didn't want to win just for my sister. I wanted to win for me.

"There's nothing wrong with that, but it put some really important relationships of mine at risk because the need to win consumed me. It consumed a lot of us. It took getting to that point for me to realize what's actually important. And I'm sorry to say it's not perfect grades or being better than everyone else or even getting crowned Champion." I take the crown off my head, setting it on the podium. "It's being there for the people who matter most, because they won't care what grades you have or who you're better than or if you're a Champion. They'll love you for you. Unconditionally."

I take a deep breath, knowing I need to hurry. I don't think the *Jaws* theme song will play if I talk too long like the score at the Oscars, but I don't want to risk it.

"I guess I just want to say that I'm grateful to be standing before you as the Champion of this year's Wilde Academy Wilderness Competition." If I'm going to do what I'm about to, I have to do it now. I look out at the sea of parents and family members and faculty. "Especially since it wasn't supposed to be me."

That sparks a few confused murmurs. From the front row, Trevor stares at me very hard.

"It's kind of a funny story, actually," I laugh, because it's so not. "But a deal was made between a Challenger and a Champion to help that Challenger win. The Challenger knew what the trials were ahead of time—scratch that, she actually helped *change* the trials to put herself at an advantage. She sabotaged other Challengers, threatening us to keep quiet or else it'd get worse. She even turned some of us against each other. And the whole time, the Champion was helping."

My gaze locks on Trevor's horrified face. He's half out of his seat, clearly torn between revealing himself to shut me up or holding on to the hope I won't name him.

"I bet the Champion would have even helped the Challenger get away with murder. After all, he did."

Jarod and Carly gawk at Trevor as a wave of gasps and uncomfortable whispering follows my statement.

"Chloe suffered a head wound during the final trial," Trevor tells the audience, jumping to his feet. He rushes up the steps to the stage. "We really should have pushed her to get it looked at once we got back. I don't think she should continue speaking given her state."

My "state" includes a barely-there scratch mostly covered by makeup and my hair. But I shrug, stepping back so I'm beside Aura. "Fine, I won't."

I turn enough to make eye contact with Soph, who has her phone in her hand. She taps the screen.

"Principal Watershed, we can move onto closing remarks—"

"Let go of me, Trevor!"

Aura's voice cuts Trevor off, but it's not coming from the Aura standing beside me. No, it's coming from the speakers that fill the auditorium with surround sound. Trevor's head whips around, looking for the source. But it's everywhere.

"Get your shit together," the recording of him snarls. *"What were you thinking bursting into tears like that after the announcement*

that this year's trials will be at the estate? You're being suspicious!"

"What was I thinking? I'm thinking I can't go back to the place where Hunter died. Where you killed him," Aura cries in the recording.

Horrified gasps rise from the audience, and even though I've watched the recording half a dozen times since Soph swiped it from Mina's Cloud storage last night, the anguish in Aura's voice still makes me shudder. I glance at Mina sitting among the graduates, her eyes wide and jaw dropped as she realizes what's playing.

"Turn this off!" the Trevor in front of me bellows, looking around for someone to help. But everyone is too shocked. Soph, controlling the speaker system from her phone, turns it even louder to drown him out with the recording of himself.

"For two weeks, you'll have to fucking deal with it," past Trevor says. "I might have killed Hunter, but that truth is never getting out. It's dead and buried, just like him."

The recording ends. It's dead silent.

Until it isn't.

The auditorium explodes with sound as faculty hop to their feet and conversation ripples through the room. Nearly every senior sitting behind me has their jaw on the floor. Principal Watershed is saying something, but I can't hear it over the blood roaring in my ears.

Trevor's furious gaze locks on me. "You."

And that's the only warning I get before he's storming across the stage toward me, his charismatic air replaced by cold rage. I wonder if this is the face Hunter saw right before he was shoved over the edge.

Aura stiffens beside me, but before I can react, Hayes is in front of me. He doesn't say anything, but he doesn't have to. Trevor stops short, and something in him crumples at the sight of Hayes, who is not surprised one bit by this news.

"Hayes, I can explain—"

"You really can't," Hayes cuts him off coolly. "Not when I have this."

Aura passes him what she was hiding in the pocket of her loose-fitting dress. He raises it so everyone can see: Hunter's journal.

38

Instead of the usual swanky party that follows the graduation ceremony, I have the joy of eating cold hors d'oeuvres while getting questioned by the police.

Following graduation-gate, the academy went into lockdown, with no one allowed to leave until the police cleared them. I was questioned for an obscenely long time. Woolf was right when he said I wouldn't hesitate to rat. I spilled everything. Recounting the atrocity of the last two weeks of my life was nothing short of free therapy.

When I finally walk out of the questioning room—in the STEM hall, of course—Professor Ruffalo is outside the door.

"Your parents are speaking with Principal Watershed," she tells me with a comforting smile. "I offered to wait here for you."

I'm eager to return to my room, where I left Cece with Emmy and Keana, but I don't want to brush Professor Ruffalo off, so I gesture for her to walk with me. "Thank you. I appreciate it."

She swallows as we make our way down the hall. "I want to apologize, Chloe."

I frown, confused. "What for?"

"I knew things weren't the easiest for you," she tells me. "That some of the other students picked on you and that coming from a different school gave you a lot to catch up on. I knew all that but I still pushed you because I knew you would rise to the challenge. I think it's much of the same reason why Diana started the wilderness competition all those years ago. She wanted to push the best to be even better. To compete to be better. But that's no way to teach, and certainly not how I want to teach. I should have supported you better."

"You helped me a lot," I reply in earnest. "You made me believe I could win."

She smiles as we stop at the bottom of the stairs. "I never doubted you for a second."

Without the watchful eye of Principal Watershed, I squeeze her in a hug, and she squeezes me back.

As I climb the steps to the living hall on my own, I pass Dodge. His parents are on either side of him, speaking to him in condescending tones. For a moment, fear strikes me that he'll reach out to hurt me.

We make eye contact, but he rips his away first, cowering as his parents berate him.

They continue down and out of earshot. I don't know what the police will do with Dodge, if anything. I didn't have as much ammo on his involvement as I did Mina's, and I'm not even sure what they'll do with her. She's been locked up in rooms with different detectives all night.

As I watch Dodge disappear downstairs, I realize I have no reason to fear him anymore. He was only brave in the forest because nobody was around to stop him. In reality, he's all bark and no bite.

For better or worse, I think I'm more bite.

I finally get to the living hall, which is peaceful compared to the constant movement downstairs. In my room, Cece is curled up on my bed, fast asleep.

"How'd questioning go?" Keana asks quietly from where she and Emmy cuddle on her bed. Keana's parents are no less happy with our treatment during the trials than mine, and I expect Principal Watershed will have a lot of complaints to deal with.

"Good, I think," I say, sitting on the edge of my bed. Cece snuggles up to me in her sleep, and I put my arm around her. "I only cried for, like, seventy percent of it."

Emmy smiles. "I would have cried for all of it, so you're better than me."

"I'll take the wins where I can."

"I got out of mine not too long ago," Keana says. "I saw Hayes talking to his parents with police. He might be almost done by now."

I haven't had a minute alone with him yet to check on him or his parents, who looked distraught when I saw them right after Trevor was pulled from the stage. I hope, like with Hayes, it gives them much-needed closure even if it dredges up a lot.

"Good to know," I say to Keana, turning back toward the door.

"Where are you going?" Cece asks, voice groggy as she sits up.

"To find Hayes." My hand is on the knob but I release it to pad across the room and sit beside her on my bed. "What's your favorite book?"

She squints at me in confusion. "Why?"

"I want to know."

"Okay, weirdo," she says with a weak smile. "I don't know if I have a favorite, but I like books with magic. Fantasy, I guess. And mysteries. Like Nancy Drew, but not as old."

The pressure that's been sitting on my chest eases. "I like Nancy Drew, too. I'll be back soon," I promise, pressing a kiss to the top of her head and slipping out the door.

Police roam the hallways. When I get to the foyer, I pass Woolf on the stairs talking to Phlip.

"Where's Hayes?" I ask, wrapping my arms around myself. I never changed out of my dress, though I did leave the silly crown on the podium.

"Getting questioned again," Woolf says. "The detective finished reading Hunter's journal."

"Can you tell him I'm waiting for him on the observation deck?"

Phlip gives Woolf a startled look, but Woolf waves it off, like, *I'll tell you later.* "Yeah, I'll let him know."

I start ascending the steps but pause, calling down to Woolf. He looks up at me with a raised brow.

"I thought you'd want to know you look very badass with that black eye," I compliment him. His signature grin crosses his face, and he gives me a salute, which I return before continuing up.

I reach the entrance to the deck and climb to the top. The clear floor beneath me still makes my vision swim, but it's easier to rein in the terror this time. I make it to the railing without my knees buckling, which is a win in my book.

From here, I can see all the way into the forest. Though I can't actually make out the estate, I feel like I know exactly where it is.

I wonder if anyone will ever visit it again or if I just brought the Wilde Trials to a crashing, catatonic end.

Up here is the most peace I've gotten in the past ten hours. I thought I'd hate the quietness and solitude of the forest, but I kind of miss it.

Though I'm not mad the silence is interrupted by footsteps behind me.

"Didn't expect to ever see you up here willingly," Hayes tells me, taking in the view. He's also still in his dress clothes, with the sleeves of his white button-down rolled up to his elbows. He rests them on the railing. "Is your fear of heights cured now?"

"Not even close," I say. "But I kind of like proving myself wrong. Old habits die hard and all that."

"Right." He looks at his clasped hands in front of him, then at me. "Chlo, I can't even begin to thank you for what you did. That was the bravest thing I've ever seen."

I finally turn to him. He looks different, somehow. Not actually, but there's a softness to his features; a relaxed tilt in his shoulders and a spark in his eyes. It's like the truth being out about Hunter lifted an invisible weight off him.

I can't help but smile. "I'm not sure this was the best way to spill the beans, but it certainly will be tough to cover up now."

"More like impossible." He bumps his shoulder to mine. "You caused quite the scene."

"It's my toxic trait." I give an exaggerated sigh, then perk up. "But hey, at least there's no flying mashed potatoes this time."

"Or pork tenderloin."

A laugh bubbles out of me. "Or pork tenderloin."

Silence descends around us, warm and comfortable. Like it used to be. And we might never be those same kids again, but maybe it's for the better.

"I talked to my parents," Hayes says. "I told them I could have never figured out the truth without you. I hope you don't mind, but I also told them about Cece and why winning was so important to you. They said they have some helpful connections they'll put in contact with your parents. Friends who do work with cancer research centers and stuff like that."

Hope blooms in my chest. My parents weren't upset in the slightest about everything that went down—aside from the fact that they were horrified to hear what happened to me during the trials—but we don't know the fate of my prize money. It's donated by the alumni society, but unfortunately, a large chunk was from Trevor's father. After trial seven, I had to return the money bags to the Champions. I have yet to get anything back.

"That's kind of them."

He makes a conflicted face. "They're . . . trying."

"It counts."

"It does," he agrees.

A lump forms in my throat. I've cried way too much in the past twelve hours, but most of all with Cece, who said over and over how she would have never forgiven me if something happened. It made me realize maybe Hayes needed to forgive Hunter. From how much lighter he seems, I think he finally has.

It's silent for a few more moments as I gather the words to say what I actually came up here to talk about. "I don't want this to be the last time I see you," I confess. "I don't want the truce to end."

Once the police are done, everyone is free to go home. Most students and their families will probably start leaving in the next hour or so.

"I do," Hayes says surely. "I want the truce to end."

I blink at him, feeling as if the clear floor beneath me shattered like I always feared it might. "Oh," I say, forcing brightness into my tone. "Um, that's fine. Great, even. We can go back to hating each other."

It's the biggest lie I've ever said. If I couldn't hate Hayes after he broke my heart, there's no way I can hate him now.

He pulls out an envelope from his back pocket and hands it to me.

"What is this?" I ask, turning it over in my hands. The only thing on the outside is his neat handwriting: *Clover*.

"The letter that never made it to you," Hayes replies.

I meant to bug him more about that, but I forgot amid everything else. "Woolf admitted he saw me put it in your room a month after our breakup and snuck in before you returned from class to steal it back. I think his defense was something like, *Dude, that's basically like drunk texting your ex, but make it Shakespeare.* He thought leaving it made him a bad friend."

"He's so weird," I say with a watery laugh, opening the letter.

"The weirdest. But he's a good friend."

Hayes watches as I read it. It takes me a second to realize what I'm looking at.

"Oh my God." I look at him, unable to hide my awe at the acceptance letter. "You got into *Juilliard*?"

I throw my arms around his neck. He laughs, hugging me

back. "I found out and wanted you to know. I didn't realize it never made it to you and was collecting dust under Woolf's bed."

"Ew," I say, brushing off the envelope. I look back at Hayes. "Are you going?"

He nods, his smile bursting into a grin. "My parents are cool with it, too. I mean, they were disappointed and upset when I first told them the decision, but since all of this, they're just happy I'm alive now. So I guess I'll be seeing you on the East Coast."

My excitement fades. "But you just said—"

"I have a proposition," he cuts me off.

"I'm listening."

"We end the truce," he says, stepping closer to me. His fingers intertwine with mine. "We go home with our families today. I visit you during the summer, and you take me to the town full of flowers we drove to on Christmas. We go to the beach together and Boston and wherever else you want to go. In the fall, I go to Juilliard, you go to Brown. We see each other on weekends and FaceTime and text. We go back to being us." He presses a kiss to my ring. "Or whatever new version of us this is. But whatever it is, we don't need a truce to make it work. Make *us* work."

I'm about to start ugly crying in 0.2 seconds, so I throw my arms around him, squeezing extra tight as if it can keep me together. I never want to let go.

"So what I'm hearing is you're trying to end the truce cold turkey," I mumble into his shoulder.

He pulls back to cup my face, grinning so his dimple shows. "You caught me."

"I'll allow it just this once. But only because I like the proposition."

Hayes's arm comes around me, and I lean my head on his shoulder as we turn to face the forest. "Hunter would be really proud of you," I say softly.

The tip of his nose reddens, but no tears fall. "How do you know?"

I grin teasingly at him. "I don't know if you're new here or something, but I'm kind of a know-it-all."

His laugh rings out into the morning, and just like that first time I heard it junior year, I'll do whatever it takes to keep hearing it again and again. "You kind of are, Clover. And I love you for it."

He kisses me sweetly and I melt into it. I may not like heights, but I've certainly never had a problem falling for Hayes.

Together, we gaze out at the forest in easy silence. Eventually, Wilde Estate will be nothing more than yellowed photographs and whispered lore. Just moonflowers and wild flora and vines. The forest will swallow the grounds, and the estate will collapse and crumble.

But we sure won't.

ACKNOWLEDGMENTS

There's a well-known saying among authors called "the book two curse," which is what it sounds like—that the follow-up to your debut novel is one of the hardest things you'll ever write. I'm nothing if not delusional, so naturally I didn't think that would apply to me. Long story short, I was humbled!

Figuring this book out was the hugest of trials, and there were many times I was convinced I'd never be able to do Chloe and Hayes's story justice. But luckily, I didn't need to tackle it alone. I first must thank my amazing agent Amy Bishop-Wycisk for believing in me and always using plenty of exclamation points in our emails to keep my spirits up. I trust you implicitly and consider myself so lucky to have you in my corner. Thank you also to the teams at Trellis Literary and Dystel, Goderich & Bourret, especially Michaela Whatnall, for your support.

I'm so grateful to everyone at Harper who made this book a reality. First and foremost, to my wonderful editors, Tara Weikum and Sarah Homer. Your heart for my stories and belief in me have shaped my writing in the best of ways and I'm so glad we got to work on another adventure together. This book wouldn't be what it is today without you both and your thoughtful vision.

To Catherine Lee and my talented design team, including my incredible cover artist, Holly Ovenden: you did it again! I'm so grateful to have an awesome cover that captures so many key components of this story. It feels so distinctly mine, and how did you know these are my all-time favorite colors?? Thank you!!

It wouldn't be a Mackenzie Reed book if there wasn't a healthy helping of friendship, and I'm lucky to say that's influenced by my own life. A billion thank-yous to Rachel Moore for believing in every iteration of this story (and there were many!!!) and for being ready to drop everything to hash out a sticky plot. To Kara Kennedy, my Aquarius big sister, for guiding me in more ways than one, hyping me up at every turn, and being my Eras tour buddy. To Kat Korpi, my type nine twin, for talking me off every hypothetical ledge and being the best fake-real-fake publicist who always makes sure I get on the right subway. I'd probably still be wandering a random platform in NYC if it wasn't for your expert navigation skills.

Thank you to my dearest HexQuills, each of whom I could gush about for hours (and I do). To Olivia, Phoebe, Helena, Brit, Sam, Skyla, Kalla, Kahlan, Juliet, Marina, Shay, Crystal, Lindsey, Abby, Alex, Morgan, Cassie, Darcy, Holly, Livy, Maria, and Wajudah. How incredibly lucky I am to call so many superstars my friends.

Thank you to Kaylynn Nelson, who reads every story I write and has been rooting me on every step of the way. And to Ellen

O'Clover, my sweet friend, for being such a rock throughout this process and never letting me feel alone in my feelings.

Thank you to everyone working behind-the-scenes to make this book a success. I appreciate you so much! And also thank you to the early readers, reviewers, blurbers, and my lovely street team for taking the time to hype up this story (and me).

So many of my stories first exist as a long-winded word vomit to my best friends Laura and Molly, who have been listening to my ramblings far before they ever made it onto the page. Thank you for never telling me to shut up, and to Ali, Sam, and all my local friends for being so uplifting. And same goes for my family, who have shown so much interest and love and support throughout this journey (especially Aunt Donna for buying copies of my book for all your friends!!). You all have every bit of my heart.

I dedicated this book to my brothers because at its core, this is a story about sibling love. It's never been lost on me how fortunate I am to have grown up with two brilliant role models who teased me just enough to give me a great personality. Danny, thank you for being so enthusiastic about everything I do and for keeping all the little libraries in Rochester well-stocked with my books. Jeff, thank you for always being ready to give advice and for having such a generous heart. And thank you to Lauren, Sheila, Gracie, and Mikey for rooting me on and sharing in all the excitement!

To Mom and Dad, my parents who double as two of my best friends, there aren't enough thank-yous in the world to convey how grateful I am to have you both. Your support and love have shaped me in so many ways, and thank you for telling literally everyone you meet about my book. I'm convinced half my sales are thanks to you guys spreading the word.

Writing books is the best, but it can be a road full of ups and downs and late nights and early mornings. Thank you, Josh, for being by my side through it all as a steady and constant force, and for always believing in me, even when I don't.

Lastly, thank you to my readers, who picked this book up and allow me to share my dream of storytelling. I hope you know you are always enough just as you are.